Penguin Books
The Unicorn

Iris Murdoch was born in Dublin of Anglo-Irish
parents. She went to Badminton School, Bristol,
and read classics at Somerville College, Oxford.
During the war she was an Assistant Principal at
the Treasury, and then worked with U.N.R.R.A. in
London, Belgium, and Austria.

She held a studentship in philosophy in Newnham
College, Cambridge, for a year, and in 1948 returned
to Oxford where she was until lately a Fellow and
Tutor in philosophy at St Anne's College. In 1956
she married John Bayley, don and novelist.

Her other novels are *Under the Net* (1954), *The
Flight from the Enchanter* (1955), *The Sandcastle*
(1957), *The Bell* (1958), *A Severed Head* (1961), *An
Unofficial Rose* (1962), *The Italian Girl* (1964), *The
Red and the Green* (1965), *The Time of the Angels*
(1966), *The Nice and the Good* – all in Penguins –
and *Bruno's Dream*.

Iris Murdoch

The Unicorn

Penguin Books
in association
with Chatto & Windus

Penguin Books Ltd, Harmondsworth,
Middlesex, England
Penguin Books Australia Ltd, Ringwood,
Victoria, Australia
Penguin Books Canada Ltd,
41 Steelcase Road West,
Markham, Ontario, Canada
Penguin Books (N.Z.) Ltd,
182–190 Wairau Road,
Auckland 10, New Zealand

First published in the U.S.A. 1963
Published in Great Britain by Chatto & Windus 1963
Published in Penguin Books 1966
Reprinted 1967, 1970, 1972, 1975

Made and printed in Great Britain by
Hazell Watson & Viney Ltd, Aylesbury, Bucks
Set in Linotype Times

To David Pears

Part One

Chapter One

'How far away is it?'

'Fifteen miles.'

'Is there a bus?'

'There is not.'

'Is there a taxi or a car I can hire in the village?'

'There is not.'

'Then how am I to get there?'

'You might hire a horse hereabouts,' someone suggested after a silence.

'I can't ride a horse,' she said in exasperation, 'and in any case there's my luggage.'

They stared at her with quiet dreamy curiosity. She had been told that the local people were 'friendly', but these big slow men, while not exactly hostile, entirely lacked the responsiveness of civilization. They had looked at her a little strangely when she told them where she was going. Perhaps that was it.

She saw now that it was foolish and even discourteous not to have announced her exact time of arrival. It had seemed more exciting, more romantic and somehow less alarming to come at her own pace. But now that the bedraggled little train which had brought her from Greytown Junction had coughed away among the rocks, leaving her in this silence a spectacle for these men, she felt helpless and almost frightened. She had not expected this solitude. She had not expected this appalling landscape.

'There's Mr Scottow's car now,' said one of the men, pointing.

She stared through the afternoon haze at the empty hillside, at the receding shelves of yellowish grey rock, bare and monumental. Smooth segments of wall here and there suggested the twists and turns of a steeply descending road. By the time she saw the Land Rover approaching, the men had withdrawn from her in a little group, and by the time the vehicle had entered the station yard they had disappeared altogether.

'Are you Marian Taylor?'

With a relieved sense of regaining her identity she took the hand and reassuring grip of the tall man who stepped out of the car.

'Yes. I'm so sorry. However did you know I was here?'

'As you didn't say when you were coming I asked the station-master at Greytown to look out for you and to send a message with the post van when he saw you waiting for our train. The van gets to Gaze a good half-hour before the train is due. And I thought you shouldn't prove hard to identify!' He gave a smile with this which made the remark complimentary.

Marian felt both rebuked and looked after. She liked the man. 'Are you Mr Scottow?'

'Yes. I should have said. I'm Gerald Scottow. Are these all your bags?' He spoke with a pleasant English voice.

She followed him towards the car, smiling and dignified, hoping that she was making a good impression. That had been a very foolish moment of fright just now.

'In we go,' said Gerald Scottow.

As he pushed her bags into the back of the Land Rover she saw in the shadowy interior what she took at first to be a large dog, but then recognized as a very pretty boy of about fifteen. The boy did not get out, but bowed to her from behind the luggage.

'This is Jamesie Evercreech,' said Scottow, as he settled Marian in the front.

The name meant nothing to her, but as she greeted him she wondered if he were perhaps her prospective pupil.

'I hope you had a decent tea at Greytown? Dinner will be late tonight. It's awfully good of you to join us in this God-forsaken spot.' Scottow started up the engine and the car set off back toward the twisting rising road.

'Not at all. I'm most thrilled to come to this part of the world.'

8

'Your first visit, I suppose? The coast-line is all right. Beautiful perhaps. But the land is dreadful. I doubt if there's a single tree between here and Greytown.'

As Marian, who had also noticed this, was trying to think of a way of turning it into a merit, the Land Rover took an abrupt turning and the sea came into view. She exclaimed.

The sea was a luminous emerald green streaked with lines of dark purple. Small humpy islands of a duller paler green, bisected by shadows, rose out of it through rings of white foam. As the car kept turning and mounting, the scene appeared and reappeared, framed between fissured towers of grey rock which, now that she was close to it, Marian saw to be covered with yellow stonecrop and saxifrage and pink tufted moss.

'Yes,' said Scottow. 'Beautiful certainly. I'm afraid I've got too used to it, and we have so few visitors to see it with new eyes. You'll see the famous cliffs in a minute.'

'Do many people live about here?'

'It's an empty land. As you can see, there's scarcely any earth. And inland where there is earth it's mostly bog. The nearest settlement is at Blackport, and that's a miserable fishing-village.'

'Isn't there a village at Gaze?' Marian asked, her heart sinking a little.

'Not now. Or scarcely. There used to be some fishermen's cottages and a sort of inn. There was a bit of moor up above and a lake, and a few people would come for the shooting and that, though it was never fashionable. But the place was killed by a big storm some years ago. The fishing-boats were all lost and the lake came flooding down the valley. It was quite a famous disaster, you might have read about it. And now the moor is just another piece of bog, and even the salmon have gone away.'

Marian thought to herself, with a sudden foreboding, that perhaps Geoffrey had been right after all. They had looked at the map together and he had shaken his head over it. Yet Gaze had been marked in quite large letters and Marian had been sure it must be a real civilized place with shops and a public house.

9

Elation and despair had so fiercely ebbed and flowed in her during the last month; she realized now how naïve it had been to envisage her journey's end as the beginning of some sort of happiness. Her love for Geoffrey had not been her first love, but it had had the violence of a first occasion together with a depth and a detail which come from commerce with the judgement. She was no longer, after all, so young. She was very nearly thirty; and her sense of her life hitherto as a series of makeshift stage-setting preliminaries had made her the more rapaciously welcoming to what seemed at last an event. Totally disappointed, she had faced her loss with fierce rationality. When it had become clear that Geoffrey did not and could not love her she had decided that she must go. She had been settled, perhaps too settled, in her job as a schoolmistress. Now it was suddenly plain that the same town, the same country even, must not contain herself and him. She admired in herself this ruthlessness. But she admired even more what came later: how, after she had ceased wanting to blot him entirely from her mind, to make him not to be, they had found that they could after all talk good sense and kindness to each other. She was, then, consciously generous. She let him console her a little for the loss of him; and had the painful gratification of finding him almost ready to fall in love with her at about the moment when she, amazingly, disgracefully, was beginning to recover.

She had noticed it quite by chance, the curious little advertisement. Geoffrey had told her teasingly that she was simply impressed by a grand name and a vision of 'high life'. She was attracted indeed by the name, Gaze Castle, and by the remote and reputedly beautiful region. A Mrs Crean-Smith was advertising for a governess with a knowledge of French and Italian. A high salary was mentioned; suspiciously high, Geoffrey said, even considering it was a lonely place. He had been against the plan; partly, Marian felt, with a rueful tenderness for him, out of a kind of jealousy, a kind of envy, at seeing her so soon whole again and ready for adventure.

Marian had written, naming her qualifications, and had received a friendly letter from a Gerald Scottow. Correspondence followed, and she was offered the job, but without having found out, or quite liking to enquire, the age and number of her prospective pupils. Nor could she quite make out from Mr Scottow's manner whether he was a friend or a relative or a servant of the Mrs Crean-Smith on whose behalf he wrote.

Marian turned her head now in a cautious manner and surveyed Gerald Scottow. This was easy to do, since he sat between her and the great view of the sea. She would have liked to turn round too and look at the boy whose silent presence behind her she most uneasily felt, but she was too shy to do that. Scottow certainly seemed to be, in a terminology which Geoffrey would have been quick to taunt her with adopting, one of 'the gentry'. His accent and his manner proclaimed him no subordinate, and Marian conjectured that he might be a relative or a family friend. Yet, if he lived here, what did he *do*? He was a big handsome man with a smooth fresh-complexioned powerful face and something of the mien of a soldier. He had a great deal of crinkly brown hair which grew in little flat circular curls a long way down his reddish weather-beaten neck. His brown eyes were rather consciously fine. He seemed in his early forties and was perhaps just thickening out of some early beauty. He now made a stouter, squarer impression, filled out yet muscular and not without grace. Marian transferred her gaze to his big hirsute hands upon the steering-wheel. She shivered for a moment. It occurred to her to wonder if there was a Mrs Scottow.

'There are the cliffs.'

Marian had read about the great cliffs of black sandstone. In the hazy light they seemed brownish now, receding in a series of huge buttresses as far as eye could see, striated, perpendicular, immensely lofty, descending sheer into a boiling white surge. It was the sea here which seemed black, mingling with the foam like ink with cream.

'They are wonderful,' said Marian. She found the vast dark coastline repellent and frightening. She had never seen a land so out of sympathy with man.

'They are said to be sublime,' said Scottow. 'Again I am no judge. I am too used to them.'

'Are there good places to swim?' said Marian. 'I mean, can one get down to the sea?'

'One can get down to the sea. But no one swims here.'

'Why not?'

'No one swims in this sea. It's far too cold. And it is a sea that kills people.'

Marian, who was a strong swimmer, privately decided to swim all the same.

The descending sun was making a brilliance now upon the water and her eyes were dazzled. She looked inland, still un-nervingly conscious of the silent boy behind her. The bare limestone desert receded, rising in clearly marked shelves to form low humpy plateaus which lay one behind the other like huge fossilized monsters. A few miserable reddish shrubs and little east-bent hazel trees clung to the rock, which the sun had turned to a pale gritty yellow.

'It's remarkable scenery, isn't it?' said Scottow. 'Not every-one's cup of tea, of course. But you should see those rocks in May and June. They're absolutely covered with gentians. Even now there's far more vegetation than appears at first sight. Weird little flowers you'll find if you look, and carnivorous plants. And there are most curious caves and underground rivers. Are you interested in geology and in flowers and things? I see you've brought your field-glasses with you.'

'I'm no geologist, I'm afraid. I thought I might do some bird-watching, though I don't really know much about birds either.'

'I know nothing about birds except the kind you shoot, but you can certainly see some rare ones around here. Ravens and golden eagles and such. I hope you're fond of walking?'

'Yes, very. I imagine one could soon get lost up there.'

'There aren't many landmarks, on the Scarren. There's hardly anything upright except megaliths and dolmens. It's a very ancient land.'

The road had turned inland and was winding between shallow shelves of rock. The uncertain tarmac was beginning to degenerate into a bumpy gravelly track. Scottow slowed down. There was something dark ahead which turned out to be a little

12

group of donkeys. Among them were two baby donkeys scarcely bigger than fox terriers. The car nosed its way up to them and they shifted lazily upon their dainty feet. A weird cry followed after.

Marian took the occasion of the donkeys to turn and look at the boy behind her. He gave her a smile of singular sweetness, but she could not make out his face.

'They're nice little beasts,' said Scottow, 'but I wish they'd keep off the roads. Fortunately there's little traffic. Though that means too that people drive like the devil. There's a saying about here that you'll meet only one car in a day, but that car will kill you.'

A turn in the road suddenly revealed in the distance a big handsome house. Its appearance was startling in the midst of the naked scene and had, in the sunny mist, something of the air of a mirage. It stood high up on the seaward side, on a promontory of the cliffs, a long grey three-storey eighteenth-century house. Marian had seen several such houses already on her journey, but always with their roofs off. 'Is that Gaze Castle?'

'I'm afraid not. That's a house called Riders. Our nearest neighbour. Gaze isn't half so grand. I hope you won't be disappointed. All the gentlemen's residences around here tend to be called castles.'

'Who lives at Riders?' From the account of the available civilization it seemed that this would be a matter of some importance.

'A curious recluse, an elderly scholar called Max Lejour.'

'Does he live there alone?'

'He lives alone all the winter, except for the servants, of course. The winter here is terrible and not everyone can stand it. In the summer he has visitors. His son and daughter are with him at present. And there's a man called Effingham Cooper who always comes.'

There was a weird high-pitched noise behind her. Marian realized that the boy had laughed. She realized at the same moment that he must be older than she had guessed. That was not a fifteen-year-old laugh. She turned quickly to look at him and saw his face more clearly now. He was a pallid rather spoilt-looking cherub of about nineteen with a long head and a pointed chin. Lank longish silky fair curls hung about his brow and half obscured his long light blue intelligent eyes, giving him the dog-like appearance. He tossed his hair back, widened his eyes, and gave Marian an impish look which made her a mock-partner in his private joke.

Scottow went on, 'That lot, together with our little gang, account for the gentry for about thirty miles around. Eh, Jamesie?' There was a slight sharpness. Perhaps Scottow had been irritated by the laugh.

Marian longed to enquire who 'our little gang' consisted of. Well, she would know, for better or worse, soon enough.

'I'm afraid you've come to an awful hole, Miss Taylor. The peasants are mostly loonies, and the others are something worse.' The boy spoke in a pleasant light voice with a touch of the local accent.

'Don't ever believe a word he says!' said Scottow. 'Jamesie is our little sunshine, but he's a dreadful romancer.'

Marian laughed uneasily. She could not place Jamesie. She could not even yet really place Scottow.

Scottow, as if guessing her thought, went on, 'Jamesie kindly tolerates my driving the car.'

'Oh, is it his car?' said Marian, and then realized her mistake.

'Not exactly. Jamesie acts as our chauffeur and generally puts up with us and cheers us up when we get melancholy.'

Marian blushed. Ought she somehow to have known that Jamesie was a 'servant'?

'Here the domain begins. You'll see a rather remarkable dolmen on your left in a minute.'

The big house was out of sight now behind a dome of limestone. The landscape had become a trifle gentler and a little dried-up grass, or it might have been a tufted lichen, made saffron pools among the rocks. Some black-faced sheep with brilliant amber eyes made a sudden appearance on a low crag, and behind them rose the dolmen against a greenish sky. Two immense upright stones supported a vast capstone which protruded a long way on either side. It was a weird lop-sided structure, seemingly pointless yet dreadfully significant.

'No one knows who put it up, or when, or why, or even how. These things are very ancient. But of course you are a scholar, Miss Taylor, and will understand far more about it than I do. Beyond the dolmen the peat bog begins and goes on for miles. There's Gaze now.'

As the car began to descend, Marian made out on the opposite hillside a big grey forbidding house with a crenellated façade and tall thin windows which glittered now with light from the sea. The house had been built of the local limestone and reared itself out of the landscape, rather like the dolmen, belonging yet not belonging.

'Not a thing of beauty, I'm afraid,' said Scottow. 'Nineteenth century, of course. There was an older house here, but it got burnt down like most of them. The eighteenth-century terrace remains and the stables. Here's our little river. It doesn't look very dangerous now, does it? And this is the village, what's left of it.'

The car slowed down to rattle very slowly over a long wooden bridge across a channel of large almost spherical speckled stones. A little trickle of water, the colour of brown sherry, forced an erratic way among the stones and spread out on the seaward side into a shallow rippled expanse bordered with tangles of glistening yellow seaweed. A few white-washed one-room cottages huddled in a disorderly group near to the road. Marian noticed that some of them were roofless. No people were to be seen. Below and beyond, framed on each side by the perpendicular black cliffs, whose great height was now apparent, was the sea, total gold. The house, Riders, had come into view again behind them. The car began to climb the other side of the valley.

Marian was suddenly overcome by an appalling crippling panic. She was very frightened at the idea of arriving. But it was more than that. She feared the rocks and the cliffs and the grotesque dolmen and the ancient secret things. Her two companions seemed no longer reassuring but dreadfully alien and even sinister. She felt, for the first time in her life, com-

15

pletely isolated and in danger. She became in an instant almost faint with terror.

She said, as a cry of help, 'I'm feeling terribly nervous.'

'I know you are,' said Scottow. He smiled, not looking at her, and again the words had an intimate protective ring. 'Don't be. You'll soon feel at home here. We're a very harmless lot.'

Behind her she heard again the high-pitched sound of the boy's laugh.

The car bumped over a jangling cattle-grid and through an immense crenellated archway. A lodge cottage with blank gaping windows and a sagging roof stood in a wilderness of wind-torn shrubs. The uneven gravel track, devastated by rain and weeds, wound away to the left, circling upward toward the house. After the dry rocks, the earth here was suddenly moist and black, covered patchily with wiry grass of a vivid green. Red flowering fuchsia blotched the hillside among dark dishevelled clumps of rhododendron. The track turned again and the house was near. Marian descried the stone balustrade of a terrace which surrounded it on all sides, lifting it high out of the peaty earth. There was a grey stone wall some distance beyond and indications of an overgrown garden with a few bedraggled fir trees and a monkey puzzle. The car came to a standstill and Scottow switched off the engine.

Marian was appalled at the sudden quietness. But the insane panic had left her. She was frightened now in an ordinary way, sick in her stomach, shy, tongue-tied, horribly aware of the onset of a new world.

Scottow and Jamesie carried her bags. Not looking up at the staring windows, she followed up the steps to the terrace of cracked weedy paving-stones, on to the big ornate stone porch and through swinging glass doors. Inside there was a new kind of silence, and it was dark and rather cold and there was a sweetish smell of old curtains and old damp. Two maids with tall white lace caps and black streaky hair and squints came forward to take her luggage.

Jamesie had vanished into the darkness. Scottow said, 'I expect you would like to wash and so on. There's no hurry. Of

16

course, we don't usually change for dinner here, not seriously, I mean. The maids will show you to your room. Perhaps you'd like to find your way down again in half an hour or so, and I'll be waiting about on the terrace.'

The maids were already whisking the luggage away up the stairs. Marian followed them through the semi-darkness. The floors were mostly uncarpeted, tilting, creaking, echoing, but there were soft hangings above her head, curtains in archways and vague cobwebby textiles which hung down at doors and corners and tugged her passing sleeve. At last she was ushered into a big room full of evening light. The maids disappeared.

She crossed to the window. She had the big view across the valley to Riders and the sea. The sea was peacock blue now and the cliffs were jet black, receding to where the distant islands were again to be seen against a tawny sky. She looked and sighed, forgetting herself.

The case containing her brand-new field-glasses was slung about her neck. Still absorbed in looking, she fumbled them out. They were yet a delightful toy. She focused them upon the valley. Startlingly close the wooden bridge sprang into view, and slowly the magic circle moved up the hill toward the opposite house. She came to a wall, discerning the uneven texture of the stone where the sinking sun struck it obliquely and cast small shadows; and then unexpectedly there was a stone balustrade, like the one at Gaze, and behind it a shuttered window. She moved the glasses slowly, pausing at a group of gay deck-chairs and white table with a bottle on it. The next moment she was looking at a man. He was standing on the terrace and looking straight into her eyes with lifted binoculars trained on Gaze. Marian dropped her glasses and moved hastily back from the window. The panic returned.

Chapter Two

'Mrs Crean-Smith is not quite ready to see you,' said Gerald Scottow. 'Would you be so kind as to wait here while I find the others.'

Marian had not lingered long upstairs. Recovered from her fright, she had quickly inspected her room, appreciating the eighteenth-century writing-desk, grateful for the empty varnished bookshelves, pleased with the ancient floppy chintz armchairs, suspicious of the powerful bedstead whose dinted brass knobs shone like soft gold, and appalled by the extremely garrulous coloured prints upon the wall which she hoped that no one would object to her removing. She washed quickly, finding hottish water in a flowery jug and basin upon a wash-stand of green and ochre tiles. Nervously venturing out into the silent stuffy corridor, she found near by a lavatory with a vast mahogany seat, which seemed warm from generations of incumbents, and a wide shallow bowl adorned with garlands of flowers. She did not know whether to be pleased or unnerved by the discovery that it matched her jug and basin.

She changed hastily into a dress and surveyed herself in a pretty satinwood mirror. There was no long glass. She powdered her long nose and combed back her short, straight, dark hair. Her face, too crowded with large features to be called 'pretty', might pass, she thought, as 'handsome', or at least as 'strong'. But there was also her expression to be reckoned with. Geoffrey had often told her she looked sulky and aggressive. She must not look so now. He had said once, 'Stop thinking that life is cheating you. Take what there *is* and use it. Will you never be a realist?' Well, whatever here there *was*, she would take it with her full and devoted attention. Perhaps the era of realism was beginning. Perhaps she had been right to think

18

that, with her love for Geoffrey, the preliminaries were over. Yet with a sudden dreadful loneliness, a sudden nostalgia for the old affectionate vanished world, she felt how desperately she would want to be needed and to be loved by the people at Gaze. She composed her face, took what courage she could from communion with herself, and went downstairs.

Scottow had ushered her into a large drawing-room on the ground floor where she now stood alone, fingering an unlit cigarette, and not at all looking forward to 'the others'. The room smelt broodingly of the past, chilly and obscure in the warm September evening. Two tall sash-windows, which reached almost to the floor, and a high glass doorway communicated with the sunny terrace. They were draped and darkened by swathes of looped-up white lace which was slightly less than clean. Thick red curtains, stiff as fluted columns, emitted a dusty incense, and the fawn-and-yellow carpet gave out little puffs when stepped on. A dark mahogany erection containing a mirror surmounted the fireplace and reached almost to the dim ceiling in a converging series of shelves and brackets upon which small complicated brass objects were clustered. A jet-black grand piano was defended by a troop of little tables draped to their ankles in embroidered velvet cloths. Amid the jumble, pieces of cut glass glittered here and there, and a bookcase with formidable doors supported hazy rows of calf-bound volumes upon shelves with leather fringes. The clutter in the room had about it little suggestion of human use or occupation. Whoever the children might be, they did not come here.

Marian looked cautiously about. There was a yellowish reflected twilight from the sunny evening outside, and an extreme quietness. Yet the room felt watchful, and she almost feared to find that she had overlooked some person standing silently in a corner. She moved noiselessly looking for a match for her cigarette. There was a tarnished silver matchbox on one of the velvet tables but no matches. She peered about near the door for the electric-light switch, found none, and merely dislodged a loose piece of flowery wallpaper. It occurred to her that of course there was no electric light at Gaze. To keep her attention on something and to steady her nerves, she crossed to the bookcase and tried to see the names of the books, but the glass was too dirty and the room too dark. She began to try to open the bookcase.

'It's locked,' said a voice close behind her.

Marian jumped violently round. A tall woman had come very near to her. She could not see her face clearly, but she seemed to have grey or very fair or colourless hair done up in a bun. She wore a dark dress with white lace collar and cuffs.

Marian's heart began to hit her so hard that she almost fell down. 'Mrs Crean-Smith?'

The reassuring voice of Gerald Scottow spoke from beyond. 'This is Miss Evercreech. Miss Evercreech, Miss Taylor.'

A glow of light grew in the doorway and three black-haired maids entered bearing big oil-lamps with opaque creamy glass domes. They set them down on various tables. The scene became different, enclosed, shadowy, and the figures drew nearer together. Now Marian could see Miss Evercreech. She was thin, with a narrow transparent high-cheekboned face and oily light blue eyes and a long fine mouth. The colour of her hair was still hard to determine. So was her age. She could have been forty or sixty. She stared at Marian unsmiling, frowning slightly, with an intensity which though a little alarming was not hostile.

'Miss Evercreech is Jamesie's sister, of course,' said Scottow. 'His big sister, practically his Ma.'

'I don't know why you say "of course", Gerald,' said Miss Evercreech, still intently perusing Marian, 'or why you permit yourself these references to my age in front of a stranger.'

'There, there, Violet!' said Scottow. He seemed a trifle uneasy with her. 'Anyway, Miss Taylor is not a stranger. She's one of us, or soon will be.'

Miss Evercreech was silent a moment, then ended her study of Marian's face. 'Poor child! Gerald, where is the key to that bookcase? Miss Taylor wants to look inside.'

'No, indeed, don't bother – ,' said Marian.

'I've no idea,' said Scottow. 'It's never been opened as far as I know.'

'It must have been opened, dear, to get the books in. The key may be in one of those brass bowls. I seem to remember that it is. Could you reach them down, please?'

With a slightly resigned look which Marian read as a private communication to herself, Scottow began to take down the brass ornaments one by one and placed them on a table where Miss Evercreech extracted from their interiors a miscellany of buttons, paper clips, cigar butts, elastic bands, and what looked like a gold sovereign, which she pocketed. The key was found at last in the pannier of a brass donkey and Miss Evercreech handed it to Marian who, rigid by now with embarrassment, turned it in the lock and affected to look at the contents of the bookcase, since this seemed to be expected of her.

'Is that all right, child?' said Miss Evercreech.

Marian, who scarcely knew whether she was being indulged or punished, said, 'Oh yes, thank you, indeed, yes.'

'Is Hannah ready to see her yet, Gerald?'

'Not yet.'

Miss Evercreech suddenly took Marian's hand in a firm grip and led her over to the window. She drew her right up against the pane so that the girl's shoulder was driven into the lace curtain, releasing dry dusty smells. Outside the evening was still bright, its colours all washed over with gold, and an orange-and-purple sunset was building up over the sea. But Marian did not dare to take her eyes off the scrutinizing face, lit up now as on a little stage.

'What is your religion, child?'

'I have no religion.' She felt guilty at this, and guilty at so intensely wishing to free her hand. She twitched the curtain off her shoulder.

'You may find us a little strange at first, but you will soon find your place among us. Do not forget. If you want or need anything in this house, come to me. We do not trouble Mrs Crean-Smith with any practical details.'

'Hannah will see her now,' said Scottow's voice from among the lamps.

Miss Evercreech still retained Marian's hand, squeezing it very slightly. 'We shall meet again soon, Marian. I shall call you Marian. And later on you will call me Violet.' Her tone made it sound almost like a threat. She released Marian's hand.

Marian murmured some thanks and backed hastily away. She had found the degree of attention almost unendurable. She turned with relief to the friendly figure of Scottow.

As if deliberately changing the key, Scottow said briskly, 'There now. Nothing left here, no handbag or anything? I'm afraid we don't use this room very often and sometimes it gets locked up. Now just follow me, will you.'

They emerged into the hall, where the orange light from without produced a blurred radiant interior. At that moment a man came in from the terrace through the glass doors.

'Oh, Denis, is that you.'

'Yes, sir.'

'Miss Taylor has arrived. Miss Taylor, this is Denis Nolan.'

A maid passed by carrying one of the oil-lamps. The drawing-room was being darkened again. By the passing glow Marian saw a shortish man about her own height who was holding a large tin bowl. He had the dark hair and blue eyes of the region, indeed Marian saw, as he turned towards her before the lamp passed, sapphire blue eyes. He spoke with a strong local accent and looked, she thought, rather sulky and servile.

Scottow went on, 'Denis is my very able clerk. He does our accounts for us and tries to keep us out of the red. Eh, Denis?'

Denis grunted.

'What have you got there, Denis? Or I should ask, who have you got there?'

The man thrust the tin bowl forward and Marian saw with a little shock of surprise that it contained water and a sizeable goldfish. 'Strawberry Nose.'

'Is Strawberry Nose going to be given a salt bath?'

'Yes, sir.' The man did not smile.

Scottow said, smiling enough for two, 'Denis is a great fish man. You must see his fish ponds tomorrow. They are one of our few diversions. Now, up we go. Mrs Crean-Smith is waiting.'

In extreme agitation Marian now followed Scottow up the

almost dark staircase, past a lamp on the landing which shone dimly as in a shrine, and some way on until they came to a large double door which he opened softly. They entered a dim ante-room and Marian could see a line of golden light ahead. Gerald Scottow knocked.

'Come in.'

He entered deferentially and Marian followed.

The room was brilliantly lit with a great many lamps and the curtains were drawn although it was still so bright outside. Marian was dazzled by the soft flooding light and by fear.

'Here she is,' said Scottow in a low voice.

Marian advanced across a thick carpet towards someone at the far end of the room.

'Ah – good – '

Marian had, without reflection, expected an elderly woman. But the person who confronted her was young, perhaps scarcely older than herself, and while not exactly beautiful was yet strikingly lovely. She had a tangle of reddish gold hair and eyes of almost the same colour and a wide pale freckled face. She wore no make-up. She was dressed in a flowing robe of embroidered yellow silk which might have been either an evening dress or a dressing-gown.

Marian took the white freckled hand that was offered to her and murmured that she was glad. She was conscious of a familiar pervasive smell which she could not place ; and there was a lot of emotion in the room, not all of it her own.

'How wonderfully good of you to come,' said Mrs Crean-Smith. 'I do hope you won't mind being imprisoned with us here miles from anywhere.'

'I hope so too,' said Marian, and then realized this sounded rude. She added, 'No one would mind being imprisoned in such a lovely place.' This sounded rude too, so she added, 'It wouldn't be imprisonment.'

Scottow behind said 'Hannah.'

Marian edged back against the wall so that the two could see each other.

'I expect you'd like to take a bit of supper with Miss Taylor?'

'Yes, please, Gerald, if that would be all right. Would you mind asking Violet? I don't want to cause trouble, but it would be so nice and I'm sure Miss Taylor is hungry. Is it not so, Miss Taylor?'

Marian, who was feeling sick, said, 'Well, yes, but anything will do – '

There was a short silence. Then Scottow bowed and withdrew and Marian detached herself from the wall.

'We keep odd hours here, I'm afraid. We have no one to please but ourselves. I do hope you had a good journey? I'm afraid it's very dull until you get to the mountains. Come nearer to the fire. These evenings are cold already.'

A small turf fire was burning in a big grate and there was fine china on the black marble mantelpiece. There were a great many mirrors, some of them pretty, but no pictures and few attempts at orderly embellishment. Two brass vases full of pampas grass and dried honesty had clearly been there for a long time. The room was decrepit and ponderously old-fashioned like the one below, but immensely, almost too much, inhabited; and Marian felt herself shut in, almost menaced, by the circle of faded armchairs piled with books and papers. She noticed upon a leather-topped writting-table littered with manuscript the photograph of a man in uniform. She joined her employer beside the fire and they looked at each other.

Marian now saw that Mrs Crean-Smith was barefoot. This observation at once defined the yellow robe as a dressing-gown; and with this there came to her a general impression of something very slightly unkempt, the hair tousled, the finger-nails not quite clean, the lovely face a little tired, a little sallow and greasy, like that of a person long ill. Marian wondered at once whether Mrs Crean-Smith were not in fact somehow ill, and she had a guilty little feeling of revulsion. Yet she felt too relief and immediate liking. This person was harmless.

'I hope you like your room? If you need anything, don't fail to ask. Please sit down. I expect you'd like some whiskey.'

'Thank you.' Marian realized now that what the room smelt of was whiskey.

'Now you must tell me a little about yourself. But I expect

24

you'd like to ask questions too. This place must seem very strange to you.'

'I can't help wondering,' said Marian, 'about my pupils. Perhaps I should have asked earlier. Mr Scottow said nothing in his letters.'

'Your – pupils?'

'I mean the young persons, the ones I'm to teach, the children.'

There was a sort of blankness in Mrs Crean-Smith's eyes which suddenly made Marian feel very frightened. Had there been some terrible, some grotesque, mistake?

Mrs Crean-Smith, who had paused with her stare, moved to the whiskey decanter. 'There are no children here, Miss Taylor. Mr Scottow should have explained. I am the person that you are to teach.'

Chapter Three

Dearest Marian, I had hoped to get a letter to you for your first day, but I've been hideously bogged down in exams and Campaign work. I don't know precisely how long a letter takes to reach your distant point. I shall note day and hour of posting this and if you will let me know exact time of arrival we can construct a working hypothesis! I shall expect a letter from you reasonably soon. I have been looking at some books and maps and when I have a second I'll do some simple itineraries. There's some prehistoric stuff that absolutely *must* be seen. Tell me, by the way, if you want your bike sent on. I think you were an ass to go without it.

I envy you the bird life more than the high life. Apropos the former, I've just tied up and will post tomorrow those two bird books you wanted, and also a book on shells and one about limestone rock formations. (Most interesting and curious that.) Nay, pray accept as presents from me! Apropos the high life, I hope you're enjoying it and finding your clothes stand the strain. (Your blue dress is quite adequate to *any* occasion in my humble view.) What are the pubs like and can you get out to them? What are the kids like, more important, and what do you teach them? I hope they aren't little morons. If you can't stand it, let me know and I'll send you a wire to say someone's died.

This is a hasty note, as I have to go to Campaign headquarters for the usual chores. I hope you will be happy over there, dear Marian, and will not fret any more about worthless me. Don't on the other hand forget me! One has so few real friends and I can't spare you.

I must fly. A fat lecherous-looking girl called Freda something whom I met at the Campaign coffee party and who says she knows you insisted that I should send you her regards, which I now do. God I'm tired and term only starting. You're well out of it. *Floreas*, and let me know the worst.   Love ever,

                                                            Geoffrey

Dear dear Geoff, heavens I was glad to get your letter. Not that it's dreadful here, but it's so terribly isolated, I'm beginning even after five days to forget who I am. I don't know how the natives stay sane and I conjecture they don't. But let me tell you how it is.

To begin with, there are no kids! I'm supposed to 'teach' Mrs Crean-Smith herself, that is read a little French with her and later on maybe teach her Italian. I suspect, and they've more or less admitted it, that they really wanted a 'lady companion' and advertised for a 'governess' so as to get an intelligent one! I give them marks for that and don't feel swindled. Mrs Crean-Smith is youngish and *beautiful* and spiritual-looking in a rather fey way. There is also a hunting and shooting type called Scottow (the one who wrote to me) who is thoroughly nice and ordinary and seems to be a sort of bailiff-cum-family-friend. Then there's a rather creepy woman called Evercreech who is the sort of housekeeper (everything is rather 'sort of' here!) and is I gather some sort of poor relation of Mrs C.-S. Her brother Jamesie (*sic*) Evercreech acts as the chauffeur. I thought he was an ordinary chauffeur at first but I suppose not as he's a relation. I can't make out if there's a Mr Crean-Smith, but he's never mentioned so I assume Mrs is a widow. There's also a gloomy little clerk called Nolan and a lot of black maids with casts in their eyes and incomprehensible accents. (One of them brought your letter in, Friday 4.30. I've no idea how it got here and on reflection it seems miraculous. Please write often!) *No grandeur!* The 'castle' is a big Victorian house with nothing near it except a few cottages and one other gent's residence. The nearest pub is in Blackport and won't allow women! Fortunately whiskey flows like water here at Gaze. Everyone drinks a great deal and goes to bed early. If I start to go mad I'll let you know.

I must stop now and go and swim. My duties are not exactly arduous! I'm even hoping someone will suggest that I learn to ride. (On a horse, you know! There are some horses. I saw Mr Scottow and Jamesie horseback riding the other day. Felt envious!) That Freda girl must be Freda Darsey, a nice *quiet* girl, not at all lecherous! I was at school with her. Greet her back from me. I hope the Campaign is going well. I haven't seen a newspaper since I arrived, it now occurs to me, nor missed one! Perhaps I am being *influenced*. All that seems far away – but not you, who are so splendidly present in your letter and present in my heart. No fretting. Don't worry about me, darling. I embrace you and will write again soon.   Much love,

M.

P.S. Mr Scottow says there are golden eagles, but I wouldn't trust him to recognize any bird he can't shoot and eat!

Marian finished her letter, sealed it in an envelope, and then wondered how she should dispose of it. There was an old-fashioned box marked 'Letters' down in the hall, giving details of postage rates of fifty years ago, but it seemed unsafe to drop her missive in there without further enquiry. She decided to ask Jamesie at tea-time. She wrapped up her bathing-togs.

It was still the deep trough of the afternoon. At Gaze people retired to their rooms after lunch and were not heard of again until five o'clock. Presumably they slept. Marian was amazed at how much they seemed to sleep, since they then retired for the night about ten; and walking on the terrace at eleven two nights running she had seen no lights.

Marian's sense of loyalty to her employers was already preventing her from admitting that she was disappointed. She had indeed expected more. She had wanted, had wanted always, as she obscurely knew, some kind of colourful up-lifting steadying ceremony, some kind of distinction of life which had so far eluded her. She had never, herself, really known how to live, had never been able to spread her personality comfortably about her; and the society she had lived in hitherto had given her no help. She lacked grace, she lacked style, she knew it. While seeming to pass for what she was, she had felt unfairly diminished and frightened into herself. In moments of self-examination, which for Marian came frequently, she had asked herself whether her desire for a more settled and confident social world were not mere snobbery, and had felt uncertain of the answer. Her love for Geoffrey, who so utterly belonged to her accustomed world, being indeed one of its sovereigns, had seemed at first a justification of that world and of her own usual *persona* which under his influence had so positively glowed. But after Geoffrey she had found her everyday life so empty and her daily bread so bitter that the old half-understood desire for something quite else had grown into the frenzy which had spurred her away and which she had so much welcomed and admired.

It had seemed like the end of her timidity. Marian came of timid parents who had moved quietly through life in a little Midland town where her father owned a grocer's shop.

Marian's earliest memories were shop. Sometimes she felt as if she had been delivered in a cardboard box marked 'This side up'. Certainly one had served as her cradle. She was an only child. She was fond of her parents and not, as far as she knew, ashamed of them; but it was her abiding fear that she might, in the end, come to resemble them. That she was clever was, in this, nothing. The University had been for her a prize competition rather than a social scene; and that, again, because she was timid.

So she had thought of Gaze as the beginning of something quite new; and if she was, at this early moment, disappointed it was not, she obscurely felt, because of the lack of ceremony, or even the lack of company and entertainment, but because of some deep lack of assurance in the place itself. The place, somehow, resembled her strangely, it was nervous too. Its quietness was aimless rather than calm and its sleepy dragging routine was expressive more of some futility than of the feudal *insouciance* which Marian was still trying to perceive. Days seemed of immense length and their simple pattern already seemed to her monstrous, as if the monotony were inherent and not cumulative. There was a sort of dragging music barely heard. Her day began with breakfast at nine, brought up to her by a squinting and uncommunicative maid. About ten-thirty she made her way to Mrs Crean-Smith and stayed there for part of the morning. So far they had merely chattered and discussed possible reading. Mrs Crean-Smith, though both more cultured and more quick-witted than Marian had at first given her credit for being, seemed in no great hurry to be instructed, and it was not for Marian, whose desire to instruct was always considerable, to force the pace. Lunch again she took alone in her own room and was left to herself till five o'clock, when a large tea was served in Miss Evercreech's room. Mrs Crean-Smith did not appear at this ceremony, which gathered Scottow, Jamesie and sometimes Nolan together and was awkwardly cheerful. Miss Evercreech attached importance to Marian's attendance and seemed to regard this meal as a sort of assertion of her sovereignty. Scottow attended a little condescendingly, Jamesie giggled and Nolan was silent. Marian talked effortfully; yet she looked forward to it. It was the nearest approach to ordinary social life which Gaze had to offer, so far. About six-thirty she returned to Mrs Crean-Smith, who was by then drinking whiskey, and stayed with her for supper at eight-thirty. At nine-thirty Mrs Crean-Smith was yawning and ready for bed.

It was not exactly a gay round, not a reassuring scene, and there were moments late at night when Marian felt curiously frightened, though never with a repetition of her panic of the first day. The people at Gaze were not exactly bored, but they had, even Gerald Scottow had, some quality of anxiety which she supposed belonged with the solitude of the place. Two things however very much supported her. One was sheer curiosity. There were many matters for puzzlement in the big self-absorbed house and she found herself still, sometimes disconcertingly, unable to 'work out' the relations of the individuals to each other. She was curious too about Riders and a little surprised that so far no one had said anything about social communication with the other house, or indeed, apart from what Scottow had told her on the first day, anything about the other house at all.

The other thing which supported her, and that more deeply, was the sense that Mrs Crean-Smith was very glad of her presence. Marian wanted and needed to love and to be loved; and she was very ready to attach herself to her employer whom she found touchingly gentle and diffident. It was indeed this diffidence, together with some curious fumbling lack of assurance, Mrs Crean-Smith's own variant of the prevalent unease, which made so far the barrier between them. Marian was also readily disposed to be fond of Jamesie, who was the person with whom, in a giggling teasing way, she got on most easily. Gerald Scottow considerably occupied her thoughts, but without yet offering her any new material for reflection. She found herself surprisingly touchy with him, while he was infinitely considerate but formal with her. She could not yet, however, quite begin to like Violet Evercreech.

There was still more than an hour before tea, and the house was silent and asleep. Marian tip-toed a little guiltily down the stairs, carrying her bathing things in a closed bag in case anyone should object to her plan. She had not yet been down to the sea and this was the first day on which she had felt enough confidence to leave the house by herself, except for brief ambles about the immediate grounds. She thought she knew by now the best way down to the bay, as she had examined the prospect carefully through her glasses. There were two gates in the wall which circled the garden on the side nearest to the sea. One gate, the southern one, gave on to a path which led toward the top of the cliff; but the northern gate revealed a steep stony track which led downhill between wind-ragged fuchsia bushes and licheny boulders and nibbled velvety stretches of grass. As Marian passed through the gate, the sun shone warmly and the sea, opening now before her as she descended, quick and goat-like on the rocky path, was blandly azure. She found herself, sooner than she expected, at the bottom of the slope and came upon the dark brown stream with its wide bed of round grey stones. The village was by now just visible behind her, the cliffs towered up on either side of the bay, and both Gaze and Riders were hidden by folds of the hill. She paused and listened to the light near tinkle of the stream and the further beat of the sea.

The stream slithered and side-slipped along, appearing and disappearing among the big grey speckled stones, winking and flashing in the sun, seeming to sink underground, then leaping out in a minute waterfall and then fanning into a little wrinkled pool. Then at once it left the stones behind and sank noiselessly into a deep cleft in the dark peaty soil, running straighter and faster now in the direction of the sea. Marian, who had been following it thoughtlessly, found her feet sinking alarmingly into earth which had the consistency of soft fudge. She hesitated, and after nearly losing her shoes made her way to the left where some grey rocks were struggling up out of the soil. She clambered past a series of dark warm glutinous sea-pools fringed with pungent goldeny-yellow weed and at last found herself upon a small pebbled beach at the foot of the cliff upon which Gaze stood. She walked along a bit. Her heart was beating very hard.

The black wall of the cliff rose sheer beside her, glistening a little and seeming to overhang. The sun beat directly upon it but its darkness hung like a shadow overhead. The beach too was black, with gritty sand at the base of the cliff, and black pebbles at the water's edge. Marian had never been afraid of the sea. She did not know what was the matter with her now. The thought of entering the water gave her a *frisson* which was like a kind of sexual thrill, both unpleasant and distressingly agreeable. She found it suddenly hard to breathe, and had to stop and take deep regular breaths. She threw her bag down on the sand and advanced to the edge of the sea.

From up above it had seemed serene and calm and indeed it still looked fairly calm a little way from the shore. But some twenty yards out the smooth surge gathered into enormous waves which with sudden violent acceleration came tearing in to destroy themselves upon the shingle, which they then sucked sharply downwards and backwards with a grinding roar. Beyond the wild snowy curl and retreat of the foam the sea now looked, in the bright sunlight, inky black. Marian studied the pebbly verge. It looked as if the beach shelved very steeply, creating an undertow, each retreating wave being sucked with positive vicious violence back beneath the tall uncurling crest of its closely following successor. Marian began to wonder what to do. Then she lifted her head and saw a face.

The face was floating in the sea directly opposite to her, just beyond where the waves began to rush in. As soon as she had seen it it disappeared. Marian gave a little startled cry into the roaring of the sea. She realized the next moment that of course it was only a seal. She had never seen one so close. The seal rose again, lifting its sleek dripping antique dog-like head and regarded her with big prominent eyes. She could see its whiskers and its dark mouth opening a little. It floated lazily, keeping just out of the surge, and keeping its old indifferent gaze fixed upon her. Marian found the animal both touching and frightening. It seemed, with its head of a primitive sea-god, like a portent. But whether it was warning her out of the sea or inviting her into it she could not decide. After a minute it swam away, leaving her trembling.

Marian was by now thoroughly frightened of swimming but determined to swim. She would just have to throw herself boldly out through the breaking wave, avoiding the undertow. She could return upon a breaker, let it cast her on the shingle and scramble up quickly. It was a matter of pride ; and she felt obscurely that if she started now to be afraid of the sea she would make some crack or fissure in her being through which other and worse fears might come. Still trembling, she began awkwardly to undress.

In her bathing-costume she approached the steep verge. The pebbles hurt her feet and it was hard to stand upright on the wet shifting slope. She was wetted by now by the cold spray, and the pounding foam touched her feet before it hurled violently back, ripping the black grinding pebbles into a great dark mass beneath the white breakneck foam of the next wave. Marian stumbled, and scrambled gasping back, already wet through. The touch of the water was icy. She tried to stand again, precariously keeping her balance on the descending avalanche of stones.

'Hey, you!'

She started back and sat down, already exhausted. A man was approaching.

She sat upon the beach until the man was near to her, and then got up and threw a towel round her shoulders. The voice from the sea and the stones was so loud that it was difficult to hear what he said. He seemed to be a local man.

'You mustn't go swimming in that sea.'

Almost in tears now, Marian said, exasperated and determined to misunderstand him, 'Why not? Is this a private beach? I come from Gaze Castle.'

'You mustn't go swimming here,' said the man as if he had not heard her. Perhaps he had not. 'You'll be drowned directly.'

'I won't be!' said Marian. 'I can swim very well.' But she knew with a premonition of deeper fear that she was defeated.

'Two Germans were drowned last week,' said the man. 'Swimming near Blackport they were. We're watching for their bodies yet.' He spoke with the lilting accent of the region, solemn, incantatory, dignified. He looked at Marian out of ancient alien eyes. He resembled the seal.

'All right,' said Marian shortly. She turned her shoulder to send him away.

'And don't be hanging about too long either. The tide comes in fast. You don't want to have to climb the cliff, do you.' He moved off.

Marian began to fumble with her clothes. Hot tears blinded her eyes. The sun had gone in and a chill wind was blowing.

'Hello.'

Marion pressed the towel quickly to her face, pulled up the strap of her bathing-costume and turned again. Another figure had come close to her, this time a woman.

'Hello,' said Marian.

The woman was dressed in honey-coloured local tweeds and had a sort of tall staff in her hand. It was evident, even before she spoke again, that she belonged to the 'gentry'.

'Are you Miss Taylor?'

'Yes.'

'I'm Alice Lejour.' She held out her hand.

Marian shook it, recalling almost at once that Lejour was the name of the family at Riders. Scottow had said that the old man had his son and daughter with him. 'I'm so glad to meet you.' She wished all the same that she had some clothes on and could look a little more dignified. The scanty towel about her shoulders flopped in the wind.

Alice Lejour seemed to be in her thirties, a big handsome blue-eyed woman with short golden hair and a good straight nose and a wide rather lined brow. She seemed stout and solid and aggressively real, planted there with her tweed skirt strained against her legs and her wet brogues deep in the shingle. Marian felt flimsy before her as she danced from one bare foot to the other and tried to prevent her teeth from chattering.

'I hear you've just come, yes,' said Alice Lejour.

'Yes, I don't know the region. I like it very much.'

'Bit lonely for you, isn't it?'

'Well, yes, there's not much company,' said Marian, and

34

then added defensively, 'I like everyone at Gaze very much though.' It looked awkward.

'Hum. Never mind, yes. Will you come and see us?'

'I'd love to,' said Marian, realizing as she found herself liking the brusqueness of the woman how much, in the last few days, she had missed the presence of ordinary simple human reactions. Reactions at Gaze were slow and clouded.

'We'll have to work out a time,' said Alice Lejour. 'Don't want to offend anyone. I don't suppose they're working you very hard, are they? Bit of luck meeting you down here, really. Some time next week perhaps when Effingham's here. My friend Effingham Cooper, that is. Effingham and I do a little entertaining when he's here and when there's anyone to entertain. You know, people will drive fifty miles for a drink in this country.'

Marian, who had just realized that the curious staff was a fishing-rod, said, 'But we're such close neighbours. I hope we may often meet, with you or at Gaze.'

'Not at Gaze, I shouldn't think. Never mind, yes. Effingham and I will be splicing the old mainbrace next week. We feel it our duty to cheer my Pop up a little. He gets a bit odd over the winter-time, you know.'

'He must be lonely. I believe you – and your brother – come just for part of the summer?'

'Who told you that? Well, anyone might have, yes. He's not a lonely man. God keeps him company through the winter. You and I must have a talk. When Effingham comes. We'll send you a note, Effingham and I. I suppose that's all right, sending you a note. Don't want to offend anyone. I won't keep you now, you're shivering like a leaf. Enjoy your swim?'

'I didn't go in,' said Marian, with a sudden sense of bitter shame. She was beginning to feel slightly bullied by this plump well-clad person. 'I was afraid to,' she added.

'Wise of you, I dare say. I used to swim a lot around here before I got so fat. It's getting in and out that's tricky. Well, I'll leave you to dress. Better not dally because of the tide. We'll send you that note then. When Effingham comes. Cheerio.'

Marian saw her recede, squelching through the stones with

firm strides. She was so cold now that she could scarcely get her clothes on, and was still chilled and shivering as she began to stumble back along the beach. A cold rainy wind was blowing, and she wished heartily that she had brought a sweater. She felt completely worn out. She looked at her watch and saw with horror that it was nearly a quarter to six. She began to run.

She passed the weedy pools, where she fell twice and cut her knee. She started to pant up the steep stony track towards the house.

'There now, there now, no such hurry, no such hurry!'

She had almost run blindly into Gerald Scottow.

'I'm terribly sorry,' said Marian, gasping for breath. 'I'm late for tea.'

'We were a little worried about you. Good heavens, you haven't been in the sea, have you?'

'No, I funked it,' said Marian, and she sat down on a rock and burst into tears.

Scottow stood tall beside her. Then he pulled her gently to her feet. His manner was both solicitous and authoritative.

'There now, don't cry. But I thought I told you not to swim?'

'You did, you did,' wailed Marian.

As they started up the hill he released her arm, 'Well, do what you're told next time, Maid Marian, and we'll have fewer tears. Eh?'

Chapter Four

'Tell him if he puts one there again I'll put it down the lavatory.'

Violet Evercreech was speaking to one of the maids on the landing. Marian, who had for some time been watching the gold-fish swimming round and round the wash-basin, became rigid and breathless, hoping that Miss Evercreech would not come into the bathroom again and accuse her of some sort of complicity with Nolan's misdeed. Idiotically, she turned down the oil-lamp.

'Well, well, and what are we doing in here in the dark?'

'I'm so sorry,' said Marian. She always behaved guiltily with Violet Evercreech.

'Nothing to be sorry about that I can see,' said Miss Evercreech. She turned the lamp up again. 'Disgusting!' She indicated the fish. 'Come along now.'

People were always vaguely ushering her about at Gaze. It was the nearest they came to treating her as a servant.

Marian issued awkwardly from the bathroom. They faced each other in the half-light by the open door. Two black-clad maids faded along the landing. Miss Evercreech always seemed to have one or two in attendance. The black and white figures seemed her shadows.

'Come to my room, Marian,' said Miss Evercreech.

Put like that, the invitation sounded menacing, as if chastisement rather than entertainment were in prospect. It had not been issued before, though Marian had felt in the unnerving quality of the older woman's attention to her some hint of a significant encounter to come.

'I can't, I'm afraid,' said Marian. 'I'm just on my way to Mrs Crean-Smith. We're going to read some poetry together.' It sounded like a lie although it was the truth.

'A bit late for that sort of thing, isn't it?'

It was indeed rather late by Gaze standards, being nearly ten o'clock in the evening. Marian had been delighted by the suggestion, made by her employer earlier that day, that they should meet after dinner and read the *Cimetière marin* together. Marian was beginning to find the late evenings at Gaze rather hard to live through. She had so often yearned, cried out, simply for time, time to read, time to write, time to think, time quietly with a cigarette to *be*, to commune with objects, to expand into being herself. But now that there was time it was time with a difference, as if it had been spoilt or crossed out or used by somebody else before it reached her. She could do nothing with those late evenings. She had tried occupying herself in one of the little downstairs sitting-rooms, hoping that someone would come and talk to her. But no one came, and the oil-lamps, which she could not relight, went out. So now she usually retired to her own room and tried to stop herself from listening to the quiet house and tried to stop herself from thinking about Gerald Scottow and tried to fall asleep early. Sometimes she stood for long in the darkened room looking out at the constellation of the lights of Riders and trying to read in them some hopeful message. But they remained enigmatic. The promised summons from Alice Lejour had not come. Marian could not read or work in these hours, and while not sleepy felt exhausted, as if her energy were sapped simply by resisting some influence upon her of her too silent surroundings. So she was glad now of a chance to shorten the night. She was glad too, in quite a simple way, of the prospect of once again instructing somebody. There was no doubt that she was a little pedagogue.

'I don't know, Miss Evercreech. Anyway, we're going to read tonight and if you'll excuse me I must be getting along.' She wondered guiltily if Violet Evercreech had noticed that she had taken all the pictures down from the walls of her room. Possibly one of the maids would have told her.

Miss Evercreech drew her hand along Marian's forearm as far as the elbow, which she held in a gentle hold as if cradling an egg. 'It's nearly time for you to call me Violet. After we've had our little talk perhaps.'

'You're so kind.'

The fingers pressed and released her elbow. 'Not kind. Just fond of you. We have so little here to be fond of. Good night.'

Something touching in the words though not in their manner of utterance made Marian for a moment attend more closely to the long pale half-illuminated face; some shudder from childhood went through her, and she reflected that if she strangely lacked curiosity about Violet Evercreech it was simply because she was afraid of her. She watched the tall figure recede into darkness through a curtained archway. A light passed in the distance as a maid emerged and followed carrying a lamp.

Marian could now find her way about all the parts of the house that concerned her in the pitch dark. Sometimes lamps were lighted when darkness fell and sometimes not, and sometimes the ones that had been lighted went out and one found one's way about through blackness to intermittent glows and distant pinpoints of light. She sped now along the murky corridor toward Mrs Crean-Smith's room. A faint last evening twilight showed through tall windows the intermittent hangings.

'Come in. Ah, hello, Marian, it's you. I thought it might be Gerald.'

'Shall I fetch him?'

'No, don't bother. Come near the fire. The wind is high tonight. Come and see what we have here.'

As Marian advanced she saw a movement and noticed someone else in the room. It was Denis Nolan, who had been standing in the shadow just beyond the mantelpiece. He shifted into the lamplight and darted her a cold ray from his very blue eyes.

Hannah Crean-Smith, who was wearing a dress tonight instead of her usual dressing-gown, was kneeling on the hearth rug scrutinizing something which lay before her on the floor.

'What is it?' said Marian.

She joined them and looked at the thing on the floor. It was a little brown thing, and it took her a moment to make out, with a slight shudder, that it was a bat.

'Isn't it a dear?' said Hannah Crean-Smith. 'Denis brought it. He always brings me things. Hedgehogs, snakes, toads, nice beasts.'

'It has something wrong with it,' said Nolan gloomily. 'I don't suppose it'll live.'

Marian knelt down too. The bat, a little pipistrel, was pulling itself slowly along the rug with jerky movements of its crumpled leathery arms. It paused and looked up. Marian looked into its strange little doggy face and bright dark eyes. It had an almost uncanny degree of presence, of being. She met its look. Then it opened its little toothy mouth and uttered a high-pitched squawk. Marian laughed and then felt a sudden desire to cry. Without knowing why, she felt she could hardly bear Mrs Crean-Smith and the bat together, as if they were suddenly the same grotesque helpless thing.

'Dear, dear little creature,' said Mrs Crean-Smith. 'Odd to think that it's a mammal, like us. I can feel such a strange affinity with it, can't you?' She stroked its furry back with a finger and the bat huddled up. 'Put it in its box again, Denis. You will look after it, won't you?' In some way she could hardly bear the bat either.

'There's nothing I can do for it,' said Nolan. He picked the bat up quickly with one hand, gently. His hands were small and very dirty. He put the creature in a box on the table.

'Help yourself to some whiskey, Marian. Have you brought the books? Good. I hope you won't mind waiting a few minutes. Denis is just going to cut my hair.'

This surprised Marian. She had connected Nolan, in so far as she had thought of him at all, with the out-of-doors. She had thought of him as something rather elusive and muddy to be associated with the mysterious horses which were kept somewhere at the far end of the rhododendron slope. She would have thought him ill enough fitted to the role of *valet de chambre*.

Nolan seemed rather embarrassed and surly at the prospect of a witness. Hannah Crean-Smith, however, had settled herself into a chair and drawn a towel round her shoulders and there was nothing for him to do but to begin. He picked up the comb and scissors and began to handle the plentiful mass of red-golden hair.

Marian felt embarrassed too, as if she were being forced to be present at too intimate a rite. Yet she noticed with a sort of admiration the feudal indifference with which her employer treated the odd little occasion.

Nolan was surprisingly competent. Once he had started, his face softened into a dignified intentness as he flicked the silky stuff this way and that and snipped at it busily. The bright golden clippings furred the towel and sifted quietly to the floor. Marian observed for the first time that he was quite a good-looking man. The dry shaggy locks of blue-black hair framed a firm, ruddy, small-featured face, wherein now the surly look could be seen as a look of cautious watchfulness. And then there were the very striking eyes. Marian met them now with a sudden shock as Nolan, aware of her scrutiny, took her gaze for a moment over the red-golden head. His glance was like the flash of a kingfisher. She shifted her attention hastily to Mrs Crean-Smith's face. It wore a dreamy expression.

'I really don't know what I'd do without Denis.' Mrs Crean-Smith, her head immobile under the still-active scissors, reached a hand back and took hold of Nolan's tweed jacket. Her hand nuzzled into his pocket. Marian looked away. Her averted gaze took in the photograph upon the desk.

'You've been singeing your hair with those cigarettes again.'

'I am bad, aren't I!'

Marian had noticed the curiously frizzled appearance of the front hair.

'That's done now.' Nolan whisked away the towel and shook the cuttings into the fire, where they flamed up. He knelt and gathered the pieces from the floor. As he grovelled at her feet, Mrs Crean-Smith caressed his shoulder with a light almost shy touch.

Marian was troubled. Yet the scene had a great naturalness about it and she sensed that it had happened, somewhat like this, many times before.

'Now my shoes and stockings. I may want to go out later.'

Nolan brought her stockings and watched expressionlessly while, with a hint of petticoats and suspenders, she put them on. Then he knelt again to put on her shoes.

Marian saw that the soles of the shoes were unworn. She said, in order to break the silence which distressed her, 'What pretty new shoes.'

'They are not new,' said Mrs Crean-Smith. 'They are seven years old.'

Nolan looked up at her.

Marian had again the rather uncanny feeling of puzzlement with which her employer often affected her. She could still not make out whether Mrs Crean-Smith were not somehow ill, or convalescing from some grave ailment. The way the people of the house treated her sometimes suggested this. The idea had also at one point come into her mind, put there by something scarcely definable in Gerald Scottow's manner, that Mrs Crean-Smith might be not always, entirely, absolutely right in the head. She was certainly an eccentric lady.

To pass off the strangeness of the moment Marian said, 'You've kept them very well!'

'I don't do much walking.'

It occurred to Marian that indeed Mrs Crean-Smith had not been outside the house since her own arrival here. She must be ill, thought Marian.

Nolan stood back, preparing to be dismissed. He was a trifle shorter than either of the women, and seemed smaller still, almost dwarfish, frowning now and bunched up.

'Stay, Denis, you shall read too.'

Marian was surprised. She said thoughtlessly, 'Oh, can you read French?'

'Yes.' He gave her a hostile look.

Marian thought, he is a little jealous of me. He sees me as an intruder here.

'Denis is very clever,' said Mrs Crean-Smith. 'You should hear him play the piano and sing. We must have a musical evening soon. Do stay.'

'No. I must go and see to my fishes.' He picked up the box with the bat in it. 'Good night.' He retired abruptly.

'Look after my little bat,' said Mrs Crean-Smith after him. She sighed. 'Has he shown you the salmon pool?'

'No,' said Marian. 'I've hardly talked to Mr Nolan. Are there salmon then? Mr Scottow said they'd gone.'

'They've come back. Only don't tell Mr Scottow.'

Ill – or deranged, thought Marian.

'He *will* show you the salmon pool, I expect. Have you ever seen salmon leaping? It's a most moving sight. They spring right out of the water and struggle up the rocks. Such fantastic bravery, to enter another element like that. Like souls approaching God.'

As Marian reflected upon the slightly unexpected simile, her employer rose and began to glide about the room. She was much given to looking at herself in mirrors. She moved now from glass to glass. 'Listen to the wind. It can blow dreadfully here. In the winter it blows so that it would drive you mad. It blows day after day and one becomes so restless. What do you think of my page?'

'Your – Mr Nolan? He seems very devoted.'

'I think he would let me kill him slowly.'

There was a startling possessive savagery in the words which was oddly at variance with the accustomed *douceur*. Yet her manner, it struck Marian suddenly, was that of a sort of despair. Ill, or deranged, or in despair.

'But everyone here is devoted to you, Mrs Crean-Smith.'

'Please call me Hannah. Yes, I know, I'm lucky, Gerald Scottow is a tower of strength. Shall we read now? You shall start, you have such a lovely accent, and later we'll see if I can translate it all.'

Transported immediately, forgetting all else, into a familiar world of delight Marian began to read.

> *Ce toit tranquille, où marchent des colombes,*
> *Entre les pins palpite, entre les tombes;*
> *Midi le juste y compose de feux*
> *La mer, la mer, toujours recommencée. . . .*

Chapter Five

'All the people round here are related to the fairies,' said Jamesie Evercreech.

Marian laughed.

She was in a good humour. It was a bright sunny day and the sea was the colour of amethyst. The wind had dropped. The base of the black cliffs steamed gently in the hot sun. She and Jamesie were bowling along in the Land Rover in the direction of Blackport, where they were to pick up a crate of whiskey and some clothes which had come on approval for Hannah. Jamesie, who was a keen photographer, was also going to get supplies for his camera. He had used up his last roll of colour film taking a large number of pictures of Marian on the previous day. She was partly flattered and partly unreasoningly alarmed at this attention.

Today all seemed suddenly gay and normal and Marian was quite simply delighted at the thought of a visit to civilization. To see a paved street, to buy a newspaper, to enter a shop, see ordinary people passing, these things seemed positive treats; and although the pubs were taboo, there was apparently a little fishing hotel where she could see a row of bottles and order herself a drink: old rites, familiar and greatly missed.

The last few days at Gaze had been exceptionally somnolent. She had started reading *La Princesse de Clèves* with Hannah and they had almost fallen asleep over it at eleven o'clock in the morning. The wind had been blowing, producing the aching restlessness of which Hannah had spoken. Gerald Scottow had been unobtrusively absent, had unobtrusively returned, had continued to be polite, dignified, charming and totally unapproachable. Violet Evercreech had been intense and attentive but had not yet again proposed the 'little talk'. Alice Lejour had been silent. Marian had reflected long and vainly about why the Lejours were never mentioned at Gaze. She had scanned Riders frequently through her glasses and had once or twice seen a youngish man and a dog on the terrace. Feeling today lively and more than usually liberated from shyness, she resolved to question Jamesie about a lot of things before the journey should be out.

'You don't come from around here, do you? I mean, have you got fairy blood?'

'No. I'm one of the other lot.'

'Of course – you're related to Mrs Crean-Smith.'

'Distantly.' He gave his little weird cry of a laugh.

The car descended steeply into a ravine where the road, behind a low buttressed sea-wall, almost skirted the waves. Marian felt an unpleasant thrill, almost like a sense of guilt, at the sudden proximity of the sea. She had not tried to swim again. She looked hastily inland up a hazy tree-entangled gully. A bright line of trembling light was a distant water-fall.

'A pretty place.'

'A rather nasty place, really. It's called the Devil's Causeway. There are some very funny-looking rock forms, further up, you can't see from here.' He added, 'Something dreadful happened there on the night of the flood.'

'What?'

'That little river you saw, like our river at Gaze, came suddenly roaring down from the bog and carried away a car from the road and threw it into the sea and everyone was drowned.'

'How awful. Were you here when the flood happened?'

'No. But Mr Scottow was.'

'How long has he been here?'

'Seven years.'

'I suppose there's no danger of it happening again, something like that?'

'Oh no. The lake had gone, you see. You must go up on the bog sometime, to the edge anyhow. It's pretty up there in a funny way. The local people are frightened of it, of course. They only go there in broad daylight to cut turf. Then if the sky becomes at all overcast they run. The bog certainly turns very queer colours.'

'I expect they think their relations live there!'

'I expect they *do* live there. I wouldn't go up there in the dark myself for any money. There are strange lights. Anyway, unless you know the paths you can sink into it. There are brushwood paths, but you can get sucked down. A man was sunk in the bog two years ago. They heard him calling all night, but no one could get near him and he sunk in and died.'

Marian shuddered not only at the tale but at some relish in Jamesie's telling of it. The boy was not all sunshine.

'I suppose Denis Nolan is a local man?'

'Yes, he's one of them. He's not really here at all. He's one of the invisible ones. We call him the invisible man. His father was a gillie at Riders.'

'At Riders, really? I met Miss Lejour the other day. She said she'd invite me over to Riders when someone called Effingham Cooper arrived.'

'That'll be a treat! Was she very full of Effingham Cooper?'

'Well, now that I come to think of it she did mention his name quite a number of times. Are they – engaged, or something?'

Jamesie laughed shrilly. 'Not at all. Though I expect she wanted you to think so! She's been making herself a fool about Effingham Cooper for years, everyone knows it. And he doesn't care for her at all.'

Marian was interested. She wanted to keep the conversation on Riders. 'Then why does he come here?'

'For the old man. But mainly – oh, mainly for Mrs Crean-Smith.' Jamesie cackled again.

Marian was very interested. She did not want to seem too curious or to want to gossip with Jamesie about Hannah, but she could not resist saying casually, 'I suppose Mrs Crean-Smith is a widow?'

'No. Mr Crean-Smith lives in New York.' Jamesie smiled his wide brilliant smile at the empty road and accelerated.

'Are they – divorced?'

'No, no.' He went on smiling and darted a quick look at her.

Marian was disturbed by his provocative enjoyment of her curiosity. She said, to change the subject and because the information had seemed for some reason interesting, 'You say Mr Scottow came to this region seven years ago?'

'Oh no. He came to Gaze Castle seven years ago. He's been in the region almost all his life. He's a local man too. He was born in the village. His mother still lives there.'

'Really!' said Marian. She was very surprised and somehow disconcerted. Yet at the next moment the figure of Gerald Scottow appeared in her imagination more fascinating and mysterious than ever. So he too had fairy blood.

'Yes. He's quite the gent now, isn't he?' said Jamesie. 'He likes to keep his old ma dark!' He giggled, seeming to enjoy the revelation. Yet it had also seemed to Marian that he was very fond of Scottow.

Jamesie went on. 'His da worked at Riders like Denis's da. Only Denis stayed on there and Gerald went off to town and got grand.'

'Oh, Denis worked at Riders?' Any connexion with the other house was a matter of concern.

'Yes. Till they chucked him out!'

'What did they chuck him out for?'

'Shall I tell you? Yes I will! He jumped on Miss Lejour one day.' Jamesie laughed so much that the car swerved.

'*Jumped* on her?'

'Yes. Tried to mount her you know. He was with her up at the salmon pool. There used to be salmon up there. And suddenly he sprung on her. Not a thing I'd do, though I suppose she was prettier then. It's not so very long ago though. After that they were afraid for the maids and everything and they asked him to leave.'

'How very surprising,' said Marian. It was surprising. She could not at all picture the subdued and gloomy Denis doing any such thing. He had not the look of a satyr. He was like a wild thing that hides, not a wild thing that pursues. Perhaps that explained the resentful yet penitential air which he carried about with him. It added a new interest to his image, however. She wondered if Mrs Crean-Smith was ever afraid of being 'jumped on'.

'This is the best view-place,' said Jamesie. He slowed down abruptly and turned the car off the road. There was a sudden silence and they both got out into the warm sunshine. The cliff edge was near and they walked towards it.

It was a clear day. The sea, at the horizon a hazier blue, faded away into azure light and became sky. To the north the bastions of limestone were a dark purple. To the south the land sloped now and the cliffs had ended. A few scattered cabins and tiny walled fields lined with blazing fuchsia appeared on the seaward shelves. Then there was the little harbour of Blackport with its yellow and black lighthouse and a cluster of sails and a long green headland beyond. Here the landscape was gentle, ordinary, human. It was the end of the appalling land.

Marian had been absorbed for some time in the delight of looking when she realized that Jamesie was staring at her. After a moment she looked at him quickly. Some significant unsmiling message passed between them. She went back to gazing, but now the scene was invisible.

Jamesie continued to stare. She was aware of his face. He said at last in a deeper voice. 'I've never known a woman like you. You're different. You're real. Like a man.'

Marian was both unnerved and pleased at the unexpected change of key. No woman minds such a sudden disarming of her traditional adversary. She became tense and still, realizing that in a moment he might touch her. She had not expected this. She said quickly and lightly, 'Well, I hope that's all right!'

'Very all right. You'll make a difference.'

To what? Marian wondered. She smiled vaguely and moved a little forward away from him toward the edge of the cliff. The sense of the sheer drop below suddenly pierced her body. She began to hear the far-off beating of the sea. She fell almost involuntarily upon her knees.

Jamesie knelt beside her. It was like a strange rite. She felt the rough sleeve of his coat touch her bare arm. She felt giddy and alarmed and said at random, 'See, what a dreadfully long way down. One could not go over there and live.'

He said something which she could not catch.

'What?'

'I said Peter Crean-Smith did.'

'*What*?'

'Fell over the cliff and lived. Seven years ago.'

Marian turned to him. He was looking at her with a kind of delight. The cliff seemed to shake with the heart-beats of the sea. She began to say something.

'Hello you two, what are you up to?'

Jamesie and Marian both jumped to their feet, jerking away from each other, and stumbled back from the cliff edge.

Gerald Scottow, mounted on a massive grey horse, was close behind them. The pounding of the sea had covered his approach. Marian felt, at the sight of him, a mixture of guilt, excitement and relief.

Jamesie went toward Scottow and stood at his horse's head, looking at him. There was a sort of confiding submissive surrender in the immediate close approach. Marian followed more slowly.

Scottow mounted looked huge. He was casually dressed, his check shirt lolling open from his long thick neck. But his riding-boots were bright with polish. She smelt their sweet resinous leathery smell as she came near him now. She was glad that Jamesie had not touched her.

Scottow and Jamesie were still regarding each other. Scottow said, 'Have you been telling fairy stories?' He laughed and brushed the boy's cheek lightly with his whip.

Chapter Six

'That suits you, Marian, look!' said Hannah. She held up the
big hand-mirror which they had brought out with them on to
the terrace.

It was a warm still evening, after dinner but not yet very
late, and they were sitting out at one of the little white iron-
work tables, sipping whiskey and trying on some of Hannah's
jewels. An unclouded sun, very soon to be quenched in a level
golden sea, had turned everything on the land to a brilliant
saffron yellow. Marian felt as if she and Hannah were on a
stage, so violent and unusual was the lighting. Their hands and
faces were gilded. Long shadows stretched away behind
them; and the big rounded clumps of wild sea-pinks which
grew in the cracks of the pavement, having each its shadow,
dissolved the terrace about their feet into a pitted, chequered
cloth. The sense of play-acting was increased too by the fact
that they were both in evening-dress. At last Marian was wearing the blue cocktail dress which Geoffrey approved of, and
Hannah was wearing a long dress, one which she had selected
from the collection which came on approval. It was a light
mauve dress of heavy grained silk with a tight high bodice and
vaguely medieval air. With a golden chain about her neck she
looked, thought Marian, like some brave beleaguered lady in
a legend or like some painter's dream of 'ages far agone'.

Hannah had suggested that they should have, tonight, to in-
augurate the dress, a little celebration, with some champagne
and a better wine than usual, and that Marian should dress up
to match. Gerald Scottow and Violet Evercreech had joined
them for the champagne, and conversation had been animated
though singularly impersonal and polite. They had dined à
deux. Hannah had complained playfully that Gerald was

neglecting her, and Marian had had the thought that Gerald was avoiding *her*. She did not know what to make of this thought. She had enjoyed the novelty of the little dinner, but it had had somehow a slightly forced pathetic air.

Now they were playing with Hannah's big box of jewels which she had insisted on bringing out and spreading carelessly about on the table. Marian had already rescued an earring which had fallen to the ground and rolled into a crevice in the cracked pavement. She knew little about jewels, but she felt sure that these ones were very good indeed.

Hannah had just clipped round Marian's neck a necklace of little pearls and rubies set in gold. She stared at herself in the mirror. The necklace was like something out of the Victoria and Albert Museum. She had never even remotely coveted such an object. It seemed to change her, to change even the blue dress. Something, whether it was the necklace or the golden light or the mirror itself, enchanted by so often reflecting the lovely face of its owner, made her for a moment see herself as beautiful.

After having been silent too long she said, 'Yes, wonderful.'

'Yours!'

'You mean –?'

'The necklace. Please have it. I have so many, you see, and I hardly ever wear them. It would give me real pleasure to give you that one.'

'Oh, I *couldn't* –' said Marian. 'It's far too – too grand, too expensive for me!' The words sounded suddenly mean.

'Nonsense! Let me bully you a little. You shall have the necklace. No, no more. And don't start to take it off. It's meant to be worn.'

Marian mumbled her thanks, upset and blushing. Yet she could not help being delighted at receiving so wonderful a present. She fingered it nervously.

They both fell silent, Marian troubled and Hannah seemingly rapt into some other train of thought. She seemed tonight, Marian thought, more alert, less somnolent than usual. The sun, round and reddening, had sunk to the horizon and was descending now into a burning sea. The golden radiance faded into a vivid blue twilight and a huge figured silver moon, which had awaited its moment, became visible above the roof. Something in the scene caught Marian's eye. It was the lights appearing at Riders. She half turned her head and saw Hannah looking in the same direction. She began to try to think of some way of at once and naturally alluding to the other house.

Hannah forestalled her. 'I shall ask Effingham Cooper over to see my new dress. You must meet him.'

Marian was stunned. After such a prolonged silence on the subject of Riders this casual direct allusion surprised and confused her. And yet she realized at once too that the allusion was not really so casual. Hannah's manner was the slightest bit awkward, as if the remark had been premeditated and a little hard to get out.

Marian tried to reply smoothly. 'Is Mr Cooper there now?' The words confessed to knowledge.

'He's arriving tomorrow.'

Then after tomorrow Alice Lejour might summon her. The two women did not look at each other. Marian desperately wanted to keep the conversation going. She said, 'Old Mr Lejour must be glad of visitors. Mr Scottow said he was a scholar. Do you know what he studies?'

'Greek, I think. Plato. He's writing a book on Plato.'

'I wish I knew Greek. What is he like, the old gentleman?'

'I don't know,' said Hannah. 'I've never met him.' She turned to face Marian.

Completely routed by this reply she hardly dared now to meet her employer's gaze. When she did she realized that Hannah was once more thinking hard about something else; and it took her another moment to understand that the much-ringed hand which was urgently thrust out towards her amid the finery was intended to be seized. She seized it.

This was the first time that Marian had looked at Hannah directly in this way. Indeed such looks, anywhere, had been rare in her life. She was suddenly aware of a vast claim being made upon her and she stiffened and lifted herself to be ready for whatever was demanded. The anxious tired beautiful defeated golden-eyed face blazed at her for a moment in the half-light as if it had been literally illuminated.

'Forgive me,' said Hannah.

'For what?'

'For so shamelessly crying out for love.' She kept Marian's hand a moment and then released it, glancing up at the house. But she returned her urgent look to the girl's face as if signalling to her that there was no breaking off and that the conversation was to continue in the same key.

'Well – you know that I love you,' said Marian. She was surprised to hear herself saying this. It was not the sort of thing she came out with usually. Yet it seemed quite natural here, or as if it were compelled from her.

'Yes. Thank you. I think, don't you, that one ought to cry out more for love, to ask for it. It's odd how afraid people are of the word. Yet we all need love. Even God needs love. I suppose that's why He created us.'

'He made a bad arrangement,' said Marian, smiling. Since uttering the word she felt that she did love Hannah more: or simply that she did love her, since she had given no name before to her affectionate feelings.

'You mean because people don't love Him? Ah, but they do. Surely we all love Him under some guise or other. We have to. He desires our love so much, and a great desire for love can call love into being. Do you believe in God?'

'No,' said Marian. She felt no guilt at this admission, she was too firmly held in the conversation. She had not realized that Hannah was a religious person. She never went to church. 'You do?'

'Yes, I suppose I do. I've never really questioned it. I'm no good at thinking. I just have to believe. I have to love God.'

'But suppose you're loving – something that isn't there?'

'In a way you can't love something that isn't there. I think if you really love, then something *is* there. But I don't understand these things.'

It was almost dark now. The outline of Riders had faded

from the sky, leaving the constellation of lights. A figure crossed the end of the terrace and descended the steps, vanishing in the direction of the fish ponds. The silver moon had shrunk into a pale golden coin and was already melting its light into the last twilight. A small breeze was blowing from the sea.

Hannah shivered and drew on her shawl. 'I hope that wind isn't going to start again.'

'*Le vent se lève – il faut tenter de vivre.*'

'Ah –' She paused, and then went on. 'This is a sad time of day – of night. How mysterious day and night are, this endless procession of dark and light. The transition always affects me. I think such sad thoughts – of people in trouble and afraid, all lonely people, all prisoners. Well – I'll go in now. You take a turn in the garden.'

'Won't you come too? Let's go out on the cliffs and see the moonlight.'

'No, you go. I'd like to think of you there. Go out that way, it's quicker. Good night. Forgive me.' She rose quickly and faded before Marian could get to her feet.

The girl stood awhile, puzzled and moved. She was glad as at the breaking of some barrier. She was touched by some appeal. She had wanted to say: I don't know what you require of me, but I'll try to do it, to be it. Only she had not at all understood the conversation.

The moon was now in full possession of the sky. She began to walk slowly through the garden. When she reached the gate which Hannah had indicated, she tried to pull it open, but it resisted her as if someone were holding it from the other side. For a moment she was nervous. Then she tugged again and it came open, spattering her with earth and sand. She tried to go out.

The moon cast behind her in the garden the black shadow of the stone wall. The smooth sheep-nibbled lawn of grass that led to the cliff top lay clear before her, empty, shadowless, appallingly stilled by the dim cold illumination. Marian stood in the doorway. Something behind her, something that she feared, seemed yet like a magnet holding her back. The garden was thick and magnetic behind her. Her desire to go out was gone. She was afraid to step outside. She stood paralysed in the gateway for some time, keeping her breathing quiet. The great lawn at the cliff top remained cold and attentive, visible yet unreal, waiting to see what she would do.

Chapter Seven

Some while later Marian began to walk back through the wrecked gardens. The moon had been quenched in cloud. She had not been outside. She had had to detach herself from the archway almost by pulling her hands off the stone, so alarming did everything seem both in front of her and behind her. She had never felt quite like this before, alone in her own mind; and yet not quite alone, for somewhere in the big darkness something was haunting her. She said to herself, I can't go on like this, I must talk to somebody. Yet to whom and about what? What had she to complain of, other than the loneliness and boredom which was perfectly to be expected? Why was she suddenly now so frightened and sickened?

She saw ahead of her a small light moving in the darkness of the garden and she stopped in a fresh alarm. The light moved, questing, hesitating. It vanished for a moment and reappeared, a little round spot of light moving over foliage and stone. Marian decided that it must be an electric torch. She moved forward silently upon the gravel path, now grown so grassy and mossy that her feet made no sound. The light was a little to the right of the path, and the breathless girl had no thought but to glide quickly past it and then run in the direction of the house. Her heart fluttered violently and she increased her pace.

The light suddenly darted at her and she stopped in her tracks, seeing her feet, her dress, abruptly illumined. The gravel crunched under her heels. It was the first sound for a long time. The light moved up to her face and dazzled her and she gasped, caught.

'Miss Taylor.'

It was Denis Nolan's voice. She should have remembered that

he sometimes went out late at night to look at his fish by torch-light.

'Mr Nolan. You frightened me.'

'I'm so sorry.'

They had remained on these formal, slightly hostile, terms. As Marian stepped towards him on to the rough grass she recalled the story of his 'jumping on' Alice Lejour. Yet now she did not feel afraid.

They stood for a moment, the circle of light between them on the grass. Then she said, 'May I see the fish? I've never looked at them properly.'

He guided her, laying the light at her feet, to the cracked stone verge. The three oval lily pools had once formed part of an Italianate ornamental garden, but the paving round about them had long ago been overgrown with broom and ash saplings and all kinds of wild flowers. The white and dark red lilies still flourished, and the torchlight now skimmed the big dry leaves and the folded heads. Then the light plunged downward.

Nolan was kneeling, and Marian knelt beside him. The wire netting which usually covered the ponds had been rolled back. 'What is the wire for?'

'For the cranes.'

'The cranes? Oh – the herons. Yes. I suppose they'd take the fish.'

She looked down into the underwater world. It was green and deep and full of shaggy motionless vegetation. The fish moved, undisturbed by the torchlight, with a meditative slowness, plump golden forms.

'Those are goldfish, those are shubunkins, those quick slim fellows are orfe, golden orfe. And you can see a tench, there the dark green one, you can hardly see him, a green tench, *tinca tinca*.'

'That's his zoological name.'

'Yes.'

'How pretty. Where is Strawberry Nose?'

Nolan turned towards her in the dark and the lighted torch broke the surface with a soft splash.

'How did you know that name?'

'You had him in a bowl when I first met you and you named him to Mr Scottow.'

'Oh. He is in the other pool. He is well now.'

Marian felt that she had hurt him. He had the humourless dignity of the local people. He could not tolerate the lightest touch of mockery. Yet she had not been mocking. She said quickly, 'How is the little bat?'

'It died.'

Marian sat back on the stone verge of the pool. She was conscious now of the fragrant bushy darkness about her and of the bulk of the house near by, outlined against the sky which the hidden moon had lightened to a bluish black. There was a light in one window, she could not identify which. The stone was still warm from the day's sun. The torch faltered, skimmed the water and went out.

Marian said, 'Mr Nolan, would you mind if I asked you a few questions?'

He was standing now, as if about to go away. She could see his head and shoulders dimly above her. 'What questions?'

'What is the matter with this place?'

He paused before answering. Then he switched the torch on for a moment and shone it quickly round about them. The dark green broom bushes and a haze of harebells and white daisies and ragged vetch were suddenly vivid and then gone. He said, 'Nothing is the matter with this place. You are just not used to such a lonely place.'

'Don't put me off,' said Marian. She had known, as soon as she stepped off the gravel path, that the moment of revelation had come. 'Sit down, Mr Nolan. You've got to tell me, at any rate to tell me something. What was it that happened seven years ago?'

He fell on one knee near to her, disappearing against the darker background of the garden. 'Nothing happened, nothing special. Why?'

'Come,' said Marian. 'I know a lot of things already. About Mr Crean-Smith falling over the cliff and so on. You must tell me more. There *is* something very odd about this place, and

58

it's not just the loneliness, I'm sure. Please talk to me. You must see how difficult it is for me here, and how awful it is in a way. Talk to me, or I shall have to ask someone else.' The speech came from her without forethought and she felt as she spoke that Nolan was caught by it. He sat down. Their knees were close together upon the warm rough stone.

'I can't tell you anything.'

'There is something to tell, then? But I must know if I'm to stay on here and not become quite deranged –'

'Like the rest of us –' he said softly.

'Please tell. Otherwise I shall ask Mrs Crean-Smith.'

'Oh, don't do that –'

He was alarmed. She had struck the right note again. 'Come on, Denis.' His name came naturally now.

'Look – well – wait a minute.' He flashed the torch all round them once more, slowly and carefully. The light in the house had gone out. 'I will tell you something. It is true that you must know it if you are to stay here. And I would rather tell you myself than have you learn it from another.'

He paused. There was a little liquid sound of a fish breaking the surface. 'You ask what is the matter with this place. I will tell you. What is the matter with it is that it is a prison.'

'A prison?' said Marian, astonished, and tense now at the nearness of the revelation. Her heart beat painfully. 'A prison? Who is the prisoner?'

'Mrs Crean-Smith.'

She felt she had half known it. Yet how could she have done? Even now she did not understand it. 'And who are the gaolers?'

'Mr Scottow. Miss Evercreech. Jamesie. You. Me.'

'No, no!' she said. 'Not me! But I don't know what you're talking about. Do you mean that Mrs Crean-Smith is – shut up here, incarcerated?'

'Yes.'

'But this is mad. What about Mr Crean-Smith, why doesn't he –'

'Rescue her? It is at his will that she is shut up.'

'I don't understand at all,' said Marian. She felt again the sick panic which had gripped her by the gateway, and which she had felt prophetically upon the first day. 'Is Mrs Crean-Smith – ill – I mean insane, or dangerous, or anything?'

'No.'

'Well then, why is she shut up? People can't be just shut up. We're not living in the Middle Ages.'

'We are here. But never mind. She is shut up by her husband because she deceived him and tried to kill him.'

'Oh God –' She was far beyond curiosity now. She felt sheerly frightened of the story to come as if it might shake her reason. She was for a moment on the point of stopping him.

But he went on in a low voice. 'I had better tell you all in order. Now that I have told you this much. It is quickly enough told. And God forgive me if I do wrong. It was like this. Hannah Crean-Smith is a rich woman, was a rich girl, rich in her own right, of the landowning families of this part. This house, for instance, and all this land for miles belongs to her. And she married very young, married her first cousin, Peter Crean-Smith. He was, God forgive me if I wrong him, a brute of a young man, though a charming one, a drinker and a runner after women and violent to his wife and other things more. It was not a good marriage. She was unhappy, and so it went on. They were at this house often enough, for he loved the fishing and the shooting and that. And so it went on. And then there came Philip Lejour.'

'Philip Lejour?'

'Yes. Him they call Pip Lejour. Old Mr Lejour's son. Young Mr Lejour bought Riders then, when it was a wreck of a place, bought it for a song, to use it as a hunting-lodge, and he rented the shooting and the fishing, and so he and Mr Crean-Smith were acquainted and Mrs Crean-Smith too. The men would be often shooting together. That would be nine years or so ago. Then Mr Crean-Smith went away to America on business. I suppose it was on business, though I know nothing of his business apart from being a rich young man. And when he went away Mrs Crean-Smith and Mr Lejour fell in love with each other, and they made love to each other.'

He paused and again flashed the torch. The garden was utterly silent.

'This was how it was for a time, and Mr Crean-Smith knew nothing about it. How long a time I don't know, and I don't know what Mrs Crean-Smith would have done. But one day Mr Crean-Smith came back unexpectedly, came back here to Gaze, and found his wife in the bed with young Mr Lejour.' He paused. 'That was seven years ago.'

He was silent then for a while as if rapt entirely into the story. He went on. 'I told you that Mr Crean-Smith was a violent man. Is, for he still is. God forgive me if I wrong him. He was very violent then.'

'To Mr Lejour?'

'To his wife.'

He seemed for a moment choked to silence by emotion. He continued. 'He kept her then in the house, kept her locked in.'

'What did Mr Lejour do?'

'He went away. What could he do? He would have taken her off, he would have rescued her. She knew that. There were letters, there were people to bring letters, though they risked terrible treatment from him, from the husband. But she would not come.'

'Why not? If Mr Crean-Smith was so —'

'She was married to him in a church.'

'Yes, but still, when —'

'How can we know her mind? Perhaps she was afraid of him, and she must indeed have been terribly afraid of him. It would not have been easy even to leave the house. She was guarded, she was watched. Besides, to leave her husband, to go into the world — remember she married very young. Possibly she simply would not. Perhaps she felt, for it all, guilt, sorrow, even then.'

'Even then —?'

'Something else happened. What I told you was only a little while. Some months, weeks maybe. I don't know what she would have done. But there was something else. One day — after some violence maybe, I don't know what — she ran out of the house. She ran out of the door to the cliffs, the door you came from just now. She ran out toward the cliff top. God in

His mercy knows what was in her mind – suicide, it might be, to throw herself from the cliff. Or perhaps she was just running away with no thought at all. Mr Crean-Smith ran after her. What happened then nobody knows for sure. But there was a struggle between them and Mr Crean-Smith went over the edge of the cliff.'

'Oh God –' said Marian. She felt sick, stifled as with a taste or smell of burning. She jumped at the flash of the torch. It was dark again.

'He lived. It was like a miracle. There is a sort of cranny in the cliff there, I don't know if you've seen it, a break, a little stony channel of an old stream maybe, and he fell into that. It was a big fall, but he lived.'

'Was he – much hurt?'

'I don't know. He lived. People say he was maimed somehow or hurt, hurt for good, but they say different things of what it was happened to him, and I don't know.'

'You haven't seen – since?'

'No. And little enough before indeed. I was not at Gaze then. He has not set foot here since that time seven years ago.'

'And she –?'

'She was – shut up.'

'You mean ever since, seven years?'

'Yes. He shut her up. It was then he brought Gerald Scottow into the house. Gerald was his friend, from childhood they were friends here though of different worlds, when he came to fish as a boy, and he trusted Gerald and he set Gerald to look to her. And so the time has passed.'

'But my God!' said Marian, 'this is all mad. She's not kept here by force, is she, she could go away if she wanted to, she –'

'You are forgetting *her*.'

'You mean she stays – voluntarily – now?'

'Who can say what is in her mind? She was at first confined to the domain. Many miles she could go either way, and she rode her horse a lot then. Then one day, five years ago it was, she suddenly left and galloped her horse to Greytown and was on the train before anyone knew. And she went to her father's house.'

'And what happened?'

'Her father would not receive her. He sent her back.'

'But why did she go?'

'Who can say what was in her mind? Remember it was her first cousin and families are powerful things, those families are. And she wed as a young girl and her not able to strike a match for herself. It's a wonder she was able to buy a railway ticket. She came back.'

'And then –?'

'And then it was a rumour that he was coming, Peter Crean-Smith, and she was near mad, but he did not come. But he confined her then to the garden.'

'You mean she hasn't been outside the garden for five years?'

'She has not. And it was then he sent the Evercreeches to be here, they were poor relatives, and he sent them to add to the watch. They are not close, but they are her nearest relatives, after her husband, now her father is dead.'

'This is an insane story!' said Marian shrilly. She lowered her voice. 'I don't mean I don't believe you. But it's all mad. You say "I am forgetting her". But what *about* her? Why does she put up with it all, why doesn't she just pack and go away? Surely, Gerald Scottow and the rest of you wouldn't forcibly restrain her? And surely there are people anyway who know about her? What about this Effingham Cooper? What about young Mr Lejour? What is he doing? What –'

'Mr Lejour watches and waits. He comes every summer here. He has done up the house and has brought his old father to live here. He comes and he watches. But there is nothing for him to do. And I don't know if there is anything he wants to do – now.'

Marian recalled the man with the field-glasses whom she had so abruptly encountered on her first evening at Gaze. 'He doesn't – see her, communicate with her?'

'He is not allowed to see her, and as far as I know he does not communicate with her. He could only make her situation worse, he could only harm her.'

'But this is all absolutely appalling. What about you? Surely you can help her? Surely you aren't on their side?'

'What is – helping her?'

'But I still don't understand. Does she *want* to stay here?'

'Perhaps. You must know that she is a religious person.'

'What has religion to do with it? Did she – Do you think that she did really push him over?'

'I don't know. Perhaps she does not know now. But there are – acts which belong to people somehow regardless of their will.'

'You mean she'd feel responsible anyway? Do *you* think she pushed him over?'

He paused. 'Yes, perhaps. But is not important to say so. She has claimed the act and one has no right to take it from her.'

'I just can't imagine it. Staying so long in one small place. I'm surprised she hasn't run mad.'

'There are holy nuns in the convent at Blackport who live forever in smaller places.'

'But they have faith.'

'Perhaps Mrs Crean-Smith has faith.'

'Yes, but she's wrong. I mean, it can't be right to give way to that sort of thing. It's morbid. And it's bad for him as well as for her. Do the people about here generally know about her?'

'The local people? Yes, they know. She is a legend in this part of the country. They believe that if she comes outside the garden she will die.'

'They think she is really under a curse?'

'Yes. And they think that at the end of seven years something will happen to her.'

'Why seven years? Just because that's the time things go on for in fairy tales? But it is the end of seven years now!'

'Yes. But nothing is going to happen.'

'Something has happened. I have come.'

He was silent, as if shrugging his shoulders.

'Why have I come?' said Marian. Her own place in the story occurred to her for the first time. The ghastly tale had become a reality all about her, it was still going on. And it was a tale in which nothing happened at random. 'Who decided I should come, and why?'

'That has puzzled me,' he said. 'I think it may be simply – some moment of compassion. Or it may be that you are to be a sort of chaperone.'

'Who do I chaperone, who with her, I mean?'

'Oh, anyone. Mr Cooper, for instance. He is one of the few people who is allowed to visit her. He is a harmless man. But there might now be a chaperone to make sure. Or else it might be some torture.'

'Some torture?'

'To make her fond of you and then take you away. I don't know. The nicer maids have all gone. You will be wise not to come too close to her. And another thing. Do not make an enemy of Gerald Scottow.'

A prophetic flash of understanding burnt her with a terrible warmth. That was what she was for; she was for Gerald Scottow: his adversary, his opposite angel. By wrestling with Scottow she would make her way into the story. It was scarcely a coherent thought and it was gone in a moment. She went on at once, 'But why don't her friends – you, Mr Lejour, Mr Cooper – persuade her to come away? She can't be waiting still for him to relent, to forgive her. It sounds to me as if she were really under a spell, I mean a psychological spell, half believing by now that she's somehow *got* to stay here. Oughtn't she to be wakened up? I mean it's all so unhealthy, so unnatural.'

'What is spiritual is unnatural. The soul under the burden of sin cannot flee. What is enacted here with her is enacted with all of us in one way or another. You cannot come between her and her suffering, it is too complicated, too precious. We must play her game, whatever it is, and believe her beliefs. That is all we can do for her.'

'Well, it's not what I'm going to do,' said Marian. 'I'm going to talk to her about freedom.'

'Do not do so,' he said urgently. 'It means nothing to her now. Whatever you believe about her heart and her soul, even if you believe only that she is afraid of the outside world, or spellbound by mere fancies, or by now half mad, do not talk to her of freedom. She has found over these last years a great and deep peace of mind. As I think, she has made her peace with God. Do not try to disturb her calm. I think you could not even if you tried. She is a much stronger person than you have yet seen. But do not try. Her peace is her own and it is her best possession, whatever you believe.'

Marian shook her head violently in the darkness. 'But she seems sometimes in such pain, in despair –'

'True obedience is without illusion. A common soldier will die in silence, but Christ cried out.'

She murmured, 'Obedience to –?'

But their talk was over. He had risen as he spoke and she rose too. She was stiff and cold now and her clothes clung to her with a damp dew. The small moon, seeming to fly along through torn clouds, showed them the path to the house. They began to walk.

'When did you come here?'

'Five years ago.'

'Were you one of the messengers, the ones Mr Lejour used to send to her at such risk?'

'Yes. I think we had better go in separately.'

They were on the terrace now. The moonlight revealed the table where she had sat, so long ago, with Hannah. The mass of jewels were still strewn upon it, scattered with sparkling points of cold light. She paused to gather them up.

The stifling fright and sickness came back upon her as she looked up at the dark veiled eyes of the house. She murmured to him, 'What will end it then?'

'His death perhaps. Good night.'

Part Two

Chapter Eight

Effingham Cooper gazed out of the window of his first-class railway carriage. The landscape was just beginning to be familiar. Now each scene told him what was coming next. It was a moment that always affected him with pleasure and fear. There was the round tower, there was the ruined Georgian house with the dentil cornice, there was the big leaning megalith, there at last were the yellowish grey rocks which marked the beginning of the Scarren. Although there was still another twenty minutes to go, he took down his suitcases, put on his coat, and straightened his tie, regarding himself gravely in the carriage mirror. The little train jolted and swayed onward. It was a hot day.

It was nearly six months since he had been there before. But he would find them unchanged. Doubtless they would find him unchanged. He continued to look at himself in the mirror. His youthful appearance always startled people who knew him only by repute. He was still young, of course, in his forties, though sometimes he felt as old as Methuselah. He was certainly young for his achievements, young to be the head of a department. He looked at himself with an amused ironical affection. He was tall, large, with a pink face and a big firm mouth and a big straight nose and big blue-grey eyes. His hair, which was inclined to be chestnut-coloured and wavy, was sleek, tamed by years of bowler hats and hair-oil. He looked like a man ; and he certainly passed, in the society which he frequented, as a clever successful enviable one. As he lifted his chin pensively to his image he recalled that Elizabeth, who was the only person who dared to mock him, had once said that his favourite expression was one of 'slumbrous power'. He smiled ruefully at himself and sat down.

He began to bite his nails. Would something happen this time? What would have passed, when he was in the train once more and going the other way? He wondered this on each occasion, and wondered, as indeed he wondered all the year round, waking at night, or at unnerving moments in meetings or on escalators or railway stations, whether he ought not to *do* something. He was, it sometimes seemed to him, and he evaded the idea with alarm, the person with the most power, the only person who could really act. Ought he not to do something drastic? Was it not his action for which they were all waiting? It was a dreadful thought.

Effingham had known Hannah Crean-Smith for four years. He had known the Lejour family for twenty years. Max Lejour had been Effingham's tutor at Oxford, and he had met the younger Lejours while he was still a student. Max's wife had died when Pip was born, and Max when Effingham first knew him was so cantankerously a bachelor, it seemed that he must have invented the two children, so undoubtedly his, without female assistance. Yet the picture of Mrs Lejour, reputedly a beautiful redhead, was always to be seen on his desk. Effingham had proceeded from his first in Mods to his first in Greats and on to a College fellowship. But he was restless, and soon, to Max's sorrow, left the academic world for the public service. He had done well, he had done very well. It was senseless now to repent of that choice.

Poor little Alice Lejour had fallen in love with her father's star pupil on a weekend visit from her boarding-school; and to Effingham's gratification and annoyance she had never entertained any other serious thought on the matter of love. He had patronized her when she was a schoolgirl, teased her when she was a student, and then much later on, in a regrettable moment of weakness, flirted with her: at the time when he was escaping from the clutches of darling Elizabeth. He was glad he had not married Elizabeth. It would be awkward to marry a relentless career woman; Elizabeth was his subordinate in the department. It would be awkward to marry a relentless woman. Elizabeth was far too clever; and in any case his present relations with her were perfect. He was only sorry that he had hurt Alice, and disappointed Max, who had always tacitly wanted him to marry Alice, and entangled the poor girl yet further in a profitless love: and there they were all growing older.

Max Lejour had been a great power in his life. Uneasily Effingham acknowledged that Max was still a great power in his life. He had been completely dominated by his tutor in a way which his academic success had tended to disguise from all eyes but his own. He had taken Max without question as a great sage; and when he could himself still pass as a youth he had quite simply adored the older man. Later when, as men, they had inhabited the same world, Effingham had sometimes found himself feeling afraid of Max; it was not malice or even criticism that he feared, but simply the inadvertent extinction of his own personality by that proximity. Sometimes for a while he had avoided his former tutor; but always came back. In more recent years, during which he himself had become successful, powerful, famous, he had felt his view of Max shift again: he had permitted himself to jest at his expense, referred to him as a 'quaint old fellow', felt altogether his shoulder twitch as for the throwing off of a load. He found Max an abstract being, an out-of-date being, a hollow sage, and wondered loudly to himself what had so fascinated him for half his life. Yet still he came back.

With Pip Lejour his relations had been intermittent and uneasy. Pip was Alice's junior by four years and had come more slowly over Effingham's horizon. Pip, as a schoolboy, had settled down to making fun of Effingham as soon as Alice's passion had become evident; and Effingham suspected that, like his sister, the boy was consistent. Yet he was fond enough of Pip and had tried several times to help him with his career. Pip was unfortunately obsessed with the notion that he was a poet; but persuaded by financial need and Effingham he had eventually turned himself into a competent journalist. One thing that seemed clear about him was that he would never actually *do* anything; and it was with interested surprise that Effingham learnt from Alice of Pip's amorous exploit and its curious consequences. Pip had, after all, altered the face of the world; hardly for the better, but he had at least altered it.

Max's retirement came a year or two later and he removed himself to Riders to finish in seclusion his immense work on Plato. He suggested to Effingham that they should revive their old custom of 'reading parties' and that he should come and stay and that they should read Greek together. Effingham was pleased: he enjoyed reading Greek with the old man; he looked forward to the holiday, he looked forward to the scenery, he even looked forward to Alice, who would then be on leave from the horticultural institute where she now worked. He was less pleased, on arriving, to find Pip there as well, mooching on the terrace and surveying the other house through his glasses in a way which made Effingham think at first that there was something afoot. However, there seemed to be nothing afoot. Pip was respectful, Alice was tactful, Pip went fishing, Alice went hunting for plants, Max was eager to settle down to the *Timaeus*. The sun shone without ceasing upon the noble coast and the gorgeous sea. Nothing, it seemed, could prevent his stay from being delightful: nothing except the disturbing proximity of the imprisoned lady.

Alice had of course told Effingham the outline of the story, and of course it had intrigued him. A sort of interest in it had been part of his pleasure in the idea of coming. But now that he was here it was different. The lady obsessed him, she took away his calm of mind, he even began to dream about her. He took walks in the direction of the other house, though without daring to come very near, and spent long periods staring at it from his window, though without overcoming his distaste for the fascinating notion of using field-glasses. He decided that either he must go away or else something must be done. Yet what could be done? The Lejours never mentioned the lady; and their silence made a frame in which her image grew and grew.

What happened eventually happened without any decision. Effingham, walking late one evening on the cliffs beyond Gaze, missed his way and was overtaken by twilight. When he had been thoroughly lost for some time in the sheep runs between the cliff edge and the bog, and was beginning to be the least bit apprehensive, he fell in with a man who turned out to be Denis Nolan, who set him in the right direction. There was only one tolerable path, so they went on together. As they neared Gaze a great storm came on and it was natural for him to take refuge in the house into which Nolan invited him with an ill enough grace. News of his presence was brought to Hannah, who at once summoned him to see her.

Effingham was of course, as he had hundreds of times since told himself, stripped, prepared, keyed up, attuned, conditioned. No space-man about to step into his rocket was more meticulously fitted to go into orbit than Effingham at that moment was ready to fall in love with Hannah. He fell. It seemed in retrospect, as he tried to recall that meeting which was now so curiously confused in his memory, that he must have fallen literally at her feet and lain there gasping ; though in fact doubtless there had been a polite conversation over a glass of whiskey. He left the house an hour later in a dazed condition and walked about nearly all night in the rain.

The rest of his stay at Riders passed in a sort of cloud of altercation and confusion and misunderstanding. He could not conceal his condition. Indeed, with that pride which accompanies falling in love at what passes as an advanced age he was but too anxious to display it to everyone. He had supposed that the clever Elizabeth was the great love of his life. But the odd spiritual tormented yet resigned beauty of Hannah seemed to him now the castle perilous toward which he had now all his days been faring. Regardless of the pain he caused, he gave way to positive raving. For he did cause pain most comprehensibly to Alice, who was disembowelled by agonies of jealousy ; comprehensibly too to Pip, whose present feelings about Hannah Effingham did not understand, but who was probably distressed, even angered by Effingham's outrageous passion ; and more obscurely to Max, who seemed distressed not on account of Alice, for he had long ago stopped hoping that Effingham would marry his daughter, but oddly on account of Hannah. Max had not attempted to establish any social relations with the other house ; but Effingham reflected later, when he was able to think, that of course the imprisoned lady must somehow have occupied the old man's imagination too.

Effingham passed two days in torment and then he went to see Hannah again. He went to the front door and knocked. He was admitted. He saw her alone. He declared his love. It was done. Hannah was startled and gently scandalized without being exactly astonished. Yet he knew that he *was* a surprise, and not only to her. She did not know how to deal with him and kept seeming to look round him and past him to see how he could fit into the scene. Meanwhile she surrounded his passion with a haze of vague deprecatory chatter which was both caressing and suffocating. She said she could not take him seriously. She hinted that he was not *persona grata*. She told him laughingly to go away. And she held his hand at the moment of departure with a sudden desperate look of appeal. He called again. And again. Nothing happened. Hannah became less agitated, more friendly, less wild, more polite. As they thus became acquainted with each other he feared at each moment the intervention of some outside force. But it did not happen. For some incomprehensible reason his visits were tolerated.

They never came, however, very near, never too near. When Effingham had stopped being afraid about not seeing her, he began to be afraid about what to do next. He did not understand her situation, he did not understand her state of mind, and there was in her attitude to him a certain determined vagueness. The absent husband began to haunt his dreams. He pictured him lame, blind, full of hate. He would like to have known what really happened that day on the cliff top, he would like to have known what really happened altogether, but it was unthinkable to ask Hannah. He said to Hannah, frequently at first, 'Let me take you away from here'; but without saying anything clearly, without saying anything at all, she returned him a negative. It was evident too, without words, that he could not become her lover.

Effingham contrived, that summer, to be in a frenzy. He prolonged his leave, he got special leave, he quarrelled with the Lejours, and was always on the point of moving to the fishing-hotel at Blackport, but did not. He was in a frenzy; yet, as he had to admit afterwards to himself, or rather to Elizabeth, in a way he rather enjoyed it. And in a way he was, even then, deeply afraid of the possibility of really having to take Hannah away. He returned at last perforce to his work, regarding the situation as unresolved, and wrote carefully allusive replies to Hannah's open friendly letters. He assumed her mail was censored.

He returned at Christmas; but already the drama had taken on a certain settled form. Hannah was glad to see him, the Lejours were glad to see him; he had his place. He fell into accepting it. He was to be in love with Hannah, he was to be Hannah's servant, he was to come running back whenever he could, he was to be tolerated by everybody, he was to be harmless. Harmless indeed, he reflected, was what they, whoever exactly they were, had put him down as being from the start. But how harmless was he really? He had certainly done nothing yet. And he had to continue to admit to Elizabeth, who had some sharp-witted things to say on the subject of Courtly Love, that the situation rather fascinated him as it was. It had undeniably the qualities of a wonderful story. And as he sat in his office dreaming of Hannah he found himself feeling a certain strange guilty pleasure at the idea that she was, somehow, for him, shut up, reserved, sequestered.

He felt later, when he considered the quality of his resignation, that he had caught it positively from Hannah herself. She was, in some mysterious way, it seemed, totally resigned, almost as if she were condemned to death or already dead. The moments of appeal were wordless, ambiguous, superficial, and rare. Some kind of surrender underlay them. What kind of surrender, what kind of resignation, he could never come quite to decide: whether she had given in to Peter, or to Duty, or to God, or to some mad fancy of her own; whether it was a great virtue in her or a remarkable vice. For it was certainly something extreme: something which, he began increasingly to think, he ought not to try to disturb with flimsy ideas of happiness and freedom.

The Lejours were glad to see him, had forgiven him. Max had got over his first curious distress and seemed now to welcome, with a straightforward curiosity, Effingham's privileged access to the other house. Alice had equally recovered from her first pains, and although retaining a certain stiffness about the whole subject, was, Effingham suspected, glad in a way to see him, if not hers, at least chained to an unattainable other. Alice had never stopped being afraid of Elizabeth. The attachment to Hannah brought Effingham to Riders and kept him single. What exactly Pip thought remained a mystery; there was in his continued haunting of the place something morbid which unnerved Effingham, and at moments he imagined that Pip derived some positive satisfaction from the spectacle of the beautiful imprisoned creature. However that might be, Pip was tolerant of Effingham's role, although the old dangerous schoolboy mockery could often be seen just vanishing from his mild and non-committal gaze.

The train began to slow down and Effingham's heart quickened, with the delight and fear of arrival. Surely he was harmless and surely all would be as before; and yet too each year he had the sense of moving a little closer to the centre, whatever the centre might prove to be. He put his hand on the door. A dazzling sunshiny haze hung like a curtain over the little derelict station where a single figure was waiting on the platform. Dear Alice. Poor Alice.

Chapter Nine

'There's a new girl over there called Marian Taylor.'

'Over where?'

'Over *there*, Effie. She's been engaged as a sort of companion for Hannah. She's quite educated, and used to teach French in a school or something.'

'How do you know all this? Have you been calling on Hannah? Bless you for that.'

Alice had in the last two years set up a tenuous visiting relationship with her rival which rather pleased Effingham.

'No. I just couldn't bring myself to call. I don't know if she knows I'm here. Denis told me.'

Alice maintained, toward the delinquent Denis, a protective attitude which Effingham found incomprehensible and irritating. He could not think how she could bear to see the little rat after that incident.

'Oh. Hannah said something vague in a letter about a girl, but I thought it was a maid. I'm glad she's got some more female company. Since you're falling down on your job.'

'It's not my job. As you know, I only went to see Hannah out of curiosity. I don't dislike her, one couldn't, but we just don't get on. Anyway, it's a bit improper. But this girl, yes. Pretty and so nice. You must meet her, Effie. I said I'd ask her over.'

Alice is jealous already, thought Effingham, as he listened to her over-urgent tones. She sees every woman as a menace, as after me. The idea of every woman after him was not displeasing. 'Where did you come across this girl?'

'She was down on the beach trying to pluck up courage to get in the sea, but she didn't manage it.'

'Sensible child! I hope you haven't been swimming again?'

75

'No, I've given up swimming since I got to look like a porpoise. That reminds me, I dreamt about you last night. We were swimming together. And not just swimming. Yes. Never mind.'

It was odd, the life one lived in other people's dreams. He wondered if Hannah dreamt about him. He had never asked her.

'You *are* a little plumper. But it suits you.' Poor Alice was now getting really thick-set: a stout, tweedy, doggy middle-aged woman. Perhaps being a professional gardener made one look like that anyway: all that stooping with feet wide apart.

They had just arrived in Alice's Austin Seven from the station and they were in Effingham's bedroom. His big suitcase was half unpacked on the bed. He noted with affectionate annoyance the mess of bric-a-brac with which Alice had lovingly adorned his room: shells on the mantelpiece, china cats and dogs, small and useless cushions, embroidered mats, and chipped saucers out of fine tea-sets. Devoid of taste, Alice was an indefatigable hunter of antique shops, from which she would come home laden with small cracked objects which she had got triumphantly cheap. Alice was mean with money. And her domestic activities had the air of a sort of elephantine play. Perhaps that too was something to do with being a gardener. 'How nice you've made my room. And what a lovely little thing of wild flowers. Are they bog flowers?'

'Yes, they're those funny carnivorous flowers. I don't suppose they'll eat you. I wish we had some decent garden flowers, but the whole damn garden is blown away. I must have a go at it again, now that I have time, yes.'

'Time – ?'

'I've given up my job. Didn't I tell you?'

'Why ever – ?'

'Clearing the decks for action. It's seven years, you know!'

'You surely don't believe that – But you're jesting. Why really?'

'Well, Father's getting on, you know. And he's practically finished his book.'

'He's clearing the decks for action too!'

'And when he finishes it – I think he'll suddenly get much older. It's been with him such a long time. It will be like the end of his life.'

Effingham was chilled. He had never known Max without that book. What indeed would he do afterwards?

'Anyway,' Alice went on, 'he can't really be left alone in the winter nowadays. You've no idea what it's like here in the winter. Well, you have, but you've never stayed long. The maids are splendid, of course, but they can't be expected to take the responsibility. Now Pip and I will both be here –'

'Pip?'

'He's given up his job too, yes. Didn't I tell you? Just brought out a book of poems, I expect you saw it. Now he wants to spend two years on poetry. Thinks he could do something remarkable.'

'I see. All three of you. You'll convince me something *is* going to happen.' Effingham had indeed seen a favourable review of the poems, but he could not bring himself to look at them. He knew beforehand that they must be feeble.

A handsome red-haired maid put her head round the door. The maids at Riders were all red-heads, belonging to one of the many Norman 'pockets' to be found along that much-ravaged coast.

'Oh, Carrie, do come in, dear,' said Alice. 'Carrie is going to lay your fire. You'll need it, it gets so cold in the evenings now. Come along to my room and look at the view.'

'Hello, Carrie,' said Effingham. He shook hands with her and saw her blush. Carrie was very fond of him. All the maids were so charming. He thought fleetingly of Denis Nolan. As he left the room he caught a glimpse of the bowl of carnivorous flowers and thought how nasty they looked.

Effingham's room faced the sea. Alice's room had the view across the valley to Gaze. Effingham was for a moment absorbed in the sudden vision of the castle, into the mystery of its real presence. It was so powerful an object in his imagination that the sight of it in reality, faded and diminished, always gave him a slight shock. Then a movement caught his attention and he saw Pip Lejour below on the terrace, with his retriever dog Tadg at his feet, his glasses levelled on the house opposite. Effingham stood back with a frown.

'Pip is such a romantic,' said Alice. She wanted to defend Pip against Effingham's irritation.

'Hannah makes romantics of us all.' He did not intend to hurt Alice. He smiled a smile of conciliation.

'I wish I could make a romantic of you, Effie. All right, don't panic, I'm not going to start.'

Effingham surveyed her short straight well-powdered nose, her short downy upper lip, her short tucked fair hair. Her cheeks were more fleshy now. She was no longer a pretty girl; but she was certainly a handsome imposing middle-aged woman, born to be the pillar of something or other. What a pity she had never married. As he looked her strong face melted and kindled before him, and he was ashamed for her vulnerability. 'You're blushing, Alice!' He leaned forward.

'Don't, Effie. I should have told you at the station. I've got an awful cold.'

Damn, thought Effingham, now I shall get her cold. It was just like Alice to have a cold. He did not want to appear before Hannah with a cold. He did not want to give Hannah a cold. He did not want to see Hannah with a cold. He kissed Alice on the lips.

She gazed at him for a moment with the old hungry persecuting gaze. Then she smiled, looking like her brother. 'Decent of you! Now come down and see Father.'

As Effingham turned he saw what seemed like a white form on the bed. Then he saw that the bed was covered with shells. Alice had a great collection of local shells, to which Effingham had occasionally contributed. 'You've got all your shells out. How odd they look. Like a girl made of shells. I remember a girl made of flowers in a story once, but I can't recall a girl made of shells. This is a new enchantment.'

'To put a spell on you! Let me give you some.' She picked up a handful of the smaller shells and dropped them into his pocket. They went downstairs.

Out on the terrace the golden retriever came rushing up to Effingham, planting its paws upon his waistcoat and then

78

rolling upon its back in a fluffy whirl of smiling mouth and waving paws. This homage took a moment to deal with. 'Hello, Tadg. Hello, Pip.'

' "Lord, behold us with Thy blessing, once again assembled here." Hello, Effie.'

While Alice got plumper, Pip seemed to get slimmer and slighter. He was a wisp of a fellow now, with a soft silky suggestion of hair upon his balding head, and a moist mobile mouth, his neat face a diminished version of Alice's. His narrow blue-grey eyes continually flashed and widened at private jokes. The ramparts were manned.

'Have a dekko?'

'No, thanks.' Surely Pip must know by now what he thought about that particular error of taste. 'Just off to see Max. See you later.'

He had a last glimpse of Pip's small head and behind it, in shadow now, the vista of Gaze with the fuchsia-red hillside below it and the dark line of the bog above.

'I'll leave you here,' said Alice. Like a priestess leading him into some higher presence, she paused on the threshold. He was touched by her always slightly absurd delicacy about his relations with her father.

Max's study faced inland with a view of stony nibbled grass and dwarfish bushes and the yellow-grey hump of the Scarren beyond. The bog was invisible.

Effingham reached the door. He had a sense of painful sobering urgency, a sense of being abruptly pulled together or recalled to himself. He respected after all Max's concern with ultimate things. In a way, Max had lived for him, had lived his other life. He had stored up so much of his good in this place and he found it, on each return, however his faith in between might waver, fresh and indubitable. Then he smiled at his sudden trepidation. He was glad after all to know that the old magic had not failed. He knocked softly.

He waited, and then heard a sound which was familiar from long ago and like no other noise that he knew. A deep hoarse chanting came from within. He opened the door.

There was a haze of cigar smoke. Oblivious of him, Max

was sitting in a twilight with his back to the door, the curtains half drawn. He was singing to a plain-song lilt of his own a chorus from Aeschylus.

Effingham sat down behind him. He fingered in his pocket the sharp crushed fragments of the shells which Alice had given him. He must have broken them nervously somewhere on the way along. He followed the healing familiar lines.

Zeus, who leads men into the ways of understanding, has established the rule that we must learn by suffering. As sad care, with memories of pain, comes dropping upon the heart in sleep, so even against our will does wisdom come upon us.

Chapter Ten

'I've never seen so many hares around,' said Alice. 'They all seem quite mad too.'

'It isn't their month,' said Effingham. 'Been fishing lately?' He hardly knew what he was saying. It was the next morning and he was walking over to see Hannah. He felt homicidal with irritation against Alice, who had announced that she would walk over with him.

'Hardly,' said Alice. 'The trout are so-so, and it's too early for grayling. Have to wait till St Martin's summer.'

There were indeed a lot of hares, darting and capering on the vivid green hillside below the bog. Effingham and Alice were walking by the inland footpath which passed above the village, crossing the stream at a higher level, where it descended in a series of small waterfalls from its dark bog-source. A pair of buzzards wheeled overhead in the sunny air.

The hillside was still scarred. A wide band of black boggy soil and a strewing of stone showed where the great torrent had descended. The innocent stream now meandered in the midst, dark as the earth itself, leaping into light as it fell. They crossed, stepping from one round glinting boulder to another. Effingham absently gave Alice his hand.

His first meeting with Hannah on each occasion disturbed him terribly. When he was absent from her he felt almost perfectly serene about their relationship. Only when he approached her again, the real, breathing, existing Hannah, did he realize how large a part of the fabric was contributed by his own imagination. That, in some deliciously undefined way, she loved him, was even in love with him, was, in absence, a dogma. In presence it had to undergo the ordeal of being changed into a fact. Though even in presence Effingham later found the combination of the fantastic and the real quite felicitous and natural. Sex, love, these were after all so largely things of the imagination. Only the first encounter was alarming.

There was, too, always the possibility that he would find that something had changed. After all, so strange a situation could not go on forever. Or could it? It was not that he really pictured Hannah as a star which gets smaller and smaller and then explodes. He did not see any gathering violence; he saw rather the opposite, the unnerving disappearance of personal will. It was not that he expected that Hannah would suddenly break out or suddenly demand to be rescued; though if she ever did then he must somehow be adequate to her need. But no, he told himself, she would never ask that. Yet the situation would have to alter, and who would alter it? Or who would begin to alter it; since once it began to alter the figures so strangely woven into the quiet tapestry would themselves jerk into unpredictable life. Effingham recalled Alice's remark about 'clearing the decks for action', and he shuddered, thinking how disagreeable any sort of action might turn out to be. Of course he did not believe in the legend of the seven years. Still it had been a long time – for somebody. For Peter Crean-Smith, for example. He shuddered again.

'Why, Tadg!' The dog came tearing up to Alice, smudged her skirt with two boggy paws, and scudded round her. 'Pip must be near. He went out early to shoot.'

A distant cry came from farther up the hill and a figure could be seen descending the rocks on the far side of the stream where the Scarren spilt itself in a series of yellowish screes down the grassy slope. As Pip came nearer, the heavy shotgun under his arm, it was apparent that he was carrying something else as well, which turned out to be a brace of pheasants. Effingham was displeased. The country as far as eye could see belonged to Hannah. Pip's casual poaching seemed to Effingham petty and tactless. Pip quite failed to measure up to the potential grandeur of his role.

Alice, who knew what Effingham felt about the poaching, said, 'Oh, Pip, you said you were going up the coast for barnacle geese!'

'Didn't get up early enough.' He grinned at Effingham. 'Off to pay homage, eh, Effie?'

Effingham said nothing. He felt for a moment almost faint with suppressed violence. He would never understand Pip. He looked at the boy now, as he turned gaily back to his sister to tell her about some ravens he had seen on the Scarren. Pip still looked absurdly young in spite of his baldness. His long neck and small head emerged from a dirty tattered shirt. His cheek was ruddy with sunshine, and girlish smooth. His face twitched and twinkled as he talked and he kept casting roguish glances at Effingham. The gun leaned against his thigh. The gun suited him. Effingham, who had a horror of firearms, apprehended this with a mixture of fascination and horror. Pip belonged to some quite other race than himself ; and for that instant he saw the boy, not as an absurd and insensitive youth, but as some slim archaic Apollo, smiling, incomprehensible and dangerous.

The dead birds dripped blood. Effingham shook himself and was about to announce that he was going on, when over Pip's shoulder he became aware of a scene which was coming into focus on the hillside below the bog. A man and a girl were coming along the path from Gaze ; and a moment later he had recognized the man as Denis Nolan.

Pip and Alice stopped chattering. 'That's Miss Taylor with Denis,' said Alice. 'I suppose I'd better ask her over to lunch or something, yes.'

Pip hailed them. 'Good morning, Denis!'

'Good morning, sir.'

Pip seemed to have a positive fondness for Denis. Effingham was thinking, if a man had attacked *my* sister, when he began to notice the girl.

Pretty she was not exactly, but she had a strong interesting face, with a long dog-like nose and smallish lively brown eyes and a compressed aggressive mouth. She was very present in her face, which was poised and grave as she looked at Effingham.

Alice said, 'Mr Cooper. My brother. Miss Taylor.'

'Hello.'

'You're new to this part of the world?' said Effingham.

'Yes. I'm rather overwhelmed by it. I hadn't expected such an extreme landscape. It takes getting used to. Sublime rather than beautiful, isn't it?' She had a pleasant precise voice.

Effingham was amused by her little desire to please him. He made some more conventional remarks and Alice joined in. By the end of these exchanges he had clearly apprehended Miss Taylor, for all her shy absurd self-consciousness, as a being of his own kind: a clever girl, a junior version of Elizabeth.

A sudden diversion was created. Tadg, who had been exploring farther down the stream, had found Denis, who was standing a little apart from the group. The dog went mad. He rushed upon Denis with strangled excited barks and waddled round him, his tail wagging his whole body.

'Tadg adores Denis,' said Alice. 'He never forgets him. Denis trained Tadg when he was a puppy, when Denis was over with us.'

Denis was immediately absorbed into greeting Tadg. He sat down on the grass and let the dog climb on to him and lick his face. Effingham found this degree of informality thoroughly disrespectful. He glanced at the two women and saw that they were both watching the little scene with soft amused faces. He coughed disapprovingly. 'I must be getting along.'

'You're going to Gaze?' said Miss Taylor. 'I think Mrs Crean-Smith is expecting you.' She could not conceal her expression of interest as she looked at Effingham.

Effingham had a moment's uneasiness. The girl was not a nonentity, she might be something to be reckoned with. But he could not see this pleasant young creature as an enemy. He smiled at her and she smiled back.

Pip, who had been talking to Denis about Tadg's prowess earlier that morning, joined them. 'This is where I turn back. I've been up since five. It's nice to have met you, Miss Taylor. I believe you are coming to see us at Riders?'

'I'd love to.'

'We must fix it, yes,' said Alice vaguely.

Miss Taylor was staring at Pip's glossy-feathered trophies. 'Poor birds!'

'Are you a vegetarian?' said Alice.

Effingham looked quickly at the girl. The malice in the remark had not escaped her, nor, it was immediately clear to him, was she ignorant of its cause. Someone must have talked to her about poor Alice. He felt both annoyed with his old friend and anxious to protect her.

Miss Taylor flushed slightly and smiled. 'No, indeed! I don't practise what I seem to preach. One is so spoilt in a town. I'm sure I would be a vegetarian if I had to kill the creatures myself.'

'Good morning all!'

The loud voice just behind him made Effingham jump. They all turned.

Gerald Scottow and Jamesie Evercreech had approached from lower down the valley and come right up to the absorbed little group, their footsteps covered by the sound of the falling stream.

'Good morning,' they said, Alice stiffly, Effingham politely, Pip jauntily, Denis not at all, and Miss Taylor with a just perceptible emotion of some kind. Effingham noticed the emotion and glanced quickly at Scottow. Then he saw Jamesie winking at Miss Taylor. There doubtless was her informant concerning the condition of Alice. Effingham bristled with dislikes.

Scottow and Jamesie were also both armed with shotguns and two pairs of brown furry ears protruded from Jamesie's game bag. Two of the mad hares would caper no more.

'Well, well,' said Scottow, 'how nice to meet you all together. We aren't usually so lucky. Mr Cooper, coming to see us, I trust? Good! We've missed you, you know. You've been neglecting us. Had a good morning, Mr Lejour? I see you have two of Mrs Crean-Smith's fine birds there.'

Pip smiled. He turned towards Denis, and Denis, as at a pre-arranged signal, stood before him. He handed over the pheasants, and then began to walk away without haste in the direction of Riders. The little incident had the slow ease of a well-rehearsed ceremony, or something out of a ballet.

Scottow looked after him with a face of comical distress. 'Oh, Miss Lejour, I hope I haven't offended your brother. I was only jesting. Do tell him I was only jesting.'

'I must be getting along,' said Effingham again. The presence of the guns disturbed him. The encounter had seemed like the shadow of a real battle with real blood flowing.

Denis had already set off with the pheasants in the direction of Gaze. Miss Taylor was visibly hesitating.

Scottow said pleasantly, 'Well, Jamesie and I must continue our slaughtering activities. I can see Miss Taylor doesn't like this bit – but she won't refuse the jugged hare, I'll be bound! Come along, Jamesie.'

The big square figure and the slighter boy went on up the hill and began to cross the stream, their military silhouettes emerging now against the blue sky. The other three began to walk on in the direction of the castle.

The incident and the sense of shared but ineffable knowledge drew them for a moment together in a complicity of silence. Effingham walked between the two women. Miss Taylor glanced at her companions and then looked ahead frowning. Apprehending that determined frown out of the corner of his eye, Effingham reflected that this uncorrupted young woman was indeed a new feature in the situation and might conceivably prove an active one. It was disconcerting, as was too his spontaneous vision of her as uncorrupted. Were the rest of them corrupted, then?

To distract himself, Effingham began to question Miss Taylor about what she had been doing before she came to Gaze, and about her university career and the time she had spent in Paris. He talked to her with a great naturalness, as if she were a young student, and he again a don, and he noticed now her increasing ease with him. The aggressive self-conscious air had gone. Alice was conspicuously silent. They reached the castle gates.

'I hear Mr Lejour is a Greek scholar,' Miss Taylor was saying, to bring Alice into the conversation. 'I do wish I knew Greek. I managed to learn German by myself, but I've never quite had the guts to tackle Greek.'

86

'I'll teach you Greek,' said Effingham.

Alice made a slight movement, throwing her head back. God, what a fool I am, thought Effingham. It was too late to recall the words. Miss Taylor was blushing. She looked at Alice, who was looking away, and then at Effingham. In a second a great deal of communication passed between them. Oh, I am a very great fool, thought Effingham. 'If you'd like to, that is,' he said hurriedly, to efface the sharpness of the impression. 'I could give you a couple of lessons maybe just to start you off.'

Miss Taylor said, 'How kind of you. I'll see if I have time, shall I?'

She's quick, he thought.

'Where's Tadg?' said Alice. 'He didn't go back with Pip. I thought he was with us.'

'Is that the dog?' said Miss Taylor. 'He went in with Denis just now.'

'Oh, damn!' said Alice. 'Now I'll have to go in and fetch him. Once he's with Denis he'll never come back of his own accord.'

'Shall I get him?' said Miss Taylor.

'No, no. He wouldn't come with you anyway. Let's walk on together, shall we, at a brisk pace? We'll leave Effie to dream along, behind. He doesn't want *us*.' Alice took the girl's arm and urged her ahead.

Effingham watched them draw away. The image of Hannah grew in front of him like a great placid golden idol, the two small hurrying figures in the foreground.

Chapter Eleven

He held her in his arms. Effingham in these moments experienced a joy so intense that he could not imagine how he could ever have gone away; or rather he could not imagine that he had ever gone away, lifted, shot into a blinding timeless beatitude. She was the only one, the great phoenix, his truth, his home, his ἅπαξ λεγόμενον. He felt a thrilling humble gratitude to her for being the cause of so great a love.

'Oh Lord, Effie, I have missed you. Bless you for coming back.'

'You should be cursing me for going away. I don't look after you properly.'

'There now. You look after me beautifully. No, don't go down on the floor. Kiss me, Effie.'

He led her to the sofa and they sat down holding hands. Effingham looked about the room. Everything was blessedly the same: the whiskey bottles, the mess of papers, the little sleepy fire, the pampas grass and the honesty a little flimsier than last time. He returned his gaze to Hannah.

'Are you all right? Nothing awful's happened? Nothing you couldn't mention in a letter?'

'No, I'm fine. Everything's as usual.'

'Not everything. There's that girl, Miss Taylor.'

'Oh yes, Marian. But that's a good thing. I did tell you, didn't I. I'm so happy to have her. I wake up every morning knowing there's something nice, and it's her.'

'And now me too! I'm jealous.'

'And now you too, dear. Have some whiskey, Effingham, and give me some. I just want to sit and feel pleased to see you.'

Effingham went to the whiskey. He was touched by what

she'd said about the girl. But how long would she be allowed to keep the girl? How long indeed would the girl want to stay in this quiet little madhouse? Hannah was so evidently pleased to see him. But would he not soon go away again, would he not this time next month be sitting in an expensive restaurant listening to Elizabeth's jokes about *la princesse lointaine*?

He began to pour out the whiskey. The smell of that particular brand of whiskey, familiar and disturbing, seized him by the throat. Some half-remembered accumulation of passionate experience, suddenly present, packed together mysteriously as in a dream, nearly choked him and he stopped pouring. Everything was the same. Yet what was he doing here, why was he lending himself to this macabre pageant at all?

He returned to stand in front of Hannah, who was looking up at him. Her crest of reddish-golden hair was combed straight back over her head to reveal the big pale brow. She became, it seemed to him, lovelier each year. But certainly no younger. Something was written on that brow, something about suffering: only he could not read the characters. Her uncannily tranquil golden-brown eyes regarded him with concern. It sometimes seemed to him that she behaved to him with the exaggerated quietness of a psychiatrist dealing with a patient. Yet was *she* not the patient? Which of them was sick in mind? He put his hand to his head.

'Effie, you're looking tired. Are you –?'

'Stop it, Hannah –' He fell down beside the sofa and pawed at the stuff of her dress. She was wearing a short dress of dark green linen. He pawed at her knees. 'Stop it –'

'Stop what? What's the matter, Effingham? Here I am. Here you are. Everything is the same –'

'That's just it. Here I am. Here you are. And everything is the same. But it oughtn't to be the same.'

'Why not? And do bring me some whiskey, I'm dying for it, and if you're going to be so wild I shall need it!'

He got up awkwardly, straightening his tie, and handed her the glass of whiskey. She had tucked her feet under her now, girlishly, compact and removed, her broad severe face lifted to his. She patted the cushion to invite him to sit. It was suddenly like being at a party. Effingham still grasped at his moment of frenzy: there was surely a truth in it.

'Hannah, we can't go on like this. It's all mad somehow. Well, isn't it?'

Her face was very still now, not frozen, but still like a hovering bird. 'You mean you'd rather not go on coming?'

'No, I *don't* mean that,' said Effingham. 'I mean we must do something, you and I, do something, even if it's only going to bed together.'

'Sssh. If you did feel – and why shouldn't you feel – that all the sense has gone out of this strange incomplete love of ours – well, you know I would be sorry. But you know too that it would be better then to stop coming to see me. I could bear that, Effingham. And it might be a great relief to you. I know you worry about me. I wish I could stop you.'

'It's *not* that,' said Effingham desperately. He clasped her hand between his own in a wild prayer. 'I love you, Hannah. And I want you, and that's no joke either. But that's not the point. I feel we must do something, anything, to break this spell. For it *is* a spell, a spell on all of us, we're all walking round and round in our sleep. And it's a bad unhealthy spell. By this endless quietness we're just killing something –'

'Perhaps we are.' She released her hand and captured his, lightly stroking him across the knuckles. 'Perhaps we're killing something that has no right to live anyhow. Never mind. I know it's harder on everyone else than it is on me. Another person's illness is often harder to bear than one's own. The other is all imagined suffering; with one's own, one knows its ways and its limits. Are you sure, Effie, that you aren't just, simply, wanting to go away and stay away? I can imagine how a sort of repulsion might suddenly come over you. You must be truthful with me here. Come, Effingham, the truth.'

He could hardly bear her calm commanding tone. He wanted to see her tears, to hear her cries. He needed her frenzied need of him. He began to stammer and then stopped himself. He must be cool here, as with an enemy.

'Look here,' he said, 'I'm not wanting to go away, you know that. I'm wanting to do something sensible and natural at last.

I'm wanting to take you away from here, to take you back into ordinary life. Hannah, let me take you away.' He had not, when he arrived, intended to say this. Had she somehow made him say it?

'Don't talk too loudly, Effie. I'm sorry to have put this burden upon you. I know it's a burden and I know it all seems to you, sometimes anyway, unnatural, unhealthy. You were something – quite unexpected, something I hadn't allowed for – and I've often felt that I ought to have sent you away then, at the very start. If it were *now* I think I would send you away, I would not let such a story begin at all.'

'Good Lord, you're not going to banish me now!' cried Effingham.

'No. Sssh. You have such a loud voice. Of course not, if you really want to go on. But it *is* difficult, Effingham, it's very difficult. I'm to blame in a way for not, from the very start, putting it in front of you as something almost impossible.'

'I don't understand,' said Effingham, miserably. 'I've just offered to take you away. Would you come? I mean, will you come?'

'No, of course not. And you would regret your offer the next moment, you are regretting it already. We just haven't got that sort of life to live, that sort of love to live. We have run out of life, at least I have. I'm doing something quite different – and perhaps I ought to have made you do it too, or else have made you leave me altogether.'

'I don't know what you're doing,' said Effingham, 'but I'm jolly certain I can't do it, and I'm not sure if you ought to do it.'

She laughed. 'Give yourself a drink, dear. You know I hate drinking alone. When I say make you do it too, of course it wouldn't be the *same* thing, it couldn't be. But I ought to have made you, in a way, suffer more.'

'More?'

'Yes. You suffer, yes. But I'm a story for you. We remain on romantic terms.'

Effingham stared at the freckled hand which still so sensitively and authoritatively caressed his. He had a sense of being deeply wounded, deeply accused. At the same time he said to himself, Ah if she knew how *little* I suffer! He said, 'Perhaps I ought to have tried to do what I *could* do, and that is rescue you, help you in a quite straightforward way, or else have let you be. But I love you, and you know it's not just a story.'

'I am to blame. I couldn't help wanting you to help me in a quite *un*-straightforward way – and at the same time I gave you no lead. I let you have your dreams. And of course I'm still romantic too. You are my romantic vice.'

'Well, don't reform me out of existence. Is it too late to teach me to help you in the un-straightforward way? I think after all I might try. I love you enough to try.'

'Now I've just frightened you.'

'No you haven't. Hannah, do talk to me more frankly. Tell me about the past. Tell me what you really feel about this strange business. Let me *see* what you're doing. Then perhaps I can be with you, as it were, on the inside –'

'Ah, but nobody can be with me on the inside. Nobody can *see*. That would be another illusion and a far more dangerous one. Now we are *really* tempting each other. Sorry.' She spoke with a sudden alarm.

'I've frightened *you*,' he said. 'You know it's only old Effie, harmless old Effie. I'm quite easy to control really. I only wish I could see more of your mind. I mean – do you see – all this – as coming to an end – and how?'

'You know, it's odd, but I've almost stopped thinking in terms of time.'

He looked into her big golden eyes. She was marvellously strange to him, a fey almost demonic creature sometimes. It was for this weird unconnectedness in her, this cut-looseness from ordinary being that surely he loved her most. Thoughts of taking her away suddenly seemed unbearably crude.

'Is it like – forgive me for being so simple – a sort of trial that you must undergo with absolute patience? Do you feel –?'

She smiled as if he had been simple indeed, uncurled her legs stiffly and rose to her feet. 'Oh, I don't *feel* much any more, except about very immediate matters – what's for dinner and Denis's fish and so on. I *have* felt frightened, guilty, many things – but not now.'

'Then why don't you clear out?' said Effingham. 'Why don't you quietly get up and go? Not necessarily with me, but just go.'

She had moved to the window and stood there in the dusty sunshine. She looked back with a kind of surprise. 'But why indeed? I belong here, it all belongs here. To go somewhere else would have too much significance now, it would make me be something.'

Effingham got up too. 'I'm a dull pupil,' he said. 'But I think I've understood a little. You want me to stop being restless and romantic. You want me to be – resigned, with you – somehow, dead, with you. I can try. I'm not a fool. I know there have been consolations –'

'In the dreams? Yes. I hadn't expected this sort of talk, Effie. But perhaps it's as well. Perhaps it's time for us to care for each other differently. Not so pleasantly, but better. With less imagination. If we can.'

'Oh God,' said Effingham. He felt confused and stunned, as if the process of becoming dead had started already.

'Why, there's Alice,' said Hannah.

Effingham joined her at the window. Alice, with Tadg pulling hard upon his lead, was crossing the terrace with Denis hurrying after her. Gerald Scottow and Jamesie were striding up the drive loaded with game. Violet Evercreech, with a big basket, and with a black maid in attendance, was disappearing in the direction of the kitchen garden. Beyond was the view of Riders, the black cliffs, the green islands, the windy sea, with near fishing-boats and a steamer at the horizon. From a great height a silver aeroplane was coming down toward the airport. Effingham saw it all with a sort of shock. There was life, indifferent life, beautiful free life going forward. But to what, in here, had he just pledged himself?

Chapter Twelve

'And how was she?' Max pushed the chess board aside. It was late that night. Max and Effingham had been sitting for some time now in Max's study, drinking brandy and playing chess. Effingham, who had drunk a lot with Hannah, after Hannah, and at dinner, was feeling rather the worse for wear. He rather dreaded anyway this interrogation by Max, which occurred at the beginning of every visit. He had a sense of being put through it, and a sense, usually, of being somehow found inadequate. It recalled tutorials, it recalled his first painful-pleasant apprehension of Max as someone to whom only the best, most accurate, most thoughtful, most truthful replies could be offered. Max had been his first real glimpse of a standard. Effingham had never entirely recovered from the shock.

Max worked at a big mahogany dining-table upon which he had cleared a space for the chessboard, thrusting aside books and papers into high precarious piles which at intervals through the evening murmurously subsided or slid to the floor. At the far end of the room, beyond the expanse of the table, the dying turf fire glowed drowsily, and a single tall oil-lamp purred a pearly-yellow between the two men, showing them to each other. Layers of cigar smoke drifted up steadily past the lamp into the darkness above where the books rose in towers. A distant pale smudge was the ever-present photograph of Mrs Lejour.

Trying to be alert, Effingham picked his words carefully. 'It's hard to say. She seemed as usual. She was quite serene, she said nothing special had happened. Yet we had a weird little conversation.'

'Weird? How? Brandy?' Max's big head loomed at Effingham as he leaned forward with the bottle. Max's smoothly polished bald dome was divided from his very wrinkled face and neck by a neatly clipped circlet of silver-grey hair, which made him appear to be wearing some sort of exotic cap. He had with this, at first sight, an oriental air, as of one whose forebears drew back heavy curtains or mumbled interminable chants in the shops or temples of the East. Yet his carefully shaven face, the indoor colour of pale parchment, wore well enough the gentle abstracted mask of the scholar, and only those who knew him very well ever thought they could see anything else looking through. His big nose had thickened and coarsened with age, sprouting vigorous little tufts of black hair, and his mouth had spread and moistened, but the blue eyes were still almost cold with clarity. His hands, which had inspired Effingham as an undergraduate with irrational fears, were big too, hairy, with broad flat paw-like fingers. He was a large broad man, but round-shouldered and cramped with arthritis and stooping over books. He rarely left the house now.

'She made some sort of appeal to me. I think.'

'You think? You're not sure?'

'Yes, I am sure. But I don't know quite what the appeal was, and perhaps "command" is a better word than "appeal". I got rather emotional and said I wanted to take her away. I didn't mean to say that, it just came out. She said no in an evasive sort of way. Then she accused me of being just romantic about her and said I ought somehow to have entered more into her own experience of the situation. Then she said of course I couldn't really enter in and it was dangerous to think that too. Then I said it wasn't too late and I would try to enter in. Then I said what the hell was her experience of the situation anyway. Then she made some remark about not feeling guilt any more and not feeling anything any more. Then I said I'd do my best to be less romantic and more resigned. And then there was a diversion and we talked of other things.'

'Mmm. I've thought all that too.'

Effingham, who had offered his remarks as a half-flippant farrago, looked up quickly, not sure how to take this reply, and whether it was intended as a sort of rebuke ; but Max seemed deep in thought, his gaze resting on the distant photograph of his wife.

'At times you know,' Max went on, and his voice became hoarse and rhythmical, 'at times especially in the winter, it has all seemed to me so delicate that any action would be too gross for it, and certainly any action of mine, and it has seemed to me that this was why I always did nothing.'

'And was it?'

'I don't know. Of course, the situation has fascinated me as it has fascinated us all. But in a way too I think I was afraid of her.'

'Afraid of her needing you?'

'Afraid of her disturbing my work.'

'Well, you have stuck to your work,' said Effingham. He felt suddenly uneasy. The quietness of the room menaced him with some possibility of judgement. He went on, 'You have stuck to your work. The book is nearly finished.'

'Yes. More nearly than I've let Alice know. She thinks I'll go out like a light when the book is finished.'

'You won't,' said Effingham. Then the vision came, incomprehensibly painful. 'Ah – when the book is finished – you will go to see her –'

Max did not reply. He said after a little silence, 'I wish I understood more.'

'So do I,' said Effingham. He swept his hand upward through the clouds of cigar smoke. He felt stifled, threatened, upset. He wanted somehow to lighten the tone of the conversation and to disturb Max's oppressive reverie. 'I'd like to know a bit more about Gerald Scottow, for instance.' This was a topic on which he was now firmly resolved to question Pip.

'I am more real in the winter,' Max went on softly. 'I can think then. And of course I've thought about her. And sometimes it has seemed obvious that the right reaction is the simple one. Alice's for instance.'

'What is Alice's?' said Effingham grumpily. He was sorry now that he had reported Hannah's words to the old man.

'Alice is simply appalled and thinks that something ought to be done. If she doesn't say so to you, doubtless she has her reasons.'

'Humph,' said Effingham. He knew it was some time now since Max had given up wanting him to marry Alice. He wondered vaguely if Alice ever discussed him. He said, 'It is appalling of course. Visiting that place today was like visiting a police state. It makes one notice the free society when one gets back to it.'

'The free society? That rag freedom! Freedom may be a value in politics, but it's not a value in morals. Truth, yes. But not freedom. That's a flimsy idea, like happiness. In morals, we are all prisoners, but the name of our cure is not freedom.'

All prisoners, thought Effingham. Speak for yourself, old man. *You* are a prisoner, of books, age and ill-health. It then occurred to him that in some curious way Max might derive consolation from the spectacle, over there in the other house, of another captivity, a distorted mirror image of his own.

'I do wonder in a way,' said Effingham, 'why I *don't* react more simply. I suppose it's partly a sort of reverence for her way of taking the thing. And partly because, honestly, I find it all somehow beautiful. But that's idiotic romanticism. She was quite right about that.'

'It needn't be,' said Max. 'Plato tells us that of all the things which belong to the spiritual world beauty is the one which is most easily seen here below. We can see wisdom only darkly. But we can see beauty quite plainly, whoever we are, and we don't need to be trained to love it. And because beauty is a spiritual thing it commands worship rather than arousing desire. That is the meaning of Courtly Love. Hannah is beautiful and her story is as you say "somehow beautiful". But of course unless there are other virtues, other values, such worship can become corrupt.'

Max's oblivion of everything to do with Freud was one of the things which made Effingham love him. He said, 'I don't know if I have those other virtues. I suppose I'd better try and grow them! I feel if I could only get the situation into focus, give myself some theory of what she's *doing*, I could at least participate in some way, be resigned or whatever it is with her, stop – enjoying it. When you said just now you'd thought all that too did you mean you'd thought that I ought to stop enjoying it?'

'That among many things. In a way we can't help using her as a scapegoat. In a way that's what she's for and to recognize it is to do her honour. She is our image of the significance of suffering. But we must also see her as real. And that will make us suffer too.'

'I'm not sure that I understand,' said Effingham. 'I know one mustn't think of her as a legendary creature, a beautiful unicorn –'

'The unicorn is also the image of Christ. But we have to do too with an ordinary guilty person.'

'Do you really see her as expiating a crime?'

'I'm not a Christian. By saying she's guilty I just mean she's like us. And if she *feels* no guilt, so much the better for her. Guilt keeps people imprisoned in themselves. We must just not forget that there *was* a crime. Exactly whose probably doesn't matter by now.'

'I should have thought it did,' said Effingham. 'Though I'm not prepared to regard her as particularly guilty even if she *did* push that bloody man over the cliff. I wish I'd pushed him myself. I hate to think sometimes that she might be – suffering all this – somehow for him.'

'Why not?' said Max. 'He is in a privileged relationship to her.'

'Because he's her husband, yes!'

'I didn't mean that. Because he's her executioner.'

'Privileged? You mean he's the person she has the power to forgive?'

'Forgive is too weak a word. Recall the idea of Ate which was so real to the Greeks. Ate is the name of the almost automatic transfer of suffering from one being to another. Power is a form of Ate. The victims of power, and any power has its victims, are themselves infected. They have then to pass it on, to use power on others. This is evil, and the crude image of the all-powerful God is a sacrilege. Good is not exactly powerless. For to be powerless, to be a complete victim, may be another source of power. But Good is non-powerful. And it is in the good that Ate is finally quenched, when it encounters a pure being who only suffers and does not attempt to pass the suffering on.'

'Do you think Hannah is such a being?'

Max was silent for a few moments. Then he said, stubbing out his cigar, 'I don't know.' After a while he said, 'I may be suffering from my own form of what you call romanticism. The truth about her may be quite other. She may be just a sort of enchantress, a Circe, a spiritual Penelope keeping her suitors spellbound and enslaved.'

'I don't care for the Penelope image. I don't want Peter Crean-Smith to come back and put an arrow through me. You said the pure being doesn't pass the suffering on. But you also said that one ought to suffer with her.'

'Yes, but she would not be the cause of the suffering. Suffering is only justified if it purifies, and this kind could.'

'You mean the compassionate kind. Yes. If we have to put in such a lot of work perhaps it won't matter in the end whether she's a wicked enchantress or not, provided she's made saints of us! But I'm not really up to this spiritual adventure story. I just wish I could *understand* her. She has a weird unusual sort of calm. She spoke today about not feeling anything any more. But that can't be right. Women are made for feeling, for love. She *must* feel, she *must* love. She loves me, in a way. I only wished she loved me properly, with ordinary love.'

'She can't afford ordinary love,' said Max. 'I think that must be what, in these last years, she has understood. If she were to give way to ordinary love in that situation she would be lost. The only being she can afford to love now is God.'

'God,' said Effingham. 'God!' He added, asking a question which seemed to have been on the tip of his tongue all his life, 'Do you believe in God, Max?'

Max paused again, and replied in the same tone, 'I don't know, Effingham.' The oil-lamp murmured in the silent shadowy room, sending up the cigar smoke in a quiet spiral. He added, 'Of course, in the ordinary sense of believing in God I certainly don't. I don't believe in that old tyrant, that old monster. Yet –'

'I suspect you of being a crypto-Platonist.'

'Not even crypto, Effingham. I believe in Good. So do you.'

'That's different,' said Effingham. 'Good is a matter of choosing, acting –'

'That is the vulgar doctrine, my dear Effingham. What we can *see* determines what we choose. Good is the distant source of light, it is the unimaginable object of our desire. Our fallen nature knows only its name and its perfection. That is the idea which is vulgarized by existentialists and linguistic philosophers when they make good into a mere matter of personal choice. It cannot be defined, not because it is a function of our freedom, but because we do not know it.'

'This sounds like a mystery religion.'

'All religions are mystery religions. The only proof of God is the ontological proof, and that is a mystery. Only the spiritual man can give it to himself in secret.'

'I always thought the ontological proof was based on a gross logical fallacy. I realize I'm in no condition to give it to myself –'

' "Desire and possession of the true Good are one." '

'God is because I desire him? I'm damned if I'll stand for that.'

Max smiled. He said, 'I shall take refuge in the *Phaedrus*. You remember at the end Socrates tells Phaedrus that words can't be removed from place to place and retain their meaning. Truth is communicated from a particular speaker to a particular listener.'

'I stand rebuked! I recall that passage. But it *is* a reference to mystery religions, isn't it?'

'Not necessarily. It can apply to any occasion of learning the truth.'

'Do you think Hannah – desires the true good?'

Max said after a long silence during which Effingham found himself nodding with sleep, 'I'm not sure. And I don't think you can tell me. It may all be to meet some need of my own. I've meant all my life to go on a spiritual pilgrimage. And

100

here I am at the end – and I haven't even set out.' He spoke with a sudden fierceness, cutting and lighting a cigar with quick precision and moving the ash-tray farther down the table with a loud clack. He added, 'Perhaps Hannah is my experiment! I've always had a great theoretical knowledge of morals, but practically speaking I've never done a hand's turn. That's why my reference to the *Phaedrus* was damned dishonest. I don't know the truth either. I just know about it.'

'Well,' said Effingham, who was getting very sleepy indeed. 'You may be right about her. There is something unusual, something spiritual, there. There is that very exceptional quietness –'

'A mouse that's trapped by a cat is quiet!' said Alice sharply behind him. She had entered without their noticing her.

She came round the table and banged a tray down between the two men. 'Here's your tea. I found that vervain stuff that Effie brought from France. I hope it's all right. It's as old as the hills.'

Chapter Thirteen

Darling Effie,

Do come back soon, the office is hell, but hell, without you. When you are here (a funny thing, it occurs to me just this moment and is probably something to do with your being a brilliant administrator) when you are here it seems as if you are doing nothing at all all day (pert words from your junior) and yet as soon as you go the whole place gets uneasy and unhinged as if we suddenly weren't sure why we came in in the mornings and sat at these desks and shuffled these papers. It seems, without you, absurd; and perhaps one time you'll come back and find we've all gone away and the office is deserted, and the telephones are ringing in empty rooms. What I am referring to, as you will of course realize, is my own psychological state, though you *are* missed here, and I'm afraid there are a lot of things which men in other departments won't refer to anyone but you. Your in-tray is a picture. Poor sweetie.

How is the lonely lady of Gaze Castle? I am getting curiously attached to her. I dreamt about her the other night. Shall I write her a letter beginning, 'As you and I will realize, my dear, poor Effingham is really terrified of women'? All right, all right, there, there! But I sincerely hope that she is well and that you are chastely enjoying her, and that she is enjoying being enjoyed. And if there is a grain of malice in my respectful interest in your adventure, I am sure you would not wish that little tribute away. I am only sorry I did not realize your peculiarities a little earlier.

Art and psychoanalysis give shape and meaning to life and that is why we adore them, but life as it is lived has no shape and meaning, and that is what I am experiencing just now. I envy you your capacity for innocent romancing. At a great price bought I this freedom in four years of deep analysis, whereas you seem born not exactly free but with the next best thing, a capacity to cheer yourself along by endless little inventions. Now don't be cross with me! And come back soon or the Rubens exhibition will be over. Cooper-less go I every lunch-time. Can you think of a greater man capable of worse taste? *Quand même.*

Don't be tempted to carry off your princess, Effingham. The fairy tales never tell us, but it has always proved a mistake. I send the usual love, and am but too much as usual your too possessable

Elizabeth

Effingham read Elizabeth's letter through and pushed it hastily back into the envelope. It jarred on him. Why were clever women always so silly? He had never met a clever woman who wasn't somehow touchy and nervy and silly. Elizabeth could, on so many subjects, be beautifully serious; but as soon as matters engaged her emotions she would become suddenly arch and smart. How he detested that smart knowing tone.

A connexion of thought led him to Miss Taylor. He was on the following afternoon to give her the first of the disastrously promised Greek lessons. He would have been glad enough to drop the idea, and he guessed that Miss Taylor would tactfully have forgotten it too; only Alice had insisted. With a perverse desire to obtain for herself as much pain as possible, and with reproachful eyes fixed on Effingham, she had declared that of course this lovely plan must be carried out, it would be so nice for both of them, wouldn't it. Non-clever women could be very silly too. Perhaps all women were silly. Not Hannah of course, but, he found himself vaguely and spontaneously reflecting deep in his mind, Hannah was not exactly a woman. Well, he didn't mean that, of course she was. He recalled with exasperation Elizabeth's remark that he was really terrified of women. Poor Elizabeth had never really recovered her common sense after that analysis.

He looked out of the window and saw Pip Lejour armed with fishing-tackle, his waders slung over his shoulder, setting off up the hill. It was the dead time of the afternoon. Max, who hated the afternoon, had just retired to rest after quoting to Effingham a poem of Alcman about sleep which Effingham had always imagined referred to the night. He murmured it now, seeing it as the account of a sinister enchanted siesta. The day was hot and still enough to seem a day of the south. The mountain peaks and deep ravines, the trees, the honey bees, the wide-winged birds, asleep: like creatures round the castle of the sleeping beauty. Alice no doubt was asleep too, and in their rooms the beautiful red-haired maids were asleep. Fleetingly he pictured Carrie. The house was silent beside a silent sea. Only Pip, blasphemously out of tune as usual, was wakeful and full of jaunty purpose. Seeing him departing, Effingham had an immediate irritated desire to follow him and interrupt him. He knew from talk at lunch-time that Pip was going to fish for trout above the Devil's Causeway. He decided to pursue him and ask, at last, those questions which within the house it was so difficult brutally to put into words. It was about time, in any case, for the elusive, fluttering, mocking Pip to be cornered, pinned down, and somehow accounted for.

Effingham had woken up that morning with a disagreeable sensation which he attributed partly to alcohol and partly to the tone of Max's conversation the night before. He had been sickened, he was still not quite sure why, by the faintly hinted prospect that Max might open direct relations with Hannah. He appreciated, he enjoyed, the old man's interest in his story, but his enjoyment depended upon his retaining his own expertise, depended upon its remaining precisely a story. He did not mind, he even relished, the strange notion that Max and Hannah were somehow in communication, so long as they were in communication through him. But he did not want Max to have an independent view of the situation. Perhaps the old man ought not to be encouraged, perhaps he ought not to talk to him at all about Hannah. These conversations were too abstract, they belonged to the world of Max's book; and Effingham felt, with a sort of chilled apprehension, that he did not want the meaning of Hannah to be drawn into that world. So today Effingham felt a deliberate desire to pull things down to a simpler cruder level; and the idea of chasing and interrogating Pip appealed to him as a piece of detective work.

Effingham had of course tried to question Pip before, though not quite at first. At first a delicacy concerning Pip's privileged position had kept him silent. But time had quietly altered their relations. Effingham had come to see Pip as an outsider, as an object belonging to the past, and he had come, as he noted Pip's voyeur-like attitude to the situation, very slightly to despise him. Then he had questioned him, tactfully, indirectly, coaxingly, cleverly, but vainly. Pip had obviously enjoyed leading him on, hinting at revelations, keeping him on tenterhooks, and telling him nothing. Angry half with himself and half with his tormentor, he realized at last that his own easily divined attitude of superiority to Pip helped to close the latter's mouth. He ought to have questioned Pip at the start, at the time when he considered Pip a sacred object, and when he himself was more abjectly in need. Yet time, still quietly working upon the relations of the *dramatis personae*, had now again made, he felt, some difference. He had gained a greater stature, a greater authority, and it seemed to him for the first time that he might positively command Pip to talk.

Pip was well up the stream and Effingham was thoroughly out of breath by the time he sighted him. He had given his quarry a good start and had set out in Max's Humber, which he had left below by the sea wall. Then he had climbed up the steep leafy gully beside the stream, which tumbled in a series of narrow deafening waterfalls into dark swirling clefts, and he had passed a number of limestone steps and pillars which he had first taken to be the ruin of some eighteenth-century folly but which he later realized to be the work of nature, and now he had come out on a piece of heathery moor where the stream was spread out between expanses of tussocky grass into wide glossy pools which the clear and vivid sky had turned to a metallic blue. And there was Pip.

Pip was standing in one of the pools, the stream half-way up his waders, casting his line on to the bright smooth surface. Effingham, who knew nothing about fishing, stood by a while to watch, aware now that Pip was aware of him. The dance of the moving line continued without interruption as it curled and uncurled in an inapprehensible yet definite pattern above the fisherman's head and deposited the fly with a caressing touch upon the scarcely troubled water.

When Pip judged that he had kept Effingham waiting long

enough, he caught the line with a deft twitch, thrust the end of the rod into his waders, and came slowly back to the shore, shoving his knees sturdily against the smooth yet vigorous stream. 'Hello, Effie. Bit out of condition, aren't you? You're still puffing like an old grampus. Come for a lesson?'

'No, thanks. I still don't want to. I just wanted to talk to you, Pip.' Of course he realized now, after seeing the lonely, absorbed, graceful figure in the pool, that it was idiotic to ask favours of a maniac whom one has just disturbed in the enjoyment of his mania.

'Always ready for a talk, Effie. Got any matches? I brought my pipe and tobacco but no matches. You're a godsend.'

Pip seemed attentive enough and not out of temper. But that was how he always seemed. It sometimes struck Effingham that the good humour with which Pip always greeted him was a result of some stifled burst of laughter which Effingham's appearance somehow occasioned.

Effingham was dignified. He produced the matches and watched Pip's moist mouth pursed round the pipe and saw Pip's eyes widen with gaiety, peering up at him as the pipe was attended to. A little breeze, rising now with the approach of evening, carried the smoke away across the pool and stroked Pip's remnants of hair into a hazy fur round his neat head.

'Caught any fish?'

'Not yet. But I have hopes. I'm using a new fly. See. Alice says you can't fish these moory streams with a dry fly, but you can.' Pipe between teeth, Pip held up a tiny bright reddish gold and blue object, tied into a sort of complex bow.

'These things never look like any flies I've ever seen,' said Effingham. 'Where are its wings?'

'Doesn't need wings. Trout can't see the wings, you know. And we're aiming at a trout's eye view.'

'What's it made of?'

'Artificial silk and human hair.'

Effingham stared at the reddish gold stuff with a sudden irrational shudder. 'Whose?'

'Carrie's. The maids always oblige. And Tadg obliges too, only his hair is the tiniest bit too heavy, I find.'

'Tadg not with you?' Effingham was still unnerved by the hair.

'No. The trout would take him for an otter!'

'You're after trout? Or anything that comes?'

'For this, nothing else will come at this season. September is the best month for trout. Not that there aren't plenty of other fish around. Pike, for instance. I saw a biggish one just now. There used to be a monster pike in the lake, the little lake you know that caused the flood. Denis said he saw a pike five feet long there once and I believe him. I wonder where those pike went to. Wonderful fish, but terrifying. The big ones are always female. They often eat their husbands, ha, ha!'

'Ha, ha,' said Effingham. He felt that that was quite enough about fish. 'Look, Pip, let's sit down, shall we, while you have your pipe. There are a lot of things I want you to tell me and which I think I ought to know. I've waited long enough. I'm sorry to pursue you out here, but somehow you and I can't talk at Riders. You understand.'

'Do I?' said Pip. 'Well, there's plenty of space and privacy here.'

They sat down on a rock. There was in a way, Effingham immediately felt, rather too much space and privacy. The sky, into which an invisible lark was ascending, was too large and too high, and they beneath it were too tiny and too accidental for any really conspiratorial talk. A heron flapped across the pool, its slow wing-beats shadowed in it for a moment, and came down to stand immobile farther off, working the upper course of the stream. A water rat, its nose just above the water, broke the surface with a neat wash and vanished into the bank. A dipper moved like a restless shade from stone to stone. Elizabeth would have said it looked like a painting by Carpaccio.

'Gerald Scottow, what?' said Effingham.

Pip looked away across the pool, whistling a little squeakily past the pipe. 'They're rising a little for their evening feed, see.' There were faintly perceptible rings upon the water.

'Come on, Pip,' said Effingham. 'I deserve it.'

'I'm not sure what you deserve, Effie,' said Pip. 'But you

credit me with far too much knowledge. I know nodings. Like yourself.' He began to touch up the fly.

'Bloody liar, aren't you,' said Effingham. He never knew what line to take with Pip: polite, jocular, brusque, insinuating, he had tried them all.

Pip laughed. He said, 'I must just try another cast or two. My intuition tells me there are hungry fish over yonder. You stay here and keep damn still.'

He moved cautiously into the water again, waited till the stream was smooth again about his waders, and began to cast. In the hazier gentler light the pool was glossy but less bright, a greyish-blue in the centre and under the banks the colour of brown ale. At the far end a little white foam outlined a pebbly beach beyond which the distant heron still stood like stone. Pip's long line curled like a quiet slow-motion stock whip, moving in a leisured arabesque behind his head and seeming to pause before coming forward in the vertical cast. The fly alighted and sailed, tiny, golden, and tempting, near to the recent faint ripples. Then Pip with a sinuous movement, during which the line was invisible, lifted it cleanly into the air. He cast again and again and again. Effingham watched dreamily and then began to think about Hannah.

The graceful regular movement of the line was suddenly interrupted and Pip jerked abruptly forward into the deeper water. Effingham focused his eyes. The line was running swiftly out with a hissing sound as the trout raced for the cover of the opposite bank. Pip, legs wide apart near the swift centre of the crown pool, let the line run, checked it, and began cautiously to wind. The trout, feeling the tug, changed direction and began to rush downstream. As Effingham advanced to the water's edge, Pip came edging backward, stumbling over the stones in the slippery shallows, and began to splash after the trout in the direction of the next pool, letting out the line again and cursing Effingham for being in the way.

The trout took the narrows, visible for a second as a silver flash in the rapid water between the rocks. Pip plunged after, the rod lifted high ; the taut line grated on a boulder, cleared it, and sped to a check in the deep centre of the next pool.

Effingham, after slipping on a wet stone and getting one foot soaked, retreated to make a more dignified inland detour over the springy grass. When he reached Pip again, it was almost over. Pip was deep in the water winding the fish in. The taut line shortened, the man leaned forward almost tenderly over his victim. As the fish came very near, rising to the light in bright twisting arcs, Pip slowly retreated, then reached for the landing-net which was secured to his back, whipped it down driving the handle between his legs, and quickly manoeuvred the fish into it. The next moment with a cry of triumph he was splashing back to the bank. 'A three-pounder, Effie! You've brought me luck!'

Effingham looked at the big struggling fish with pity and revulsion. It was dreadfully alive. Pip took it by the head, pulling it out of the net. He disengaged the line, and before Effingham could look away he had killed the trout, putting a thumb in its mouth and breaking its back by a quick pressure of his hand. Such a rapid passage, such an appalling mystery. Effingham sat down on a rock feeling slightly sick.

Pip was soaked in water and muddy almost to the waist. His face was glowing and exalted and his damp wisps of hair were lacquered to his little round head. He began to pull off his waders, revealing dark cotton trousers clinging wetly to his legs. He seemed a long, thin, brown water sprite. 'All the same, I'll have no more luck today.' He crouched beside the beautiful dead trout which lay glistening between them on the grass. He stroked it. 'What was it you wanted me to tell you, Effie?'

Effingham, who had been humped over the trout staring at it sadly, jerked up. Pip was half kneeling. The exaltation had passed into a gay, tense, teasing expression. The sky behind him was becoming golden. 'Everything, roughly,' said Effingham, alert now and cautiously sensitive to Pip's precarious mood. 'But first of all about Scottow. I've never understood how Scottow fits in. Perhaps you can tell me.'

Pip sat back on his heels and then subsided on to the grass, one hand upon the dead fish. He looked away from Effingham across the pool, now become sleek and still again after the recent violence. The trout were rising again. 'Hannah's never talked to you about Gerald?'

'No, I've never asked.'

'You're a funny chap, Effie. I wonder why I've never wanted to talk to you? Well, there are hundreds of reasons. I'll tell you a bit about Gerald if you like. There could be no harm in that. You know Gerald's as queer as they come?'

'Homosexual. Yes. I suppose I thought Gerald might be *anything*,' said Effingham slowly. Yet he hadn't quite thought that. Out of some sort of weird respect for Hannah he hadn't had any clear thought about Gerald at all.

'Gerald's a local boy, you know that. He and Peter Crean-Smith are just of an age and they knew each other well as children when Peter's father, that was Hannah's mother's brother, used to come to Gaze for the shooting. Then when they were grown up a little Gerald went off and got himself some education and a new accent. Whether that was all Peter's idea I don't know. Maybe. Anyway just after Peter's marriage Gerald was back in the neighbourhood and Peter settled him with some sort of vague job in a cottage on the estate.'

Pip paused, still looking away across the pool. The golden glow deepened, outlining his head against the seaward sky. He was tense and grave now as if surprised at the emotion which his own speech had aroused in him. He went on softly as if for himself.

'I think Gerald and Peter must always have been very attached to each other, if one can attribute attachments to their natures. Obsessed with each other, anyway. Peter was queer too, you know. I don't know why I speak of him in the past, a wishful thought no doubt. Peter is queer, though of course he chases women too. *Inter alia* no doubt. That was the least of the things Hannah had to put up with.' He was silent again, his eyes widening thoughtfully.

'Anyhow, Peter's marriage didn't stop Peter from carrying on with Gerald, though at least he kept it from Hannah. Peter's attitude to Gerald at that time was a sort of sexual feudalism. I dare say it has fancier names. Gerald was his man,

110

his servant, his serf. He encouraged Hannah and everyone else, as I remember, to treat Gerald as a menial, even to kick him around a bit. And of course that was all part of the game. They both enjoyed themselves enormously. Then two things happened more or less at once. I fell in love with Hannah and Peter fell in love with an American boy called Sandy Shapiro.'

'I've heard that name,' said Effingham. 'He's a painter, isn't he? Lives in New York. Is Peter still –?'

'I don't know,' said Pip. 'Anyway, Peter was wild about this lovely boy and Gerald was wild with jealousy. Gerald had always rather made up to Hannah in a servile sort of way, as part of the game you understand. And then, when Hannah and I – Gerald helped us.'

'Gerald helped you and Hannah? Out of jealousy? But how – helped?'

'In a quite natural sort of way Hannah herself brought him into the picture. She'd got quite used, you see, to treating him as a servant. Hannah is half feudal too. She'd almost have undressed in front of him, she regarded him so much as a domestic. And oh, he was very useful. He carried messages, arranged meetings – and eventually betrayed us to Peter.'

'Good heavens,' said Effingham. 'I've often wondered – sorry –'

'How we could have been such fools as to be discovered so together? Yes. That was Gerald.'

Pip was silent again, and as if he had come to the end of the story. He relaxed on the grass, pulling up a damp trouser leg to massage his calf. The sun was going down now in a blaze of soupy reds and the near scene was vividly greenish and yellowish about the darkening pool.

Effingham leaned forward, almost beseeching. He must make Pip go on talking. The spell must not be broken. He murmured softly, coaxingly, 'And then, and then –?'

'That was Gerald. Well, then – Ah, God – Anyway.' He stopped again, as if this were the curtailment of the story. Then he went on in a rush. 'And then, you say. Well, and then Peter just went berserk –'

'But Peter did really love her?' This was the question that had haunted Effingham for years.

'Oh yes. Why doubt that?' Pip spoke suddenly in his old jaunty tone, as if it were not important.

Effingham felt, I have come too near. He looked down on Pip with awe and envy. This boy had known the simple Hannah of the ordinary world.

Pip went on the next moment, gravely again. 'That is his mystery. And her mystery. What Peter feels. Anyway he behaved like a jealous husband and like a jealous man.'

'And Gerald –?'

'I don't know what passed between them. But when Peter went away he left Gerald in charge.'

'As her gaoler. So that was Gerald's punishment – to become Peter's eunuch. But why should he endure it?'

'Gerald? Oh, for hundreds of reasons,' said Pip, lightly and impatiently, tearing up the thin grass and strewing it upon the damp scales of the trout. 'Why be complicated? Gerald has no money. Peter must pay him handsomely, oh, handsomely, handsomely, for what he does.'

'But Gerald is in effect imprisoned too –'

'You romantic ass, you don't imagine Gerald stays at Gaze? He's there a lot of the time. But in between he's stepping on and off aeroplanes. The airport is less than two hours from here by car – and from there he can take off to anywhere in the world. I've heard of Gerald in Rome, in Paris, in Tangiers, in Marrakesh –'

'In New York?'

'Ah – that's another mystery –'

'But will Peter come back – for her, for Gerald? Will he set Gerald free, will he set him free after seven years? Is there unfinished business between them?'

'I don't know,' said Pip. 'I'm damned cold,' he said, and began to get up. He was shivering.

'After all,' said Effingham. 'Whatever the advantages for Gerald, surely he wouldn't stay here unless there *was*, between him and Peter, unfinished business?'

'I don't know, I don't know. We shall be late for dinner.'

A darker greenish sky was pressing the sunset down into the sea. 'I've got the car below. What will end it, Pip?'

'His death. Or if her nerve breaks. Or, or, or. I don't know.' He tossed a pebble into the pool, full now of its own boggy darkness. 'Good night, fish.'

Chapter Fourteen

'What are we going to do, you and I, about Mrs Crean-Smith?'

Effingham had not expected this. Or had he? Had he not, ever since he had set eyes on the clever long-nosed girl, expected to be thus brought to the point? If this *was* the point, to which he was so sharply being brought. He had certainly been nervously awaiting *something* from this quarter: a sensation which had merged not unpleasantly with a straightforward interest in the girl and a desire to know her better.

The Greek lesson had gone well. Of course Alice had insisted on making coffee, bringing biscuits, installing them in the drawing-room at a specially erected table. And of course Miss Taylor had proved a delightful and intelligent pupil. Armed beforehand with Abbott and Mansfield, she had learnt her alphabet, mastered the inflections of the first and second declensions, and discovered a remarkable amount about the verb 'to loose'. They had jested together in a sophisticated way about the fact that one starts Greek by saying 'I loose' and Latin by saying 'I love'. Effingham had taken her through some elementary sentences in a severe pedagogic manner which pleased them both. There was an immediate rapport; and Effingham found himself suddenly nostalgic for the days when he had been a teacher. There was something singularly purifying in the business of teaching. He got pleasure from the presence of a hard lively mind eager for instruction. It was nice too to be looking, with an attractive girl, at some third thing. More than an hour had fleeted away.

It was still early in the afternoon. Miss Taylor had come to lunch and had got on well with Max. Alice had made a cheerful friendly show. Pip had been witty but preoccupied. They sat now at one of the big drawing-room windows. The terrace

114

outside was empty except for a somnolent, bored Tadg, and the sun shone intermittently, so that Gaze Castle opposite alternately sprang into shadowy relief and was blurred back into the hillside. A lot of small woolly golden clouds were crowding in from the sea and falling quickly down behind the peat bog. It was restless weather. There was rain in the air.

Effingham glanced quickly round to see that the door was shut. He said rather sternly, 'I don't know exactly what you mean, Miss Taylor.'

'Yes, you do. Forgive me for being so blunt. Of course, I know all about the situation and I've been dying to talk to somebody. Surely something must be done, something pretty drastic – we can't let things go on like this.'

Effingham was silent, staring at her with a stern mask. He was alarmed. He said then, 'You've only just arrived here, and –'

'I've only just arrived here, and that's why I've still got some common sense. Everyone else seems to have become completely stupefied.'

Effingham closed the books. He would have to be alert and quick to deal with this fierce unclouded young mind. He would have to be strong too. He was alarmed; but he was also exhilarated. He kept his face grave. 'All right. I'll assume you know the outline of the situation. And I won't tell you to shut up, why should I. What was it you wanted to say?'

'That we must rescue her.'

Effingham spread his hands, and a smell of hopelessness was wafted to him from the shabby furniture. The room had old memories of his visits to Riders. The sky was darkening outside. He had been in all these places before. He said, 'Naturally that is what one thinks at first. But believe me, Miss Taylor, it is not so simple. Mrs Crean-Smith doesn't want to be, as you put it, rescued. She's all right as she is, more all right I suspect than you and I have any means of knowing, and we must respect what she has chosen.'

'Rubbish,' said Miss Taylor.

Effingham felt a thrill of delight. He could not determine whether he was thrilled simply at being contradicted by a handsome clever girl with the face of a Michelozzi angel, or whether he was somehow pleased at the prospect of being forced to think in some new and dramatic way about his imprisoned lady. He had had, after Pip's revelations of yesterday, a night of bad dreams; and his visit to Hannah this morning had had a painful exciting quality.

'Look,' he said, 'this is something which it's very hard for an outsider to understand. It's something very delicate and curious, like one of those strange shells that Alice picks up on the beach. Any violent or clumsy interference could only do harm. Hannah has lived with this business for a long time and has made her peace with it. Her life is her own property, and however odd or painful it may seem to us to be, we have no right to try to alter it against her will. There's a great deal here that we can't see, a great deal in Hannah and a great deal else. We can't even remotely know the consequences of actions. Damn it, we must respect her enough to let her decide for herself how she wants to live! There's no place for arguing or pressing or persuading. There's plenty we can do for her just by letting her know we care. But there's no place for action. Come, Miss Taylor, you must see that. And now let's just wind up our lesson, shall we? It seems to have ended anyway. I suggest for next time –'

'I'm sorry,' said Miss Taylor. 'And do please call me Marian, by the way. I've thought about all this too, I've thought about it in exactly this way, but I'm still not convinced. You say we don't know the consequences of actions. But we don't know the consequences of inactions either, and inactions are actions.'

'And please call me Effingham, well, Effie. I was an existentialist when I was your age, Marian. Now I suggest you read –'

'Please, please don't put me off,' she said, stretching out her hands across the table. 'I'm tormented by this business, I really am. And there's no one to talk to.'

Effingham hesitated. It was true that inactions were actions. What was it that had given him such bad dreams last night? Pip's remark about 'if her nerve breaks'. Yet why should her nerve break, had she any nerve left to break? He felt a strong desire to unburden himself to Marian Taylor.

It was beginning to rain. Tadg scratched at the door and Effingham got up to let him in. The wet dog shook himself

116

and then made much of Marian, who had knelt to greet him. Effingham said, 'I think I'll light the fire, it's getting cold.'

They moved over to the fireplace and while Effingham crouched to set a match to the paper and sticks, Marian and Tadg settled themselves on the rug. The girl was wearing a big blue skirt of light local tweed which she must have bought in Blackport. She spread it out and the dog sat upon it, beaming up at her. Effingham seated himself on a footstool, tending the fire. It was another scene, suddenly more intimate.

'How do you get on with the people over there, apart from Hannah I mean? I know you get on splendidly with Hannah.'

'Oh, well enough. Denis Nolan is quite nice and Jamesie is perfectly sweet. I'm a bit nervous of Violet Evercreech, but she doesn't bother me. I think Gerald Scottow is charming – oh, very very charming – only I can't make him out.'

Effingham was slightly irritated by this eulogy of Scottow and for a second tempted to give Marian some further information, but he restrained himself. 'No one you talk to – about Hannah? Who was it told you about the situation?'

'Nolan did. But I haven't discussed it with him. I think he's – well, hostile to any idea of doing anything.'

'He'd be out of a job!' said Effingham. He mustn't be spiteful about Nolan.

'It's not that,' said Marian seriously. 'He somehow really believes she *ought* to stay there. I think he's rather religious or something.'

'You're not religious, are you? I'm not either. I certainly don't think anything like that about Hannah.'

'So you see,' said Marian, pursuing her own train of thought, 'there's really no one over there I could count on, for the rescue I mean. I've thought of Jamesie, but he's rather young and silly. And I haven't managed to get to know Scottow – yet.'

'Leave Scottow out. But you speak as if you were really planning something! Be realistic. What on earth could you do?'

'That's what you'll help me to decide.' She turned her fierce brown eyes upon him. 'You're the only person who can help, so you've got to help.' She sat there, near to his knees, stroking Tadg and glaring with purposes.

'You're mad,' said Effingham. 'I've already told you there's nothing to be done. But perhaps you'd better get rid of it all by talking to me. Then I can send you back with more sense in your head. Go on.' He was dying to hear what she was going to say.

'My first thought,' said Marian, 'was simply to talk to Hannah and persuade her to make arrangements to leave. I couldn't at first believe that any rational person – and of course she's rational – would tolerate the situation at all – or having tolerated it, wouldn't take the chance to clear out if some well-disposed body were ready to help them. I thought perhaps she just hadn't gone because she was afraid of – someone in the house – or because she just couldn't manage to make the arrangements by herself. She's dreadfully unpractical.'

'I hope to God you *didn't* say anything to her?'

'No, I didn't. I somehow became sure that she wouldn't let me persuade her. She'd answer with some nonsensical kind of talk. And there was no point in just upsetting her. So then I started to think about kidnapping her.'

'*Kidnapping* her?'

'Yes. I thought if I could get someone to help me we might well, just hustle her into a car and drive her away.'

'You perfect romantic fool!' said Effingham. This was no longer agreeable. The vision conjured up by these words frightened him very much indeed. He pictured Scottow on the road behind them. There was violence, violence asleep in that situation. He did not want to be the one to waken it. 'That is perfectly unthinkable, as surely you realized when you'd thought about it?'

'I thought about it, Effingham. I think I'll call you Effingham, as Mr Lejour does. And yes, I decided it was no good. It was too unfair to her, and anyway it could easily go wrong. Then I had a third idea.'

'Well, I hope it was better than the other two!' He booted some turf into the fire. The rain was pelting down outside.

'My third idea is this,' said Marian. 'It's the idea of a modified rescue. You see, it depends on what you think about her frame of mind. As I see it, her frame of mind is pretty mixed up. She began – forgive me for talking about her in this way. You've known her far longer than I have. But I'm a new broom, and I can't help behaving like one – and I *do* care about her very very much. She began, this is how I see it anyway, by simply being afraid of that beastly man, just paralysed with fear. Then she became rather apathetic and miserable. Then she began to find her situation sort of interesting, spiritually interesting. People have got to survive and they'll always invent some way of surviving, of seeing their situation as tolerable. At the time when Hannah might have survived by just hating them all, or might have survived by just bursting out and kicking it all to bits, she decided to become religious instead.'

'You don't think much of this solution?'

'I've nothing against religion in general, though I can't do it myself. But if it's to be any good it's got to be freely taken to, out in the open as it were. Hannah took to religion, or the spiritual life or whatever the hell it is, like someone taking to a drug. She had to.'

'I suppose that is *a* way of taking to religion, because one has to. But I see what you mean. Go on.'

'Well, and all the time she was being more and more hypnotized by the situation itself and by all those people surrounding her and murmuring into her ear in different tones, but all murmuring it: you're imprisoned. And now she's simply spellbound. She's psychologically paralysed. She's lost her sense of freedom.'

'And what would you propose to do about it?'

'Give her a shock. Pull her out of it just far enough to make her realize that she *is* free and that she's got to make her own decisions. This will, I'm afraid, also involve a little kidnapping.'

'Marian,' said Effingham, 'go on.' He spoke sarcastically, but his heart was suddenly in a flurry. To hear someone speaking in this calm analytic tone about the situation, speaking as if there were alternative actions which could be rationally considered, was a refreshing sacrilege.

'What I suggest is this,' said Marian. 'And I shall need some-

119

one to help me, and I hope it will be you. We decoy her into a car. That shouldn't be impossible. You often drive up to the house. We offer her a little lift up the drive, say. Then we turn round and drive like hell as far as Blackport to the fishing hotel.'

'And then –?' It was quiet and dark in the room now.

'I don't know what happens then. That will depend on her. Perhaps we have some lunch and take her back to Gaze. At least it will convince her that she won't die if she goes outside the walls. You know sometimes I think she half believes that. Anyway, it will be a shock. And if she shows the slightest hesitation, the slightest desire not to go back, we drive her to the airport.'

'Good God,' said Effingham. He looked at her with admiration and horror. He apprehended her as beautiful, invigorating, dangerous, destructive. He must listen to her no more ; and as he immediately reflected that this conversation must never be revealed to Max, he measured how far for a moment she had tempted him. But it was all an absurdity, a wicked irresponsible absurdity.

Alice came bustling in, pushing a well-laden tea trolley. 'Well, did you have a good lesson? Why, you're almost in the dark. Carrie will bring the lamps directly.'

'Fine, thanks,' said Effingham getting up.

The golden lamplight entered the room and as it shone on both their faces he held Marian Taylor's gaze for a moment and slowly shook his head.

Part Three

Chapter Fifteen

Dearest Marian,

Thanks awfully for your letters. I owe you one, I know, I've been awfully bogged down. You remember I said I'd write that leaflet for the Campaign, well that's come home to roost, and there's the Fifth Form play which I'm alleged to have agreed to produce (I can't recall *that*, can you? I must have been drunk!) and they've just decided to change the G.C.E. syllabus, as I expect you've seen in the paper, and I've got some sort of beastly virus that I can't get rid of – and well, that's enough to start with by way of excuses! Gosh, I envy you, old girl, with nothing to do but read the *Princesse de Clèves* with Mrs Thing until you both fall asleep! (I did laugh at your description.) Seriously though the country must be magnificent. I hope you're doing plenty of walking. Tell me about the birds as there doesn't seem to be much else going on. And don't think I'm getting at you with the above remarks! A little lying fallow does no one any harm. I wish I could lie fallow even for a couple of hours. Whatever the reverse of fallow is, that's me!

However there is one bright spot on the horizon, which is that I'm going to fly to Madrid at half term. I know it's immoral to pass one's pennies on to old Franco, but I've decided I don't want to be blown up without having seen Las Meninas and Las Lanzas. So several of us have arranged to go in a party on the cheap. That girl Freda Darsey, the one you were at school with, is coming too. She'll be handy as she knows Spanish. She doesn't seem a bad stick, though too bulbous for the taste of yours truly. I'll send you a postcard.

I must stop now, I've got such a pile of IVA's nasty inky little exercises to wade through. Devil take all children, why can't their parents keep the scrofulous little blighters at home! Do write, Marian, you know I love hearing from you. Your last two letters were so short, I feared you might have been hurt by my silence.

But just recall that you've got more time than I have! With best wishes to you, you lucky girl, and love as usual from your old pal

G.

Marian pushed Geoffrey's letter into a drawer. It filled her with gloom and irritation and a frightened little homesickness. Since she had learnt from Denis Nolan the true nature of what was happening at Gaze she had not been able to write frankly to Geoffrey. She had screwed out, for the sake of appearances, two limp missives about the scenery. It would have been impossible to tell him what was really going on; he would have found it all quite insane and would have given her very crude counsel. But it *was* all quite insane, and was she not giving herself very crude counsel?

She looked in the mirror. She was wearing a new terracotta-coloured shot silk evening dress which Hannah had insisted on giving her, after ordering it, with several others, secretly on approval especially for Marian. Marian had felt uneasy at accepting the present, but the idea and the charming way the dress fitted her and suited her had delighted Hannah so much that the girl had not in the end had the heart to say no; and of course it was a wonderful dress, and one which, quite apart from its price, she would never have had the discrimination and the nerve to buy herself. Since the ruby and pearl necklace didn't look quite right with it, she was wearing, as a finishing touch, a collar of irregular amber beads which Hannah had selected, after minute research, from her own store, and which she patently intended Marian to keep, though she had tactfully not said so yet.

Geoffrey had always quite rightly told Marian that she did not know how to dress. She favoured a formless exoticism, he favoured a muddy simplicity: in fact neither of them had any taste at all. But now already Marian was aware, since she had been at Gaze, she had by some process of osmosis acquired certain elements of good taste from Hannah. These elements existed in Hannah in a state of unconsciousness, but they were infectious; and although Hannah was now careless of her appearance and surroundings she had long ago, in respect of both, been beautifully trained. So it was that Marian had quietly

122

put upon the retired list quite a number of the garments and accessories with which she had arrived, including the sensible but she now saw quite horribly ill-cut blue dress in which Geoffrey had expressed such great confidence.

Marian had lately found that she was living to an alarming degree upon two different levels of mind. Upon one level she entered brightly into the tiny dramas and gaieties which made up life at Gaze, and which seemed so totally to occupy Hannah's consciousness. Marian had never seen anyone live so entirely in the present; and she too lived in the present, looking forward to her meals and to the ritual of the evening whiskey, making little ceremonies out of views of sunsets or walks to the fish ponds, and enjoying literature as those alone enjoy it who have little else to enjoy. There had been a lot of reading aloud. There had been a lot of looking at reproductions of paintings. There had been a little phase of rhyming games and drawing games. There had been a phase of trying on hats, of which Hannah had a great store from some years ago. There had been talk of fancy dress, there had been talk of charades, there had been talk of a musical evening. Tonight, in fact, was the musical evening, which was why Marian was thus arrayed. After dinner, which was shortly to take place downstairs with all present, a rare enough treat, there was to be music in the drawing-room.

So things went on in this curiously childish Marie-Antoinetteish manner; and so, with half of her mind, Marian took part in them, joining gaily with the tirelessly cheerful and prankish Jamesie in being the life and soul of the party. But the rest of her mind was concerned furtively with other things. Since her talk, now some days ago, with Effingham Cooper about the possibility of a rescue she had felt so upset and agitated that she could not sleep properly and sometimes found it difficult to behave normally with Hannah, with whom she would find herself suddenly breathless and blushing. She had spoken to Effingham with vehemence and decision as if she had thought all these plans out beforehand, but in fact they had only become really clear to her while she was actually talking to him. His very presence, his big, intelligent, rational,

123

familiar sort of face, the splendid ease of their pupil-teacher relation, all this made what had seemed nightmarishly difficult and obscure suddenly, for her, crystallize; and she had seen with an appalling clarity what ought to be done.

She had not since then wavered much. She had thought about the problem continually and she felt fairly sure that the shock tactic, the attempt to shatter the spell by a piece of planned violence, could do no harm and might do much good. Even supposing, at Blackport, Hannah asked piteously to be taken back to Gaze: well, they would take her back. No one could blame *her* for what had happened; and the insidious idea would have been planted in her head that she could leave the place with impunity. She *could* leave the place.

The horrible aspect of the thing was of course the strong possibility, which Effingham had brought to her attention when they talked again on the following day, that should Hannah return to Gaze the perpetrators of the *coup* would be forever banished from her. Effingham had refused, on this ground and on many other grounds, to have anything to do with the idea; but Marian thought it possible that, if she decided to go on, she might yet talk him round. He had already confided to her that a friend of his had once told him that a clever woman could convince him of anything. She would probably go on though, she now felt with a kind of fatalism, with or without Effingham. As she had pointed out to him in the argument, he or she or anyone else might at any moment by an obscure fiat be expelled from Gaze. It was not as if one at all liked or even understood the status quo; and for all they knew the sands might be running out.

Effingham had not liked this metaphor. He enquired what she meant, what sands were running out, had she any real reason to think that time was short or that the situation was becoming dangerous or urgent? What positive harm, surely none, could come to Hannah from the continuance of things as they were? No, Marian had no real reason. Yet she did feel in her bones a kind of urgency, a sense of being now in a position of power or trust which she must exploit while she could. She felt above all, as a sort of categorical imperative, the desire to set Hannah free, to smash up all her eerie magical surroundings, to let the fresh air in at last; even if the result should be some dreadful suffering.

So she had half decided to go on with or without Effingham. But without Effingham was impossible unless she found someone else. She herself could not drive a car, and she had to have somebody who could. Who? This brought her up against the continually puzzling question of her relations with the other inhabitants of Gaze. She had kept a constant but unprofitable watch upon Gerald Scottow. She noted his comings and goings, his frequent absences on estate business, his gay returns. She enjoyed his slightly bullying charm and the nervous badinage into which he spurred her. His physical appearance affected her with tremors. She had never before wanted so much to touch a man with whom she could not converse. For, alas, she could *not* converse with him, and her plan, if it had ever been a plan, of helping Hannah by subduing Scottow had certainly so far misfired. She did not despair of coming, somehow, to know Scottow, of coming to know him much, much better: but he was, for immediate purposes, irrelevant. Violet Evercreech was unthinkable. Denis Nolan would never approve. That left Jamesie.

Marian had by now seen a lot of Jamesie, laughed a lot with Jamesie, been driven by him here and there, without coming to know him really any better than she had on the occasion of their first drive to Blackport. There had been no repetition on Jamesie's part of that little approach to a greater intimacy. It was as if Jamesie had been warned off or had decided, after the warmth of a first enthusiasm, that he preferred a simple, cheerful relationship with Marian. Simple and cheerful he certainly was with her, and she with him; but would he do as an ally?

Jamesie could drive a car, and had indeed complete control of the Land Rover and the old Morris which made up the mechanical establishment at Gaze. This would be handy, as it occurred to Marian that at the moment of flight all other means of transport had better be disabled. But could Jamesie be trusted, and even if he could be trusted was he not too vulnerable to reprisals? Marian on reflection decided that she was prepared to risk Jamesie if he was prepared to risk himself. She felt, with the brutality, already growing upon her, of a desperate general, that Jamesie would probably be better off anyway if he were fired out of Gaze. The place did him no good. The matter of his trustworthiness she could not yet decide. He seemed, in the midst of it all, oddly uncommitted, a jocose observer. His flippancy might indicate that he could be won. She wondered.

A bang on the bedroom door interrupted her reverie and she jerked quickly away from the mirror. Whenever anyone knocked on her door she was divided between the hope that perhaps it was Gerald Scottow and the fear that it might be, even now, the arrival of her order of banishment. She opened the door to one of the maids from whom, after several repetitions of a gabbled message, she understood that she was being summoned to see Miss Evercreech.

'Come in, my child.'

Marian entered nervously. Ever since the unnerving promise of the 'little talk' she had been trying, with an uneasy conscience and no very clear mind, to avoid Violet Evercreech. She had never been near her room before, and was even now not sure where it lay in the house, so quickly had she been conducted and so agitated had she been on the way.

It was a corner room, high up on the north side of the house, facing towards the Scarren; and while most rooms at Gaze contained their share of junky relics, this room looked soberly modern. Marian took in white painted bookshelves, a white furry bedspread, wild flowers in a black vase. Violet Evercreech was sitting in a chintz armchair, dressed in a purple dressing-gown, with a bottle of sherry and two glasses on a small table beside her. Her evening-dress was laid out upon the bed, a gawky spreadeagled form.

'I thought we might take a little glass together before dinner,' said Miss Evercreech. She spoke as if this were something customary; yet there was about the occasion, about the room, a strained sense of the impromptu.

126

Marian murmured her thanks and sat down in a chair which had been drawn close to Miss Evercreech's own. She noticed, half with pity and half with a shiver, that the glasses were thick with dust.

'What a pretty dress. Where did you get it?'

'Mrs Crean-Smith gave it to me.' Marian looked down, blushing with an immediate mixture of guilt and resentment.

Miss Evercreech said slowly, after a pause during which she savoured Marian's blushes, 'Well, and why not?'

'No reason why not, Miss Evercreech.' Her voice sounded sharp and grating, and she felt, already, almost ready to weep with annoyance. Miss Evercreech had a quality of sheer attention which made her writhe.

'Please call me Violet.' The glasses were smartly polished on the purple silk sleeve, and the sherry tinkled in.

'Yes. All right. Thank you.'

'Well, say it then. "Yes, Violet." '

'Yes, Violet.'

'That's better.' Violet Evercreech, still seated, turned to look at Marian, and sat thus for some time, staring at her. Marian did not know where to look. She felt her profile being outlined as if a burning finger were being drawn down it from her brow. Her nose began to twitch. In desperation she turned her face to Violet's, and saw at uncomfortably close quarters the pale powdery skin, the dry colourless hair, and the long moist eyes which were fixed upon her with a hungry intensity.

'My dear child,' said Violet Evercreech, 'give me your hand.'

Embarrassed and alarmed, quickly averting her gaze, Marian extended her left hand as far as the arm of the chair, gripping her glass firmly with her right. Violet took the proffered hand in both of hers, gave it a slow hard pressure and retained it.

'In a way I can only talk nonsense to you,' Violet went on, 'and if I talk about myself I can only talk in riddles. I didn't ask you here to talk about myself, but one has needs, old needs.'

Marian, her hand and arm stiff as a puppet's, said, 'I'm

sorry – ' And then, to fill a silence which might soon become significant in some intolerable sense, said hastily, 'You're a second cousin of Hannah's, aren't you – ?'

'Yes. Do you know it is many years since I touched another human being in this way.'

'Really – ' said Marian. She looked down at where the purple silk parted to reveal a knee clad in a pearly brown cotton stocking. Some emotion from the past choked her utterance. She wriggled her hand in what might have been a caress or a defiance.

'You love Hannah, don't you?'

'Yes – yes, of course,' said Marian. She wondered if she were going to receive some warning, some crushing reprimand.

'So do I. Extremely.' Marian's hand was crushed again and released. Marian retrieved it and took it to safety on the other side of her knee.

Violet went on, 'It is good to have you here in this room. So unexpectedly good, it took me by surprise. It is good to be reminded that love was once a simple natural thing. Perhaps you will come here again, and perhaps I will hold your hand like that again. Or perhaps not. You may have to pay for having seen a moment of weakness. But no, no. It was not for this I summoned you.' She pushed her chair back a little. 'I wanted to tell you something else, to tell you that you have made a conquest.'

'A conquest?' Marian's thoughts flew to Gerald.

'Yes. My little brother. You have captured Jamesie's heart.'

'Oh – Jamesie – '

'You are disappointed, because you have other interests in this house. Yes, yes, I have been watching you! But I wanted to ask you to be kind to Jamesie.'

'Kind to him – why, I adore Jamesie,' said Marian with a confused overflow of emotion. She almost stretched out her hand again.

'I'm glad. I know he must seem a child to you. But a deep devotion, any deep devotion, is a precious thing, and woe to him who spurns it. Jamesie would do anything for you, anything.'

'I'm very touched indeed – and surprised. I didn't realize he felt – '

'He is a secretive boy. Everyone in this house is secretive. Even you are becoming secretive.'

'Me? Oh, no – ' said Marian hastily. 'But Jamesie – I hope he's not upset – he'll get over it – he's very young.'

'He's very young and he needs looking after. I think an affair with an older woman is often just what a young fellow needs, don't you? I mean, with an older woman who doesn't love him – but who just – adores him.'

Marian withdrew herself into her chair and put her glass down. 'Well, really, I don't think I – if you mean – I'm sorry, but – '

'Never mind, never mind. Perhaps it was for myself after all that I summoned you – even if I never refer to this occasion again, even if I never see you alone again.' She rose, as if the interview were at an end, and Marian rose too. They stood looking at each other.

Violet was taller. She moved first; but Marian knew afterwards that she had moved too, impelled by some immediate irresistible magnetism towards the purple dressing-gown. Her head was upon Violet's shoulder. She felt Violet kissing her hair and her brow. Next moment she was thrust fiercely away and found herself outside the door.

Marian fled down the stairs, scarcely touching the floor, and ran along a corridor to a big window where she could see the familiar reassuring view of the sunless garden and the green lift of the cliffs beyond. She leaned her head against the glass and found herself panting and trembling. She sat down on a chair beside the window. She had never been approached in this way by a woman before and the experience had been both weird and exciting. She had found Violet touching and repulsive; yet her whole body was roused and if Gerald Scottow had appeared in the corridor at that moment she would have fallen at his knees. She hoped there would be no sequel; yet she had not wholly, not altogether, disliked it, the drama, the sheer unexpectedness. She rearranged her dress. How curious too about Jamesie.

With Jamesie she recalled the whole range of her preoccupations. 'He would do anything for you.' If he would do anything for her he would drive the car which was to take Hannah away. Marian jumped up. A rapacious desire for action, for sensation, had been put into her by Violet. She felt so strong, so physically alive, she felt she could persuade anybody of anything. She would hunt for Jamesie now, now this minute; and the possibility that she might well, on seeing him, hurl her arms round his neck did not deter her in the least.

She turned along a dark intersecting corridor. These rooms faced the garden, and she was fairly sure one of them was his. She knocked on a door and opened it on a totally empty room. The next room looked like a maid's room. The next, the corner room, must surely be Jamesie's. She knocked again, softly, and then cautiously opened the door. The corridor, as she glanced back, was empty.

Clothes which she recognized as his lay in heaps upon the floor, and the room had the slightly menacing personal silence of a very inhabited place. Marian looked about her and saw another door, leading perhaps to a bedroom or inner sanctum. Stepping over the clothes, breathless with nervousness yet bold, she knocked on the further door and opened it. The inner room was dark and smelt of chemicals. There was no one there.

Marian stood still a moment, finding her breath. She made out an unmade disordered bed and a heap of detective novels on the floor. On a table there were trays and bottles, presumably something to do with photography. There was a curious patterned wallpaper on the walls. Marian moved instinctively to the window and pulled back the curtains. She looked, she stared, she looked closer. As the room lightened she could see that what the walls were covered with was photographs, a mass of photographs, large and small, fitted neatly edge to edge covering three sides of the room. She peered at them curiously. It took her some moments to realize that the photographs represented, every single one of them, Gerald Scottow: Gerald grave, Gerald smiling, Gerald mounted, Gerald on foot, Gerald clothed, Gerald unclothed, Gerald in some very strange postures indeed. . . .

With shocked amazement and appalled fascination Marian looked at the pictures. At that moment the sun came out, the garden was lighted up behind her, and a ray of sunlight fell on her shoulder. She started guiltily, as if suddenly revealed and discovered, turned round toward the light, and found herself looking down at the terrace and straight into the raised horrified face of Denis Nolan, who was looking up at her. His face for a moment expressed horror and a sort of anger and disgust. Then he made a violent gesture with his hand and turned away into the garden.

'Wait, Denis, wait!' Marian caught up with him just as he was reaching the gate in the wall. Her dress kept dragging and catching among the brambles and ash saplings. He turned.

Denis was dressed, for the evening's music, in a dark blue suit and wore a collar and tie. The unusual clothes made him look awkwardly thick and burly, big in the shoulder. He turned an uneasy face toward Marian, his blue eyes screwed up angrily. For the first time she felt a little frightened of him.

'Denis, please – '

'What is it?'

What was it indeed? 'You looked so strange, when I saw you just now from the window, from Jamesie's room – '

'It is nothing to me whose room you are in.'

'No – I didn't mean that. Jamesie wasn't there of course. I went to look for him, but he wasn't there. I'd never been there before.'

'That is nothing to me.'

'Denis, don't be angry. I don't understand. Why did you look so terribly savage when you saw me and make that gesture? I thought you were calling to me.'

'I was not calling to you. I think you are meddling too much and thinking too much. If you get yourself sent away now, it will nearly break her heart.'

131

'Well, I can't stay here forever,' said Marian. She said it in exasperation, meaning: I cannot serve her in *that* way, that is a palliative not a cure.

Denis looked at her for another moment, his blue-black locks all jagged in the breeze. Then he turned away through the door, banging it in her face.

Marian tried to pull the door open to follow him, but it had jammed itself once more and she could not get the trick of opening it. It took her several moments of pulling before with apparent ease it came open. She ran after him. He was walking up the slope of short grass toward the top of the cliff, the blue afternoon sky beyond him full of light.

'Denis, Denis – '

'What is it now?' He stopped again, looking at her sadly rather than angrily.

'You know I didn't mean it in that way. I'm just as troubled about her as you are. Denis, why do you think I'm meddling too much?' The breeze, stronger here, rippled and rustled the cinnamon coloured dress. The emerald and amethyst sea was in sight.

'Leave alone Jamesie and Scottow.'

'Jamesie and Scottow – Do you know, Jamesie's room is full of the most extraordinary pictures of Gerald. I – ' The significance of what she had seen came to Marian with a rush. 'Denis, those two, are they – ?'

'Yes. And you'd better leave them alone. They are jealous and spiteful, the pair of them. I've seen you looking at Scottow. And I've seen Jamesie looking at you. And there is enough trouble and violence here already.'

'Oh God – ' said Marian. A variety of confused aches and pains drummed in her heart. Gerald lost, Jamesie useless. She said, 'Have they – always been like that, I mean, ages? I had no idea Gerald was so inclined. He doesn't look like it.'

'Those ones often don't. Nearly three years. You didn't know about what Jamesie did, or rather tried to do?'

'No, what? Please tell me, Denis. You'd better tell me. It'll stop me from meddling.'

They had reached the top of the cliff now and the house

was almost hidden by the humped green slope behind them. The black cliffs were lonely, majestic, old.

'He tried to take her away.'

'Jamesie – tried to take Hannah away?'

'Yes. She had no part in it, she did not know of it, but he planned to kidnap her. When he first came, with his sister – that was five years ago, he was a boy really – he was with her a lot, with Mrs Crean-Smith, he was very close to her and she doted on him and called him her little page. Then he began to be a man. Ah, but he was quite different from what he is now. And he made up this scheme to take her away, to put her into the car and drive her away. He might have done it only he was found packing her up a bag. He didn't want to take her away suddenly without any clothes to change. And Scottow found him packing the bag and made him confess.'

'What happened then?'

'Scottow gave him a tremendous whipping.'

'Good heavens, poor Jamesie. But –'

'And after that he was Scottow's slave.'

'You mean – he abandoned Hannah – he went over to Gerald?'

'After Scottow had laid hands on him like that, Jamesie worshipped Scottow and Scottow took Jamesie. That's how it was.'

'But surely things like that can't happen so suddenly.'

'We shall be late for dinner. Remember the music.'

'How very strange.' They began to walk back. 'Everyone here seems to have some weird secret or other.' She looked quickly at Denis. She had not meant to hint at his.

He took her up sombrely. 'Everyone here is involved in guilt.'

'Except me,' said Marian half to herself after a moment. 'Except me, except me, except me.'

Chapter Sixteen

The drawing-room, whenever it was periodically resurrected, managed to look a fine enough room, especially now with the lamps lighted, a big log-fire burning, and the tall windows opened to the fragrant air of the terrace which came in with a crisp smell of sea and tamarisk. The soft light made the furniture glowing and hazy, and the various odd old pieces seemed to join hands as if remembering some great days of fifty years ago. The room encircled the people in it with a sort of tottering pride. Outside there was a big night of stars.

The 'music', while simple enough, turned out to be more ambitious than Marian had expected. One or two of the handsome redheads from Riders were to be seen sitting in the group of servants near the piano, and one of these, a big girl called Carrie, had opened the programme by playing with little expression but great correctness a small piece of Mozart. This had been applauded frenetically ; and Marian, although she had grave and painful matters on her mind, could not help being rapt into the touchingly absurd and endearing atmosphere of an amateur performance. She smiled and clapped with the rest, catching Hannah's eye. It was hard to believe that all in this cheerful little family party was not as it seemed.

The next item was a performance by two of the black maids of Gaze upon a sort of stringed instrument which Marian had not seen before, rather resembling a Jew's harp. The noise was twangy and confused, but not unpleasant. Everyone liked that too. Then another pair of black maids sang songs, one in English and two in their own language. The songs were pretty and sad, the voices thin. After that there was a pianola performance. Marian had not noticed that the grand piano had a pianola attachment. Operated by another maid, the pianola played, a little jerkily in places, the Moonlight Sonata of Beethoven.

Marian had not expected this assault upon her feelings. She had expected to be embarrassed and touched, but not to hear any serious music. Marian was not musical and on the whole shunned musical occasions. She did not understand music and it upset her, it had only sad, tragic things to say. These leaping forms, these pursuits and insistences, these elusive desperate repetitions, always seemed to her like one long cry of agony. She could not, in this company, allow herself the luxury of self-pitying tears, which was her highest tribute to the art. She looked about her and let the music gather to her the people with whom she was so deeply concerned.

The gentry were seated in a semicircle stretching across the middle of the room from the fire to the open windows. The circle was curved enough for everyone to be able to see everyone else, and there was a lot of polite exchanging of nods and smiles during the applause. The relations of the inhabitants of Gaze were, in public, remarkably formal. Hannah sat in the middle. She was wearing the mauve silk evening-dress and a collar of blue stones. She looked very young in the soft light. Effingham was on her right, on the side nearest the fire and Jamesie next to him in the bright glow of the logs. Gerald sat on Hannah's left, and Violet a little behind her. Marian sat near the window. Denis, who didn't count as gentry, was sitting, one leg crossed over the other, against the wall. Alice had been asked but had pleaded a cold. The maids were scattered, some near the piano, some behind the semicircle. Some very large men, whom Marian had not seen before, were standing at the back near the door.

Marian raised her eyes cautiously. The music, almost unheard now, had drawn her into a solemn meditation wherein she must try, so much more deeply, to understand these people for whom she suddenly felt responsible. Jamesie was looking enchanting, wearing a sort of Teddy boy evening-dress composed of tight black trousers, dark blue corduroy coat, white silk shirt, and purple choker. He had sleeked his curly hair well back and looked older, his long bony face, from which the light of play and mockery had been withdrawn, grave and in repose. His gaze, which had been cast down, lifted quietly to rest upon Gerald. He looked, as if taking a long draught, and looked away again. Marian recalled Denis's words about Jamesie having changed. He had been broken and remade by Gerald Scottow. With a long internal shuddering sigh she looked now at Gerald. His big face looked brown and southern and he inhabited his evening clothes hugely and yet with ease. His slightly bloodshot brown eyes glowed reddish in the hazy light. He was looking up, his expression quite serene, and yet he was patently not listening to the music. He turned his head slightly and caught Marian's eye. Something went through the middle of her like a shot and she looked away. Gerald might be untamable, unattainable, taboo; yet he was still for her the centre from which the furies came.

She now turned her gaze upon Effingham. Dear Effingham. Dear, dear Effingham. Dear, dear dear Effingham. What was she saying? Able now for a moment to contemplate him, as he sat there large and round and bland in the hurly-burly of the music, Marian measured how deep was her sense of relief at having Effingham upon the scene. The more dangerous that scene appeared to her, the more she needed Effingham; for he was one of her own kind. She would indeed need him, and for most precise services, she would need him now to drive the car: if she ever carried out her plan. At that moment Effingham looked at her and smiled. Marian smiled back, warmed by a sudden rush of affection for him; and found herself reflecting that it was perhaps something of a pity that the rescue of Hannah was so likely to be equivalent to the definitive withdrawal of Effingham from circulation.

Yet how seriously did she intend her rescue plan? Was it not merely a dream? Hannah was a provoker of dreams, her many shadows fell round about her in the fantasies of others; and the plan of the rescue, which had seemed the product of plainest sense and reason, was already beginning to look a little crazed. The very solidity of Marian's only possible confederate made her idea now seem flimsy. It was not just that she would never persuade Effingham to help her; his very mode of being, felt as so kin to her own, now made her lose confidence. The whole notion was too mad: it must figure as but one more of those lurid private consolations which those concerned with her plight continued to generate about the unconscious and unconcerned figure of Hannah.

The music came abruptly to an end. There was clapping, and Marian, startled and shivering a little with cold beside the open window, turned her head and saw behind her the stony figure of Violet Evercreech. Violet, who had been clapping, had her hands held up before her in an attitude of prayer. She was looking at Hannah. Marian looked away quickly. The strange guilt which she had always felt before Violet had been a shadow of which she now confusedly apprehended the substance. With what hope of good or malicious intent toward confusion and chaos, out of what love or what hate, had Violet spoken to her today? For Violet too had her fantasies, her own version of an imperfect and frustrated love.

Denis had moved to the piano. There was some expectant whispering, and Marian's embarrassment returned. She blushed already on Denis's behalf. She looked down at the floor while in a profounder silence he touched the keys. Then he began to sing. Marian lifted her head. With a relieved surprise, with a strong shock of pleasure which drove all other thoughts from her mind, she realized that Denis had got an exceedingly beautiful tenor voice.

There was a slight nervousness in the first notes, but then with confidence and authority the rich sound took possession of the room. Nothing is more beautifully and acceptably self-assertive than good singing. The sound filled and honey-combed the collected room, making the rapt audience one with itself, a great golden object rising slowly through space. The song ended, and after a homage of acute silence there was rapturous applauding. Marian exclaimed aloud, and found that several people were looking at her, evidently enjoying her surprise. She leaned forward to exchange looks with Hannah, smiling and nodding her head.

The song had been simple enough, a local ballad sung to a sad monotonous little tune. There followed two Elizabethan songs full of grieving intervals and grave spondaic cadences. There was in the singing an elusive sense of drama, a mounting atmosphere, as if the audience were sitting forward in their chairs ready to participate in some marvellous transfiguration. Yet Denis himself seemed by now almost invisible, so much had he made sound sovereign over vision.

He began another song. She knew it slightly, had heard it somewhere long ago.

> O what if the fowler my blackbird has taken?
> The roses of dawn blossom over the sea;
> Awaken, my blackbird, awaken, awaken,
> And sing to me out of my red fuchsia tree.
>
> O what if the fowler my blackbird has taken?
> The sun lifts his head from the lap of the sea –
> Awaken, my blackbird, awaken, awaken,
> And sing to me out of my red fuchsia tree.
>
> O what if the fowler my blackbird has taken?
> The mountains grow white with the birds of the sea,
> But down in the garden forsaken, forsaken,
> I'll weep all the day by my red fuchsia tree.

As the last notes died away, in the breathless moment before the crack of the applause, there was a cry of pain. Hannah was sitting with her head thrown right forward in her lap. It looked for a moment as if she had been physically struck. Then she gave a moan, lifted her face and covered it, and there followed the sharp rhythmic wails and gasps of a hysterically sobbing woman. The applause, which had begun uncertainly, faltered to silence and was succeeded by a rising murmur of voices.

Marian stood up. People all round her were getting up and either hurrying forward toward Hannah or else retreating from her with a sort of fearful respect. In the centre the dreadful sobbing continued. As Marian moved she caught a glimpse through the throng of Denis, who was standing by the piano, looking down at his hand on one of the keys. She tried to get to Hannah and had almost reached her when she was thrust aside. The tall figure of Violet Evercreech loomed and swayed over the little group in the centre where Effingham distractedly and Gerald with a kind of sympathetic annoyance were patting and exhorting Hannah from either side. Violet said, 'Get up.'

Hannah rose, still hiding her face, and let Violet lead her away stumbling toward the door. The hubbub rose as people pushed each other back out of the way. The bowed, weeping figure seemed to inspire fear as well as pity. They shrank from her. The door closed behind the two women. A moment later, from farther, and then farther, away in the house there arose a sort of howl, the scarcely human cry of a soul in agony.

Marian found that there were tears upon her cheeks. She looked around for Effingham and saw that he was standing beside her. He instantly took her hand and led her toward the open window. There was a desperate childish spontaneity in their departure together, as Marian's last glimpse of the room took in the figure of Denis, seated now by the piano, frowning, his eyes closed, and the alert, interested glance of Jamesie as he observed her flight with Effingham. Gerald was giving instructions to two of the maids. He still wore his air of annoyance. The noise subsided behind them. The musical evening was at an end.

There was no moon, but the stars gave a kind of light. Effingham held on to her hand as they half ran across the terrace and over the drive and on to the soft peaty grass among the fuchsia bushes. At last they stopped in the middle of the blackness and the stillness and turned to face each other.

'Oh, Effingham –' The cold sea breeze chilled her cheeks where the tears were yet coming.

'Marian,' said Effingham, and there was a coolness, even a coldness, in his manner which affected her with an increased sense of the violence of the occasion, 'You were quite right.'

'Right –?'

'Your reaction was right, was the right one. The rest of us have been bewitched. We must get her out of this.'

Marian reflected; and I was just about to become bewitched

too. She said, 'Yes. We have thought her sane when she was half mad and serene when she was in torment.'

'I don't know about that,' said Effingham. 'She has achieved a kind of peace, a kind of centre for herself – it's not just an illusion. But it suddenly seems to me that the whole structure is just too dangerous. There are these – awful cracks. And she might lose her nerve.'

'What would happen then?'

'I don't know. I'm just suddenly terrified. We're all eating her up somehow, all of us. It's got to stop. I suggest we do exactly what you proposed, the other day – take her off in the car and hope to God she won't want to come back.'

'All right,' said Marian. Her teeth were suddenly chattering with cold and fear. 'Shall we fix the details now?'

'No. You must go back to her now. She mustn't be left with Scottow and Violet tonight. Come to Riders tomorrow afternoon. Of course, I won't tell Max or Alice.'

'Nor I anyone. Goodnight, Effingham.'

They stood staring at each other's darkened faces. Then in a quick movement they drew together, once more like frightened children, and without kissing hugged one another fiercely. Marian thought, soon we shall leave them all behind, soon we shall be off on the road together, Hannah and Effingham and I.

Chapter Seventeen

The day had come. They had been over the details a number of times and there seemed to be nothing now which could possibly go wrong. The main uncertain factor had been the weather and that, as Marian rose early from a sleepless bed, seemed likely to be perfect.

She could scarcely believe it, as she dressed herself, trembling and shivering already with excitement, that she, today, was to be the one to break the spell which had dazed and defeated so many. This day, whatever it brought, and whether it would count in the end as victory or disaster, would surely be the last day of the prison and the end of the legend. What would come after would be inconceivably different, would be real life.

That she was on the brink of some terrible act of destruction had at moments occurred to her, but without in any way affecting her resolution. It did at those moments seem possible that the sudden violence might produce, not the vanishing of the dream and the reassuring appearance of the ordinary good world, but some shapes yet more Gothic and grotesque. There might be some terrible shaking to pieces of Hannah, some terrible dissolving of the beloved face; and once late at night Marian shuddered to find herself half believing that by removing Hannah from Gaze she would indeed procure her death. Yet with daylight, and recalling again the cries, the howls, which she had heard on the evening of the music, she told herself that it was leaving her here, not taking her away, which would be the end of Hannah.

Hannah herself had apparently recovered almost at once from the musical upset. When Marian had returned from her brief talk with Effingham she had found her employer in her

141

room drinking whiskey with Violet Evercreech and laughing shamefacedly over her exhibition. Yet Hannah had been somehow exhausted by that overflow of feeling and for the next few days was, with Marian, more touchingly dependent and apologetic than usual. Violet had visited Hannah assiduously, and with something of the air of a doctor, on the two days following, and had then withdrawn again into her isolation. She had ignored Marian.

Effingham was now splendidly firm. Having made up his mind, he was fiercely anxious for action, as if he feared the relentless movement of a clock which might suddenly bring down with a clang some impossible portcullis. Of course, they were both quite straightforwardly afraid of discovery. Their looks, their meetings, must sooner or later suggest that something was afoot. But apart from this, Effingham conveyed to her, infected her with, a dreadful sense of urgency. Half sadly she reflected that in him it was, it must be, the desire, how exquisitely fearful at the last, to gain possession of what he had so long worshipped. What her own role would later on be she did not pause to consider. Her thought ended with the breaking of the barrier.

They had decided to proceed like this. Marian was to accustom Hannah to taking a little walk in the grounds in the late afternoon. This was easily done, as the stroll was already half customary and Hannah never in practice opposed any suggestion which Marian made. On the day in question they were to walk down the drive toward the entrance gates. Effingham would then appear in Max's Humber and offer them a lift back to the house. The likelihood of Hannah's refusing a lift back to the house was small, especially as Marian would at once profess exhaustion. Once Hannah was in the car, Effingham would turn it round and accelerate out of the gates.

They would then drive very fast, not to Blackport, which Effingham thought was too obvious and risky, but to a remote little hotel in the mountains which he knew of, which was also reasonably on the road to the airport. There they would stop, lock themselves in a private room and reason with

142

Hannah. It was unlikely that they would be successfully pursued. The hotel, one after all of many possibilities, was hard to find; and they had chosen a day when Scottow and Jamesie would be absent on one of their regular jaunts. 'Going to market,' Gerald called these expeditions, but the two usually came back late, smelling of burgundy and not especially laden with merchandise. The Land Rover then would be absent; and the Morris, Effingham explained, could easily be disabled by pouring sugar into the petrol tank. The plan seemed simple enough to be foolproof, provided Scottow and Jamesie departed as usual, and provided it did not rain.

Recalling what Jamesie's blunder had been on a similar occasion, Marian very carefully and surreptitiously packed for Hannah a small selection of old and out-of-favour clothes whose absence would not be noticed. She then packed for herself a little bag containing the precious minimum of her belongings, and both bags had been conveyed to Riders by Effingham on the previous night. Marian was resigned to losing the rest of her things; for although she tried to be open-minded about what Hannah would want them to do, she could not really conceive of herself returning to the castle, she could scarcely indeed conceive of the castle as, after today's act, continuing to exist.

Marian got through the morning somehow. She and Effingham had synchronized their watches, but she was terrified that hers would stop, and kept trying to wind it every half-hour. She was so incoherent with Hannah that the latter thought she must be ill and tried to persuade her to go to bed. After lunch, to her intense relief, Gerald and Jamesie left the house together, and she watched through glasses the disappearance of the Land Rover along the road to Greytown. In the dead depths of the afternoon she dealt with the Morris. But when that was securely done and she had returned unseen to the house it was still too early to go back to Hannah. She sat in her room chewing her knuckles and feeling faint.

At last it was time to go. She took a last look round her room, put on her coat and hurried to Hannah's room. Hannah was not there. After a moment of sickening panic she saw from the window that she was already walking on the terrace. She ran down and they began to stroll with their usual extreme slowness along the winding sunny drive.

Marian had timed it on several occasions and knew exactly how long it would take them to reach the desired point. She kept glancing at her watch while Hannah talked. The timing was perfect. Only let Effingham not fail.

'I really must try to grow camellias here,' Hannah was saying. 'The peaty soil ought to suit them, oughtn't it? I just wonder if they could stand the wind. Though there are some sheltered spots. I must ask Alice. Give me your arm, would you, dear, I still feel so tired. Aren't you hot in that coat? Why not leave it under a bush and we could pick it up on the way back.'

'I think I'll keep it,' Marian mumbled. She could hardly speak.

'Or shall we turn back now?'

'A little farther.' She wondered if Hannah could feel her trembling. She cast a quick look at the wide-eyed rather sleepy face beside her. It was the last drowsy moment for the sleeping beauty.

The gravel drive was bordered on each side by black soft boggy soil, and there was only one place about half way along the drive where the car could turn, where there was a circle of gravel and a little sundial. They were just passing this, Marian the slightest bit urging Hannah onward with her supporting arm. Effingham was exactly due.

'You were right to put your coat on after all,' Hannah was saying. 'There's a cold wind. Ah, my dear, I wonder how you'll stand us all in the winter time. I mustn't start taking you for granted just because you fit in so beautifully. You must have plenty of holidays, you know, as much as you want. And I feel you ought to be doing more of your own work. I'm so glad about the Greek. We must make it pleasant for you –'

'I love it here,' muttered Marian. Effingham was half a minute late.

'Why, how nice, there's Effie in Max's old car.'

Thank God. Marian drew Hannah a little aside off the

144

drive. Their shoes sank into the soft soil as the car slowed up.

'Can I gave you two a lift back?'

Effingham's face was so white and his eyes so bulging that it seemed that Hannah must notice. But she said gaily 'Splendid!' and got into the back of the car at once. Effingham had thoughtfully piled a lot of books on to the vacant front seat. Marian gave him a hard encouraging look and stepped in after her. The door banged, for better or worse, upon their enterprise.

According to a plan which they had arranged beforehand Marian began immediately to complain of having hurt her foot. It had been hurting all the way down the drive, she said, and, see, she must have cut it without noticing on some glass for it seemed to be bleeding. She leaned down, dropping her head below the back of the seat. With an exclamation of concern Hannah leaned right down too to examine the wounded foot in the gloom of the back of the car. Head well down, Marian could feel the car turning in a circle.

Hannah must have felt it too, for she immediately straightened up. But by now the Humber was moving with swiftly increasing speed in the direction of the gates. Hannah stared for a moment and then cried out in a shriek, 'Effie, don't!'

As she leaned forward to tug at Effingham's shoulder Marian seized her in her arms and rolled back embracing her into the back of the car. The Humber was going very fast.

The next things that happened happened very fast too; Marian recalled them afterwards with a strange photographic clarity with which she could scarcely have perceived them at the time, locked as she was with her face half hidden in Hannah's shoulder. Hannah moaned and struggled, but Marian was far stronger. Then when they were about sixty yards from the gates another car appeared in the gateway. It was the red Austin Seven driven by Alice.

The Austin, going fast, bore straight down on the Humber as if it meant to collide with it head on. Effingham did not slacken speed, but put his hand on the horn and kept it there. As the cars rushed upon each other, the Austin keeping its course, Effingham swerved slightly, skidded on the loose gravel, and the Humber left the drive and careered across the soft earth into a clump of fuchsias. It was twenty yards short of the gateway. The engine stopped.

In the silence that followed Marian could hear the engine of the Austin. Alice had braked hard and had put it into reverse. She reversed until she was level with them and then switched off the engine, leaning on the steering-wheel and looking at Effingham. Effingham did not look at her. He got out slowly and opened the rear door of the Humber. The wheels were sunk into the black earth and it was clear that a tractor would be needed now to move the car. The enterprise was over.

Effingham thrust both his hands through the door and supported Hannah out. She was deadly white and uttered little gasps as he gently drew her out of the car. Then she leaned against him in silence. He put his arms right round her and clasped her very closely to him, closing his eyes, and they stood there absolutely still in silence. Marian got out.

The enterprise was indeed over. It did not for a second occur to Marian that, even now, she and Effingham might have hustled Hannah out through the gates. But if she had had that thought she would have had to dismiss it soon, for yet another car appeared in the gateway. It was the Land Rover.

The Land Rover drove in slowly and stopped just behind the Austin. Gerald and Jamesie got out. Jamesie stayed on the far side of the car, leaning on the bonnet, while Gerald advanced to the edge of the drive. He surveyed the scene: the Humber embedded among the fuchsia, with scored earth and scattered gravel behind it, Marian standing beside it, and Effingham on the other side holding Hannah in his arms. Effingham slowly released her.

Gerald said, 'Hannah.'

She moved towards him like a sleep walker, and as she almost stumbled he moved to give her his arm, and led her to the Land Rover. He handed her in, and then quietly started the car again, nosed it slowly round the Austin, and proceeded

146

up the drive in the direction of the house, leaving Jamesie still motionless at the edge of the drive.

'Effie.' Alice opened the passenger door of the Austin.

Effingham looked vaguely across at her. His face was empty and flattened as if the outside layer of expression had been removed. Then he frowned, shook his head almost absently, and went across to the car. He got in and the door banged. The Austin briskly started, ran up to turn at the sundial, and then shot back down the drive and out of the gates.

Marian began to pick her way back to the gravel. Her shoes were covered with black soil.

Jamesie was still standing where he had been left, and as Marian looked at him he seemed to be glowing with some sort of secret pleasure. He stood, a hand poised, like one who wishes to retain before him the vision of some rapturous scene. He slowly turned his head towards her and smiled. 'Marian!'

'Hello,' said Marian. One of her shoes came off. She began to cry quietly.

'Ah, don't!' He moved at last and put an arm round her, supporting her as she dealt with her shoe. He still clasped her as they began to walk back toward the house. 'Here's just you and me left behind. That's nice, isn't it? Here, let me show you some pictures of yourself. I had them specially done in colour at Greytown.'

Chapter Eighteen

She went straight to her room. The house was very silent as she came in with Jamesie, and after they crossed the threshold his chatter at once subsided and he faded away into the shadow of the stairs.

She entered the room and shut the door. It was still and bright in the room, the sun making great squares on the floor. Her clock was ticking. She had been sorry to leave her clock behind. Well, she had not left her clock behind. She looked at the room in a kind of amazement. Here it was, inhabited, fresh, not yet fallen into the staleness of absence. A jersey and some underclothes lay tossed upon one of the chairs. Yet she had intended never to return.

There was something new lying on the table, a picture postcard. She picked it up and stared at it. It represented the Velasquez picture of the Surrender of Breda. She turned it over. It was from Geoffrey in Madrid. He announced that everyone else had cried off the expedition, so he and Freda Darsey had had to go by themselves. He said he thought the Titians were really . . . Marian threw the card into the wastepaper basket.

She slowly took off her coat. She had so naturally and immediately been thinking about herself. But what about Hannah? They *must* know that it was not Hannah's idea, that it had all been planned by herself and Effingham. She must explain, they must forgive. Yet why 'forgive'? Already her mind was back in the cage. And even if they regarded Hannah as blameless, would they let *her* now stay at Gaze, since she had proved so dangerous? Would they not send her instantly away, and forbid Effingham the house forever after ; so that Hannah would be punished indeed, losing her two best friends. She groaned, and the accusing image of Denis came before her.

He had warned her not to meddle ; why had she not listened?

She got up and walked about the room, walking fast and then stopping suddenly to think and walking again. It all now seemed a terrible mistake. She ought to have respected Hannah's condition. And was there not a sort of fate about it all. They *could not* have passed those gates. Yet this was mad. She paused at the window and looked across at Riders. The windows were twinkling orange in the western sun. Over there Alice and Effingham were having God knows what to say to each other. Marian felt a resentful lack of interest in whatever it might be. How had Alice known anyway? Effingham must have committed some blunder ; and somehow on reflection it seemed inevitable that he would. He had lacked faith. Perhaps she had lacked faith herself. All the same, poor Effingham.

She looked at her watch. It was the time when she was usually with Hannah. Would she ever sit with her again doing the good ordinary things? The narrow quiet life of Gaze, the prison life, suddenly seemed to her the best life of all. It was large enough for love. So it was large enough.

As time passed and she moved restlessly, sometimes talking to herself aloud, she became quietly aware that she was waiting for something, she was waiting for something with a deep tense excited expectation. It did not take her long to realize that what she was waiting for was Gerald Scottow's visit.

It was nearly an hour before he came. Marian was sitting by the window, and it was getting redder and goldener now outside and darkening in the room, when he softly entered after a little knock. She rose at once.

He closed the door and moved at once to her bed and sat down upon it. 'Come here.'

Marian came to him.

'Sit down.'

She sat upon an upright chair beside the bed.

'Give me your hand.'

She gave it to him.

'Maid Marian, wasn't that a foolish thing to do?'

'Look,' said Marian, her words all fighting to rush out together, 'it wasn't Hannah's fault at all, she didn't even know anything about it, we were kidnapping her, well not really that, we were just going to take her a little way, to show her the outside as it were, and then bring her back if she wanted to. We wouldn't have taken her away if she didn't want. And she knew nothing about it, nothing whatever, she tried to jump out of the car when she realized. It was all my fault really. Effingham didn't really approve, I just argued him into it. It was all my fault. Please don't send me away, please.'

Gerald, who was still holding her hand, turned it over and tapped the palm with one finger. His big brooding face hung over her in the twilight. He did not smile, but his eyes seemed to glow and lengthen. He said, 'I'm touched by your anxiety to spare Effingham.'

'Please don't send me away,' said Marian, 'and please don't send Effingham away. You must understand – '

'I understand all right. And of course I know that you planned this without Hannah. I think it is you, Maid Marian, who do not understand. You are very young and you know very little about life and suffering, and since people here have been very ready to become attached to you, your little head has been turned, eh? You have imagined that you know our ills and you have imagined that you have the power to cure them. But neither is the case. Eh?'

'I was thinking only of Hannah – ' Marian began miserably. She could feel herself being sapped and broken as if the rigid parts of her mind and body were giving way one by one.

'But indeed – we are all thinking only of Hannah. But it is not so easy as you seem to imagine to think about Hannah. What can you do for her, do you think, for *her* with her years and years of this solitude within her, by simply, as you say, "showing her the outside"? Do you think this would mean anything? Do you think there really *is*, for Hannah, an inside and an outside any more? You thought, didn't you, for I can see into your little mind, that if you could pass the gateposts something would snap, something would be broken. That shows you don't begin to see what's in front of you. In a way of course Hannah would be upset. It would make a nasty trivial little incident to be got over, a little wound. But in another way, you know, she would hardly notice, she would hardly even notice.'

'You confuse me, you confuse me,' said Marian, near to tears. She was clinging on to his hand now. She felt she was being entangled in some dreadful coil of thoughts. If only she could find the words to bring it all back to simplicity and truth. 'You can't think it right to shut her up, she can't want it really, she oughtn't to want it, it can't be right –'

'Sssh, Marian, there. There are things which are appalling to young people because young people think life should be happy and free. But life is never really happy and free in any beautiful sense. Happiness is a weak and paltry thing and perhaps "freedom" has no meaning. There are great patterns in which we are all involved, and destinies which belong to us and which we love even in the moment when they destroy us. Do you think that I myself am separated in any way from what goes on here, that I am free? I am part of it too. It does not belong to me, I belong to it. And that is the only way it can be here, because of the way the lives of several people are working themselves out, because of the pattern that is what has authority here, and absolute authority. And that is what anyone must submit to, if they are to stay here, and what you must submit to, my Marian, if you are to stay here.'

Marian's tears were flowing, 'You know I want to stay here –'

'Then I must have an undertaking from you. No more games of this kind. Will you promise? Think carefully before you answer.'

'I promise, I promise –'

'Well, there's a good girl. Come here and be more comfy, eh? And let's mop up those tears.' He drew her gently on to his knee.

Marian leaned against his shoulder sobbing and let him dab her face with a big white handkerchief.

'There now. No more tears, my child. Everyone loves you here. I love you. Come put your arm round my neck, that's better. Come, Maid Marian, no grief, this is a good moment.

151

Lift your face now and let me see you. Let me see your pretty face, there now, let me kiss you.' He was murmuring to her, moving his hand back over her face and tilting her head. It was almost dark in the room now. Marian leaned helplessly back against his arm, closing her eyes and seeking for his mouth.

He held her in a long hard open-lipped kiss. Time and place fell about her in a dark warm jumble and she seemed almost to lose consciousness. Then, moving her firmly back, he edged her off his knee and on to the chair, and smoothed her face over again with his big hand inside the handkerchief. 'There now –'

Marian got awkwardly to her feet, holding on to the back of her chair. Something seemed to have happened to her knees and she could scarcely stand up. She began to say something.

Gerald rose. 'No more now, child. I must go back to Hannah. Some supper will be sent up to you here. Then you can give your face a good cold wash and comb your hair, and come along to Hannah's room. Hannah will want to see you. We're all good friends now, eh Marian?'

She mumbled assent as he faded across the room and left her. She sat down abruptly on the floor. She could not have been more defeated if he had treated her as he had treated Jamesie. Her appalled heart, her appalled body, submitted utterly.

Chapter Nineteen

Marian knocked on Hannah's door. It was some time later. She had not been able to stop weeping, and had had to wash and powder her face several times over.

She entered the lighted room from the darkness outside. It seemed as if everyone was in the room, and there was a sub-dued cheerful murmur as if a decorous little party were in progress. The curtains were cosily drawn and the persons grouped about the fireplace were in fact holding glasses. As she advanced the forms before her were jagged and hazy; she looked for Hannah. A moment later she had a vision of Hannah's face, swept and pale from recent tears, but wearing the peaceful ecstatic look of someone saved from a shipwreck. Then Hannah was embracing her and kissing her. A moment later she too was holding a glass which had been thrust into her hand by Jamesie.

It was not for a while clear whether anyone was really talk-ing or not or whether the murmur was all inside her head. The golden group about her still seemed sheathed like seraphim from head to foot in serrated wings of light. Everyone seemed to have become very tall and elongated. She rubbed her aching eyes. Jamesie was indeed now saying something to her and giving her a cigarette and lighting her cigarette. She sipped the strong clean familiar whiskey.

She took in the little gathering. Hannah was standing close to Violet Evercreech and every now and then their hands en-twined. Violet looked beautiful, serene and shadowed over, as if a slightly mauve light were touching her face and hair. At one point she reached out a hand, smiling, to Marian and the tips of their fingers touched in a strange salute. Marian found that she was smiling too and felt dawning upon her face the same rapt serenity which glorified the others.

Jamesie was darting round the outside of the group, filling glasses and lighting cigarettes, but always returning to the proximity of Gerald. Jamesie was exalted, drunken with some sort of exhilaration, his face beaming and twinkling as if about to dissolve into a peal of purest gaiety. He kept looking at Marian and opening his mouth as if about to call to her and then closing it again in a sort of friendly nip. He touched her arm every time he passed her by; and then he would go and brush against Gerald, returning always to stand very close to him, hunching himself a little as if in conscious collected homage to Gerald's greater bulk.

Gerald himself beamed over the scene like a benevolent giant. He kept glancing at Hannah with a pleased look as if asking for her approbation, which she constantly gave him in quick little pleading darts of attention which seemed to express a sort of timid exhausted gratitude. What is she grateful for? thought Marian. Because he's let me stay? Hannah and Gerald seemed like the mother and father of a united family. Gerald even spread out his arms now and then as if embracing them all, holding them all together. He looked about upon them, and when his gaze met Marian's, it expressed a sort of bracing unsentimental pride, the sort of look a father might give his daughter when he sees her being a brave good girl. Marian said to herself, I have been accepted into the family, that is what has happened, I have become part of the pattern. That is what we are celebrating tonight. She felt a strange relief. Nothing dreadful had happened. Everything would be as usual. She drank some more neat whiskey.

The sense of them as a family brought with it an uneasy feeling of something missing. Something or someone was not there. She began to move her head about searching for it as if it were always just outside her field of vision like a ghost or doppelganger. Then she realized what was missing – it was Denis. She looked round again. But no, Denis was not missing, he had been there all the time, standing in the shadow, behind the little group, near to the picture of Peter Crean-Smith. He held a glass too and had evidently been receiving the hospitable attentions of Jamesie. Not for a moment seeing him clearly Marian gave him a little smile. He too belonged here. Then she saw his face.

The faces of the others were gilded. Denis's was black. He stood stiffly holding his glass and his features looked like blackened iron. The knobs of his cheekbones and of his brow stood out in the shadowed lamplight as if some terrible pressure was being put upon him. His eyes were black and his mouth a black line. His shirt was hanging open, his hair tousled, and as he held his glass as if it were the top of a rifle he looked strangely like some small tough partisan, irregular and lonely and full to the brim with relentless judgements and grim purposes. He did not return Marian's smile and she could not even make out the direction of the fierce darkened eyes.

The shock of the encounter sobered her; while at the same time she realized that she must have become half tipsy with drinking so much whiskey on an empty stomach, as through excitement she had eaten nothing all day. She swayed slightly and took hold of the mantelpiece. What had she been thinking, what had she been doing, since she entered this room? And what before? The previous scene seemed like a dream. And yet it had happened and had somehow caused this one. She had been taken to some place of ultimate surrender, and she had given in without a movement, without a moan. Gerald could have had anything he wished of her in that dark room. He must have known it, even as he patted her like a child and led her back chastened into the bright approval of the family. And Marian recalled her words to Denis when she had said that she alone of them was not involved in guilt. Well, she was involved now.

Something sudden was happening. Marian shook her head confusedly and made an effort to pull herself together. She somehow got rid of her glass and the scene took shape again. Everyone had turned towards the door, where one of the black maids was standing and saying something unintelligible to Hannah, and Hannah was saying, 'Yes, yes, of course. Bring her in at once.'

155

There was a little flurry in the room and a little buzz of talk and then the door opened to admit Alice Lejour.

Alice advanced into the circle of light. Her appearance was dishevelled and she wore a frightened, strained, aggressive look. She went up to Hannah. 'Is Effingham here, here in this house?'

'No, my dear.'

'Well, then he's lost!' She spoke it as a desolate cry.

'Lost?'

'He was angry and I let him get out of the car and he started walking inland and it's after midnight now and he must have got lost in the bog.'

Part Four

Chapter Twenty

It took Effingham some time to realize that he was indeed lost, hopelessly and completely lost. He had had, as the Austin Seven drove away from Gaze, some furious exchanges with Alice; and then, unable to contain himself for the anger, misery, disappointment and remorse that was in him, he told her to stop, got out abruptly and walked away up the hill. She had waited on the road, and he had seen from far above, as he went inland over the skyline, the little red car still waiting. But she had not followed him or called after him.

Effingham was angry with her not so much for having occasioned the disaster as for having offered him such a quick safe means of retreat. He ought to have stayed, he was telling himself even as he closed the door of the Austin, he ought to have stayed and done *something*, he ought to have confronted Scottow, to have protected Hannah, to have *explained* at least. Or he might even have commandeered the Austin and pushed Hannah into it. But no, he could never have done that. Yet he might at least have stayed and had something to say for himself. As it was he had simply shown them all a clean pair of heels and left the two women at Scottow's mercy. And yet what else could he really have done? It was, first of all, to resolve this debate, whose thunderous beginnings were in his ears even as the car shot out through the castle gateway, that he had had to get away from Alice and be by himself.

One thing which had been established in their short angry conversation was how it was that Alice knew. Effingham had been betrayed by his own vanity. He had for several years now vaguely taken it for granted that the maid Carrie was a bit in love with him and would do anything that he wished. The idea that he might, in some earlier and more brutish age, have taken

Carrie into his bed as a matter of course occurred to him as a piece of agreeable fantasy; and he assumed without reflection that even now *she* would have no objection. When he had made his preparations for the *coup* he had written a letter of explanation to Alice. He had given this letter, together with a large tip, to Carrie to be delivered to Alice at dinner-time; by which hour Effingham would be far away. He had not of course hinted to Carrie that he was leaving. But his manner must have been sufficiently conspiratorial; and although he had planned to remove very few of his things, one of the maids might have seen him packing. In any case, Carrie's suspicions were aroused and she had taken the letter to Alice the moment Effingham was out of the house. Alice had set off, as she said to him, very upset indeed, and with no end in view except to find out what was happening; and when she had seen the Humber coming down the drive full tilt with someone in the back she had been just violently determined not to let it through the gates. She was sorry, she mightn't have done it if she'd reflected, she mightn't have done anything if she'd reflected, only Effingham had not given her much time to reflect.

Effingham had strode blindly on, groaning to himself. It now all seemed a piece of perfectly horrible loutish idiocy, this that he had done. Why ever had he let that clever long-nosed girl persuade him? The whole plan, he could see now, was hopelessly ill-conceived. Hannah would never have consented to be taken away in a hurly-burly like that. It was the proximity of the airport which had confused them both. He seemed to make it out now that it was when Marian mentioned the airport that she had set the fatal seed in his mind. They were both stupidly, frivolously, romantically intoxicated with the idea of taking Hannah on to a plane, it was such a perfect image of escape. He had been influenced too, in a quite irrational way, by the scene at the music. That, for no good reason, had seemed to settle it, that cry of a soul in pain. And of course he had been moved sheerly by Marian, because she seemed so decent, because she argued so well, because he respected her, because he liked her.

And now look where he was. He had put Hannah in peril, laying her open to retribution from people who had power over her, he had almost certainly helped Marian to get herself the sack, he had wounded Alice perhaps irrevocably, and worst of all he would himself be under sentence. He might never be allowed to go to Gaze again. This was a thought so agonizing that he almost had to bend down over the pain. If they banished him he really would do something desperate. Yet what on earth could he do? Had he not now forfeited the *only* thing which he could do for Hannah? Even if the opening part of today's plan had succeeded what could have come of it? He recalled Hannah's cry of 'Don't Effie!' as they rushed towards the gates. It would have been no different later. They would have driven to the hotel, Hannah would have been tearful, perhaps frightened, and would have begged them to take her back quickly, and they would have had to do so. She could not now confront the outside world like that, and it was unfair as well as foolish to expect her to do so. But if, from within the gates, there was nothing he could thus do for her, what from outside the gates could he hope to achieve.

He stumbled on, and the accusing remorseful thoughts buzzed in his mind, making him blind and deaf. What should he do now, go back to Gaze and camp woefully outside? It was too soon, they would spurn him from the door, and rightly. He had better let things settle down. Yet what reception would await him at Riders when he went back? How would Alice treat him? What would Max say to him about this piece of irresponsible lunacy, Max with his curious view of Hannah's spiritual adventure, Max with his deferred attachment to Hannah?

The thought of returning to Riders brought back to him some vague sense of time and place and he began to slow down. He had been walking fast, gesticulating and talking aloud, and the raging to and fro of his thoughts had provided an impression of continual din. He now, as he checked them a little, began to apprehend what was outside him, and became gradually aware that he was surrounded by a vast silence. He came to a standstill.

Silent within himself now he looked about. The big sky was crossed with lines of fluffy reds and golds, weighted and blurred with the approach of twilight. The land on every side, already darkened to a purplish brown, was entirely flat and empty. Effingham reassembled his wits. Where was he exactly? He had mounted the hill near to the stream and had started following the path that led to the salmon pool. But there was no sign of the stream now, he must have somehow turned away from it. There was no sign indeed of *anything* now which could serve as a landmark.

Fortunately he had only to retrace his steps. He turned about. After all, the sky would guide him. He had been walking east. Now he would walk west toward the sunset. He looked at the sunset. The sky was certainly brighter and redder in one quarter and darker and bluer in another, but the bright quarter was unnervingly large and did not clearly determine a direction. Also it occurred to him that the coastline played odd tricks with east and west in this part of the world. Still his way must lie roughly toward the brighter part of the sky, and he could simply walk back along the path he had been on.

He began to walk. After a few steps he began to wonder if what he was on was indeed a path at all. There was a scattering of stones under foot; but the stones, he now noticed, were intermittent, and round and about among the humps of wiry brownish-green grass he saw other similar lines of dotted stones which might equally well be or not be paths, be or not be the way he had come. He quickened his pace. His direction was surely right, and there was nothing to be done except to get along quickly. There was plenty of light left. He would soon see something he recognized.

He strode on, scanning the flat low uniform horizon. The uncertain light troubled his too intently peering gaze and the land seemed to jerk occasionally in an odd way. He had to stop now and then to rub his eyes. He walked on steadily but fast. He should in a little while be able to see the big dolmen which stood on the road above the village, and he kept looking for it and thinking that he saw it, only to see when he had blinked that the land was as flat and empty as ever on every side.

At last he did begin to see something. There was on the horizon, considerably to the right, something vertical. It must be the dolmen. How far off the straight course he must have wandered. He changed direction and hurried on, falling over moist tussocks of grass, occasionally seeming to lose sight of the vertical object and then finding it again. The light was going fast. After a bit of blind going, when he seemed to be stumbling all the time, he lifted his head to find the object near him, and saw that it was not the dolmen at all, but a tree.

He approached the tree more slowly. It was not a tree that he knew. Trees were individuals in that part of the world. He must be well away from anywhere where he had ever been before; and now, after leaving his previous course to pursue the tree he was not at all sure where his previous course had lain or how to get back to it. The sky was still a little light, with the hazy fuzzy blue of the darker twilight, and a narrow reddish rim outlined three quarters of the horizon. The land all round was a mottled purplish black. Effingham came up to the tree and stopped to listen to the silence.

Since he had realized that the tree was not the dolmen he had known that he was lost; not seriously or badly lost of course, but annoyingly lost. It would probably take him some time now to walk back. Of course, his sense of direction was not entirely gone, and anyway if he headed firmly for the centre of the red arc of the horizon he would be certain to hit the road, or to come to the Scarren and then to the road. He did not fancy the idea of descending the Scarren in the dark, but it would be all right if he went slowly. There would be starlight and perhaps a moon later. So he was resigned to being, for a while at any rate, benighted.

He hesitated. He felt suddenly a curious reluctance to leave the tree, which was at least a thing upright like himself. He reached out and touched it. Effingham was a town-dweller. He had always found the countryside at night rather alien and unnerving: the darkness, the emptiness, the absence of human activity, the presence perhaps of other activity. He shook himself. He had better move on before the faint red arc, his only guide now, should have quite faded away. If he walked briskly

161

he would soon reach the road; he might even now be just a few hundred yards away from it. Cheered by this idea he set off quickly and walked for about five minutes. The red arc faded. Effingham walked.

He came again to a standstill, he had been putting off the moment of stopping. The sky was now almost completely dark, though he could still see a short distance about him. Stars had been visible for a little while. He had put off stopping because he knew that as soon as he stopped he would begin to feel frightened. He now did feel frightened. Of course, not very frightened, it was ridiculous: there was nothing to be frightened of. The worst that could happen to him was a summer night in the open air, and he was certainly not frightened of that. All the same, it was an eerie sort of spot to be lost in.

He wished now that he had not left the tree. The tree was at least a sort of shelter, a sort of house, a sort of *place* with some kind of significance. Now all around him there was nothingness and nowhere. He wondered whether to walk on. But surely he had to walk on. To stand still all night in this appalling quietness would be unthinkable. Walking was at least activity and made, to surround him, a comfortable little bit of human noise. Besides, he couldn't really be far from the road now. He wondered for the first time whether it was worth shouting. But what was the use of shouting up here in this desolation? Nothing human lived up here. Still, it was worth trying just in case; but what did one shout? He meditated a while and then, with an effort, managed to call out 'Hullo!'

It was weird. The sound seemed to die on him at once as if a thick blanket, hanging some ten feet away on every side, had stifled it. It was no good shouting, the surroundings were too hostile, the cries would be choked in his throat. He began to walk on hastily. The sky was now a dark night blue and full of stars, and although he could not really see the ground before him there was a semblance of diffused light and he felt able to go on. He wished passionately that he had some cigarettes with him, but he had left them behind in the Humber. He made out from the luminous dial of his watch that it was after midnight. As he walked he could not prevent himself from looking round and keeping his hands ready in front of him as if he expected suddenly to touch something or to see something. But what he now expected to see was not the headlights of a car. His heart was beating rather uncomfortably hard.

He became suddenly aware of something very peculiar behind him. He had caught sight of this thing from the corner of his eye just a moment before and had thought it was a trick of his vision. Now it came again, and as he turned with a gasp of alarm he saw it. There was a strange bright light, a brilliant green light, which seemed to have been switched on on the ground. It glowed there with an intense hard brilliance in the middle of the blackish scene, suggesting a vivid, incomprehensible, menacing presence. It was as if something were coming up from below, something very full of life indeed. Effingham backed away from it.

As he moved he saw two things. There was, round about him in a great arc, almost encircling him, a fainter line of green light; and there was, at his very feet, the same light again, even more brilliant, lighting up the ground and tumbling on his shoes like small creatures of luminous green. Effingham's moment of unreason had not lasted long, but it had shaken him right down into his bowels. Of course he realized that this was not a supernatural phenomenon, but the well-attested though rarely seen 'fairy fire', which had chemical causes and constituents and which could be analysed in laboratories. All the same he hated and feared it, and tried desperately and without success to shake it off his shoes. It clung to him, coming into being as he trod, and covering his feet and his footsteps with a weird glow. He hated and feared too the message it gave him as he looked at his luminous trail. He had been walking in a circle. Heaven knew where the right direction lay now. Perhaps after all he had better stand still.

Effingham had no special tendency to fear the supernatural, at least he had not thought that he had. He knew perfectly well that there were no such things as fairies or spirits or malevolent non-human agencies. Yet people in this part of the world believed in them. And as he stood now listening, feeling, looking in a futile way into the thick silent air he felt not a faint belief but almost a certainty of the presence of evil round about him. He was, in this place, an intruder ; and he felt the menace round about him of presences to whom human things were abhorrent. He reflected on evil as he had known it. Surely it was a great force, a great dark positive force ; it could inhabit human beings, it could inhabit where it pleased. He began to wish that he had a crucifix.

It was again impossible to stand still, he was by now too much afraid. He would like to have called out now, but he feared to receive some appalling answer. Who knew what a cry would summon. He moved on ; and after some way was only half relieved when the fairy fire vanished from him as mysteriously as it had come, leaving him in almost total darkness. The going was more difficult now. The ground seemed damper under foot and once or twice he slithered on muddy lumps of grass. He wondered if he were approaching the stream. Then another thought struck him. The fairy fire was a phenomenon of the bog.

The notion that he might be wandering into the depths of the bog had vaguely occurred to him once or twice and he had hastily put it away. It was so unlikely. The bog, the real bog, was a good way inland in this region, and between the bog and the Scarren was a long stretch of scrubby moor on which he had assumed he was still walking. After all he had not gone far, and some of his walking had been circular. He looked at his watch. It was nearly two o'clock. He could not possibly be in the bog. The ground was still absolutely firm under foot.

Or was it? He tried the earth round about him, patting it with his hand and his foot. It was a little quaky and mushy. There didn't seem to be any stones any more. He missed those stones. They were at least things solid like himself. He rose and sniffed the air. There was a damp sourish smell of peat. Well, even if he were on the edge of the bog there was nothing to be afraid of. It would fairly soon be light and he would get a sense of direction again. Only he had really better stop walking. He would just find some nearby spot that was a little less damp and sit down in it and wait for the day. He walked on another ten yards.

Effingham stopped. The ground had become very mushy and was coming up over his shoes. He pulled his feet out with a sucking sound and took two steps. At each step his feet sank into the gluey stuff and had to be pulled out of the hole they had made with a little effort. He decided he had better get back to where he was a minute ago, and he turned about; but after five steps it was no better. The ground seemed suddenly quaking and diluted with water. His trousers, soaked and muddy now to the knee from the splash of his footsteps, clung to his legs. The night seemed darker, colder, and in the intervals of his movement aggressively silent. He paused; and found himself sinking in.

Effingham had of course heard the local stories about men lost in the bog. He had been told of morasses there which would engulf a man, of slimy wells and pits and sudden muddy descents into the limestone caves below. For the first time he began to conceive himself in danger. He wondered what to do. If only he had stayed by the tree, if only he had stayed by the stones. But he must not let his imagination frighten him absurdly. The ground was certainly muddy, but had he never walked on mud or wet sand before? Whether he walked or stood nothing would happen which was worse than wet feet. All the same the gluey stuff was gripping him rather unpleasantly hard. In a sudden panic he wrenched one foot right out. It was not easy.

Walking had now become something else. Effingham, standing on one foot, panted with effort. The other foot had, in the struggle, sunk farther in. To get it out he would need a new foothold. What was he trying to do anyway? In a panic, and because he could balance no longer, he plunged forward, dragging the other leg out, and was able to take two or three staggering jumps before he found himself stuck again with the bog well over his ankles. His running heartbeats almost stopped his breath. What was the point of these antics? Had he not better stay perfectly still? Nothing could happen to him if he stayed still. At that moment something seemed to give way under his left foot, as if it had entered some watery chamber, some air bubble of the bog. He lurched, tried to take another

165

step, and fell violently on his side. The ground gave and gurgled all round him.

He stayed still now perforce. He stayed still for several minutes with his eyes closed trying to control his mind before he was able to determine the position of his limbs. He was sitting upright with his right leg curled under him, the sticky mud gripping his knee. The other leg was stretched before him, inclining downward into a hole in which he could hear a licking lapping sound of water disturbed. He was perhaps on the brink of one of those bottomless slimy wells of the bog. He held his hands in front of his breast like two animals that he wanted to keep safe. He lifted his head slowly and saw the few stars of the night.

He began to tell himself things. It was not so very long till day; and when it was daylight they would send a search party. They would surely know that he must have gone into the bog. Or would they? They might think he had come back to the road and got a lift to Blackport or to the railway station. He might have gone anywhere. They simply might not think of the bog. Or if they did, would they be able to find him? And if they found him could they reach him? He recalled a story of a man perishing horribly within call of his helpless rescuers. In any case, when daylight came, would he still be there?

Effingham shifted slightly. There was no doubt that he was very very slowly sinking. The thick toffee-like mud was creeping up the length of his thigh and he could feel the cold gluey stuff gripping the lower part of his back. He had known for some time that it was now quite impossible for him to get up; and he feared to move in case he should simply slither down into the liquid hole which now seemed positively to be sucking at his left leg.

Effingham had never confronted death. The confrontation brought with it a new quietness and a new terror. The dark bog seemed empty now, utterly empty, as if, because of the great mystery which was about to be enacted, the little wicked gods had withdrawn. Even the stars were veiled now and Effingham was at the centre of a black globe. He felt the touch of some degraded gibbering panic. He could still feel himself slowly sinking. He could not envisage what was to come. He did not want to perish whimpering. As if obeying some imperative, a larger imperative than he had ever acknowledged before, he collected himself and concentrated his attention; yet what he was concentrating on was blackness too, a very dark central blackness. He began to feel dazed and light-headed.

Max had always known about death, had always sat there like a judge in his chair facing toward death, like a judge or like a victim. Why had Effingham never realized that this was the only fact that mattered, perhaps the only fact there was? If one realized this one could have lived all one's life in the light. Yet why in the light, and why did it seem now that the dark ball at which he was staring was full of light? Something had been withdrawn, had slipped away from him in the moment of his attention and that something was simply himself. Perhaps he was dead already, the darkening image of the self forever removed. Yet what was left, for something was surely left, something existed still? It came to him with the simplicity of a simple sum. What was left was everything else, all that was not himself, that object which he had never before seen and upon which he now gazed with the passion of a lover. And indeed he could always have known this for the fact of death stretches the length of life. Since he was mortal he was nothing and since he was nothing all that was not himself was filled to the brim with being and it was from this that the light streamed. This then was love, to look and look until one exists no more, *this* was the love which was the same as death. He looked, and knew with a clarity which was one with the increasing light, that with the death of the self the world becomes quite automatically the object of a perfect love. He clung on to the words 'quite automatically' and murmured them to himself as a charm

Something gave way under his right leg and it seemed without his will to be straightening out below him. He leaned sideways, thrusting out his hands involuntarily to try to pull himself upward. There was nothing firm, and his hands plunged desperately about in the mud. He became still, lifting his muddied hands to his face. He was now fixed in the bog almost to the waist and sinking faster. The final panic came. He uttered several low cries and then a loud terrified shrieking wail, the voice of total despair at last.

He had not meant it as a cry for help. He had for some time thought himself beyond help. He listened to it roll away and seem to echo and then he uttered another, like a desperate animal. There was again an echo.

Suddenly Effingham's mind returned to him. It was as if he had indeed, during that time, been depersonalized, abandoned by his self. It returned now with an exact awareness of his situation, an awareness of the sky lightening with hints of morning, it returned with a frenetic desire to live. Had that been an answering cry?

Effingham now called out in a quite different voice. 'Hello there, hello! Help! Help!' The answering cry, a long way off, came again. It was certainly a human voice. Effingham continued to call. The light increased, still within darkness, but he was able now to apprehend his own form, to see his arms dimly, to be aware of space about him. He went on calling and the other person went on answering though without seeming to move. Then after a short silence the voice called out, suddenly much nearer. 'Mr Cooper!' It was the voice of Denis Nolan.

'Denis!' cried Effingham. It was the happiest sound he had ever uttered in his life. 'Denis, Denis, Denis!' The tears started into his eyes. His old unregenerate being was with him again. He would live.

'Are you stuck, sir?'

Effingham could still see nothing clearly. The darkness had become a light brownish-blueish haze. 'Yes, dreadfully. I'm almost in it up to my waist. I can't move any more. For heaven's sake be careful what you do or you'll fall in too. There's a sort of pit here. Perhaps you'd better wait till there's more light and fetch some people with a ladder. If you can find your way back to me. I think I'm good for some time yet.'

Silence followed and then Effingham could see the figure of Denis approaching him. It was a marvel to see at last something upright, to see a man. Denis seemed to be walking lightly over the surface of the bog, his feet scarcely touching the ground. A small dark shape was following him which materialized a moment later as a donkey. Denis and the donkey stopped about thirty yards away. The light increased.

'What in God's name are you standing on, Denis?'

'There are paths in the bog, old brushwood paths. Only one has to know them. This is as near as I can get to you on the path.'

Effingham groaned. 'You'll never reach me. There's a morass all round. You'd better get helpers. Only for God's sake be quick.'

'I'll reach you. It's not too bad for a little way just here. I'm going to lay down brushwood on top of the bog. It won't take long. Keep quite still and don't struggle at all.'

Denis unloaded a bulky bundle from the back of the donkey. Swiftly and deftly be began to cast the lengths of brushwood on to the dark surface of the bog. He pressed it in a little and laid more on top. The dawn light now showed the flat unfeatured land all around. The path lengthened toward Effingham.

Denis worked quickly padding to and fro. Effingham saw that the plimsoll-clad feet were scarcely muddied. He began cautiously to move his legs in the mud, preparatory to taking control of his body again, and with a gasp slipped a little farther. The bog clasped his waist. He was indeed not 'good for some time yet'.

'Keep still, I told you.' Denis was now almost near enough to touch him. 'Listen, when I reach you we'll do it quickly. I'm going to take you under the arms and pull gently and you will swim with your legs as if you were in the water. Here I am now. Now move quietly and as I tell you. I've got you, there, I'll kneel and you hold on to my shoulders. Now swim with your legs and come upward, upward.'

It seemed afterwards to Effingham as if Denis's very words had given him a new power. He was not able to 'swim' with his legs, which seemed paralysed, but he agitated them a little and urged his body upward in unison with Denis's steady pull.

169

'Now stop. Now again. Stop. Again. Now I can pull you on to the brushwood. Yes, use your hands a little. Don't try to get up, just lie. Rest now. And in a minute you'll crawl along to the firmer place. Rest. Now crawl. Give me one hand. Just slither along. I'll keep pulling you.'

Panting with exhaustion, Effingham managed to propel his sodden muddy body along the surface of the brushwood, which was already beginning to descend quietly into the bog. At last under his groping hand he felt a firmer surface and in a moment was sitting on the path. The sky was a cloudy blue and the sun was rising. 'Denis, what can I say. Thank you.'

'It's nothing, sir. You'll walk soon.'

'Don't call me "sir". I think I can walk now. If you'll help me up.'

'No hurry. There. Try your legs a little. I'll just undo the donkey. It's a little wild one. We can leave it here.'

'Won't it fall into the bog?'

'No, those creatures know the paths. It'll follow us along a bit, you'll see, and then it will go off to its own people.'

'How beautiful the bog looks in the sun. So many colours, reds and blues and yellows. I never knew it had so many colours. I can walk now, Denis.'

'We'll go, then. The path is firm but quite narrow, and it's hard to see. You'd better take my hand.'

They set off along the path in the first sunshine, Denis leading Effingham by the hand and the donkey following.

Chapter Twenty-one

'Lift your arm, Effie, into the sleeve, that's right.'

'Forward a bit, let me tuck your shirt in at the back.'

'Feet up, while I put these slippers on.'

He was dressed in Gerald's tweeds, fragrant with Hannah's bath-salts, and alone with the three women. Their handsome faces, lit with tenderness and love, hovered over him angel-like.

'In the eastern church,' said Effingham, 'the Holy Trinity is sometimes represented as three angels.' He had drunk a great deal of whiskey since his return. Now he seemed to be being patted all over by three pairs of hands. He added, 'Automatically, quite automatically.'

'What do you mean, Effie? You've said that several times already. You were saying it when Denis brought you in.'

'I'm trying to remember something—'

'It's just as well Denis was here. None of the village people would have gone up at night. Had you been shouting for long when Denis heard you?'

'Oh, I called out "Help" every now and then. I expected someone would turn up.'

'You're very brave. I should have just panicked. Wouldn't you, Marian, Alice?'

That wasn't quite right though, what he had just said, Effingham thought. He tried to focus his gaze upon the women, but they drew together into a single fuzzy golden orb. His body felt limp yet glorious, as if he had been reborn, as if he had crawled forth into a new element and lay yet upon the shore, weary but transfigured. He wished he could remember what he was trying to remember.

'I'm sure I should have panicked. It was such a long time.

Whatever did you think about, Effingham, when you were just sinking in?'

'I'd rather not know,' he said. That was a nonsensical sort of answer. But he could scarcely yet bear to think of the recent past as real. It was a vague blackness rapidly receding like a nightmare which remains present to the waking mind as a terrible dissolving something.

'Don't worry him, Marian. Give him more whiskey, Alice.'

'I want to help him to remember. I'm sure it's better. What is it that happens "quite automatically", Effingham?'

Effingham concentrated. The three angels were a radiant globe out of which light streamed forth. He had seen this before. The globe was the world, the universe. He said, 'I think it is love which happens automatically when love is death.'

'I think you're sozzled, Effie.'

'Sssh, Alice, let him talk.'

He sat up. He was still not sure, but he thought now that he could explain it to them. Perhaps after all he could recapture his vision, though he did not yet know its name and awaited his own words to tell him. He could not in memory determine how long the vision had lasted. It might have been only a minute or only a second; and it had faded utterly with the return of his will to live. Yet he felt that it was in some sense still there, hidden in the core of the nightmare object. He must fix his attention upon it before it was engulfed and darkened and made as black as the bog itself.

He looked up at Hannah and found himself suddenly able to see her quite clearly as if a light had been shone on her and as if the other two faces had been merged in hers leaving only one image. 'You see,' he said laboriously. If only he could play a little for time the vision might announce itself quite simply through his speech. 'You see, it's not a bit like what Freud and Wagner think.'

'What do you mean, Effie darling? What about Freud and Wagner?'

He stared at Hannah. Her beautiful tired face was smiling down upon him. After all she was his guide, his Beatrice. It came to him that she must have been somehow connected with

172

the revelation which was made to him in the bog. Perhaps this was the truth, this the very truth, which resided in her in a sort of sleeping state and which made round about her the perpetual sense of a spiritual disturbance. Surely she would understand him. 'You see. You see. You see, death is not the consummation of oneself but just the end of oneself. It's very simple. Before the self vanishes nothing really is, and that's how it is most of the time. But as soon as the self vanishes everything is, and becomes automatically the object of love. Love holds the world together, and if we could forget ourselves everything in the world would fly into a perfect harmony, and when we see beautiful things that is what they remind us of.'

'I think he's delirious. That's just a garbled version of something Father –'

'It can't be quite as simple as that, Effingham –'

'I see what you mean, Effie, go on.'

Effingham looked up imploringly into the angelic face. No it couldn't be as simple as that, and yet he was sure these were the right words. He felt that it was all fading and that he was going to forget it after all. He would be left with an empty description, the thing itself utterly gone from view. He tried to repeat the words again, like a prayer, like a charm. 'It's automatic, you see, that's what's so important. You just have to look in the other direction – ' But he no longer believed what he was saying. And as he looked he saw the three heads sliding apart, unfolded, unwrapped, spread out in front of him. The big thing had gone ; and yet perhaps something remained.

He loved Hannah. But did he not in loving her love the others too? How beautifully they were now drawn together in spiritual amity, in a lovely configuration by their joint concern for him, and what a perfect object of love they made, they-loving-him, together. So love, making an unchecked circuit, returned to himself. He contemplated them. This at least he could explain. It was not the big thing, but it was surely an exquisite little thing.

He began again. 'Us four, for instance. With so much good will between us, why aren't we perfect with each other? What stops us being? We can't make the whole world into a republic of love, but one can make a little corner of our own here –'

'I'm sure we are ready to try, dearest Effie –'

'The trouble is, until the whole world –'

'Effie, I think you'd better come home –'

'You and Alice, for instance. You both love me. Well, you ought to love each other too. And, Marian, I love you of course. Love is so easy, it's practically *necessary*, if only –'

'I'm sorry to break in on this metaphysical discussion, but I have some very grave news for all of you.' The voice of Gerald Scottow spoke from the door.

Hannah, who had been sitting close to Effingham, rose at once, and the group drew apart, as Gerald closed the door and advanced upon them. He was a little breathless and plainly agitated or excited. For Effingham the scene was suddenly collected, focused, over-vivid in its precision, and dark. The golden glow had faded. He was aware of a rainy light at a murky window pane.

'What is it, in God's name?' said Hannah, her hand going to her throat.

'Peter is on his way back to Gaze.'

'Peter?' said Effingham stupidly.

'Peter. Peter Crean-Smith. Hannah's husband.' Gerald raised his voice.

'When will he arrive?' said Hannah. Her voice was quiet but suddenly weak and thin.

'In a few days. He sent off the cable as he was getting on to the ship.'

'So the seven years are at an end,' said Effingham. He tried to get up. Something seemed to be wrong with his legs.

Hannah stood perfectly still with her arms hanging at her sides. She was wearing her long robe of yellow silk and she looked like a priestess in the moment before the rite, pregnant with some strong emotion. She stared at Gerald. 'Peter,' she said softly. Effingham had never heard her utter that name and it rang and jangled mutedly about the room. 'Peter. Coming here. In a few days. Is that really true, Gerald?'

'It is really true, Hannah. Would you like to see the cable?'

She gave her head an irritated little shake and twitched away the sympathetic hand which Marian had laid upon her shoulder. She said again, 'Peter,' as if trying to get used to the sound. And then, 'It's not possible. Is it really true, Gerald?'

'Really true. Sit down, Hannah. Have some whiskey.'

'I've had enough,' she murmured, and turned away to the window and looked out. They all looked at her figure, so decisively detached from them. There was silence in the room.

Alice said at last, clearing her throat, 'I'm sorry, I'm afraid we're in the way. Effie and I had better go. Come on, Effie.' With a quick pull she had him on his feet.

Hannah said without turning round, 'Don't go Effingham, *please.*'

Alice, surly and firm, said, 'He's drunk. He'd better sleep it off. I'll bring him back when he's sober. Come on, Effie, lift your big feet.' She began to propel him towards the door.

'Effingham, please stay here, please –'

'I tell you I'll bring him back.'

'It happens quite automatically,' said Effingham to Scottow.

Effingham was unsteadily descending the stairs, clinging on to Alice's arm. The sunlight hurt his eyes. As he went out of the glass doors he heard a sound behind him in the depths of the house. It was his own name uttered in a cry which rose to a shriek. He got into the Austin Seven and went to sleep.

Chapter Twenty-two

'Effingham! Effingham!'

They were shouting and calling again. He listened lazily for a while. The voice came from far far away across the dark bog. He turned a little and sank again into blackness.

'Effingham!'

I won't wake up, he thought. In a moment there would be silence. But now someone was shaking him roughly by the shoulder and going on and on. He murmured protestingly and half opened his eyes. It was night and there was a dim lamp burning on his bedside table. Max was sitting on his bed.

'I've been trying to wake you for so long –'

The great shadowed bulk of the old man, suddenly so heavy and close, was menacing. Effingham shrank away into the bed. Something appalling had happened which he could not at the moment remember. He began to close his eyes again.

Max was shaking him once more, digging his fingers savagely into his shoulder. 'That hurts!' murmured Effingham petulantly. He had always disliked Max's hands, feared them. He had a violent headache and his legs were hurting. He remembered the night in the bog and more vaguely the morning at Gaze. Peter Crean-Smith was coming home. 'What time is it, Max?'

'Late, late, Effingham. It's nearly eleven o'clock.'

'Have I slept so long? How did I get here?'

'You fell asleep in the car. Alice and I put you to bed. How do you feel?'

'Terrible!' It was too late to go to Gaze now, everyone would be in bed. It was a comforting thought. Whatever was happening it was not happening now. There was nothing he could do now. Sleep was overwhelming him again, great clouds and folds of sleep like a warm fog.

'Wake up properly, Effingham. It's time to get up now.'

Effingham felt weak and prostrate and sorry for himself and safe in his bed. The darkness crouched behind Max, thick and heavy and full of strange smells. He said, 'My legs are hurting and there's no point in getting up now.' Sleep, sweet oblivion, had not yet abandoned him, it still covered half of his consciousness. 'Let me sleep again, Max, for God's sake.'

'No. I oughtn't to have let you sleep for so long. You must get up now, Effingham. Oh, why did you have to be drunk on this day of all days!'

'It wasn't my fault! Didn't Alice tell you what happened? I can't go to Gaze now anyway, it's too late.'

Peter Crean-Smith was coming back. This was a terrible yet quite incomprehensible fact. Peter's actions seemed to belong to some other dimension of being. Surely tomorrow he would go to Gaze and find that all was as usual. Hannah would make all well. She would swallow it all up, she would assimilate the evil news and make it not to be, she would suffer Peter internally as she had always done, and there would no more be heard.

'You must go there at once, Effingham. Do you think there is any sleep in the castle tonight or that anything is in its place? God only knows what today has been. You must go back.'

Effingham lay still and looked at Max's huge shadow crouching on the wall and ceiling. Only let it be tomorrow, let it be daylight. He shrank utterly from the idea of a night-time arrival at Gaze. He had always feared the violence that lay behind the legend of the sleeping beauty. It had hung behind the figure of Hannah like a dark cloth, perceptible but not stirring. He now feared dreadfully to find that background suddenly alive with movements, with faces. And what he feared most of all was to see Hannah afraid. Then he suddenly remembered the cry which had rung through the house as he went out through the doors. He sat up abruptly.

'But what could I do if I did go over now?'

'Just be there. Your presence in the house will prevent some things. You ought never to have come away.'

'You're being very alarmist,' said Effingham. But he began to get up all the same. 'Damn it, how much strength and sense do you think Hannah's got?'

'That is just what we don't know. But she's certain to need help. And if you aren't there she may take it from someone else.'

Effingham brought the Humber to a halt close to the front door and switched off the engine and headlights. The bulk of the house crept into view above him, against a clouded almost black sky, with lights very faintly glimmering in several windows. He got out on to the terrace and stood still, afraid of the sudden silence and of the sound of his own footsteps. The noise of the car would have announced his arrival; yet he felt himself, before the dim consciousness of the house, unwanted, ignored, invisible. He began to walk quietly along the terrace, stumbling every now and then against the soft clumps of wild sea pinks until he could see Hannah's window. There was the same faint light there. He went back to the front door, found it unlatched and entered.

The hall was dark, but a lamp on the upstairs landing murkily suggested the stairs, and a faint glow came from the open drawing-room door. He cautiously pushed the door.

'Effingham! Thank God!'

Marian appeared in the half darkness and in a moment he was holding her tightly in his arms. Only then did he remember what he had been saying to the three women that morning. He must have been thoroughly drunk. He realized that there were other people present in the room and he let her go.

The room was lit by two lamps and by the irregular flickering of the log fire Denis Nolan was sitting in front of the open piano staring at the keys. In a corner beside one of the lamps Jamesie was sitting at a table with a whiskey decanter and a glass. Neither of them paid the slightest attention to Effingham or to the little scene which had just occurred.

'Thank heavens you've come,' said Marian, leading him to the fire. 'I simply haven't known what to do. I was longing for you to come. Today has been a nightmare.'

Today. There had been, while he slept, a whole eventful day.

'What's happened? Oh, Marian, why did you let Alice take me away?'

'I know. I've thought of that too. I was stupid, I should have interfered. I've done everything wrong. Have some whiskey? No, I won't. I was drinking the stuff for hours. I'm quite light-headed, I've eaten nothing.'

'What's happened, Marian?' Now in complete possession of his wits, Effingham felt the full apocalyptic terror. A world was about to end, and he knew not how.

'I don't altogether know what's happened. Something has happened or is happening –'

Denis played a scale on the piano and then a few odd notes and phrases like the song of a bird. It rang weirdly in the dim flickering room, like a distant nightingale. Over Marian's shoulder Effingham saw Jamesie's pale self-absorbed face. His face was grubby like that of a child, perhaps from weeping. He seemed far gone in drink.

'But what have you been doing all day, what has Hannah done –'

'I'll tell you what I know. After you went Hannah started to cry, and she cried in a hysterical way for nearly an hour. I don't know whether you've ever seen anyone in real hysterics, wailing and gasping for breath. Well, it was terrible. I stayed with her of course and kept trying to calm her and kept saying the same things to her over and over again. We were left alone together during this time. Then she did become quieter – that was about midday – and I'm not sure that it wasn't worse then. She just cried quietly with occasional little moans and whimpers. I'd been fairly sensible all the time she had hysterics, but this was just too much for me and I started to cry too. So we sat together and cried for another hour. It sounds idiotic, but I was so tired and something about her frightened me so much. During this time various people came in and looked at us, but no one tried to talk to us. Then Hannah became quite silent and I stopped crying and I tried to talk to her, but she wouldn't reply to anything I said.'

'Had she said anything earlier on?'

'No, nothing at all. Well, then Violet Evercreech arrived with

179

some coffee and things to eat, but Hannah paid no attention. Violet wanted me to go away and leave her with Hannah, but Hannah wouldn't. She held on to me and motioned Violet to go. She still didn't say anything, it was as if she'd been struck dumb, it was very frightening. Violet went away very upset. I drank some coffee and tried to make Hannah take some, but she just shook her head and wouldn't even look at me. During this time Gerald came in once or twice but didn't try to speak to Hannah. Denis came and did try, but she paid no attention to him. Then she settled into a chair near the window and sat looking out for another hour. Then quite suddenly and quite calmly she said to me that she was going to rest and she thought I should rest too. That was about half past three. I was stupid then. I ought to have lain down on the sofa in her room. But I was so dead tired I was practically unconscious. I saw her to bed, and then I went to my room and slept there and didn't wake up till nearly nine. I was mad, I should have told someone to wake me. Anyway, I rushed to Hannah's room and found that the door of the ante-room was locked. I got terrified and began knocking on the door, but almost at once Denis appeared and said that Hannah had woken up about six. He'd been lying on her sofa in the place where I ought to have been. She asked for some tea and that was brought. She seemed perfectly calm, he said, but awfully pale and weird. Then she sat for a while quite quietly, frowning a little as if she were thinking. Then she asked for Gerald to be sent to her. Gerald came and told Denis to go. And a little later when Denis tried the outer door he found that it was locked. Oh, I forgot to say that when she woke up she asked if you had come back.'

'Oh God! And then?'

'Well, and then I don't know. They've been in there ever since.'

'We must go to her at once,' said Effingham. 'Gerald's probably trying to brain-wash her about Peter.'

'Effingham, don't you think – she just mustn't be in the house when Peter comes back?'

'And why not, pray?' said a voice behind them. Violet Evercreech was standing in the darkened doorway.

'Violet, what shall we do?' said Marian, starting up.

'I don't see that you and Mr Cooper are called upon to do anything,' said Violet. She moved forward and picked up one of the lamps. 'I've come for a lamp, I see you have two in here.' The lamplight made her face ghostly-bright. 'Peter Crean-Smith is coming home to his wife. It is about time he established some order in his own house.'

'He might kill her.' The fierce words made a silence round about them. Denis, who had been softly playing a scale, paused in the middle.

'Really, Marian, you are too imaginative.' Violet spoke wearily, contemptuously. 'Hannah's admirers have been perfectly happy up to now to assume that she knew perfectly well what she was doing. She and her husband will continue to know perfectly well what they are doing. They have a concern with each other which is nobody else's business at all.'

'No, no, no, we must protect her – '

'Rubbish,' said Violet, at the door. 'She is grown-up, which you seem to forget. She is also, which you seem to forget, a murderous adulterous woman. You had best pay her the compliment of leaving her to her husband and to her own private and personal destiny. Good night.'

'Violet hates her,' said Effingham.

'No, Violet loves her. But it comes to the same thing. We might go up now. Gerald must still be with her. I asked one of the maids to tell me when he came out.'

'But what shall we say?'

'We'll tell her we're taking her away at once, and we'll stand no nonsense this time. You've got the car outside, haven't you? This time we will drive her to the airport.'

Effingham felt an immediate sharp pain of fear. He was not ready for this. He said, 'Wait, wait. Need we be quite so hasty? We've still got another day or two. We mustn't do anything mad. We must at least consider the possibility that she might *want* to stay for Peter. After all, why not? We all knew it was possible, didn't we, that Peter would come back some time. She knew it was possible. We can't assume just because she weeps that she doesn't want to see it through. Perhaps we shouldn't interfere, at least not in such a hurry, not tonight when we're all exhausted and distracted. Let's wait till to-morrow and have a long talk with her then.'

'Someone's had a long talk with her already. That's just what I'm afraid of. Denis, tell Mr Cooper what you think.'

Denis played an arpeggio. He turned towards Effingham. The room was very dark now and the fire had ceased to flicker. 'She must not be here when he comes.'

'Why not?' said Effingham. He was annoyed at the appeal to Denis.

'She must not be here.'

'It's true,' said Marian. 'You say we all knew perfectly well that he might come. But we didn't. Really we thought he wouldn't come ever. It's so clear now, I can't think why I didn't see it before. The whole thing made sense only if one assumed he wasn't coming.'

Effingham thought, she is right. We never really faced it. We never really *believed* in Peter. But he said, 'We must at least reflect upon it now. Why should they not be somehow – reconciled?'

'You don't know Peter Crean-Smith.' Denis spoke again. He played another phrase, a wild faint piece of song.

'Effingham! Are you really resigned to losing her to a man who is certainly a brute and possibly a lunatic? Are you re-signed to never seeing her again ever? To just leaving her behind in some sort of awful bondage we shall never know anything about? Come. Let us do something, and do it quickly.'

Effingham still hesitated. 'Suppose Gerald – objects, resists? As of course he will. He won't want to lose his reward at the last moment.'

'Let him object. As for resisting, we outnumber him. Come.'

Effingham was not prepared for this sudden dissolution of the situation into violence. He did not want to be pressed into a gang with Denis. He felt that something confused and ill-considered was going to happen. Yet he was impressed all the same and frightened by her urgency and somehow quite directly tempted by the idea of the waiting car. And he was indeed not resigned to having the story end so suddenly, to simply not knowing what happened. He pictured himself slinking away or being put out of doors by Peter. He rose to his feet.

'Oh, you poor fools.' Jamesie spoke softly into his whiskey.

Effingham turned to stare at the boy, where he sat in the corner beneath the single lamp examining his glass like a crystal-gazer. Whatever images of disaster were visible therein he could be no more appalled by the future than Effingham was at that moment. He became aware that Marian had moved past him toward the door and he followed her without more thought.

At the foot of the stairs Marian paused. She took hold of his hand carefully and firmly as if it were a large piece of china and began to draw him after her up the stairs. They moved slowly as if impeded by the air like people in a dream. The lamp was still alight at the top of the stairs and as he passed it Effingham could hear its quiet dangerous purr. They turned into the long corridor and he sensed a shape behind him which was Denis noiselessly following. They moved along the curtainy corridor past the lamplit shrines toward the door of Hannah's ante-room. It was only then, as they glided like murderers to their scene of action, and Effingham began to wonder about exactly what was going to happen, that he really took it in that Hannah had been cloistered for nearly five hours with Gerald Scottow. And he recalled Max's words: 'She'll need help, and if you aren't there she may take it from someone else.'

When they were about five yards from the door Effingham stopped abruptly beside one of the lamps and pulled Marian back towards him. 'Listen, listen.' He spoke in a trembling whisper. 'What do we do if the door is locked and he won't open it?' He felt confused and frightened.

'It will be locked and he won't open it.' She spoke in a whisper too.

'Well, what do we do?'

'First we call and shout, then we bang and kick, and then if need be we break the door in.'

The silence of the house hung its foul night about him in

thick ragged folds. Effingham felt that he would be unable to raise his voice, let alone to do violence to the door, let alone – He was about to start again when someone said softly, 'Look! Look!'

Effingham turned to look. He shaded his eyes against the bright glow of the nearby lamp and took a step backward. He saw that the door of the ante-room stood open.

There was a golden recess which at the first moment seemed empty. Then within the shining frame a great apparition assembled before his astonished eyes. Gerald was standing in the doorway, his arms spread wide, dressed in a long pale garment. The next moment, as the scene came into focus, it became plain that Gerald was carrying Hannah in his arms with her yellow silken gown hanging down in front of him. He moved slowly forward out of the doorway.

Effingham cowered back against the wall. As Gerald passed him by, moving in the direction of his own room, as the silk sleeve brushed lightly in passing, as the lamplight for a moment illumined her, Effingham saw Hannah's head resting quietly against Gerald's shoulder, her eyes wide open.

Chapter Twenty-three

'I must stop crying. Just tell me to, will you, Effingham.'

'Stop crying, Marian.'

She was lying on the sofa in the drawing-room and he was sitting on the ground beside her holding her hand. It was four hours later; four hours since they had heard the key turn in the door of Gerald Scottow's room. It would soon begin to be light.

They had perceived nothing further since the sound of the locking door. Jamesie had taken the decanter of whiskey and was sitting out on the stairs. He seemed to have fallen asleep against the banisters. Denis Nolan was sitting on the floor on the upper landing, hugging his knees and keeping Gerald's door in view. Most of the lamps had gone out and blackness had gradually crept over the house. The drawing-room lamp had failed an hour ago and the fire was out. Effingham had lit the two candles in the silver candlesticks on the mantelpiece.

What had happened? A consciousness of what had happened and of what was happening sat upon the house like a stifling cowl. Effingham felt paralysed. He could not, as he saw Gerald recede along the lighted corridor, have lifted a finger or uttered a sound. He could not remember whether he had not fallen on his knees. He was paralysed, like a creature bitten by an insect or a snake, and lying there living, breathing, and waiting to be eaten.

'Effingham, she is destroyed.' Marian had been saying things like this in paroxysms of weeping for an hour.

His own task, his own moment, laid up for him since the beginning like a precious jewel, how neatly and how absolutely he had lost it. 'Stop it. We know nothing. Oughtn't you to eat something? I'll go and find some bread. I know where the kitchen is.'

'No, not for me. When it gets light the maids can bring us something. If there are any maids. Oh God, I wish it were light. I can't bear this darkness. This night seems to have been going on for twenty hours. The house smells horrible at night. And there's no air. Are the windows open? Effingham, don't go away!'

'I'm not going away. I'm getting myself some more whiskey. Marian, for Christ's sake stop crying. Or for my sake.'

He sat down again beside her and stroked her flushed face with his hand and she became quiet. It was odd, sitting so close to her in the dark quiet room. He stroked her face. Then he stroked her breasts. She captured his hand and stilled it upon her heart, holding it there. They gazed at each other. Effingham thought, I don't desire her, yet I feel as intimate with her as if we had been lovers. He leaned forward and kissed her upon the brow. Then he kissed her upon the lips.

She participated in the kiss and then lay there looking at him with a gentle defeated look. He thought, she feels as I do: and in a moment he was feeling infinitely sorry for himself. She squeezed his hand and sighed and closed her eyes. He contemplated her. He was comforted by her silent steady acceptance of his kiss. He found himself murmuring, 'I do love you, Marian, I wasn't just drunk!'

'I love you too, Effingham,' she said without opening her eyes. 'But we are talking in our sleep.'

He did not know what she meant, but he was content with the answer. He knelt down and laid his head on the sofa against her arm and instantly fell asleep.

He was awakened by a murmur of voices. He had the feeling as he woke that the voices had been going on for some time. He lifted his head. One of the candles had gone out and the room was very dark indeed and cold. Two people were sitting and talking softly at the far end of the room near the door. It took him a dazed moment to realize that it was Alice and Denis. He got up stiffly and went towards them. They became

186

silent, lifting their faces, shadowy and light brown in the indistinct candlelight.

'I'm sorry to come chasing you and bothering you, Effingham,' said Alice rather stiffly. Her loud precise voice rang absurdly in the dark airless room. 'But Father wanted to know what was going on.'

'I want to know what's going on! I can tell you all I know —'

'It's all right, Denis has told me everything. I thought I wouldn't wake you, you were sleeping so peacefully. I'd better go back to Father now.'

She rose and Denis rose too, and they confronted Effingham as a pair, drawn together by confidences in the dark. They seemed to accuse him and he almost quailed before them. Alice, solid, handsome, her wide face surly with a sort of conviction, had already lapped strength from the new situation.

'Don't go away, Alice.' Marian's voice spoke from behind him.

'Why not?'

'Don't go yet. I feel there's safety in numbers. Wait till we know what's happened. I'm so afraid.'

'Surely we know what's happened,' said Alice slowly. 'Surely it's all over. There's nothing for *us* to do here any more.' She drew them all together with her, all together as outsiders.

Marian gave a little exclamation and Effingham drew in his breath. But neither of them answered. Denis moved quietly away and began to pull back the heavy curtains from the windows. It was getting light outside. The new grey pale light came into the room, making the candle desolate, making the figures into different ghosts.

'Marian, Marian!' A loud urgent cry rang out from somewhere in the depths of the house.

They stood for a moment open-mouthed with fright, staring at each other. It was as if all their previous conversation had been a silence, and here was a sound at last.

'Marian!'

Marian ran to the door. It was the voice of Gerald Scottow. The faint appalling daylight, entering through the window at the top of the stairs, made the hall and staircase dimly present. Jamesie, who had just risen, was standing on the fifth step looking up. Denis was standing in the hall. Gerald was at the head of the stairs, his great bulk outlined against the window.

'Here I am,' she said, her foot upon the first stair.

Jamesie moved away from between them, half stumbling, half slithering down, and joined the others who were standing close together in the hall.

'Marian, will you please go and pack Hannah's things.'

There was a silence. Then Marian said, thickly and heavily, 'Why?'

'Because I am going to take her away.'

There was silence again. The scene seemed to shift and shimmer in the dim greyish bluish light. The little crowd below huddled together, aware of their insubstantial faces raised to the stairhead.

Then Marian said slowly, 'No, I don't think I will.'

Everyone stood still with held breath as if thinking about this response. Then a voice said, 'Well, I will then.'

Violet Evercreech, who had joined the group in the twilight without anyone's noticing, swept suddenly forward to the foot of the stairs. Effingham felt himself pushed aside with a positive and brutal violence. Violet paused beside Marian and seized her arm. She hissed into her face. 'I told you. Whore and murderess!' Then she ran up the stairs.

'Thank you, Violet,' said Gerald Scottow in a calm voice.

Violet passed him and vanished down the corridor towards Hannah's room. And as she went she suddenly cried out aloud, 'End! End! End!' The strange cry receded. It was an invocation; and the watchers at the foot of the stairs shuddered with an instant sense of the proximity of the power invoked.

Gerald was about to go. But Violet's loud cry had awakened an echo. 'Wait a minute!'

Denis Nolan had run lightly past Marian and half-way up the stairs. The daylight was increased and Gerald's face was now faintly visible as he turned back to look down at the poised defiant figure below him. 'Well, Denis?'

'Wait a minute. You say you will take her away. But you

188

will *not* take her away. Not against her will, and it must be against her will. You must let us see her. We will see her. We will all talk to her. And then see how she will go away.'

'Denis,' said Gerald, as one talking to a child, 'you are really very naïve. I am not taking Hannah away against her will. Hannah, as usual, knows exactly what she is doing. Hannah and I understand each other very well and we have always understood each other very well. And now may I suggest you all go away and get some sleep and stop prolonging a pointless vigil.' He turned again to depart.

'No!' Denis was not shouting, but his voice rang. He mounted another two stairs. 'We will see her first, and we will see her without you. We will see her now.'

'My dear Denis, you will not see her,' said Gerald quietly. 'Go away, all of you. Go away and go to bed. Don't you see, it is all over.' The words quivered in the air, mingling with the pale composing daylight.

'No, no, no!' Denis was shouting now. 'We will go to her. Come on, then, come on!' He turned to the little group behind him.

There was a paralysed stillness. All that Effingham could say afterwards, when in some black penitential hour he told the story to Max, was that they might have all swept forward, they might have all rushed up past Gerald towards where Hannah was: but they did not. It just did not happen. Effingham felt an immediate rigid coldness in his limbs. He could not afterwards swear but that Alice had not laid a restraining hand upon his arm. However that might be, he could not, he felt, in any case have moved an inch. He was already, and well before that moment, defeated. Everyone stayed still and silent.

Denis waited a few seconds. Then he turned and ran up the stairs.

Effingham saw, with a horrible detached precision, how Denis bent low and tried to take a wrestler's hold of Gerald to hurl him over his shoulder. But Gerald used his advantage of weight and his higher position. He simply butted his opponent away with brute force; and in a moment Denis was tumbling and crashing back down the stairs. He came to rest in a

189

heap at the bottom and lay still. Gerald faded from the stairhead and disappeared.

After another stunned moment there was a low piercing wail. Alice ran forward. She fell noisily to her knees beside him, patting him and pawing him, trying to turn him towards her, to raise him, to undo his shirt. 'Denis, Denis, Denis –'

'Yes, yes, don't be after taking on so, Alice, there, let me go, I'm all right.' He pushed her roughly off and leaned back against the lowest stair, rubbing his head. 'I'm all right, I'm fine.'

He began to scramble to his feet. But Alice remained kneeling. She looked up at him as he stood now, a little withdrawn from her, dusting his coat with an almost embarrassed air. The firm daylight showed her resolute broad face, her solid presence, as she knelt with her hands spread wide upon her thighs. She said in a loud voice, 'I am going to tell them the truth.'

Denis stopped. He looked at her quietly, urgently, imploringly. 'No, no, *no* – ' He went down on one knee, stretching out a hand towards her.

She took his hand, and they remained there in an awkward yet formal pose. 'Yes.' She turned her head to Effingham. 'Listen. You know, everyone knows, the story about how Denis sprang upon me at the salmon pool. Everyone knows the story. But a little detail is wrong. Denis never sprang upon me. I sprang upon him.'

There was silence. Denis slowly rose again. Then in a gentle courteous way he helped Alice to her feet. She rose heavily, leaning on his arm which she held on to, and they stood together, suddenly, strangely, connected.

'Yes,' said Alice going on in a softer voice. Her eyes were fixed on Denis's face while he looked down at her hand. 'I let that convenient lie cover up my situation.' She grasped the material of Denis's sleeve and twisted it in her fingers. 'Oh, I was in love with you all right, Effie. But I wanted Denis. And I tried to take hold of him, up there at the salmon pool, like some old marquise might have had her stable man. Only he turned me off. And then I let that lie get about, to cover up the fact that he left Riders immediately.'

In the violent pause after her words Denis, still looking down moved his lips soundlessly, like one expected to speak who can find nothing to say. He gave her a quick look and then hung his head again. 'Ah, Alice, now there was no need – '

'Yes, there was need, Denis. I've suffered such pain for this, as I've deserved to do. I could not *now* live with that lie any longer. We must all live – out in the open now.' She stroked his arm with long gentle strokes. 'You know it wasn't just like the marquise, don't you?'

'Yes, Alice.' He took her hand, detaching it from his sleeve as if it were some intrusive but pleasant animal. He held it for a moment. Then he faded from them and vanished under the stairs in the direction of the kitchen quarters.

Effingham stared at Alice. Her words, the scene, the two joined figures, had stricken him with amazement and pain. 'Is that true?'

'Yes,' she said loudly and angrily, glaring back. 'I didn't really invent the lie. It just happened and I didn't contradict it.'

'Oh *God*!' said Effingham. He was stunned and wounded. He could hardly conceive that Alice, his Alice, could have stooped so low. He waited for her to utter words of justification, of conciliation. It could have been nothing serious. He was deeply hurt, almost angry now, but ready to forgive her.

'What's more, I want him still,' said Alice in a low fierce voice. 'I would follow him to his bed if I thought I had the slightest chance!'

She turned away and went quickly through the glass doors of the hall. He saw her for a moment outlined against the light blue morning sky and then she was gone.

'Go with her, Effingham.'

Effingham had forgotten Marian. He turned upon her now. Why was this intrusive child telling him his duty? Alice was his old, dear friend, his Alice, his own. Without a word he moved quickly to the doors and passed out into the day.

Chapter Twenty-four

When Effingham came out of the house he looked at once at the Austin Seven, which was parked next to the Humber. The cars looked crudely ordinary, vividly modern, over-bright, sitting there neatly side by side upon the gravel. He blinked at them. It seemed strange that they should be still there. They did not belong to the world, to the time, from which he had just emerged. He looked for Alice, but she was not in the car. He looked quickly about him and saw the garden gate shutting which led out to the rocky path down to the sea. She must have gone that way. He followed.

He opened the gate with difficulty. A strong warm wind from the sea was trying to keep it closed. He saw the sea before him now, a metallic silvery pale blue expanse, glittering, empty and sterile in the morning light. The sun was not long up, and the short sallow grass was overrun with huge shadows of rocks. The rocks themselves, scattered senseless lumps, were yellowed with lichen and diamonded with quartz. Then in the scene below him, like a figure in a painting, he saw Alice running.

He called out, but the strong wind took his voice inland. He began hastily to descend the path. Jumping and stumbling he zigzagged downward between the boulders which seemed slowly to grow larger and then to jerk past his head. There was a roaring in his ears which could not yet be the sea. His limbs swung and jolted about as he ran, like those of a broken puppet. He felt weak and giddy, and when he paused for a moment the blue space before him seethed and boiled with particles of light.

He could not see Alice now. By the time he reached the more level ground he could no longer run and had no breath to call out. He walked along panting and holding his side, while the light from the sea seemed to be running through his head like a wide piece of silk pulled through a small hole. He was vaguely aware of the night that had passed, a great dark object, a black obelisk, looming behind him; and somewhere behind that, seemingly lost in the same endless dark, was the bog. He seemed to have lived in continuous darkness now for days, and the light found him blanched and eyeless like a hapless grub.

He was not able yet to begin to think about Hannah. He had a sense of her having died. And Marian was a frail elf, a little ghost that ran away squeaking and gibbering when the daylight came. What emerged from the wreck of everything, with an authority which drew him panting onward, was the reality of Alice. When Alice had spoken her words of truth in the house he had felt, as it seemed to him now, suddenly and unexpectedly unwound, unbound, as by a spell repeated backwards. He had dabbled in necromancy, had held communion with the dark powers; and he almost felt, with a premonitory thrill of fear at what this idea would later do to him, that he himself had somehow brought about the whole wreckage of the long night: conjuring too rashly with the unknown he had pulled the house down upon them all. But Alice was his health, his crucifix, his redeemer.

He had assumed in her an eternity of unselfish devotion, letting her stand near to him, never quite looked at but vaguely seen, a stone idol, a great mother, while he played at love. He had accepted her sufferings with but casual attention. But now, when things had happened which were too appalling to think about, when his romantic love was a corpse and his cleverness a ghost, he knew where it was that he wanted to lay his head. He needed her to shield him from thoughts of Hannah, from Max's anger, from the consequences of his acts. 'Alice! Alice!'

The sun dazzled him and he paused again. He was now at the bottom of the hill where the rocks and the weedy pools stretched away toward the base of the black cliff which as he turned to look, seemed to come gliding up out of the earth. The cliff glided on and on up and came to rest, blackening half the sky. Now the rocks were humps of gleaming saffron seaweed, and the sea pools were dark brown between. He saw Alice not far off, detached from him as in some other space, moving slowly across the line of the sea.

'Alice!' She did not heed him. Perhaps she had not heard. She went on steadily from rock to rock, sure-footed and without haste, towards the sea. Effingham stumbled after her. His feet splayed and slithered upon the golden weed which heaved and popped and breathed under him like a sea animal. When he had caught up on her a little she stopped abruptly upon the brink of a brown pool and turned to face him. The acknowledgement of his presence forced him to stop too and they regarded each other.

She looked at him, not with any expression of intensity, but moodily, morosely, almost crossly. There were tears or sea spray upon her face. The breaking waves were near now and he could see behind her the hypnotic movement of their nearing lines. 'Alice —' He said it with an imploring confidence. He wanted to clasp her, to reward her, to make certain of her protection. She was turning away from him again ; and as he was slipping upon the next rock and saving himself with outstretched arms, she put her hands in her pockets, took another step, and hurled herself full length into the pool.

The shock of her sudden movement made Effingham stumble to his knees. By the time he had got himself up and reached the edge, all was strangely quiet again, the surface rippling a little and Alice lying immersed in the pool, her head resting against a gently sloping rock at the far end. The scene, wrapped about by the loudly roaring waves, had a weird stillness, as if Alice had lain there already a long time, a fish-like sea goddess, brooding since antiquity in some watery hole.

She lay there so still, reposing in the brown weedy pool, her head and shoulders raised against the rock, her hair darkened by the water and quietly dripping, that Effingham thought for a moment that she might have struck the rock and become unconscious. But her eyes were open. He stared at them, remembering Hannah's eyes. He looked down, paralysed and fascinated, as at something suddenly metamorphosed. He could not speak to her now, she had made herself too much other. Yet he noted how grotesquely her hands were still in her pockets, the soaked collar of her tweed coat turned up about her neck, her clothed body disappearing between the reddish stems of flowery seaweed. Shells glittered like small jewels on the floor of the pool, and he remembered the woman of shells that he had seen laid out upon Alice's bed.

The strong sun cast his shadow upon the pool. He must find his way to Alice. The sides of the pool were too steep and high for him to be able to reach down and touch her. He stood on one leg and took off one shoe. The action seemed grotesque. A seagull passed his head with a shriek and flashed out to sea. He pulled off his sock, removed the other shoe and sock, and then took off his watch and put it in one of the shoes. He took off his jacket and began to loosen his tie. He paused. Something in the ritual of the actions touched him and he felt a sensation which he identified almost at once as sexual desire. Well, was he not going to bed? Without undressing further he began to slither down the side of the pool.

The water was warm and thick with weed. Effingham sank into the brown gluey liquid, on his side now, his head descending close to Alice's. He felt his clothes resist and then drink. Now he was soaked and heavy. His face was close to hers now, their brows almost touching, as he edged his shoulder to the sloping rock. He seemed to intercept Alice's vague gaze. She showed no intensity, looking at him quietly with a sort of casual dignity, her hands still in her pockets. He did not try to raise her yet. He leaned towards her and kissed her on the lips. She was calmly ready for the kiss. As he touched the new Alice he was obscurely aware that something was broken, someone had gone: but he could not at the moment remember what or who.

Part Five

Chapter Twenty-five

'How much farther is it to the salmon pool?'

'Another mile maybe. Shall we go on?'

'Yes, please, Denis. Anything to stay out of the house.'

Hannah was still there; but her trunks were packed and Marian had hourly expected to see her departure take place, like the carrying out of a coffin. It seemed probable now that she would leave on the morrow. The sensation was indeed very like that of having a dead person in the house.

It was only the evening of the day which had dawned so violently, but everyone at Gaze seemed to have been changed as by some vast tract of experience. Marian had waited about, slept a little, waited about, hoped to be summoned, feared to be summoned, decided to go to Riders, decided not to go to Riders, tried the door of Hannah's old room and found it locked, sat for an hour on the stairs, retired to the drawing-room with Denis, and at last, in a sick frenzy to get out of the deadly atmosphere, set out with him for a walk.

She had wept earlier in the day but felt, for the moment, a sort of mad calm. She was almost surprised at the completeness with which she despaired for Hannah. And yet, was it despair? She had wanted Hannah to leave the house and Hannah was leaving the house. The due time had passed and the princess was going to be rescued. Did it matter so much how and by whom? She had felt it, in the night, to be appalling that Gerald, who had watched over her for so long, should so suddenly and easily, in her moment of need, have taken her. While her other friends, who had protested so much, had simply not known what to do for her. But Gerald's long vigil was perhaps the very thing that had mattered, and that had made him, at the crucial moment, more real to her than the others.

Gerald had had no theory about Hannah. Gerald had not been paralysed by an allegory. It was right after all that he should be the wondrous necessary man.

However that might be, everything would be different for her now, and her end was in darkness. She moved from one mystery into another. As the huge endless day went on, Marian felt less of the horror and more of a sick sadness of a more selfish kind, her own sense of a total deprivation of Hannah; and it was a part of this pain that she said to herself: I did not love her enough, I did not *see* her enough. Hannah would need her, would ask for her, no more, and there was some justice in this. Still later in the day, as a grotesque and unnerving consolation, came a weird feeling which Marian identified, though not at once, as a re-awakening of her sense of freedom. It was exhilarating though not altogether pleasant. She felt light-headed, giddy with exhaustion and freedom, not exalted, not guilty, almost at moments foot-loose and ordinary. Hannah's great act of destruction had indeed transformed the world.

Marian supposed that she had better start packing her cases too. Yet the sense of a strange interval, almost of a holiday, was too strong. Everyone sat about drinking tea. The maids abandoned work and invaded all parts of the house, chattering in their own language. No ordinary meals were served. Marian wondered vaguely what would happen when Hannah was gone and they were all left behind. Perhaps they would stay on in the house like a pack of witless abandoned servants, quarrelling among themselves. They would stay there till Peter Crean-Smith arrived, and he would whip them into the stables and change them into swine.

'Go on telling me about the salmon, what they do.' Marian asked this as much to distract Denis as to distract herself. He had been in tears, she thought, in the morning, and was in some deep mood of desperation now. He had been touchingly anxious to stay near her all day.

'Well, when they are about two or three years old they leave the pools and go down the rivers to the sea. And they live in the sea for maybe three or four years – people don't really know, I think, and particular ones may stay for longer in the

197

sea. And they eat and eat and become big powerful fish. Then one spring they come back up the rivers to spawn, and come back to their own birthplaces.'

'Up a river like this one? How can they? You'd think they'd be dashed to pieces on the stones.'

'Some of them are. But they have great strength and cunning. Both are needed to move upward against such a power coming down. It is nature against nature. I have seen one trying to leap up that waterfall there and banging himself on the rocks and falling back, and then at last he leapt sideways on to those stones at the edge, and wriggled along on the land and got himself into the water above the fall. They are brave fish.'

'Brave fish. Yes. I remember Hannah saying that once. She said their going up the rivers was like souls trying to approach God.'

'They are certainly possessed by a strange desire.'

'But to suffer so much –'

'Suffering is no scandal. It is natural. Nature appoints it. All creation suffers. It suffers from having been created, if from nothing else. It suffers from being divided from God.'

'Yours is a melancholy sort of religion, Denis. I'm afraid I don't believe in God.'

'Ah, you do. But you do not know His name. And I who know His name am only the better of you by one little word. Here is the salmon pool.'

They paused. By a trick of the land, the sound of the waterfalls was, as they came over the brow, quite cut off. The sky ahead was greenish with the evening and gave a green tinge to the big expanse of unrippled water. Hooded crows rose from the heather and took to slow flight casting a fugitive reflection. Ahead at the flat horizon was the dark line of the bog, and a little to the left, far off against a pinker evening, the lop-sided figure of the distant dolmen. Otherwise there was just water and sky and heather and silence.

Marian breathed deeply. She was tired with the hard ascent. But the place had some power too which took her breath away. She felt a sudden embarrassment with Denis, as if they had entered a church and must now talk in a different key.

Denis seemed to notice nothing and was picking his way along the heathery verge. He was saying, 'There's a place here, where you can usually see them. Don't come too near the edge though. Here, if you crawl out and lie on this stone. Make no sudden movements, that's right. Now look into the shadowed places. Wait. Now do you see them, the big fellows?'

Marian lay down cautiously on the stone which projected a little way into the pool. There were dark ledges beneath it and the water seemed deep and very brown now that one was close above it. She looked down for a while but could see nothing except the speckling of the light in the dappled water. Then the speckles seemed to assemble into scales. A great form passed by like a shadow. Then another. The deep brown world was filled with slow majestic silent forms.

'Do you see them now, Marian? Those are the big fellows. Thirty and forty pounds, some of them. Please God they'll be left alone.'

Marian suddenly could not endure it. She pulled herself back off the stone into the dry crackling heather. Denis was sitting near, his arms about his knees, his eyes still straining after the fish. Marian felt that she was going to weep. To prevent herself she turned directly to look at Denis. He turned his head slowly in a moment to look at her and she saw against the green eastern sky his bony face of polished bronze, his jagged blue-black hair, his long eyes of sapphire blue, his sad lost face, his face of a man from altogether somewhere else. She said, 'Whatever could we have done for Hannah? Forgive me for having been a coward.'

He frowned with distress, quickly looking away again. 'There is nothing. Since she – gave herself – away.'

'I feel this too, but it's quite irrational. Still I suppose there's nothing to be done now. We must just be glad she will be gone – when he comes back. You said yourself that she must not be there when he comes. Well, she will not be there.' Marian thought with a sort of shock, shall I be there? She pictured Peter approaching and approaching.

'Yes, but not like that. Ah, she should have kept herself away from him, she should have kept herself!' The little cry shook

199

with jealousy. Yet it seemed also the primitive word of some untouched puritan.

'I suppose somehow or other he deserved her. And somehow or other we did not.'

Denis shook his head. 'She has destroyed herself.'

'Or set herself free. Time will show.'

Well, she is gone, thought Marian. And whether she will be free or destroyed I shall probably never know; and that is as it should be. No one should be a prisoner of other people's thoughts, no one's destiny should be an object of fascination to others, no one's destiny should be open to inspection; and for a moment with her pity, she felt almost a resentment against Hannah for having so totally fascinated her. Then she thought again, I did not love her enough. Then she thought, she is gone into privacy, she is gone, and now we can all see each other again. She lifted her head and felt the giddy sense of her returning freedom. She stared at Denis. And a second later, quite suddenly, she knew that she was going to do what Alice Lejour had done.

The warm sea wind was risen and blew over them now bringing a salty leafy smell of the autumn. It blew over the wide greenish surface of the salmon pool, rippling it a little, and blew on toward the solitary places of the bog. The evening air thickened about them and the heather began to glow.

'Denis.'

He turned again, giving her his full face, still sad, still pensively elsewhere. Marian edged forward until her knees touched his. Then she took his hand, then his arm, and leaning forward a little awkwardly she kissed him on the lips. She withdrew a moment. His face was calm now, with a dignified serenity which made him very present to her. Then, edging well up to his side, she kissed him again, holding him longer and letting one arm creep round his shoulder. His lips were closed and unresponsive, but he looked at her still with a solemn detachment which was neither hostile nor surprised.

'I'm sorry,' said Marian. 'I didn't expect this. I see these things can happen suddenly. I didn't believe it when you said about Gerald and Jamesie.' She added, 'I think I've wanted to do this for some time, only I couldn't *see* you properly.'

He still stared at her. Then he closed his eyes and began to rub the back of her hand to and fro against his brow, uttering little grunting sounds.

Marian felt suddenly pierced and transfixed by tenderness for him. Her first movement had had a sort of abstract purity about it. She had seized him because she must, and emotion, refined to some point of extreme necessity, was scarcely something felt. Now came the torrent of feeling. She drew him close against her shoulder and saw above the black cherished head the salmon beginning to rise.

He was helpless and silent in her arms. She shifted them both into a more comfortable position, her knees leaning against his thighs, and then moved herself back a little so that they could converse. This was freedom, the freedom to love and move which she had so terribly lacked. She was deeply shaken by the suddenness and beauty of it. This at last, after what seemed an interval of stifling in some tapestried room, of simply looking at herself in a mirror, was the real other, the real unknown.

'Denis, look at me. How old are you? I've often wondered.'

'Thirty-three.'

'I'm twenty-nine. Denis, you're not angry with me?'

'Marian, Marian –' He looked at her and his face was full of hollows and shadows. His eyes were narrowed to dark slits which showed no flash of blue. He moved slightly back, stroking her hand as if to control and conciliate it. 'I didn't expect this either. I don't know what it is. But I am glad of you, I have been glad of you from the start.'

'And now we are, as it were, released to each other.'

He smiled. 'It sounds like a mating of animals.'

'We are animals.' She felt this to be true for the first time in her life. She desired Denis.

'We are a little mad today, Marian, because of what has passed. Let us go back now.'

'Not yet. You don't want to, do you?' He lowered his eyes and she saw that he did not. 'Dear, dear Denis, perhaps we are a little mad, but it is a mad place and a mad time. And I feel

much more real with you than I do with any of the others.'
Or indeed with anyone else at all, she suddenly felt. This encounter was the unclassifiable encounter that liberates. Always before she had been a kind of person meeting a kind of person. But she did not know what Denis was, and this ignorance cast a darkness back upon herself which made her quiver with reality. They were two unique things meeting one another.

An orange glow from the west was spreading over the zenith and the salmon pool had turned to a sheet of gold which the rising fish fretted with darker rings. Marian still stared at Denis and saw his eyes gradually widen for her. He was wearing his usual faded blue open-necked shirt, and he looked shabby and young and hard like a lad following a tinker's cart. There was a marvellous equality in the way she was able to meet his still rather suspicious gaze. Still sitting as they were, knee to knee, she began to caress his head, drawing her hand down over his cheek and his neck. She undid the top button of his shirt and let her hand slide down inside. He trembled.

His eyes became vaguer, and then without haste he removed his hand and laid his arm across her throat, forcing her back into the heather. He lay full length beside her, his shoulder covering hers. He did not attempt to kiss her, but pressed his closed mouth against her cheek. She felt the hard pressure and the continued trembling.

Marian looked up past the dark head at the high orange sky with its little scarfs of fiery cloud. She felt a great blank joy and with it a sense almost of free playful gaiety.

'Denis, I do love you. I've never felt like this. Don't tremble so. You're not frightened, are you? Denis, tell me, how many girls have you had?'

He withdrew his lips from her cheek, but did not otherwise move. 'How many – how do you mean?'

'How many girls have you made love to, been to bed with?'

'None.'

Marian's gaiety left her, but her joy darkened and deepened. She still looked at the sky. Her desire became deep and quiet and solemn as if something from the bog, something not hostile but very old, were hovering over them, presiding over the rite.

202

Denis went on, since she was silent. 'It is not the custom here – to do those things – if one is not married.'

Marian was silent still, not for unsureness of her feelings, but for very sureness. She would let the words find their own way out. She said at last. 'I said that I loved you. Perhaps I still don't know what I mean. But I do know that for me this, now, is well, is good. And I have never really felt this before. I feel totally innocent. It is the first time. But it may be that it would not be right for you, not innocent for you –'

The silence between them was serene, almost sleepy, inert as their two bodies.

'What – are you wanting?'

'Whatever you want – anything, this. I feel we are like children together.'

He raised himself a little and looked at her. Then he began to fumble awkwardly with the neck of her dress. She helped him.

Later, much later, when his darkness moved above her and she saw stars overhead she heard him murmur very softly, as if to himself, 'Ah, but we are faithless, faithless.'

Chapter Twenty-six

'Marian, I think I must be honest with you. And please forgive me if I cause you pain.'

Marian listened distractedly to Effingham. They were standing at the window of the drawing-room. Hannah would be leaving the house any moment. She knew this not from any definite intelligence, but from a sense of increasing urgency, a sense of climax which pervaded the rooms and the stairs and trembled upon the terrace in the morning sunshine. Several times she had thought she heard the engine of the Land Rover.

Last night she had returned, not very late, with Denis, to find that all was as before. They were both relieved, and determined now to stay inside the house until the end. Denis had gone away to his own room, and she had leaned for long upon her window sill, watching the full moon, a great golden globe, rising over the sea, and she had watched it until it had become a flat silver plate high up in the blue black sky, and the sea was almost dazzling, barred with light.

She had wept tears of a sort of exhausted broken joy. With the return to Gaze she felt again her connexion with the house and with the drama it had contained. But she felt towards it rather as one who is leaving a theatre after some tragic play, worn, torn, yet rejoiced and set free with a new appetite for the difficult world. Heaven knew what she had landed herself in with Denis. But what would be would be. She had never, she realized, really felt before that certain recklessness of love; and that she was now suddenly, unexpectedly, genuinely in love she did not doubt. It had been no momentary magic of the salmon pool. Denis was real to her, mysterious, awkward, unfamiliar, infinitely to be learnt, but real.

They returned to Hannah, to the hidden Hannah, with a sort

of bold shame. They did not speak of her, and Marian did not know or ask exactly what Denis felt. But she herself felt as if her pity had been, as it were, purified by gratitude. It was almost as if Hannah had sent them forth together, had released them from their former bond, had absolved them. In the breaking of the seven-year vigil it was not only she who disappeared into a terrible liberty. Her servants too were amazingly set free.

'What did you say, Effingham?'

'I said I must speak frankly to you. Will you forgive me?'

She must talk to Denis soon about what they would do next. Marian could not see that it was necessary in any way that they should stay at Gaze until the arrival of Peter Crean-Smith. They had no moral obligation to Peter; and Marian was, when she thought about it, more than a little afraid of this dark figure. She had had enough tragic drama. Her encounter with Denis, for all its surprisingness and oddness, had so much of the feeling of coming into real life. What would be enacted between herself and Denis she could not foresee: she was prepared for difficulties, she was prepared for pain. But this would be the real business which one human being has with another. She felt obscurely that if they waited until Peter came they might become involved in some further pattern of magical events. If they waited until Peter came they might be unable to leave Gaze. They must flee sooner. But first they had to attend, as kneeling figures at the fringe of some sombre procession, upon the departure of Hannah.

'Yes, do talk, Effingham. Is it about Hannah?'

'Well, not exactly. Marian, I hope you won't think me irresponsible and mad. I've known Alice for a very long time –'

'Yes, Effingham?' Was that Denis now? No, it was Jamesie, tripping along the terrace. She glimpsed his face for a moment and it looked strangely, even wildly happy. She had not, it occurred to her, seen Jamesie since yesterday morning, when he had looked so gaunt and tearful. Perhaps the departing Hannah had dispensed to him too some gift of joy.

'I suppose I had better explain, tell you everything. Yes, it will be a relief to do so. A relief in many ways. Even if you find me hopelessly – disappointing.'

'I'm sure I won't do that, Effingham. What is it?' When Hannah had gone she would make Denis play the piano and sing. There would be a time for tears then.

'Ah, I'm sorry. You understand so quickly. But let me say it all in order. It will be a sort of confession.'

'Yes, Effingham?' Whatever was he talking about? If only Hannah would go. That was a moment of suffering, a moment of birth, that must be gone through before the new life could be born.

'My love for Hannah – you might have asked me *then*, the night before last, what I made of it, and whether I was being faithless –'

'Faithless,' said Marian. She caught at the word. 'We are all faithless.' She said it objectively, with a pain which had its place, which was not confusing.

'*You* are not faithless, Marian dear, sit down and look at me properly. I know I'm causing you pain.'

They moved from the window and sat down in two of the big humpy sagging armchairs beside the fireplace. Charred logs and mounds of feathery ashes strewed the hearth. Marian looked at Effingham. His fair hair was still wispy and tousled from the morning breeze and his big face was pale and shiny with tiredness; and with something else. There was a vague wild look in his eyes which Marian could not place. She began to attend to him.

'I loved Hannah, Marian. I *love* her. Oh, I could give all kinds of explanations of that love, but they would insult her and be always less than the truth. I loved her and there were a great many things I might have done for her. I certainly suffered for her. And I would have suffered more. You believe that?'

'Of course –' Marian was distressed and troubled by the urgent confessional tone.

'I can't really explain or justify what happened. I know now that I never at all had the measure of Hannah. Perhaps none of us had. Perhaps none of us tried to have –'

'Except Gerald.' The remark sounded suddenly cynical, but Marian had not meant it so and was relieved that Effingham did not take it so.

'Indeed. Perhaps Gerald really loved her best. I don't know why, but it never occurred to me for a second to think of Gerald as capable of having any interest in Hannah as a human being –'

'It never occurred to me either.' How funereal it was, talking about her as if she were dead, or at least gone.

'Anyway, that remains a mystery. And I suppose it is our last tribute to her to let it remain a mystery.'

'Yes.' Marian bowed her head. She began to think of Denis once again.

'Well, perhaps indeed Gerald understood her as a human being, as a real person. And I realize now that I didn't. At least not sufficiently, evidently not sufficiently. I was too moved by – the story. But then so was she –' He looked away in a sort of puzzlement. 'Marian, do you think we could have some *tea*?'

'My dear, I'll make you some. It's no use ringing. I think half the maids have gone.'

'No, no, stay here, let me go on talking. Anyhow, whatever it was which would have made me able to help, I hadn't got it, I couldn't even *see*.'

'So – she has set us free,' said Marian, returning to her idea. She felt for the first time, perhaps Hannah is now herself happy, and not just the cause of happiness in others. It was a strange beautiful thought.

'Oh, Marian –' said Effingham, as if much moved. He covered his face for a moment. 'I am sorry.'

Marian looked at him with puzzlement. 'Don't grieve for her,' she said. 'She is free too.'

'You don't understand me. I must go on and say it all. Alice –'

'Alice –?'

'Well, yes. There it is. And I didn't know. I didn't know, really fully know, until she said all those things about Denis, you remember, about Denis and the salmon pool.'

'Denis and the salmon pool. Yes.'

'Marian, I've known her so long. And things can grow up inside one without one's noticing. And then suddenly they leap out into consciousness, into the world. It can happen.'

'I know it can happen!'

'And when it happens in that way it happens with such completeness and such authority. You see, I've so much relied on Alice, so much taken her presence here for granted. In a way she's – the real side of the story, the real person, the real object of love. It's as if I'd been, all the time, looking into a mirror, and only been vaguely conscious of the real world at my side.'

'I've felt something like that too, Effingham –'

'Oh, understand me! This is so painful. I'm telling you that I'm in love with Alice, suddenly, deeply in love.'

Marian rose to her feet, and he rose with her. So that was it. The dazed look in Effingham's eyes had been happiness, the achievement at last of a real action. Hannah had so beautifully sent them all away in their different directions.

'Marian, Marian, please don't grieve or judge me harshly. I've known Alice so long. Ever since she was a child. Please understand and forgive. We have known each other such a little while, you and I. You are young, you'll soon feel better –'

What on earth is he protesting about, Marian wondered. Then it suddenly came to her: he thinks I'm in love with him! The idea filled her with such a rush of hilarity that she had to turn away from him to conceal her face.

'Please, don't be in pain –'

Marian composed her features and turned back. 'Dear Effingham, don't be upset for me. I shall be all right.'

'Ah, you are so kind.'

'These things happen, Effingham. One must be brave.'

'You *are* brave. And so considerate.'

'What would be the point of being otherwise. I wish you and Alice every possible happiness.'

'And so generous! Honestly, it's all happened so quickly, I hardly know where I am. I feel much better now I've told you.'

'Don't worry about me. I shall recover.' It was naughty perhaps to deceive him. But he would suffer no sleepless nights for her. And she was, with that enlargement of one's sympathy for others which one's own happiness can bring, genuinely glad for him and for Alice. It was like a comedy by Shakespeare. All the ends of the story were being bound up in a good way.

She was facing the door, looking away with her composed face over his head. The door opened and Denis came in. Her face scarcely changed, but she greeted him with triumph.

'Oh, Denis,' said Effingham, 'good morning. Do you think you could get us some tea?'

'Certainly, sir.'

'And some whiskey, if you can find any,' said Marian.

'Surely. I've got some locked up. It's been disappearing lately.'

They smiled at each other. I am free, thought Marian, as she watched him out of the room, we are free. She lifted her hands in a gesture of expansion and well-being.

'You see, I just didn't *expect* it,' Effingham was going on. He was obviously fascinated by his predicament.

The tall sash-windows to the terrace had been pushed right up and a warm breeze stirred the yellowish lace curtains. Listening to Effingham's murmur, Marian looked through the window at the sea beyond, a very pale blue washed with silver. There was a distant ship. The scene, just as she was about to leave it, was becoming real to her. It had been too beautiful before.

A tall figure darkened one of the windows and Violet Evercreech entered the room. Marian rose with the slight chill which Violet's advent always brought, and Effingham fell silent.

'Well, children –'

'Good morning, Violet.'

'Packed your bags, Marian?'

'Not yet. Is Hannah going – now, soon?'

'You want to get it over, don't you? You both feel you are sitting out the end of some rather tedious film, don't you, where you already know what's going to happen?'

Marian felt uneasy, guilty, before Violet. She hoped Violet had not seen her looking happy. She said lamely, 'No, not like that –'

'But perhaps you *don't* know what is going to happen, perhaps there are still surprises, turns of the story –'

'What do you mean?'

'While you are playing ring-a-roses others are working the machine.'

'The machine?'

A figure appeared at another of the windows and Alice Lejour stepped into the room. 'Morning all. Hello, Marian dear.' She kissed Marian.

Marian thought distractedly, now I shall have to keep up this fiction with Alice for ever. Perhaps she would not, in the future, see them again, perhaps that would be better. But what was the future? She was frightened by Violet's presence and by her enigmatic words.

Denis entered through the door with a large tray with teapot and cups, whiskey and glasses. He set it down and began without a word to pour out. Alice sat on the arm of Effingham's chair and Marian and Denis drew together near the bookcase. Alice and Effingham began to murmur to each other in low voices. It was like a funeral party. Marian thought, now we are all gathered together, it must surely be the moment of departure. She listened to sounds elsewhere in the house.

There was a distant sound, and her heart jerked, half with fear, half with a sort of exhausted relief. Someone was coming noisily down the stairs, but not slowly, not solemnly. It was a sound of running feet. The sound approached and a moment later Jamesie threw open the door and came running into the room.

Jamesie was transfigured. He had resumed his dandified fancy-dress appearance and his eyes were alight with a strange glee. All his features seemed to have been pulled upward so that he even looked taller. He bounded in, like Puck, like Peter Pan, a graceful youthful authoritative apparition.

He advanced lightly, almost mincingly, into the centre of the room.

There was a tense silence which Marian broke nervously. 'Hello, Jamesie. Is Hannah just going?' The words sounded suddenly mean. Violet Everscreech laughed.

'No.'

'When, then, do you know? Soon?'

Jamesie looked at them all, his gay intent look moving from face to face. 'Good news. She is not going. She is not going at all.'

Effingham and Alice rose to their feet. Marian looked at Denis. His face was strained back as if a great wind were pressing it. Violet laughed again.

Effingham moved forward as if taking charge of the party. He said, 'Look here, Jamesie, don't joke with us. Would you please explain what you mean?'

'Just that. Hannah is not going. Everything is going to be just like it was before. Isn't that splendid?' He twirled about on one foot, harlequin-like, spreading his arms.

'Look here,' said Effingham. He looked tired and stupid. 'What on earth do you mean? What about Peter?'

'Peter isn't coming. It was a false alarm. He didn't get on to the boat after all. He sent another cable. He's going to stay in New York. So we can all settle down again. Isn't it too lovely?'

Marian stared at him, dazed and horrified at things not yet fully understood. Over his shoulder she could see the men carrying Hannah's trunks back into the hall. One of the black maids came in and removed the tea-cups. So everything would be the same as before. And yet it could not be, it could never be.

Effingham said, 'Is this true, Violet?'

'So, my friends,' cried Jamesie. 'Back to your posts! Back to your tasks! Unpack your suitcases! Our happy family will not be broken up. For all shall be restored, revived, renewed, and far more beautiful than it was before!'

'Do not listen to him!' Violet spoke quietly not vehemently, looking at her brother. 'Do not listen to him. You are all on the point of departure. There is no occasion for you to change your plans. You have all found good reasons for going, you have been longing to go, you could hardly wait. Take your good hour and go. Later on, it may be too late. Go now, I tell you. Leave this place. You can do no good here any more.'

Effingham was looking at Alice. Alice's face was grey and

211

lumpish. She stared stolidly in front of her. Marian's first thought was, yet let us go!

'Of course we are not going.' It was Denis.

Marian turned, almost surprised, to look at him. It was as if something had physically pushed her from him. Then, from the doorway, another voice joined in.

'I am glad to hear that, Denis. I trust that after this little upset we can all settle down amicably and get on with our jobs as before. There is no need to prolong this drama, which was based anyway upon a misunderstanding. So may I suggest that we all disperse to our usual places and let this rather unhealthy atmosphere dissipate itself.'

Gerald Scottow was leaning against the door. He looked larger, browner, healthier than ever before. His big well-shaven face glowed, ruddy with power. He smiled upon them and his eyes especially sought out Marian. She sat down abruptly on the arm of a chair.

Jamesie sprang to Gerald, poised in his familiar way under the shade of Gerald's tallness, ready to dart away like an arrow in any direction to do his bidding.

'Go, go, I tell you! This will end in blood!' Violet's voice wailed and faded. She receded through the white lace curtains. The sky outside had darkened. It was beginning to rain.

'I'm going home to lunch.' Alice set herself in motion and tramped across the floor. After a moment's hesitation, during which he tried to look at Marian but didn't quite manage it, Effingham went with her.

Denis turned to Marian. 'We will go and see her now.' He marched toward the door. Jerked into motion, Marian followed. Gerald and Jamesie stood back on either side to let them go by. As she passed Gerald, Marian flinched and dropped her eyes.

Chapter Twenty-seven

Marian crossed the ante-chamber and knocked on the door of Hannah's room. Denis had sent her on alone. 'Come in.'

She entered. The room was dark, shut in by the rain which was falling outside. A lamp was lit on the writing-table. The turf fire flickered. Hannah was standing by the fireplace wearing her old yellow silk dressing-gown.

Marian came half-way down the room. She felt she was confronted by a stranger. She felt positively afraid.

Hannah had been fumbling in her pocket for a cigarette when Marian appeared. She went on doing so, after giving the girl a quick sideways glance. She looked sallow, older. And as Marian now came near she saw the familiar beautiful features marked all over as if something hard had been pressed down upon them. The face was broken up with little twists and frowns. The rounded radiant look was absent. It seemed another person.

'Marian.' It was more like a statement than a greeting. Hannah found the cigarette, lit it, and then as an after-thought offered one to Marian. The familiar smell of whiskey crept like incense through the room and pervaded the plump figure in the dressing-gown.

Marian did not know what to say. Hideous pity filled her and a sudden rising sense of guilt. She felt like a member of a personal bodyguard confronted with the mutilated corpse of her master. She sought for words. Could she say: I'm so glad you're staying after all? What could she say? There was nothing to say. She bowed her head and felt a burning flush rising through her cheeks. The next moment with an almost cold sense that there was nothing else to be done she fell on her knees at Hannah's feet.

It was the right thing to do. Hannah pulled her up with an incoherent exclamation, and they embraced, holding each other in silence. Marian felt the unhoped-for tears overbrimming her eyes and darkening Hannah's silken shoulder. And with the tears, half with despair, she felt ebb away the hard free person that she had momentarily been. And yet it was true too that nothing could be the same again. Pity for herself, for Hannah, possessed her till she shook.

'There now, there now, have some whiskey.' Hannah was comforting her. She too had shed tears, but was dry-eyed now.

The familiar sound of the liquid entering the glass rang like an angelus and they paused, more calm, and then looked at each other. 'So you didn't go away, Marian.'

'Of course not! I didn't dream of it!' But that was not true. She felt, as she looked into the golden eyes, suddenly Hannah's equal, her adversary, an inhabitant of the same world. It was a sickening yet pleasant feeling. It was now possible to lie to Hannah.

Hannah turned away shaking her head and looked out at the rain. 'It's strange. I thought I might – come round – come back – and find everyone had gone away. Like in a fairy tale. Has anyone gone?'

'No.'

She sighed, and Marian said sharply, 'You're not *sorry*, are you, that we haven't gone?'

'Ah, of course not!' Hannah turned, smiling. It was like the old smile, but not quite. 'How could I be? Yet, you know, it will be difficult, for a while. Don't feel you have to stay.'

Marian said at once, 'Of course I shall stay, Hannah.'

They stared at each other. The golden eyes held their own. Marian looked down into the whiskey which, touched with the lamplight, was almost the same colour. The day seemed to be getting darker. What had happened to Hannah? It was not exactly that she was 'broken', but she seemed different, as if by some great loop or shift she had joined some other phase of her being. Many years seemed to have passed in two days.

Marian, feeling her way, and testing out her new sensation

of being Hannah's equal, said cautiously, 'How will it be —
difficult – exactly, Hannah?'

'That would take a long time to say. And anyway you know.
After all that – here we still are.'

'But we love you, Hannah.' It had such a false ring that
Marian could not lift her head to help the words. She had
never really *loved* Hannah.

'We'll see, shall we? Sit down. I feel so tired. I want to talk
at random. Oh, how it rains! The winter is starting. Say something to me, Marian.'

They sat down on the sofa, facing the fire, the lamp behind
them. The flames lit Hannah's tired face, with that strange
dislocation of the features, as in someone who has had a
stroke.

'I don't understand what has happened,' said Marian. 'Why
did – your husband – change his mind?'

Hannah shuddered, perhaps at the word. 'I think he didn't.
I think he didn't send the cable at all. That it was a fake. But I
shall never know.'

'A fake?' Marion was chilled. Yet more dark galleries opened
out behind the scene. 'But who – why –?'

'I don't know.' She smiled into the fire, the sort of smile that
might become a hysterical laugh. She closed her lips on it, and
the light of the smile gave to her features a slightly crazy lift.
'I don't know who sent the cable or why, though I could make
one or two different guesses.'

I couldn't, thought Marian. Who could have played such a
stupid aimless trick? Or was it a stupid aimless trick? She felt
fright, as at a glimpse of madness, and to cover it up said
quickly, in a tone that sounded ridiculously chatty, 'Well, it
certainly turned things upside down for a while, didn't it.'

'It made me temporarily mad.' She spoke in a high voice as
if near to tears. And then, to reassure Marian, turned and
smiled at her.

God, poor Hannah. Marian thought desperately of what to
say. She felt a nervous itching desire to speak of Gerald. She
said, 'We are all mad sometimes, but it passes.'

'The consequences do not pass.'

'What are the consequences?' Marian was breathless, gripping her glass and looking into the fire. Although their conversation was slow in tempo, almost as in the days when they fell asleep over the *Princesse de Clèves*, she felt she was fencing with Hannah, or rather building up with her, very delicately, some sort of precarious edifice; something dangerous yet essential, something within which, however crazy, they would have to take shelter in the future.

'Oh, well they remain to be seen.' Hannah rubbed her eyes. She wriggled her shoulders and shuffled her bare feet in the thick rug. She seemed to be choosing more words. 'I've always had, of course, a very special bond with Gerald, a mysterious bond –' She paused again, and seemed to be seeking some greater elaboration, but then ended, 'because of the way things are, you know.'

Marian felt now that she was being made the recipient of a very precious and very important confession. Certain things had got to be said between them before they could look each other again in the face and go on to build some how-much-altered relationship. This seemed to matter to Hannah. Marian could feel her almost trembling with eagerness to be most delicately interrogated. Marian again felt shame. She was not worthy of this role. Only a humble person could have played it properly. She wished that she had persuaded Denis to go in first. But Hannah would not have talked to Denis. This reminded her too that she was on the brink of a large deception: would she tell Hannah about Denis? How could she, and yet how could she not? How quickly they had all consoled themselves! She was blushing. She felt the silence demanding her speech and, with an effort at precision, said not looking up, 'But your relation with Gerald is different now?'

'Yes. Different, quite different.'

What does it mean? Marian wondered. A pain which was certainly jealousy goaded her on. She must find out more before this delicate moment of their being open to each other should be quite past. She was cold, and yet it was like a climax of love. She lifted her eyes to Hannah's and took the shock of the beautiful changed face again. 'Hannah, why don't you go

216

away with Gerald anyway? After – what has happened – why should you and Gerald stay here any more?'

This was the point toward which Hannah had been drawing her. And Marian saw something which was almost cunning in the golden firelit eyes: cunning, or caution, or perhaps the look with which someone offers a secret hint in a precarious situation. There was a sort of imploring: as Hannah answered, 'There just wasn't sufficient reason for going away.'

With a sudden sense of Hannah's courage, of her sheer indestructibility, Marian took the look to her heart, but without understanding it. Then she thought, My God, Gerald wouldn't take her! And she recalled the transfiguration of Jamesie, Jamesie's triumph, and the figures of Gerald and Jamesie dominating the scene below. Gerald had, with one quick twist, as of one manipulating a whirling rope, bound her, enslaved her, a thousand times more: and then proposed that the situation should continue. Gerald must surely have known almost at once that the telegram was a fake. He must have telephoned New York. He might even have sent the telegram himself. Or Jamesie might have sent it. Or, with a different view, Violet. Or Peter might really have sent it, but only to torment and confuse. As Marian opened out the long fretted sheet of possibilities she apprehended Hannah as hopelessly, catastrophically, beset by enemies, caught. Her own guilt struck her and she hid her face and lowered her head to her knees.

'Come, come. Look at me.' The command was sharp.

Marian straightened up. She had to face her now, she had to try to understand what was required of her. Some apex or crisis in the conversation had passed, and Hannah looked now no longer cunning or begging but very determined, as if she were now going to explain to Marian some important and difficult scheme of work. The change in her face now seemed to Marian to be this: the spiritual veil or haze, the strange light, had been taken away, to reveal the irregularities of the features beneath. But she was still beautiful.

'None of that!' said Hannah softly. Then she went on in a more ordinary voice, as if she were talking of quite ordinary things. 'I must live here and go on with this business of mine,

217

whatever it is, and be prepared to do so alone if necessary. For what has happened will have results. I have a feeling that if it means anything at all I must live it all through from the beginning, since everything up to now has been a false start. *Now* is the start.'

Marian felt immediately; this is intolerable, she cannot do this, although she did not clearly know what this was. The seven years could not be thus folded into nothing. Were they at the beginning of another seven years? Marian felt as if the prison doors were closing on herself. 'No, no, no!'

'Indeed, perhaps better alone. I may decide to send you all away, even if you don't go of your own accord. Ah, Marian, it is possible to go on and on and to suffer, to pray and to meditate, to impose on oneself a discipline of the greatest austerity, and for all this to be nothing, to be a dream.'

'Oh, Hannah, stop it!' said Marian. It was a bitter cry. The enchantment was beginning again, the first words of the spell were being hoarsely murmured; and it was the more terrifying since Marian realized obscurely but at once that this was a far far stranger and more dangerous spell than the old one. This was a spell which had absorbed the old one; it was a higher, more majestic, more terrible spell. She almost wanted, like someone in the presence of a moving, whispering enchanter, to freeze Hannah to stone before her own wits should be stolen away.

'A dream. Do you know what part I have been playing? That of God. And do you know what I have been really? Nothing, a legend. A hand stretched out from the real world went me as through paper.' Her voice became deeper, resonant, like a chant, with touches of the dovelike purr of the local accent. Her eloquent voice was suddenly almost like Denis's voice.

Marian shivered. She wanted to break the mood which was being imposed. She did not want to hear these confidences, to know these plans. She said, with an attempt at briskness, 'Playing God? Surely not. God is a tyrant.'

'The false God is a tyrant. Or rather he is a tyrannical dream, and that is what I was. I have lived on my audience, on my worshippers. I have lived by their thoughts, by your thoughts – just as you have lived by what you thought were mine. And we have deceived each other.'

'Hannah, you are talking wildly.' Marian did not wish to be rushed along so fast, not so fast, and not in this direction at all. Yet Hannah was not speaking in an excited tone. She was regarding the fire and twisting her hands as if delivering some sober much-debated judgement.

'It was your belief in the significance of my suffering that kept me going. Ah, how much I needed you all! I have battened upon you like a secret vampire, I have even battened on Max Lejour.' She sighed. 'I needed my audience, I lived in your gaze like a false God. But it is the punishment of a false God to become unreal. I have become unreal. You have made me unreal by thinking about me so much. You made me into an object of contemplation. Just like this landscape. I have made it unreal by endlessly looking at it instead of entering it.' She rose as she spoke and wandered to the window.

Marian saw her, a dark figure now against the grey rain. Gerald had entered the landscape and made it real. But what would happen to it now? What *was* there, in that strange desolate landscape? Marian had risen too. She said rather harshly, 'But you *have* suffered –'

Hannah turned, and her face, touched by the distant lamp, seemed to glimmer and tremble against the dark grey window. 'You all attributed your own feelings to me. But I had no feelings, I was empty. I lived by your belief in my suffering. But I had no real suffering. The suffering is only beginning – now.'

And Gerald is its instrument, thought Marian. She was already, as if affected by some strange drug, beginning to see new patterns, new colours. She shook herself. The idea that Hannah was mad shot across her mind like a meteor and disappeared. It was herself she must keep a hold on. In desperation, but quietly, she said, 'Hannah, you are the most sublime egoist that I have ever met.'

'Am I not after telling you just that?' The voice was very like Denis's. And with the deliberate aping of the local brogue Hannah laughed briefly, and Marian laughed too.

She moved to join Hannah at the window and together they looked out at the legendary landscape. As she watched the rain falling on the wrecked garden and on the dull grass slope and on the gleaming streaming black cliffs and on the sullen iron-grey sea, Marian felt a shock of despair, a shock of mortality, as if Death were passing close before her face and, not yet ready to take her, had blown a chill breath into her mouth. The rain fell into the dark fish pools with a jumpy jerky rhythm. Would she have to stay here with Hannah perhaps forever? The real suffering was only beginning now.

As Marian looked down the lines of the rain confused her eyes, so that she could not at first make out whether something which seemed to be happening below were not just some trick of the grey uncertain light. There was a movement, an unrolling of dark shapes. Then she saw that two figures dressed in black oilskins had emerged on to the terrace and were standing there together, looking ahead as if waiting for something. She recognized them from their stance and from the particular way that in standing they seemed to belong together, like a sculptured group, as Gerald and Jamesie. Hannah too stiffened, watching them. The two women looked down in silence.

A minute or two later, materializing out of the blanket of rain, a grey darkness gathering out of the sheeted greyness, another figure appeared, slowly approaching. Hannah gave a soft exclamation, a little gasp or cry. Marian stared at the unfamiliar figure. It was also wrapped up in a mackintosh with a cape over the head. Then with a gasp too, and as she turned in a terror of surprise to Hannah, Marian recognized it. It was Pip Lejour, and he was carrying a shotgun.

Chapter Twenty-eight

Denis leaned against the door. 'Will you see him? Shall I let him in?'

Hannah was still standing by the window. She had not moved when the figure of Pip entered the house. She was still looking out at the rain. She spoke over her shoulder. 'So Gerald – didn't mind.'

'Mr Lejour was very determined.'

'Is he outside now? Let him in. No, wait a minute.'

She turned back to the room, drawing the silk gown closer about her and re-tying the cord. She went to one of the mirrors and looked at herself. She did not touch her face or hair. 'Let him in.'

Marian moved toward the door. 'Wait, Marian, I want you and Denis to stay here while I talk to – him.'

Marian looked at Denis, but his face was frozen, grim, his face of a mountain man, of a partisan; and he would not look at her. With a sense almost of physical danger at what was to come Marian retired again to the window, getting as far away as she could. Hannah sat down on an upright chair, turning it a little towards the door. Denis opened the door.

Pip had taken off his coat but he still carried the gun. His boots were thick with mud and a smell of rain and earth and sea, a smell of damp tweed, entered the room with him. For all his rough country clothes, he looked slim, elegant, feline, or with his small sleek head and long neck, like a beautiful snake. He took a step or two, and stood before Hannah, very straight, soldier-like. Denis closed the door softly and sat down against it on the floor.

Pip and Hannah looked at each other in silence for a long time, he reflectively grave as if before a great picture, she gloomy, almost morose, taking her eyes off him, glancing about, returning.

'You don't mind my coming?' It was a cool question, as if he had been with her yesterday.

'Of course I mind. What do you want?'

'To take you away.'

'Why do you say this now? You could have come and said this at any time in these years. You have been here often enough, watching me. Marian, my cigarettes please.' Her tone was calmly irritable. But when Marian lit the cigarette Hannah's hand was trembling so much that the operation was almost impossible.

'It is different now. There is no point in your staying now.'

'You are brutal.'

'Not that. I am not going to witness what happens next. Everything has changed now. When I go away from here now I shall never come back. But I want to take you with me.' He spoke softly and rhythmically as if with the authority of a priest.

'Some things may have changed, but my intentions have not changed.' She answered him with an equal resonance, leaning back in her chair, one arm drawn back, one foot extended. Their still figures were connected by lines of force which made them seem without witnesses, a closed capsule of quiet violence.

'You can't do it again. It is all spoilt now. Don't deceive yourself, Hannah. You are *tired*.'

She closed her eyes and the truth of it for a moment seemed to weaken her. 'You say it is spoilt *now*. What was it before?'

He was silent for a moment. Then he turned and leaned the gun against the desk. He crossed his arms, looking down on her, and seemed to reflect as if for the first time on her question. 'Does it matter exactly? You attempted something which was too difficult.'

'Well. Now I am going to attempt something even more difficult –' The cigarette was singeing her hair. She drew her hand away. The smell of burnt hair drifted through the room.

'No, no. You *cannot* do the thing that you intended. You

222

simply do not know how. Come out through the gates into the real world.'

She was silent as if she had been listening to him attentively. Then she said conversationally, 'With you?'

'With me. I have had my own vigil, Hannah, the counterpart of yours. And I have learnt on the last day what I should have known on the first day. Come.'

'And what would we do,' she said in the soft voice of someone listening to a story, 'if we were to go out of the gates together?'

Pip gazed at her. The mere sound of the hypothesis uttered in her voice seemed to make him glow as with some imminent metamorphosis. He grew not tenser, but looser, like a ballet dancer about to move. 'We would decide that – when we got outside. We would decide it as people in the world decide things, considering this and that, considering possibilities. You know that you could dismiss me forever as soon as we were away.' A smile lightened for a moment behind the sad poised mask.

Hannah sighed a long sigh and looked away from him. 'I doubt if you really want this. But why do you think you deserve it?' She spoke as a queen, one who highly disposes of herself.

'I am the only one who has loved you and not used you.'

'What were you doing all these seven years if you were not "using me"?'

'Waiting for you to wake up. You *have* woken up. You are awake now. Come, move, act, before you fall asleep again.'

'You think Gerald woke me up?'

Pip unfolded his arms and opened his drooping hands before her in a gesture of prayer. 'I have a right –'

'You mean if someone's going to have me it may as well be you. Perhaps it was you that Gerald awakened!'

She said it brutally, and for that second Marian, watching from the window, stilled and almost without breath, saw her not as a queen but as a great courtesan, saw her, she suddenly thought, as Violet Evercreech saw her: a woman infinitely capable of crimes.

Pip looked at her, and the dignity of his face dissolved into

223

supplication. Then he moved. Everyone in the room flinched. But he merely stepped forward and fell on one knee. There was still a space between them. 'Don't ask what it meant for you, for me, that interval. Fold it away. You loved me once. Call up the remnant of that love. It is your only hope of life.'

Hannah was silent, in repose, staring at him thoughtfully, as at a beautiful boy brought to judgement. She did not seem so much debating as contemplating.

Marian could not bear it. She said in a clear voice, 'Go with him. Your clothes are still packed. Tell Denis to go and get the car. You are mistress here.' She moved up behind Hannah's chair. Denis had risen and moved forward too.

Hannah and Pip went on looking at each other as if no one had spoken, and a moment later Marian wondered if she had uttered the words only in her mind. The immobility continued; and then Hannah began to move and fidget. It was like the moment after the host has been lifted, when the silence of adoration is quietly broken. When she spoke it was in the old irritable almost whining tone. 'No, Pip. I wish you hadn't come. It's no use.'

Pip rose slowly where he was. 'Why not?'

'I thought it would never matter. I thought I would never see you again. You may not have used me, but I have used you.'

'No, no –' he said softly, putting her words away with a gesture.

But she went on, fidgeting with the neck of her gown, turned now a little toward the rainy window. 'I suffered too much for you. At the beginning. The suffering did not end in me. I thrust it back towards you in resentment. If you do not understand that, you are a dupe of the story after all. Did you expect me not to blame you? Did you expect me to go on loving you? Did you expect me not to curse you?'

He said quietly after a moment's silence, 'Yes, I think I did expect these things.'

'Well, you expected too much!' It was the voice of an aggrieved querulous woman. 'You are a blackened image. You can work no miracles for me, Pip. You ought not to have come to watch me. Go away. Go away, as you said, from Riders and don't ever come back. Go, go, go!'

He looked down at her and his face became quiet, as if she had receded from him into the remoteness of art. Tears gathered in his eyes and he blinked to release them. They were large still tears such as men weep in solitude over beautiful things. To weep like that over a human being was a most desolate homage.

He began to withdraw slowly, collecting himself towards the door. He paused. 'Shall I send my father to see you?' The question seemed detached, the beginning of another subject.

Hannah rose, and anger and resentment inhabited her whole person. 'No! What have I to do with your father? Let him keep to his choice and leave me to mine. Go.'

Denis began to open the door. Pip had paused and had turned back as if he might implore her again. Then Gerald entered.

There was no doubt that he had been waiting and listening outside and that he came now to terminate the interview. Marian felt at that instant how Gerald attracted the hatred of everyone in the room, and although no one moved it was as if they all swirled about him. There was a black hole where he was.

It was dark in the room now. The rain hissed steadily outside. Gerald was smiling. Hannah moved slowly across to the window and lay against it with her head touching the pane. Gerald held the door wide open and Pip passed through it without haste, and then Gerald was closing the door. It was the defeat of a man by a beast.

There was silence. Hannah said in a low voice to herself, 'Oh dear.' Gerald waited, leaning against the closed door, to give Pip time to leave the house. He was still smiling. Then he opened the door again. 'You two can get out. Get moving.'

Denis, who had been standing perfectly still, gave a sudden exclamation and for just a second Marian expected him to strike Gerald. But instead he ran out of the room. Marian moved slowly to follow him. She tried to bring herself to speak to Hannah, to touch her, but she could not, she could not even look at her. All she could see was Gerald's grinning face. As she neared him he shot out a hand and gripped her arm hard.

She hung in his grasp like a terrified punished child. 'Go to your room, Maid Marian, and stay there. I shall want to talk to you.' He pivoted her to the door. The last she saw were his teeth, wide, white and metallic. Then she was outside and the door was bolted.

Chapter Twenty-nine

The light inside the house was sallow and cold. She ran along the upper corridor but could not see where Denis had gone. The tasselled curtains flicked her face as she passed through. She stopped at the stairhead and called him softly. The place was silent, yet with a sense of people brooding behind their doors. In fear of the house she moved to the big landing window. The rain was leaking in through the closed window and lay in pools upon the floor. She looked out at the yellowish rain-lashed garden and saw with a shock a figure standing still beside one of the fish pools. Then she saw that it was Denis. Yet his solitary presence there in the rain and his quick translation from the house to the garden lent him an eerie quality.

Marian ran down the stairs and out through the back of the house on to the slippery glistening terrace. The rain had abated a little. It enclosed her in a cold, fragrant, drifting, penetrating cloud as she ran towards Denis. He was standing looking down at the black trembling surface of the pool. His hair was flattened to his head in long dark streaks and the water dripped from his nose and chin.

'Denis, Denis, come inside. You're getting all wet. Come with me, come inside.'

He let her lead him back into the house and on into the drawing-room. The rain water stood out in drops upon the close tweed of his coat and as Marian tried to brush them off he stood preoccupied and silent, staring over her shoulder. She went to fetch a towel, and when she returned he had laid himself face downward on the couch. Marian looked at him for a while and then began slowly to dry her own face and hair. Isolated from her by his grief, he seemed an almost frightening object. She sat down on the floor beside him.

Now everything was the same as before. Yet everything was also different and much worse. That earlier time, which had at moments seemed a nightmare, looked now like a period of innocence and unconsciousness and peace. She had imagined that something had been wound to a conclusion and that she had been set free. She had been ready to go. Yet it was merely the turn of the screw, the turn to the next spiral. She was not free to go, she was more deeply involved than ever; and if Hannah chose to suffer, she chose a suffering now for all of them which they could not avoid.

Marian took hold of Denis's hand. It was as cold and as limp as a dead fish. His face was still buried in the cushions. How little she knew about this being with whom she felt now so connected. Had she, by coveting him, by seizing him, done him a harm for which he would detest her? She recalled his cry of 'We are faithless, faithless.' How much more faithless did they not seem *now*, recalled to their former places. And as Marian looked at Denis's humped shoulder and at the streaks of black hair upon his neck she thought: I am not Hannah's equal, for I am connected with her through him.

She thought too: he is now connected with her through me, and he may hate me for this. The shadow of Hannah had been upon her at the salmon pool. Denis must now doubly, because of Gerald and because of her, think of Hannah as a woman who might be possessed. His pains, which had been simple and pure before, would be darkened now. But they were all darkened now by what Hannah had done, and because Hannah was no longer innocent she could no longer save them.

It's odd, she thought, there is no one to appeal to any more, not even Peter. There is no outside any more. Everything is inside, the sphere is closed upon itself, and we can't get out. Pip had gone, he would wait and watch no longer. Effingham had deserted to the world of ordinary life and reason. She and Denis were ruined servants. The human world was at an end. Now they could only wait for Gerald to come down and whip them to the stables and turn them into swine.

Marian found herself crying quietly. She thought, I am becoming a bit mad. Gerald had told her to go to her room and wait. Through Hannah Gerald now had them all at his disposal. Gerald towered in her imagination: it was as if he were indeed a black man, a colossal Moor. And Marian apprehended with prophetic terror the quality of the new spiral. She feared and detested Gerald; yet something in her also said quite clearly: do what you will.

In a sudden fright she knelt up beside Denis, shaking him. 'Please speak to me. I am having terrible thoughts. Denis, what can we do? What can we do for Hannah, for ourselves?'

He rolled over slowly. His face, upon which she had expected to see agony, was curiously serene and thoughtful. He leaned his head back, looking wide-eyed at the ceiling, silent for a while. 'Ah, if she had only not done *that*. She has changed us all.'

'I know.' It was a relief just to talk, like the consolation of prayer. 'Denis, I'm so frightened of Gerald.'

Denis murmured, still regarding the ceiling, 'He has become like him. He has *become* him. That is what has happened.'

'You mean –?'

'Gerald is Peter now. He has Peter's place, he is possessed by Peter, he even looks like Peter. He is no longer what keeps Peter away from her. Nothing keeps him off her now.'

'So it is – like it was at the beginning – it is the beginning –'

'Only worse. Peter, Gerald, they have learnt a lot in seven years. This is a spiritual not a physical thing.'

Marian was silent. She was afraid to look at the apparitions which Denis was calling up; she was afraid of Denis, this suddenly cool, savage, preoccupied man. His face was beautiful though, and younger, as if a wind had swept away all the wrinkles of human fret and worry. She could not understand this sudden calm and it did little to quiet her. She said at last, 'What are you thinking?'

'Whether one must not in the end fight evil with evil.'

'No!' But she said it, she knew even then, not because she abhorred evil, but because she too much feared it.

Her word had scarcely sounded when a great deafening noise rang thunderously through the house. The house shook with it. Marian leapt terrified to her feet, but not more quickly than

Denis, who was already at the door of the room, uttering, in the echoes of the strange sound, a great wail of pain. Then Marian realized what it was. It was the sound of a shotgun being fired upstairs.

Denis and Marian crossed the ante-room. They could hear behind them the sound of running feet converging from different parts of the house. Denis had been gabbling something to himself as he ran. Now he hurled himself against the door. It was still bolted. Marian had an impression of many people crowding behind her. Denis had begun to kick the door, splintering the wood, when suddenly the bolt was withdrawn and the door was opened slowly from within.

They fell silent outside. Then Denis entered the room and Marian followed. Hannah was standing by the window looking out at the rain. The shotgun was leaning against her thigh. Her face had the calm angelic look which Denis's face had worn a few moments since. Gerald was lying on the floor.

Denis ran to Hannah and took the gun away from her. Marian looked down at what was at her feet. There could be no doubting what she saw. She was aware of Hannah sinking slowly to the ground and Denis kneeling beside her. She heard the slight bump as the red-golden head struck the floor. She stepped back so as to see no more. The sphere was shattered now and the open sky looked in. Hannah had brought the day of judgement upon them.

Part Six

Chapter Thirty

Effingham and Alice paused in the darkened hall. There was a disagreeable stifling smell, perhaps of something burning. A weird sound was issuing from the drawing-room, a lilting, singing, whining sound, rising and falling continuously. Effingham had been long enough in that part of the world to know what it was, and he shuddered. Alice took his hand. There seemed to be no one about. Yet they had come at once as soon as they got Marian's note with the dreadful news.

They whispered to each other, not daring to speak aloud. Then Marian materialized upon the stairs. 'Not in there. Come upstairs to my room, will you.'

They followed her up into the darkness. The rain was still falling heavily and the leaden evening sky could send no light into the house. A lamp was lit in Marian's room.

Marian closed the door and then turned to face them with a little moan. Alice put her arms round her. Effingham looked at the two women clinging together with their eyes closed. He felt paralysed, stupefied, filled with blind horror and revulsion. He could still scarcely believe what Marian had said in her letter.

Alice slowly released her. 'Who is that keening?'

'Gerald's mother. She's been in the house – ever since.'

'Why didn't you let us know at once?' said Effingham.

'So much has been happening all day. We've had the police here. Jamesie had to go to Blackport to contact them and to telephone New York. And someone's had to look after Hannah. Denis is with her now. And I couldn't find a man to take the note. Oh God –'

'Steady, steady,' said Alice. 'We'd have arrived sooner only we had to take the inland road because of the rain. The lower road is rather silted up. And half your drive is washed away, we could hardly get up it. What happened with the police?'

'It was very weird. They were terribly simple men. Violet just told them there had been a ghastly accident, and they wrote it all down as she said.'

'They will treat what we do as our own affair. I don't suppose you'll hear anything more from them. We've destroyed your note, of course. Did they say there'd be an inquest?'

'They said there was no need for one. The undertaker has been too. He somehow knew and came of his own accord. He says we can't – bury Gerald anyway until the rain stops. Oh, Alice –'

Effingham went over to the window. He looked out into the depths of the rain. Nothing could be seen but grey rain behind rain.

He said, 'What happened about New York?'

'Peter's coming over by jet. He should be here some time tonight or early tomorrow morning. Someone will have to meet him at the airport.'

'And Hannah –?'

'She hasn't spoken a word since then. I've sat with her, and Denis has sat with her, and Violet. She just stays quite quiet, looking rather puzzled. She ate some lunch and some tea in an ordinary way, but she won't speak. We kept her away from the police of course. Violet said Gerald was cleaning his gun when it happened.'

'Do you think she's –' Effingham choked on the words. 'Do you think she's – deranged – that her reason has given way?'

Marian wiped her eyes. 'I don't know. She's in a terribly shocked state, but so she was before and got over it. I don't think she's any more – deranged now than she ever was.'

'And how much that is is anyone's guess,' said Alice shortly.

'Shall I go and see her?' said Effingham.

Since his departure from the house that morning Effingham had been talking almost continuously to Alice. The subject of his talk had been Hannah, or rather, that is, Effingham. He had explained it all to Alice from the very beginning. He understood it now, he saw exactly how it had been. Hannah had been to him the chaste mother-goddess, the Virgin mother. The sin which Hannah was, through her own sinless suffering, redeeming for him had been the sin of his own mother's betrayal of him with his own father. Hannah was the mother who sequestered, immaculate, chaste, the unmoved mover. Because of his unconscious resentment of his own mother's sin of sex, he had been, he explained, unable to establish any satisfactory relations with women other than those of Courtly Love. He would identify the woman he loved with his mother and then make her unapproachable and holy.

Hannah of course fitted this role perfectly. Or had done. Of course it was all impossible now. He had not really loved Hannah, he had loved a dream figure which he had been able to superimpose upon her – as long as she was chaste and untouched. Now he recognized, through the very collapse of his whole structure of emotions, what it was that he had been up to. It was interesting and curious, really. When he searched his heart it seemed as if his love for Hannah had ceased, had been abruptly switched off. Of course, things didn't really happen as quickly as that, and he could not regard himself as 'cured'. The difficulty always was to bring to the passions the news which the reason was so much readier to learn. He would have slowly to take in what he had done, to take it in to his whole self. And when he had thoroughly learnt it perhaps he would be free to love properly, to escape from this frustrating pattern. He understood himself at last; but he would need to recite the solution, like a charm, many times over before he should be really free. Alice should help him. She would hear his lesson. And when he had recited it to her enough times he would become hers in wholeness and truth in the present, as he was already hers prophetically, and through their long common past. He felt, with her, home. *She* was real to him and had been all along. Only let her hear him repeat the exorcism and all would be well.

Alice had listened to him with a sceptical face, with sudden bursts of tears, but she had held his hand as he talked wildly hour after hour. She had twice suggested that he should talk to her father, but Effingham had refused. He was not yet ready to face Max. He had not yet repeated the charm enough times. Max would not understand. He had to strengthen himself further, he had more fully to convert Alice, before he could face Max. Alice herself had of course been in to see her father to tell him what had happened at the other house, but Max had apparently sent no summons to Effingham. So the hours had passed.

The arrival of Marian's note had put an abrupt end to Effingham's self-analysis, which was by then becoming rather feverish and repetitive. His immediate feeling on learning what had happened was, after the first extreme shock, a sort of violent guilt which was indistinguishable from resentment. How could he be so horribly put in the wrong, just when he was beginning to extricate himself and to talk honesty and sense about his position? His next feeling was one of pity which was indistinguishable from horror. What had she done? What had she done now, and what in the past? For the new crime suddenly cast back upon the old crime a certain lurid light; and Violet Evercreech's cry rang in his ears again, 'a murderous adulterous woman'. Then he felt compassion and then he felt fear. He had never, he knew now, understood Hannah, or seen in her the violence which lay behind her apparent resignation. He had seen her as an innocent, as a lamb led to the slaughter. Yet why? He had had his own good reasons for suffering at her hands; she doubtless had had her own good reasons for suffering at Peter's. If it had been, for him, a psychological masquerade, so had it been for her something which had, in reality, little to do with the spiritual world whose light he had been pleased to see so purely shining all about her. It had been, after all, violence all the way. This new violence was the almost casual expression of a fierceness of character which it now seemed amazing to him that he had not previously seen and shrunk from. The change in Hannah's situation which had begun to effect his own liberation had let that violence loose. And now, since a man had died, some unimaginably different state of affairs must come to be, just as he was beginning to understand the old one. He looked with sick amazement at Gerald's clothes, which he still had in his room at Riders. Some transforming mystery had come upon them all. Then it was that he wanted desperately to speak to Max, but the old man refused to see him.

Effingham felt bound to ask to see Hannah, but he did not feel at all ready for it. He felt frightened, guilty and ashamed. He could not help feeling that what had happened must somehow, though he could not quite see how, be his fault. At Hannah's greatest moment of need he had abandoned her for Alice. Or rather, he had abandoned her for some more urgent, and it almost now seemed to him abstract, concern with his own destiny. Alice's love for him had made the place, the vacuum, into which he had been able to step aside to reassemble himself. Yet there had been some inevitability in this, and it was as if Hannah's own destiny, assembling itself for a violent dénouement, had simply thrust him aside. He had been cleared away as useless. He felt his guilt merge with resentment, and with a sheer fear of her, as of something poisonous or radioactive. He shivered and sickened at the thought of what she had done, he felt the shock of it through his whole body as if he were being threatened himself. He did not really want to see her yet.

'I don't know that there's any point in your seeing her,' said Marian. 'She won't talk to you and I don't think she should be troubled any more.' Her voice trembled tearfully. 'Anyway, I don't think Violet and Jamesie will let anyone see her, except me and Denis, before Peter comes. One of them is always in the ante-room. They're keeping her shut up.'

'So Violet and Jamesie have taken over?' said Alice.

'Well, someone had to,' said Marian rather fiercely, as if she were being accused. 'Denis isn't concerned with anything except sitting with Hannah and he'll hardly utter a word. Someone had to deal with the situation, and I just couldn't by myself. Violet really took charge.'

'Was Jamesie – very upset?'

'Yes, I suppose so. He behaved oddly. He was quite hysterical first of all. Then he suddenly stopped that and began to rush round the house looking for things.'

'Looking for things?'

'Yes, for letters and things. He and Violet have practically taken the house to pieces looking for papers and things. One of the maids said they were looking for Hannah's will.'

'For her *will*?' said Effingham. He was chilled by the murky room and by the silence of the house in his back. It was getting dark outside. He shivered.

'Yes. I think Violet thinks Hannah made a will in her favour and she wants to get it to a safe place before Peter comes. And there are a lot of other things, things they want to hide and destroy. Jamesie has burnt a lot of photographs. And they've been burning letters and all sorts of things. They couldn't burn them outside, so they've had a sort of perpetual bonfire in the kitchen boiler. You must have smelt it as you came in.'

'I can imagine,' said Alice drily, 'that the house would need some sweeping and garnishing before Peter's arrival.'

'Peter, yes. I can hardly believe he's coming. This time to-morrow he will be here.'

They were silent. Alice turned up the oil-lamp a little. The rain continued its dull roar. The sound of keening was distantly heard from below. Effingham thought, poor Gerald. Then he thought, and it might have been me. Who knew if the violence which Hannah's quiet years had stored up between these walls had yet spent its force? He began desperately to want to leave the house.

Alice said, 'You must let us stay, Marian.'

Marian rose. The lamp lighted half her face. She quieted her mouth with her hand. Now it was dark outside. She said, 'I'm awfully frightened. I'd be very glad if you would stay. I've hardly talked to Denis, but I know he's afraid that Peter, when he arrives, will just go berserk or something.'

Effingham said, 'But our presence here, as outsiders, will only make him madder.' He was appalled, terrified, at the idea of being found in the house by Peter.

'I've thought about this. I'm even more frightened of what will happen if you're not here. I want to crowd the house with people. It may be just a matter of getting through the first twenty-four hours without something dreadful.'

Effingham started to protest again, but Alice spoke more

loudly. 'Effie, one of us must go back and tell my father we're staying. Shall I go?'

'That's just it,' said Marian, and her high-pitched nervous voice rang decisively. 'I want you to go and fetch your father. I want him to be in the house when Peter comes. If he is here, I feel everything will be all right.'

'Fetch Max, bring him here!' Effingham jumped up. This was another kind of violence. He needed time to decide upon his own view of the story, to regroup his emotions, to sketch out his own salvation. He did not want Max to enter suddenly upon the scene. He did not want Max to contain him in any picture of the destiny of Hannah. The story, after all, was his, he had suffered enough for it.

'Capital idea,' said Alice, as if it were the most ordinary of suggestions. 'I'll go and get him, Effie.'

'I'll come with you,' said Effingham. 'He may need persuading. And anyway I must get some clothes and things.' He would not stay behind in the dark house with Hannah imprisoned and Peter approaching.

'Then we'd better go at once,' said Alice. 'The roads may soon be impassable.'

'Yes, yes, go. And bring your father back, whatever you do. Here, take this lamp. It's all right, I have a candle. I won't come down with you. I'll go back to Hannah. But, oh, come back soon, soon. I shall be waiting for you, listening for the car. Come back very soon. I am so frightened.'

She opened the door for them and the lamp in Alice's hand showed the empty corridor and the red looped velvet hangings. The sound of keening was louder, regular, endless. The smell of burning paper floated up from below.

Chapter Thirty-one

Marian woke with a start, and terror immediately, with consciousness, invaded her limbs and made them rigid. It was pitch dark in the room, but she knew that someone was standing beside her bed. She tried to move and speak, but it was as if her throat were being held. She gasped and cowered back.

Then with a sharp sound a match was struck and she saw the face of Jamesie close above her.

It must be many hours now since Denis had set off in the Land Rover for the airport. 'Has he come?'

'Ssh. No, no one's come. It's only four o'clock.'

Four o'clock. Why had not Alice and Effingham come back with Max? She should never have let them go away.

Marian had been asleep on a couch in Hannah's ante-room. She had remained with Hannah until the latter had showed signs of wanting to go to bed. Hannah had still not spoken, though she had begun, in the later evening, to murmur various things to herself. Marian could not make out what these murmurings were, and she had several times tried in vain to make Hannah speak to her. She had helped Hannah to bed, and seen her instantly fall asleep. The beautiful face, which had all day been wrinkled in a puzzled painful frown, became smooth and young, flooded with innocence and forgetfulness. Perhaps Hannah had now forgotten and would never more remember. Perhaps, it occurred to Marian as she sat watching beside her, she had forgotten Gerald, and had earlier forgotten Peter, forgotten what she had done to Peter. And with that there rose the image of the maimed returning husband, and Marian had shuddered and turned to find a tall figure in the doorway.

It was Violet Evercreech. She had come to lock the room. She told Marian that she might stay inside or come outside, but

238

locked the room must be until the morning. Marian did not want to be separated from Hannah by a locked door. But she decided she had better be on the outside. She was momently expecting the party from Riders. So she had come out, leaving Hannah sleeping, and had seen Violet turn the key in the lock of Hannah's sitting-room and depart. After that Marian had fetched blankets and lain down on the couch in the ante-room. Sleep had come at once.

'Light the candle. Here it is.' She spoke softly. Hannah's bedroom was beyond the sitting-room, but she did not want to risk waking her. She feared Hannah's return to consciousness.

Jamesie lit the candle, and placed it on the table beside her. He went on looking at her.

Marian felt afraid of Jamesie. She was afraid of everyone now. She had even been frightened by Denis, by his long silences, by his air of being elsewhere. It was as if his spirit had taken flight from his body. He had held on to her hand, when they sat together, and caressed it. But he had been looking through her at something else. With Hannah he had behaved quietly, hovering about her silently, and she had seemed somehow glad of him, more aware of him than she was of Marian. But he had not touched Hannah. He moved about her as if compelled by an aura which both attracted and protected, and he looked at her through it as one might look at some weird but holy relic in a casket. Marian touched her, partly in the natural course of her tasks, but partly too through some compulsive fascination; and Hannah's flesh felt inert and cold, as if from her too the spirit were being slowly withdrawn.

Denis had shown considerable hesitation about whether he should go to the airport himself or send one of the men. Jamesie had refused to go, and neither Marian nor Violet could drive. Denis had hesitated long, holding Marian's hand in an absent childish way, but without at all discussing with her which he should do. He decided in the end to go, and set off into the black darkness and a rain so opaque and thick that it completely deadened the headlights. The interior of the Land Rover was soaked, through its rickety hood, a moment after it left its garage. Marian had run across the terrace in her mackintosh and sat with him for a moment in the front of the car, while a dim light from the dashboard illumined his dripping head. They embraced, hugging each other awkwardly in the narrow space. 'Be very careful. The road to Blackport may be dreadful. Hadn't you better go inland?'

'No. The coast road is quicker. It will be all right. God bless you. Look after her.'

He had started the engine, and as she got out the car moved off and instantly vanished into total darkness. There was a roaring sound behind the rain which was perhaps the sea. She had waited a while under the porch, trying to imagine that she made out the lights of the Humber approaching, but nothing came, and she had gone back past the now silent drawing-room to rejoin Hannah.

'What is it, Jamesie?' Marian stood up and drew on her overcoat. She had lain down in her clothes. It was very cold in the room now, and the candle flickered in a draught. Marian glanced at Hannah's door, but it was closed as before.

He did not reply, but sat down near her and seemed to listen. Marian listened too. There was complete silence in the house. The rain could be heard all about them pattering noisily on the roof and gurgling along the gutters and battering the terrace and the garden, merging into a deep continuous roar, which seemed to surround the house's silence and make it more intense. Marian sat down again and drew a blanket over her knees. Four o'clock.

The image of Gerald suddenly rose before her like an apparition. She had not, in all yesterday's mad anguish, had a full thought, a full heart, to spare for him. She had been appalled for Hannah, in terror about the police. Now in the cold dark he seemed to rise. She had not seen them carry him downstairs, and had only known of his whereabouts when the cries of his mother had echoed from the drawing-room, to be followed by the long undulating whine. She thought of him lying there now in the dark with the old woman beside him, lying there lonely and without power any more, reduced to nothing. She whimpered at the thought, and found her tears coming, tears of pity and fear, tears for him and for herself. Now in the black middle of the night it was the fact of death that mattered most, the translation of a big, healthy, powerful man into a piece of senseless heavy stuff.

Marian felt that in a moment she might break out into hysterical gasping. She took a deep slow breath and gripped the blanket, feeling its thick furry texture. She must not show her fear to Jamesie. If Jamesie knew how afraid she was he might, like some wild animal when its human opponent falters, break out in some way, occasion some new appalling thing, she knew not what. In this darkness everyone was dangerous; and Marian felt it all round about her, the accumulated vicious savagery of the house, ready to rush through again when any weak point should be found. She must hold on to her courage and her sanity or she herself would become that weak point and let through the terrible flood.

'Jamesie, can you not light the lamp? It's so dark.'

'There's no oil. There is no oil in the whole house.'

'Why did you come and wake me up?' For her too the return of consciousness was hateful. It would have been better to have slept on.

'I wanted to watch with you,' Jamesie was sitting near her, still looking at her, his legs crossed and his hands in his pockets. He suddenly seemed to her to have the air of a gaoler. But was she not herself now a gaoler? The house was now more totally a prison than it had ever been.

Jamesie stared. She could see his eyes, darker and larger in the very dim light. The wavering candle flame cast moving shadows across his features, making them mobile and grotesque. It came to Marian that he was full of purpose, he was going to do something, he had come to her with some end. She shrank back from him. She had not let her mind dwell upon the mystery of his relation with Gerald. It confronted her now, and she felt in the staring boy the new madness of the house collected and wakeful.

Wakeful. Jamesie was listening again. He became very still, seeming to urge her to listen too. But she could hear only the endless mingled battering of the rain. She thought of Peter coming steadily through the darkness toward the house.

Jamesie got up. He kept his alert questioning stare upon Marian. Though he was so quiet he seemed excited or very frightened. He lifted the candle from beside her and went to stand in the middle of the room. Then he slowly raised the candle above his head and looked away from her.

She could not at first understand the ritual. She watched him breathless, still straining her ears. Then she heard a tiny sound in the room itself, and she followed Jamesie's gaze. The handle of Hannah's door was quietly turning. It turned, and then slipped back, and turned again. Hannah was trying to get out.

Marian felt the hair rising on her head. There was something hideous and uncanny in the quiet desperate little movement. She knew that she ought to dispel her sudden crazy terror by speaking out loud to Hannah. But she could not speak. Hannah was imprisoned now in the small centre, in the very heart of things; and perhaps it was there that Peter would keep her shut up now, imprisoned in that room for ever. The handle turned again.

She stared at Jamesie, who was looking at her with his enormous night eyes. He had lowered the candle which made his face golden from below. His lips were parted and he looked at her with a fearful urgency, trembling with purpose.

Marian said in a low whisper, 'Have you got the key? Should I go in to her?'

Jamesie put his finger on his lips. He motioned her to rise and took her arm and led her outside into the corridor. He closed the door of the ante-room and put the candle on the floor beside them.

'What is it? Jamesie, you're frightening me.'

The long corridor stretched away behind them, dark and quiet. She could not see Jamesie's face now. The light of the candle seemed to swirl about their knees and get lost. He still gripped her arm.

'We must let her out.'

Marian heard him, but without understanding. 'You mean you must let me in. Have you got the key?'

'Yes. I tell you we must let her out.'

Marian stood quiet while the sense of the words expanded round about her seeming to fill the house with resonant echoes. It was as if now everybody must awake, must be awake, standing in the darkness beyond the candle flame, listening to what would be. Had it come at last then, the moment of liberation? Hannah now *wanted* to get out. The idea was terrifying and painful.

She said, still whispering, 'You are mad, Jamesie. Where could she go, what could she do, leaving the house like this at night and in this rain?' The answer seemed to echo, booming round about them under the dome of the rain. She held on to Jamesie now. They clung together like conspirators, like threatened children.

'We must let her out,' he said again. 'It is her right. We must let her go before Peter comes.'

Marian felt a sharp spasm of pain: why should it be to me, to me that this comes? She said, 'No, no. We can take her away tomorrow in the car.'

'Take her away? Where to? What for? Peter will be here any moment. No, this is the time and this is the way. We must simply open the door.'

'No. Jamesie, I can't. Why did you wake me, anyway? Why didn't you just open the door yourself?'

'I had to have you too. Don't be afraid, Marian. This is how it must be. Come.'

He opened the door of the ante-room and began to draw her back. As the door opened the candle flared up for a moment and then went out. They stood immobile together, still holding on to each other, in the dark room. Then Marian saw that there was a little grey light. The morning was coming.

She murmured again: 'No!' pitifully. But Jamesie was fumbling for the key. She watched him with fascination as he found it and quietly inserted it in the lock and turned it. He pushed the door open a little and stood back.

Marian shrank back against the wall. She felt that some dreadful apparition was about to pass through the room. Jamesie stood opposite to her, his eyes fixed on the dark gap of the door. The light was increasing.

They waited, perfectly still, for several minutes. Then there was a little sound from within. Marian was open-mouthed, almost gasping. Then the door moved and a shape was there in the doorway.

After a moment's pause she moved noiselessly forward through the room and passed between them. Her face was indistinct but her figure was clearly seen in the first cold twilight. She was wearing an overcoat and her feet were bare. She disappeared into the corridor. Marian became aware that Jamesie opposite to her had fallen to his knees. As she moved to the window he slowly stretched himself out full length face-downwards on the ground.

The terrace was grey and empty, glistening with running water. The rain had become less fierce and it was just possible to see across the battered garden to the wall and the gate. The next moment Hannah was there on the terrace. She glided with unhurrying swiftness down the steps and past the fish pools and along the path between the ragged yews, a figure so blurred and uncertain that it might have been a ghost. She passed through the door in the wall and disappeared into the rain beyond.

Chapter Thirty-two

'Take her inside.'

Violet slowly opened the glass doors, and the men, who had laid their burden down upon the terrace, lifted it again and began to shuffle in. It was still raining.

Marian followed them. She was scarcely able to walk and held on to the glass doors as she went through. She stood uncertainly behind them as they passed into the drawing-room. She saw the other white draped figure within. As Violet led the men and told them what to do, Marian met her long fatigued eyes through the closing door. Violet looked at her not with hatred but as if she were a complete stranger. She was now, in this house, a total outlaw. She began to go slowly up the stairs.

The time, she supposed, must be about nine o'clock. Or it might be earlier. All the clocks seemed to have stopped. Hannah had been found almost at once. A fisherman had seen it happen, and her body had been recovered without much difficulty from where it lay among the rocks. It had been brought up to the house soon after the arrival of the first messenger with the news.

When she had emerged from her trance, or prayer, at Hannah's window she had found Jamesie gone. She had returned to her own room and lain down. She kept dozing off into a nightmare-ridden half-sleep, to wake quickly each time in a fright, listening and wondering. Once she imagined she heard Hannah calling her just as she woke, and once she set off to Hannah's room to see if she had come back but gave up half way. She could not see that place again. At the stairhead she found herself suddenly expecting to meet Gerald, and she ran all the way to her own room. After that she sat at the window until she saw first the running panting messenger and then the slow cavalcade. She looked now along the drive. She dreaded the appearance of the Land Rover.

The gathering daylight had brought with it, as she gazed from the window, another shock. She had been looking at the grey composing shapes of the valley and had become aware that they seemed to be composing in a very strange way. She almost for a while wondered if she were dreaming, in one of those weird dreams where a waking consciousness seems to accompany the dreamer. The scene outside looked entirely different. She turned back several times to the room to make sure that she was indeed in her own room and not in some quite other part of the house which had a view she had never seen before. But her room was familiar, and on the far side of the valley she saw, as the light gained, the unaltered silhouette of Riders. But the valley between was utterly changed: and then at last she realized what had happened and why it was that Effingham and the others had not come back. There was a huge torrent, wide, brown and turgid, roaring down the centre, dividing the two houses. The bog had released its waters.

The bridge had completely disappeared, and the white cottages were submerged to half their height. The stream had cut a steep-walled cleft at the top of the valley through which it descended, straight and very fast, its former meanderings forgotten. Further down it spread out, boiling and foaming among the boulders, casting thick lines of debris upon the shore, and surging forward in the centre with the violent motion of a big fast river. The bottom of the valley had become a surging lake, hundreds of yards wide, where with a churning of brown and white, in a series of whirlpools, the waters met the sea.

It must have become, soon after Effingham and Alice had departed last night, quite impossible to get across. Marian looked upon the wrecked, altered scene with appalled amazement, and then with a kind of dazed relief. The general cataclysm dulled her own pain. She trained her field-glasses upon the valley. The lower slopes were strewn with a wide debris of stones and bushes. She made out the bedraggled corpse of a sheep. Further up there were pale glistening streaks among the heather which she later saw to be dead salmon lying broadcast upon the hillside. The river must, in the night, have been even more tremendous. No one could possibly have crossed it.

The rain was gradually abating now and the sky was lightening, turning to a dirty light yellow and bringing a new sharp clarity to the devastated scene. Marian looked through her glasses at Riders, but could see no signs of life whatsoever in the other house. It lay above the rushing waters like a stranded and abandoned ship. It seemed to her confused mind a very long time since she had said in such imploring tones that she wanted to crowd the house with people. Crowds were no use now any more. This was the end game.

Marian had not yet dared to think fully or properly about what had happened in the night. At times it seemed like a dream, something done in unconsciousness; and in certain moments of half-sleep she thought that perhaps it was just a fantasy in her mind and that she had imagined it all. Yet, with a pain which had not yet fully claimed her, she knew that there had been an act and that it belonged to her. Even Jamesie seemed like an accessory; she did not even trouble to reflect upon Jamesie's motives, so little did he seem responsible. It was she who had done the thing that mattered. Had she done right to give Hannah this last thing, the freedom to make her life over in her own way into her own property? When at last Hannah had wanted to break the mirror, to go out through the gate, ought she *then* to have been her gaoler? It was not any more the old image of freedom which could move her now. It was Hannah's authority which had moved her, her sense, in the pathetic scene of her final imprisonment, of Hannah's sovereignty, of her royal right to dispose of herself as she would. Marian could not at that moment have been her keeper. The memory came to her of Jamesie kneeling upon the floor and Hannah gliding past. But had she done right? She could not yet give the words a sense. But she knew, as she moaned and rubbed her forehead upon the cold window pane, that she had taken upon herself a blood guilt which would make its own reckoning.

No one could be her judge. But there was one person who could help her and that was Denis, because he was innocent and because he loved Hannah. And although he could not be her judge he could, she felt, at least if necessary be her executioner. Denis and Peter were coming together. Now their figures merged strangely in her mind. Her task had been to protect Hannah. She had performed it, but too perfectly. And now she stood, as it were, in Hannah's place and it was perhaps on her that the axe would fall. She turned to look for the hundredth time along the length of the drive.

A car had appeared in the distance near to the gates and was approaching slowly over the devastated gravel. It was not the Land Rover. It was not the Humber either. It was a completely strange car. Marian gazed at it with fear and confusion. Was this some quite new person coming, some quite strange person coming to Gaze from the outside world, some doctor or some inspector, someone who would assess, clear up, explain and punish? The car approached the house and stopped. Then the door opened and Denis got out. He was alone.

Marian turned about and shot out of her room. Her flying heels made an echoing din along the corridor and down the stairs. The house she ran through echoed as if it had already been emptied of its people and its things. There was no one about and no one on the terrace when she got there just as Denis was mounting the steps. She saw his face, strained and exhausted, strangely blank. When he saw her the features seemed to droop with a sudden relief and he opened his arms to her. He looked familiar now, renewed, restored. But she closed her eye against his shoulder with a groan. It was clear that he did not yet know.

She became aware that his clothes were dripping wet and stiff with mud and sand. She held him off a little, gripping him hard and careless who saw them from the windows behind. 'Where's Peter?'

Denis held her two forearms firmly as if to prevent her from falling. They stood there like two wrestlers.

'Peter. You haven't heard?'

'No –'

'Peter is drowned.'

Marian leaned back against the balustrade, drawing him to

248

her. Behind his head the sky had become a soft bright fawn colour. It had stopped raining.

She could hardly speak. 'Drowned. How?'

'I should not have come back by the coast road. There was a great flood coming down at the Devil's Causeway. The car got out of control and went into the sea. I got out quick enough but Peter did not.' He went on holding her and staring into her eyes as if her attention could rescue him from the appalling memory. He added, 'They are bringing him now.'

Another car had appeared distantly on the drive.

He said, 'Let us go in now and tell Hannah.'

Marian's grip restrained his movement. Her mouth opened mumbling but she could find no words. Then she threw her head back and uttered a long harsh cry. After that she said, still staring at him, in a very low voice. 'It is too late. Hannah is dead.'

He closed his eyes for a moment. Then he removed her clasp from her arm and turned his back to her. As she began to whimper and to paw at his shoulder she saw beyond him the second car coming slowly nearer, bringing Peter Crean-Smith home at last.

Part Seven

Chapter Thirty-three

Effingham, driving the Humber through the rain from the night on into the morning, learnt the news about Hannah and Peter at one of the inland villages. Max and Alice were with him. They had taken an inland route which was very round-about and had been lost twice and once stopped by flood water. Carrie and two of the maids and a man-servant were following them in the Austin Seven, but they had lost touch with them far back while it was still dark. They had paused at an inn for some breakfast and been told the news.

The Humber came crawling up the drive at Gaze, bumping across the deep rain-channels, just as they were carrying Peter Crean-Smith into the house. Effingham left Alice to help Max. He ran on to the terrace and stood watching. He felt stupid, curious, excluded. The emotional current of the scene did not pass through him. He followed the procession into the house. Marian was in the hall. She was pointing to the drawing-room door, her handkerchief pressed tightly against her mouth. Denis was lying on the stairs, his face hidden. He looked like some-thing that had fallen from a great height. No one paid any attention to Effingham. He was suddenly a stranger. He wanted, like a stranger, to find someone to whom he could say, 'Oh, I am sorry, I am so sorry.'

Alice and Max were coming slowly through the door and he could see beyond them that the Austin Seven had arrived. Marian pushed past him and sat down on the bottom step. She laid her head against the banisters and began to weep in a series of low cries, 'Oh, oh, oh –' Effingham stared. It did not seem to him that he could establish any communication with Marian and Denis, and the spectacle of their grief sickened him. The others were gathered behind him. Quickly he stepped over

Denis's legs and ran up the stairs and along the corridor to Hannah's room.

He rushed in and paused in appalled confusion. The sun was shining now and the room was bright, almost welcoming as if it did not know what had passed. A clock was ticking jauntily. A last remnant of fire glowed in the grate. There was a dark stain on the carpet near the door, and the drawers of the desk were open and papers were strewn about everywhere upon the floor. But otherwise everything was the same. The pampas grass and dried honesty were stiff and immobile in their vase. Peter's photograph gazed across the room at exactly the same angle. There was the familiar smell of turf and whiskey. Surely in a moment Hannah would emerge from the inner room. Then as he stood there alone he heard the heavy dragging tread of Max and Alice's shuffle as they came along the corridor after him; and for one violent moment he was tempted to hurl himself against the door to prevent the old man from entering.

Effingham stood stiffly, staring into a corner. Something was lying there. It was Hannah's old yellow silk dressing-gown, lying there in a heap. Max moved slowly past him and sat down in Hannah's chair. Effingham gave a moan and descended abruptly on to a stool. He felt almost delirious with tiredness.

'Open the windows, would you,' said Max. He spoke with his usual authority but very wearily, letting his big head, yellow and hollowed like some Chinese object, fall heavily back against the cushions. He looked like death itself usurping Hannah's place.

Carrie, who had followed them up, ran to the window. The room seemed to be full of people.

'Brace up, Effie. Drink this.' Alice was pouring whiskey out of Hannah's decanter. She thrust it into Effingham's hand and he sipped it. It tasted of Hannah. His eyes were closing.

Fresh cool rainy air blew through the room, carrying away the close quiet smells, lifting the litter of papers along the floor and stirring the honesty and the pampas grass. Two of the maids were gathering up the papers and stuffing them back

251

into the drawers. Alice had picked up Hannah's dressing-gown and hung it on a hook.

'What is this? What are you all doing here, this great crowd of you? Why are you walking about and giving orders in this house?' Violet Evercreech stood in the doorway, leaning upon a stick. Her voice was high and piercing with anger. Jamesie stood just behind her.

Alice answered, 'Forgive us, Violet. We came to see if we could help. We only heard the news on the way.' She pushed a chair forward for Violet.

'And coming into this room, and drinking. Have you no shame? No, you cannot help. I can bury my own dead.'

She ignored the chair. Jamesie swung it to the side and sat down on it himself. He rested his elbows on his knees and covered his face. The maids retired into the ante-room.

No one spoke. Violet crashed her stick upon the floor. 'You can go. I don't need you to open windows in my house.'

Max turned his head slightly to Alice, who was leaning back against the mantelpiece, her feet wide apart. Alice said, 'Don't turn us out, Violet. We have a sort of right to be here.'

Violet looked venomously at each of them. 'Oh yes! You've lived like vampires on the sorrows of this house and now you are even come to gape at the dead.'

'Violet, don't be angry. My father is tired. We'll –'

'You'll go now, the whole gaping crowd of you. I am in charge here.'

'Anyway,' said Alice, her voice sharpening a little, 'it's a matter to be decided, I suppose, who all this *does* belong to now.'

'It belongs to me. I am Hannah's next of kin and there is no will.'

'Well, there is a will, actually,' said Alice, looking down. 'Hannah made a will in favour of my father.'

Effingham opened his eyes and jerked his head up, spilling his whiskey. Jamesie got up slowly. Alice looked at her shoes and shuffled them in the carpet.

Violet said at last in a whisper, 'Your *father*. I don't believe you.'

'Yes. She gave me a copy of it when I came over with some books and things last Christmas time. She asked me then not to tell him, and I didn't till very lately, when I thought I should. There's another copy with the solicitor in Greytown.'

Violet stared at her. Then her eyes became hazy and vague. 'What a bitch she was, what a perfect bitch!'

The words stood up in the room like an epitaph, like a monument, and there was a silence round about them. Then Alice began to say, 'Of course, we don't intend to accept –'

But Jamesie stepped into the centre. He took his sister by the arm. 'There is no more for us to say to each other. The play is over, the Vampire Play let us call it. The blood is all shed that we used to drink. We shall go away now and you will hear no more of us at all and you'll clean the house of our traces. We leave them all to you, the dead ones. You can have the house, you can conduct the funeral, yes, you can bury them and weep too if you have tears for them. They are yours now, made over to you, part of the property, all yours now that they are dead, my lord of the underworld!'

He pulled at Violet's arm. Leaning heavily upon him she turned, her eyes still vague, and they went out of the door.

Alice began to say, 'I'll go after them, I shouldn't have upset Violet like that –'

But Max shook his head. 'Not now –' Carrie closed the door from the outside.

Effingham jumped up. 'Is that true?'

'About the will? Yes. She left Father everything. Of course we –'

'Oh, shut up!' said Effingham. He strode to the window. He wanted to yell. The sun was burning the sea, searing it with a long golden scar. The sky was a pale but cloudless blue. The battered garden was entirely still. Of course, he had not thought that Hannah would leave her wealth to him, he had not thought about it at all, he had not expected that she would die. But how grotesque and hideous it was that she had made Max her heir. Why Max, the person who deserved least of her? It was like a senseless insulting joke. Now the invasion that he dreaded had taken place indeed, and it all belonged to *him*, her

253

desk, her dressing-gown, her decanter of whiskey, the pampas grass, Peter's photo, everything. Effingham found himself suddenly coveting the things, and not only the little things, but the house, the acres of moorland, the stocks and shares. She had made herself into a piece of property and given herself insanely, spitefully away. This was her death, this mean thing. It was a vulgar trick.

Max said, 'What's the matter, Effingham?' His voice was tired and cross.

Effingham thought, she is taken from me entirely. Max will scatter the earth upon her, Max will speak her funeral speech, Max will tell the world what she was.

Effingham said out of his immediate distress, 'It was an unkind decision, and rather mad, don't you think?' He was near to echoing Violet's epitaph.

Max said slowly, 'It was a romantic decision, if you like a symbolic decision. Hannah was like the rest of us. She loved what wasn't there, what was absent. This can be dangerous. Only she did not dare to love what was present too. Perhaps it would have been better if she had. She could not really love the people she saw, she could not afford to, it would have made the limitations of her life too painful. She could not, for them, transform the idea of love into something manageable: it remained something destructive and fearful and she simply avoided it.'

Alice said solemnly, 'She could have loved *you* in presence too, father. You are the person she was waiting for. I felt this very much at Christmas. Perhaps the will was a sort of hint.'

Max just shook his head.

Effingham stared at the old man, the great hollow mask, the crumpled dangling body. He said, 'So Jamesie was right. You are the owner of her death and she was waiting for you. You *are* her death and she loved you.'

He uttered the words in a sudden angry cry. Then he felt that he must get out of the room, away from that little shut-in silken scene with Max's hollow stare in the centre of it. He fumbled desperately at the door-handle. The maids, who were talking quietly in the ante-room, fell silent to let him pass. He ran down the stairs. He felt cornered, harassed, menaced. He was being driven out too, like Violet and Jamesie. He was being, in the course of some ruthless rite of purification, simply cleared away. He paused in the hall. Marian and Denis had moved and were sitting side by side on the floor near to the glass doors. Marian had turned her head so that her brow rested on Denis's shoulder. They both had their eyes closed. They looked unnecessary, absurd, like some sculptured group in an auction sale. He looked at them with a shrinking disgust. They too ought to be cleared away. He moved nearer to the drawing-room door.

The sun shone on to the gleaming terrace raising a gentle steam. There was a profound quietness outside as if nature were exhausted and resting. He had not yet really understood that she was dead. He could think of her as lost, blackened, destroyed, he could think of her as transformed into stocks and shares, he could think of her as diminished into a little idea in the mind of Max, he could not think of her as simply dead. He could not think of *her* as dead, so utterly was she now veiled from him. He had been ready to feel her death as an affront, as an act on her part of unwarrantable self-assertion. Now, with the sudden intense quietness in front of him, he felt the awful mystery of her absence sweep over him like a cloud. He opened the drawing-room door.

The lace curtains were drawn and there was a yellowish light in the room. Effingham had a strange vague memory of childhood, of lying in some sick-room in summer. He saw in the engraved twilight, as in a picture by Blake, the three recumbent forms and the folds of the white sheets reaching to the floor. They seemed already like three funereal monuments. He stood quite still. They slept together now, those three entwined destinies, they lay now helpless and complete before whatever judgement there might be in earth or heaven.

There was a slight movement in the room and Effingham started violently. Then he saw in the brown shadows a little black old woman sitting hunched on a low chair beside one of the white forms. He saw the pale round of her face, oblivious of him, herself a little grotesque image of death. Her presence made the scene suddenly more personal, more dreadfully real. He looked down at the shrouded body nearest to him. It was long and large. If that was Gerald, this must be Peter, and *that* at the far end must be her. He looked at the quiet, quiet, face-less form, but he could not stir his feet to approach nearer. She was her death now, that death which she had so much striven to emulate in life, which she had studied and practised and loved. She had succeeded, and death and she had converged into a single point. Who knew if that was victory or defeat? His last vision was of the white veil that hid her now. After all, and at last, she had become utterly private.

He felt no sharp grief only a rather frightened awe. He gazed down at the nearer figure. Perhaps it was here that he belonged, with Peter Crean-Smith. He felt then, like a sudden chill, a sense of ghoulish curiosity which he recognized as such almost before he knew its object. What had really happened to Peter when he fell over the cliff? In what way was Peter maimed or disfigured? Effingham breathed hard. There was a smell of sea-water in the room and the carpet at his feet was damp and darkened. He felt a stirring in his hand, a desire to whisk off the sheet and see what lay beneath. But again he could not. Perhaps he feared to see, not some terrible disfigured face, but laid thereupon, like a hideous mask, the likeness of his own features.

Chapter Thirty-four

Marian thrust the letter from Geoffrey into her pocket unopened. She went to the window wondering what time it was and how long she had slept.

The sky suggested that it was late afternoon. The wind had risen again and a great mountain of purple cloud was growing out of the sea. Max and Effingham and Alice had gone back to Riders that morning, not very long indeed after their arrival. Jamesie and Violet had driven away in the Morris, whether temporarily or for good was not known. Denis had gone to his own room to sleep. He would not let Marian stay with him. She had crept upstairs at last and lain down and dropped her brow into a pool of blackness.

The awakening was terrible. She awoke to the aggressive reddened afternoon and the sound of the wind. She got up and noticed Geoffrey's letter which a maid must have left there heaven knows how long ago. She washed her face which was stiff with weeping as if it had been coated with enamel. She opened the door of her room and seemed suddenly to apprehend the house as empty. There were distant creakings and murmurings and shudderings but there were no human sounds. It came to her that she might have been left behind, that everyone might have gone away and left her there alone. She stood there for a while paralysed listening.

She forced herself to move at last and went very quietly down the stairs. She feared the house was empty, yet she also feared what might be behind those many many closed doors. She paused in the hall, controlling her urge to rush outside and run and run. She felt the presences in the drawing-room. She turned back, compelling herself to re-enter the heart of the house. She must find Denis.

She both needed him and feared him now. Now that he was separated from her by her action, now that he was separated from her by the special quality of his grief, she realized that she had never for a second known him. He was as wild to her as an unfamiliar animal that has briefly let itself be caressed. She could not see his mind or predict his movements. She feared him yet she needed him: to wait at his feet, to gain from him some sense of what had happened, to receive some hint or vestige of a judgement. He would protect her against the dead.

She knocked very softly on the door of his room. There was no answer and she slowly opened the door upon the twilit curtained room. Her heart beat painfully. It took her a moment to see that there was no one there. The bed was disordered, a number of drawers stood open, there were clothes scattered upon the floor. Marian retired. She ran on into the kitchen. The huge deal table had been cleared and scrubbed, but the place was empty. The big clock ticked in the interior silence. Marian called 'Denis', quietly at first, and then with a voice high, cracked with tears and fear. There was no answer.

She kept turning to see what was behind her. Now she retreated step by step toward the window, as if something invisible in the house were cornering her. In desperation she looked out into the garden. There was a figure moving. The figure was too starkly clear in the intense light, detached from its surroundings, the same daylight spectre that she had seen before. It was Denis, standing beside one of the fish pools and staring down into it. Marian exclaimed almost with a new fear at seeing him. Then she ran from the too empty kitchen and out through the labyrinth of damp echoing stone-flagged rooms on to the wet-slippery terrace. She nearly fell and then went on more slowly.

'Denis!' She was connected with what had happened only through him. Only he could set her free from the gathered dead.

He looked towards her with a vague wild look. 'Hello, Marian. Are you feeling better?'

'I was so frightened when I woke up, I thought you'd gone. Oh, Denis, come inside and talk to me, you must talk to me.'

He focused his eyes upon her now, frowning, a small alien

258

man, his hair fanned up by the wind, hunched and shrivelling inside his overcoat as the wind blew. He looked down again at the dark brown rippling surface of the pool and was silent.

'*Please,*' said Marian. She took a step forward and reached out timidly to touch his sleeve.

He moved back from her. 'Not that.' He turned his shoulder to her and knelt down beside the pool.

Marian looked at the crouching figure. Then she saw beside him a small neat suitcase, and beyond that a gaping canvas hold-all, out of which there emerged the wide mouth of a plastic bag. The plastic bag contained water and she saw a quick movement of gold in the darkness within. A small fishing net lay by Denis's hand.

'You're catching the fish – Oh, Denis –' Marian felt her tears again. She could not bear any more crying. She knelt down beside him. 'Why are you catching the fish?'

Denis spoke in a quiet way and his accent made his speech sound almost jaunty. 'I thought I might just take some old friends away with me.'

'You're – going?'

'Yes.'

'When, where –?'

'Now. I don't know where. Why should I stay here? Don't you grieve now –'

'Denis,' said Marian. She was trying hard to be calm. 'You can't go away and leave me here. Stay a little and we'll go together. Or if you won't stay, then let me pack some things and come with you.'

He looked at her gently now as they knelt close together, and she saw above him the purple clouds parting for the evening sun. 'No. What have we to do with each other, Marian? We are strangers really to each other. We have been able to converse, we have seemed to understand each other, *here*. But even here the spell is broken and the magic is all blown away. I ought not to have let you persuade me of things. Only evil, and more evil than you know, has come of those things. We did not really love each other. We could not. You know that now, don't you?'

Marian looked at him and then looked down into the water. It was true. She had wanted to possess this sprite. But they had had no real knowledge of each other. And she had brought him an illness of the spirit almost innocently, carrying it like a germ to a remote island. She began to weep again but very quietly. She said through tears, 'Are you taking Strawberry Nose away?'

Denis paused before answering and she knew that he took her words as an acceptance of his. 'Yes. I can't catch him yet though. He's very quick. See, there he goes.'

Denis picked up the net again. The brilliant red fish glided from the shade of the lilies, darted through a cloud of dark weed, and was gone. Denis trailed the net cautiously in the water. The fish reappeared near the end of the pool, circled and approached the net. Denis made a rapid gesture and the next moment the net was lifted high, full of wet, flashing, struggling fish. Strawberry Nose fell with a plop into the plastic bag.

'What will you do with them? You said you didn't know where you were going.'

'Well, I'll likely go first across the bog. I know where there are some gipsies would lend me a horse. Then I'll go to a big house far beyond where I worked a short while once. They've a little pond there would take the fish. And then maybe I'd stay at that house or maybe go on. But the fish would be well and I could visit them or take them to where I am. You see,' he said apologetically, in case Marian was worrying about the fish, 'the cranes would get them surely if they stayed here. The nets will blow off in the winter, no one will put them back and the cranes will come.'

Marian gazed through her tears at the blurred golden movements of the fish that remained in the pond. 'But, Denis, you can't just leave me behind. You must talk to me. You must tell me that you don't blame me. You must tell me that it was somehow for the best.'

'It was not for the best. But of course I don't blame you.'

'You see,' said Marian, speaking quickly, 'I thought it was better. I wasn't to know that Peter would be drowned. I had to let her be free. I had to let her be herself at the end. It would have been like destroying her entirely to keep her shut up till Peter came. It was so terrible keeping her a prisoner –' She knew as she spoke that she would say these things to herself many many times again, perhaps to the end of her life, but she would never more be able to say them aloud to another person. She turned desperately to Denis as they knelt together like penitents on the hard stone. 'Denis, you mustn't leave me like this. You must help me, you must cure me. It's not really what I ought to have done. I ought to have had hope. I killed her –'

Denis shook his head. 'We all killed her. I most of all.'

'No, no. You least of all.'

'I ought never to have left her for a moment.'

Marian groaned. The words accused her. 'You weren't to know –'

'Oh, I could have known, I could have feared, I did fear. But I did not only love I also hated. And hatred can corrupt the love that makes it be. That was why I was not there when I should have been.'

'I don't understand. Who did you hate? And why did that make you be away?'

'Peter.'

As Marian stared at him he gave her the full gaze of his blue eyes, solemn, sad, and a little ruthless, a little crazy. 'I don't see –' said Marian.

'What do you think really happened, down there by the sea, at the foot of the Devil's Causeway?'

'I don't know. I suppose the water –' She stopped. She felt her face violently burning. 'You didn't –?'

'Yes. The wall was broken down, I saw that as I went out along the road. I drove the car straight into the sea. I jumped out as it went in. He is not an agile man and I thought the car would sink before he got out. And he was not expecting it. But he did begin to get out. And I had to go back into the sea and push him back in the car. Then the pressure of the water kept the door shut, and the car sank.'

Marian had covered her face as he began to speak. She uncovered it a little now and looked up at the house. The blank windows took the rich sunlight and the house seemed ablaze. No one was near to hear what she had just heard.

Denis rose. He held out his arm and she pressed upon it to rise too. His arm was hard and rigid as iron. She saw the car plunging into the sea, the terrified man trying to get out. 'You hated so much – because of –?'

'Because of what I saw at that other time. And what I feared for her now. So you see, Marian, this is your cure.'

'Why is it my cure?' She turned to touch him, touching his arm again. She did not want to seem to shrink from him after what he had told her. But she looked on him with a strange awe.

'I should have loved only and not hated at all. I should have stayed by her and suffered with her, beside her, becoming her. There was really no other way, and I knew that before. But I let myself be driven mad by jealousy, by her actions, and I was faithless to her and so became mad. I am the most guilty. The guilt passes to me. That is why I must go away by myself.'

'But does that leave me – free?'

He regarded her sadly without replying and picked up the suitcase and then more carefully the bag containing the fish.

Marian stared at him. Then she said softly, 'Yes, you are becoming Hannah, now.' She came close to him and after a moment's hesitation kissed the rough shoulder of his coat.

'Good-bye.' He touched her cheek with his hand and turned away.

With a most heavy sense of what must be, Marian watched him tramp along the garden and out of the gate. The gate clanged loudly after him. The sun was becoming yet more golden and turning the hillside beyond to a brilliant saffron.

She was shocked and appalled at what he had said and yet she felt a sort of deep release which may have been no more than a sort of resignation. All her life she would, with differences, be re-enacting that story. And with Denis's words she had an eerie sense of it all beginning again, the whole tangled business: the violence, the prison house, the guilt. It all still existed. Yet Denis was taking it away with him. He had wound it all inside himself and was taking it away. Perhaps he was bringing it, for her, for the others, to an end.

She moved slowly away from the edge of the pool. She noticed that one of the wire nets had not been replaced and she pushed it back into position with her foot. Later on no doubt, but not yet, the herons would come to eat the fish. She walked slowly back to the terrace.

On the golden yellow hillside a little figure had appeared, climbing up the path toward the bog. Marian watched it recede. It was the last flicker, the last pinprick, that showed the light through from that other world which she had so briefly and so uncomprehendingly inhabited. And as she watched the climbing figure, and thought, with a last effort of the imagination to reach so far away, of Denis there alone, going onward, with his fish in his hand and his clear knowledge of what he had done, she remembered the story about his having fairy blood; and she did not know whether the world in which she had been living was a world of good or of evil, a world of significant suffering or a devil's shadow-play, a mere nightmare of violence.

'Oh, Marian, there you are!'

She turned to find Alice standing beside her, with the dog Tadg held closely on a lead.

'I thought everyone had vanished into thin air. Where's Denis?'

Marian looked at Alice, dear, solid, real, ordinary Alice. Good Alice. Then she threw her arms round her neck.

'My dear,' said Alice, trying to manage Marian's embrace and Tadg's lead, 'are you all right? You really should have come over to Riders. I think I must take you back now, I shall insist.'

'You're very good,' said Marian, letting her go. 'But no, I must start packing my things up. I think I must see it through here.'

'Where's Denis?'

'He's gone.'

'Gone?'

'Yes. Gone to the bog, gone to the gipsies, gone.'

Alice's face became blank and stiff. Her voice trembled a

little as she said, 'I see. I thought he *would* go, of course. But I wanted to give him Tadg to go with him. It seemed right.'

'Quick, then,' said Marian. 'He's not quite out of sight. He's up there on the hillside, see, see. Would Tadg go after him, do you think, if we released him?'

They ran across the sunny garden to the gate, their long shadows flying before them. The figure on the hillside was clearly visible.

Alice undid the lead. 'Denis, Denis, Denis!' she whispered intensely to the attentive dog, pointing her finger. Tadg hesitated: looked at her, looked about, sniffed the ground, and then set off slowly. He ambled, sniffing and looking back. Then he began to run and disappeared into a dip in the ground. A little later, much farther up the hill, they saw the golden dog streaking upward in pursuit of the man until both were lost to view in the saffron yellow haze near the skyline.

Alice and Marian began to walk slowly back toward the house. Marian thrust her hands into her pockets looking for a handkerchief and encountered Geoffrey's letter. She pulled it out and opened it.

Alice was saying, 'The upper road is more or less clear now. It's a good half-hour to Riders all the same. I'd have come back sooner only I had a chance to arrange a cottage for old Mrs Scottow. You know hers was destroyed in the flood. I've brought Carrie with me. I told her to make us some tea. And I've brought a cherry cake. No bad news in your letter, I hope?'

'No, no,' said Marian, 'good news. A friend of mine is engaged to be married. He's going to marry a girl I was at school with. They've just been in Spain together –'

'Good show.' Alice's face was wet with tears.

In silence Marian handed her her handkerchief. Yes, she would go back to all that now, to the real world. She would dance at Geoffrey's wedding.

Chapter Thirty-five

Effingham pulled his overcoat more closely about him and entered the waiting-room. There was still a while to wait before the train. A little fire was burning in the dark room. The afternoon was grey and overcast and there was a streak of winter in the air.

Effingham had left Riders two days ago. After the funeral he had not felt able to return to the house, and he had gone away to be by himself at the little fishing-hotel at Blackport. It had been a curious and not unpleasant interval with a sense of holiday about it. He had strolled on the quay watching the fishing-boats and had sat for long hours dreaming in the bar. He had eaten well and felt generally better. Today his taxi had brought him back along the road. The small railway line from Blackport only served the aerodrome, so he had returned to the more northerly station, passing on the road between Gaze and Riders. He had taken in the grey yet clear rainy light what he now felt to be a last look at the two houses. They had glowered upon him like Scylla and Charybdis, but they had let him go through.

Effingham's departure from Riders had been hasty and absurd. He had prepared Alice for it by a number of vague remarks beforehand. Then after the long slow business of the funeral, the awkward jolting cortège through the narrow muddy lanes to the tiny distant church, he had acted with frenetic speed, hurling his clothes into suitcases with a sort of wild relief. He had not been able, until they were all safely hidden in the wet earth, to think, to feel, to stir a finger. Now it was as if his will to live had returned with some overplus. He had vitality, purpose, action, stored up to his credit.

He had had, on the previous evening, a talk with Alice. It

was a curiously impressionistic talk. They had sat on the terrace, wrapped in coats and rugs, drinking whiskey before dinner and looking at the fading view of Gaze and the black cliffs, and each of them seemed to pursue an intermittent monologue. Effingham's purpose was to free himself from Alice with as much gentleness and dignity as possible. Alice's purpose was to let Effingham go without being tearful or troublesome. Together they managed it, as if lowering a heavy weight between them to the ground.

Alice had said, I seem to have mislaid you even as an object of love. I loved you when I was eighteen with a real passion. Perhaps my love for you never grew up. I remember times of real suffering. But lately in a way I haven't suffered. Perhaps it was something to do with Hannah. As soon as you began to love her, that made my love for you into something else. I became a sort of spectator. I had a role of being the generous rejected one. And since your love was hopeless too there was a structure and a story on which I could rest. And so I stopped just loving you and I was consoled. Then there was Denis, and he might have awakened me with some real pain if only I could ever have stopped regarding him as a servant. But I never did. So I will let you go at last, Effie. Hannah kept you for me for a few dream years, but she has gone and she has set you free. I shall always remember with gratitude that you turned to me for a moment. Let us call it a gift that you gave to a girl of eighteen who really loved you.

Effingham had said, this adventure is over for me, and you, through having become a part of it, are over too. I could only love you, and I think I did love you for a day, as an incident in that story. I loved you for Hannah, against Hannah, and not for yourself. Whether I did right, whether I abandoned Hannah at her moment of need, whether I could have done otherwise, I do not know. I feel that perhaps it was all inevitable and we were all something in Hannah's dream. And Hannah's death, that was the most inevitable thing of all, that was what we were all the time waiting for. We were all the attendants upon that ceremony and we are all now dismissed. So we return to our real life and our real tasks: and God knows if we shall be the better for this dream of death, this enactment of last things.

Effingham had not seen Max alone before his departure. The old man seemed to have aged to a mysterious degree in the last weeks and now seemed a remote wizened sage who had long ago forgotten all about life. It was as if the funeral were Max's funeral and they were conveying him ceremonially out of the world, as if those others were dream deaths while Max wore the real garb of mortality. Effingham had let it be known that he was going shortly, and after lunch had shaken Max by the hand and uttered vague good wishes and thanks. The old man had smiled upon him but had not drawn him aside into privacy or given him any admonitions or any blessing or made any comment whatever on what had passed. And why should he? Effingham had rather resentfully reflected. He had had enough of Max's visions and interpretations. One could not go on forever regarding one's old tutor as an infallible source of wisdom.

Effingham had left the house in haste, his bulging suitcases trailing ties and shirt-sleeves, dragging his coat on as he ran down the stairs, before Max had emerged from his afternoon rest. Alice had not made his departure any easier by trying to load him with gifts as if he were leaving for a long journey: the long journey of life without her. She gave him her fountain pen, which he had once borrowed and liked, a Japanese print from the bathroom which he had admired, a pretty edition of the poems of Marvell which they had once read together, a familiar china cat from his bedroom mantelpiece, and several of her favourite shells. These objects made such a bulky and fragile collection that he had had at the last moment to beg her to pack them carefully and send them after him. The little presents touched him very much; and he anticipated that he would weep in the taxi all the way to Blackport. But on that journey he was in fact chiefly engaged in wondering whether he had not been too forward in kissing Carrie at the moment of departure.

With the image of Hannah he had not made his peace and perhaps he never would. It haunted his dreams and shifted

267

before his waking eyes, sometimes piteous, sometimes accusing, always beautiful. He did not feel that he had killed her. It was rather as if she had attempted to kill him, a beautiful pale vampire fluttering at his night window, a *belle dame sans merci*. But he had never really let her in, not really inside. If he had let her in he might now be dead himself. What, he wondered, had saved him? Was it merely his colossal, almost with satisfaction he recognized, really fat and monumental egoism? Or was it some streak of health and sanity in a nature also but too prone to be fascinated by the weird and the deathly? What had made the noticeable, the crucial difference at the end was her terrible descent from her pinnacle of isolation, her unspeakable surrender to Scottow. And if that made so much difference did it not suggest that her vigil had had a spiritual meaning after all? She had been their nun and she had broken her vows.

Yet it was a strange nun that she had been. How little time ago it was that he had been sitting with her in her tired, crowded, golden room, her cluttered cell. The memory was smooth and rounded like a piece of amber. It smelt of an old degenerate happiness. He had been glad to have her reserved, sequestered, caged. Max had been right perhaps when he said that they had all turned towards her to discover a significance in their own sufferings, to load their own evil on to her to be burnt up. It had been a fantasy of the spiritual life, a story, a tragedy. Only the spiritual life has no story and is not tragic. Hannah had been for them an image of God; and if she was a false God they had certainly worked hard to make her so. He thought of her now as a doomed figure, a Lilith, a pale death-dealing enchantress: anything but a human being.

If what was over had indeed been a fantasy of the spiritual life, it was its fantastic and not its spiritual quality which had touched him. He had, through egoism, through being in some sense too small, too trivial to interest the powers of that world, escaped from evil. But he had not either been touched by good. That vision, true or false, he would leave to Max, of the good forced into being as the object of desire, as if one should compel God to be. He himself would hurry back to his familiar ordinary world. Ah, how he looked forward to it now, how he looked forward to the round of office and pub and dinner parties and dull country weekends. He even anticipated the pleasure it would be to catch up on the gossip. He would try to forget what he had briefly seen.

It was raining now. The train was late as usual. Effingham idly undid the copy of the *Blackport Gazette* which he had bought that morning and had not yet had time to read. Newspapers, unobtainable at Riders, were still something of a treat, a diverting little repast of triviality. Then his eye was suddenly caught by a familiar name. He turned the page back. *A Tragic Accident. It is learnt with regret that a sad accident occurred yesterday on the estate of Mr Max Lejour, the well-known writer. Mr Lejour's son, Mr Philip Lejour, accidentally shot and killed himself while cleaning his gun....*

Effingham folded up the paper. For one agonizing moment he wondered whether he ought not to go straight back to Riders. But with a sense of craven relief he thought: no. It was the merest chance that he had seen the news before he left. For all they knew he might be far away by now. And in any case there was no place for him there, he could have no part any more in comforting the Lejour family. He would never go back. He thought of Pip, at first with pain and pity, and then also with a strange sort of satisfaction. There was a time when he might have envied him, but that time was gone. Pip's long vigil was over. And his death rounded the thing off, gave it a tragic completeness which made it all the easier to cut free of it, to let it drift away like a great buoyant sphere into the past. Hannah had claimed her last victim.

Effingham heard the distant train. He was now in a frenzy to be off, to have escaped. He gathered his cases, and as the little train came rumbling slowly in he made a dash through the rain towards the first-class carriage. As he bundled his things hastily in he caught a glimpse further down the platform of Marian Taylor getting into a second-class compartment. He wondered if she had seen him. He sat quietly, breathing hard after the exertion of lifting his cases, leaning well back and waiting for the train to start. He could not, until then, feel entirely safe.

The train moved at last. The shabby station slid away. The bare domes of the Scarren were grey as lead in the drifting rain. The train went with gathering speed through the treeless land. Effingham sighed and crumpled the newspaper in his hand. This was his defeat, this was his triumph, that he had lived to speak their elegy. 'There are no voices that are not soon mute, there is no name, with whatever emphasis of passionate love repeated, of which the echoes are not faint at last.' He was the angel who drew the curtain upon the mystery, remaining himself outside in the great lighted auditorium, where the clatter of departure and the sound of ordinary talk was coming now to be heard. He sighed again and closed his eyes upon the appalling land.

At Greytown Junction he would telephone to Elizabeth. And perhaps, the thought did not displease him, when they had got on to the other train, he would summon little Marian Taylor to his carriage. He was still touched by her attachment to him. She would be delighted. And she too belonged out in the big well-lighted world. They would talk the whole thing over as the express carried them away across the central plain.

More About Penguins

Penguinews, which appears every month, contains details of all the new books issued by Penguins as they are published. From time to time it is supplemented by *Penguins in Print*, which is a complete list of all available books published by Penguins. (There are well over three thousand of these.)

A specimen copy of *Penguinews* will be sent to you free on request, and you can become a subscriber for the price of the postage. For a year's issues (including the complete lists) please send 30p if you live in the United Kingdom, or 60p if you live elsewhere. Just write to Dept EP, Penguin Books Ltd, Harmondsworth, Middlesex, enclosing a cheque or postal order, and your name will be added to the mailing list.
Some more Iris Murdoch novels in Penguins are listed overleaf.

Note: *Penguinews* and *Penguins in Print* are not available in the U.S.A. or Canada

The following novels by Iris Murdoch are in Penguins

'Of all the novelists that have made their bow since the war she seems to me to be the most remarkable . . . behind her books one feels a power of intellect quite exceptional in a novelist' –

Raymond Mortimer in the *Sunday Times*

THE BELL

BRUNO'S DREAM

A FAIRLY HONOURABLE DEFEAT

THE FLIGHT FROM THE ENCHANTER

THE SANDCASTLE

A SEVERED HEAD

UNDER THE NET

AN UNOFFICIAL ROSE

THE ITALIAN GIRL

THE NICE AND THE GOOD

THE RED AND THE GREEN

THE TIME OF THE ANGELS

Not for sale in the U.S.A.